The Most ELIGIBLE HIGHLANDER In SCOTLAND

MICHELE SINCLAIR

ZEBRA BOOKS
KENSINGTON PUBLISHING CORP.
http://www.kensingtonbooks.com

ZEBRA BOOKS are published by

Kensington Publishing Corp.
119 West 40th Street
New York, NY 10018

All Kensington titles, imprints, and distributed lines are available at special quantity discounts for bulk purchases for sales promotion, premiums, fund-raising, educational, or institutional use.

Special book excerpts or customized printings can also be created to fit specific needs. For details, write or phone the office of the Kensington Sales Manager: Attn.: Sales Department. Kensington Publishing Corp., 119 West 40th Street, New York, NY 10018. Phone: 1-800-221-2647.

Zebra and the Z logo Reg. U.S. Pat. & TM Off.

First Printing: February 2018
ISBN-13: 978-1-4201-3882-5
ISBN-10: 1-4201-3882-0

eISBN-13: 978-1-4201-3883-2
eISBN-10: 1-4201-3883-9

10 9 8 7 6 5 4 3 2 1

Printed in the United States of America

THE MOST ELIGIBLE
HIGHLANDER IN SCOTLAND

Conan stood up abruptly. Mhàiri reopened her eyes to see that he was packing his things. "We're leaving?" she asked, rising to her feet as well.

"Aye," he said, clearly disgruntled.

"I promise we will get together again in two days and I will show you how to draw buildings, castles, or whatever you want."

Conan dropped his things to the ground. "You think that's what I care about right now?" He reached out and his hands gripped her arms, not painfully, but with enough force Mhàiri could feel the tension raging in his body. "If you wanted to know what a kiss was like so damn bad, you should have asked me."

The desire Conan had worked so hard to suppress suddenly erupted and was beyond his control. His mouth came down on hers before Mhàiri could even think of moving. He caught her face between his hands, pulled her close, and kissed her—hard and deliberately—letting her feel the frustration and temper she had aroused in him.

Surprised, she clutched his forearms and resisted, but Conan did not lessen his hold. The pressure against her mouth was deep and persuasive and undeniable. And before she realized what she was doing, her mouth opened and welcomed him in . . .

Books by Michele Sinclair

THE HIGHLANDER'S BRIDE

TO WED A HIGHLANDER

DESIRING THE HIGHLANDER

THE CHRISTMAS KNIGHT

TEMPTING THE HIGHLANDER

A WOMAN MADE FOR PLEASURE

SEDUCING THE HIGHLANDER

A WOMAN MADE FOR SIN

NEVER KISS A HIGHLANDER

THE MOST ELIGIBLE HIGHLANDER IN SCOTLAND

HIGHLAND HUNGER
(with Hannah Howell and Jackie Ivie)

Published by Kensington Publishing Corporation

To my father.
He was the absolute best,
and I was a very lucky daughter
to have had him in my life for as long as I did.
Thank you, Dad—for everything.

And to Joseph Campbell,
who once said some profound words about moving on.
"Sometimes you must give up the life you planned
in order to have the life that is waiting for you."

Chapter One

October 1317
Loch Coire Fionnaraich

"*Chruitheachd!* The damn man's naked! I told you to stay hidden and wait for me, not pull a sword on him."

Conan arched a brow at the angry older man yelling at his younger redheaded companion. Conan kept his expression unconcerned as the man's dark eyes wandered cautiously down his completely exposed body. He was aware that even in the nude he made a somewhat imposing impression. Like most of his brothers, he had thick dark brown hair, bright blue eyes and was unusually tall. But it was not those features the man was gauging. And while Conan did not possess the bulk of one who trained every day, his powerful, well-muscled body looked like what it was—that of a skilled warrior who was deadly even without a sword.

The older man's eyes continued their scrutiny until they reached Conan's feet. "*Mac na galla!* He's still standing in the *fuar* loch!"

Standing in ankle-deep water near the loch's shoreline with his hands on his hips, Conan shifted his gaze from the much heavier, angry man approaching his companion to the tip of the shaking sword the thin redhead had pointed at his chest. To survive, most Highlanders were tough men, regardless of how they made a living. If they weren't, they would eventually succumb to Scotland's harsh northern environment, which made the scrawny man in front of him an anomaly. The redhead was tall, but his thin frame was frail and the shaking of his arm indicated what strength he had was waning. It would take little effort to incapacitate him.

His hairy beast of a friend, however, was enormous. He was almost a half a head taller than Conan, and based on the sizeable gut he was carrying, the man easily outweighed both him and his friend together. The giant knew these facts as well, and by his assertive walk, Conan sensed his size gave him a false sense of confidence, which would make him hard to rattle. Things were about to get interesting.

"He . . . he saw me." The thin one swallowed, keeping his malevolent gaze on Conan. "I had no choice. I didn't want him to get the upper hand."

"Well, he's obviously terrified," the darker-haired man sneered with sarcasm, making no effort to hide his disdain. "And now he knows about us and we don't even know if it's him!"

"It has to be! No one else has been around since we got here. Then he comes, exactly where we were told, to this loch. And . . . and his tartan matches the piece we were given." The redhead used his chin to gesture to Conan's clothes lying on top of a large rock near the shoulder. "Look."

Dark brown eyes narrowed with warning at Conan before taking a quick glance at the rock. The man's gaze widened a bit, and he gripped the sword a little more firmly. "What's your name?"

Conan inhaled deeply, slowly licked his lips, and replied, "McTiernay."

The man's lips twitched, but instead of walking away in realization of his mistake as Conan had expected him to do, he did nothing. It was almost as if he had never heard of one of the largest and most powerful clans in the Highlands. The idea was so unthinkable Conan suspected the man was just extremely good at hiding his emotions. The real question was whether he knew that he was not just facing a Highlander who belonged to the powerful clan, but actually one of *the* McTiernays.

"I've heard of the McTiernays," the giant growled, cold dark eyes remaining steady on Conan's blue ones. "But that is not what I asked. What is *your* name?"

"Conan," he answered, keeping his look of boredom. The man's unreadable expression also remained unchanged.

Conor was his eldest brother and chief of the McTiernay clan and all its chieftains—two of whom were his brothers, three when including his brother who was to become the next Schellden laird. There were seven McTiernay brothers total, and though Conan was the second to youngest, he had a strong reputation of his own. Or so he'd thought, for it did not look like either the giant or the redhead recognized his name.

If they were ignorant, Conan was not interested in educating them on their mistake. He had not been in a good mood for days, and in just a few moments, he was about to add another reason to his long list of things for which to blame Laurel McTiernay.

Despite their quarrelsome relationship, Conan loved his sister-in-law and appreciated her loyalty to his brother Conor, but she was by far the most exasperating, annoying, and altogether frustrating person he had ever met. And he would not be in this humiliating situation—naked, wet, and weaponless—if it were not for her. Worse, if Laurel ever learned of it, she would laugh until she cried, sharing her mirth with anyone with working ears.

Important details, however, would be lost. Laurel would not ruin her storytelling with pesky truths, such as that he had not been taken unawares or that, despite being temporarily weaponless against two men who did have swords, he was not in any real danger. Nor would she remember to relay that he had spied the two would-be thieves long before they approached. All Laurel would care about was that he had been caught unarmed in the nude by two men who had mistakenly been bold enough to wave a sword at his chest while demanding he answer their questions.

Conan prayed he could scare them into silence because he was not in the mood to kill anyone. Death was messy, and he had just gotten clean. Last thing he wanted to do was deal with bloody bodies.

"You *would* have to be one of them," the large man snarled as he stared Conan in the eye.

Conan lifted his chin slightly in surprise, and then nodded once. An odd sense of joy went through him at learning that his name was as recognizable as he had thought.

"Unfortunately for you, it doesn't change anything," spat the redhead, recapturing Conan's attention. The man had bright red frizzy hair with a matching beard. The color matched the almost tangible anger rolling off him.

The giant lifted his hand to hush his mouthy partner. "It might."

Conan arched a brow at the comment. Perhaps he had been wrong to assume these two men were mere thieves. Both were more interested in him than they were in his horse or his sword, which was still sheathed to his saddle. And Conan had no idea why, but the redhead's hate seemed personal as if he wished him dead—and that was *before* he'd had any idea who Conan was. His partner, however, had gone suddenly quiet.

"Just take my clothes and leave," Conan prompted, testing his new theory.

"We don't want your clothes, *cac*," the frail figure snarled.

Unfazed by the insult, Conan sighed. *Not thieves*, he thought unhappily. "Well, if you do not want them, I do. My toes are numb and I would like to get out of the water."

The thin arm that was holding a sword stiffened. "Don't move."

Conan renewed his bored look. The redhead jabbed his weapon in his direction, in an obvious attempt at intimidation. Running out of patience, Conan threw his hands up in the air. "What do you want?"

The thin man laughed in a pathetic attempt to show bravado. "*We* don't want anything. It's—"

"*Cum do theanga ablaich gun fheum!*" his companion shouted, cutting him off. The redhead closed his mouth and glowered. Whether it was from being told to shut up, being called an idiot, or just his hatred for

Conan was unclear. What was clear was the giant did not care. "This would have been a hell of a lot easier if you had simply *listened* to me. Now he knows our faces, and neither of us have ones that are easy to forget."

"We could kill him." The redhead's thin lips smiled at the idea.

If not thieves, Conan thought, ensuring he kept his face impassive despite the threat, *assassins?*

The giant scoffed. "Nay, we take him with us. He's a McTiernay. That means I want more money."

So not assassins. They were mercenaries. If Conan had to guess, they had been sent here on reconnaissance. But by whom? No one knew he was coming this way, which meant they were not looking for him.

The redhead opened his mouth to argue, but the giant cut him off. "And if I'm wrong, he can have the honor of killing a McTiernay."

Capture, death, threats . . . all three annoyed Conan and it was becoming increasingly clear that he was not going to learn anything more this way. He needed to end this.

With hands already in the air, Conan took advantage of the brief sideways glance the larger man gave his companion and lunged for the redhead's weapon. When his fingers circled the grip, he spun, yanking it out of the man's weak grasp just in time to block an attack from the larger foe.

Conan deftly twirled the blade, leaving no doubt at his level of skill with a sword. The scrawny attacker's eyes grew wide before he scurried back, letting his friend take charge. The large man did not look worried. Conan grimaced, knowing how this was going to have to end. "*Go n-ithe an cat thú is go n-ithe an diabhal an cat,*" he murmured, cursing Laurel once again under his breath.

Thinking fear was the reason behind Conan's mutterings, the giant's stony expression broke into a malicious smile. His dark gaze quickly swept down and up Conan's naked form and his smile grew larger. Conan stifled a sigh. The man was an imbecile if he thought nudity diminished a man's ability to fight. The state of one's dress—or lack thereof—had nothing to do with wielding a weapon. The only reason Conan cared even a little about his lack of dress was that if this ever got back to his brothers, or especially his sister-in-law, he would never hear the end of it.

The massive man changed his stance and adjusted his grip, announcing not only that he was about to attack, but how. Believing his size compensated for his lack of skill, the giant swung wide, and Conan easily dodged the blade before thrusting his sword up and at an angle, forcing the large man to stumble backward.

"I'll ask one more time. What do you want with me?" Conan knew he was giving the man time to regain his balance, but he wanted him to feel empowered enough to answer his question.

"I don't want anything," the giant snorted. "All I know and all I care about is the coin being offered to the one who finds the man who bathes in this loch and wears that tartan. That seems to be you."

Conan's eyes widened in shock hearing the flimsy description. They could be looking for anyone. "These *are* McTiernay lands. Anyone bathing here would be wearing a McTiernay tartan," he retorted.

The large man sniggered. "We've been here weeks. No one ever comes to this loch. That is, until you."

Conan inwardly groaned. Whoever this giant

mercenary was looking for, it was not him. It probably was not even a McTiernay. That he was even *here* was sheer coincidence and prompted by his miserable attempt to prove to his sister-in-law that he was not someone willing to address any whim she had, even if she was Lady McTiernay. That was his brother's job. Conor was laird and Laurel was *his* wife.

"This is my first time at this loch. I'm not who you want," Conan stated unequivocally, still clinging to a little bit of hope that this could end without bloodshed.

"Maybe not." The large man gave a half-hearted shrug. "Don't matter. You're coming with us, and that dull blade isn't going to stop me from making that happen."

Conan exhaled, all hope gone. His trip was ruined, and the possibility of studying the area any further was as dead as the man in front of him was going to be. Conan cursed under his breath. He *really* was not looking forward to bringing a colossal, fetid corpse with him for the remainder of his journey.

The man grinned, largely this time, exposing rotten and missing teeth. Then, with none of the speed necessary to make his thrust effective, he attacked. Conan easily blocked him. He took several steps back, knowing a quick way he could end this battle victoriously despite using a dull blade.

The man took the bait. He raised his sword high above his head and surged forward, preparing to put all his weight behind his downward thrust, knowing it would be impossible to block. Only at the very last moment did he realize that Conan had no intention of blocking his attack and instead had planted his feet. With a single lunge, Conan impaled the man's stomach so that his arm dropped as he fell forward. The dull tip pierced his chest all the way through his back.

The sound of hooves riding away captured Conan's attention. He spotted the bright red hair of the dead man's companion as it disappeared behind the large rocks that partially surrounded the small loch. Conan groaned. He could go after the man and had no doubt of his ability to catch him eventually, but it would not be until after nightfall. And when he did, Conan was not sure what good it would do. The coward knew nothing more and was undoubtedly stupid enough to attack rather than answer questions if confronted. The only thing almost guaranteed in a pursuit was that he would have *two* bodies to carry back to Cole's.

Conan knelt down and stared at the immense man as he took his dying breath. He studied the man's filthy tartan and thanked God he had not killed a MacCoinnich—even if the man had deserved it. There were dozens of small clans that ran up Scotland's western coastline and he knew very few of them, but like the McTiernays, the MacCoinnich clan was well known, just as large, and arguably almost as powerful. While Laird MacCoinnich and Conor respected each other, neither felt inclined to be anything more than civil toward the other.

Conan took one more look at the dead man and wished he had asked for the name of the one who actually sent him and his friend. He wondered just why they were so interested in the man who supposedly regularly visited this remote area. While the loch was nestled on the far eastern edge of his brother Cole's territory, he had not seen signs of someone living this far out. It was cold, rocky, and impossible to farm, and had practically nothing for cattle to graze on.

Most clansmen lived closer to Fàire Creachann, Cole's home. The castle was set on a stretch of land that extended out into the blue waters of Loch Torridon, where one could glimpse the *An Cuan Sgìth*, the strait of sea separating the homeland from its islands. With only one access point, it was protected by the sea with enormous cliffs on almost all sides and therefore nearly impenetrable to attackers. Living close to the fortress gave clansmen protection.

This loch was so far from Fàire Creachann, it was highly unlikely his attackers were looking for an actual McTiernay. Whoever swam in these waters was probably a squatter, a nomad, or even a thief. He could have just found a McTiernay tartan and been using it as his own, thinking the appearance of being aligned with a powerful clan beneficial.

Conan put his hand on his knee and pushed himself back up to his feet. Speculating was a waste of time. Cole was his best chance of learning who had attacked him and why. As the third brother and McTiernay laird for this region of the Torridon Hills, Cole knew the tartans of all the larger clans in the area, and hopefully a majority of the smaller ones.

Conan went to the shore and quickly washed the blood off his arms and stomach. He then walked over to the boulder where his clothes lay drying and yanked on his leine. He grabbed his tartan and belt and was about to put them on when he spied the dead body near the shoreline. The man reeked. Everything about him was dirty, and Conan did not relish hauling his corpse up onto his horse.

One puffy hand floated in the water, and Conan considered rolling the mass into the water and rinsing it off in an effort to help reduce the stench. "Damn you, Laurel," Conan hissed and pulled off his leine so that he was naked once more. The idea of the man's dirt and grime on his skin was enough to turn his stomach, but unlike his clothes, his body was easy to wash and quickly dried.

Grabbing his sword, he went off to find the man's horse. Minutes later, he returned, glad that it had been easy to locate with reins wrapped around the tree. It also served as further proof that the dead man's companion had been an idiot since he had not freed the animal when he was making his own getaway.

Using rope, ingenuity, and a lot of energy and strength, Conan managed to get the large dead bulk lying across the saddle. After tying the body down so that it would not slide off, Conan once again headed toward the loch's shore and dived into the icy waters, thinking of ways he might take revenge on his sister-in-law without it costing him his own life.

Nestled high within the Torridon Hills, Loch Coire Fionnaraich's waters were always cold, but right now, its cool temperature felt soothing after the exhausting hour he had spent in the abnormally hot sun. Scotland's fall weather could be unpredictable, bringing in cold winds or even seemingly ceaseless rains, but for the past few days, it had felt more like August than October. It had been perfect for trekking and plotting out the mountains that lay between the McTiernay and MacCoinnich borders.

Conan broke the water's surface and took a deep breath, feeling slightly better. He did not really want to overly antagonize Laurel. He, in fact, begrudgingly liked his eldest brother's wife when she was not annoying him. But lately, she had been more than irritating, she had been unusually demanding, and he was not the only one to think so. Laurel had been taking her frustrations out on everyone.

Her pleasant, mischievous demeanor rarely made an appearance lately. Instead, she was so moody that it was impossible to tell whether her over-the-top threats should be taken seriously. Her latest tirade had been the worst. And the one thing that kept his own anger from growing anew was knowing how furious Laurel would be to learn that he had gone against her wishes to take the shortest route to Cole's and instead had selected a more circuitous path. And she would have only herself to blame for her anger. Laurel knew what happened when someone *demanded* anything of him. She knew it from personal experience.

When word had come that the McTiernay priest needed help—specifically *his* help—and Conan had not immediately jumped on a horse and taken off, Laurel had leaped to the correct conclusion that he never intended to go. But just because he was not inclined to make the journey himself did not mean he did not plan on dispatching someone to help the priest. But would Laurel listen to reason? No.

She knew he was very busy prepping hides so they could be turned into vellum. Halting the painstaking and time-consuming process midway to go north to help Father Lanaghly had cost him to lose *three* much-needed vellums for his trip this spring. But Laurel had not cared. To her, his trip was months away and therefore three vellums were a negligible loss. Father Lanaghly's need, however, was important. Monumentally important. Conan disagreed. It was upsetting to learn that a small priory had caught fire and was no longer habitable, and even more disheartening to know that two people had died. But the church was already in the process of relocating the nuns and the undamaged artifacts to a larger, more established abbey in the Lowlands.

Conan cared nothing about some uninteresting religious scrolls that had miraculously survived a fire. It annoyed him greatly that, because he was highly intelligent and kept a lot of written scrolls and books, people assumed he wanted to read just anything. Maybe in his youth that had been true, but never had he aspired to be a scholar who consumed any type of knowledge whenever he had the chance.

Out of all his brothers, he might be the one who valued written knowledge the most; however, that did not mean he was the only one able to protect some religious documents. Anyone could put them in a crate, a trunk, or a bag. How hard was that? Even Conor could manage such a feat, and he was already up north visiting Cole. Then again, why did Father Lanaghly need send for help at all? He was as capable as anyone of carting some scrolls and keeping them safe from poor weather.

Instead of seeing the logic of his rather straightforward arguments, Laurel had become highly emotional and issued him a fiery command—ride north to Cole's immediately and help Father Lanaghly or deal with not just her wrath, but that of Conor's, when he returned.

His eldest brother, Conor, would indeed have been furious. Not because Conan had done anything wrong, but, because like many around the McTiernay Castle, his brother's concern was mounting about his wife and her increasingly fragile emotional state. Conor had almost not even made the journey to Cole's, and he had made it clear when he left that he was entrusting certain people to see to her happiness. That included Conan, especially if the clan was to provide him any precious vellums for his upcoming journey.

Happiness. A completely outrageous concept to demand. But that was what love did to a man. It made him unreasonable and caused him to issue crazy orders that no sane, cogent person could follow, even if they wanted to. And yet, in part to keep Laurel *happy*, Conan had left as she had demanded.

But not as she had intended.

Conan had proclaimed his departure was driven by his need to get away from her nagging voice, but in truth, once he had decided to take a longer route, he had been almost eager to leave, for he had wanted to come to this area of the Highlands for a while. He had always taken the most direct route to Fàire Creachann, but this time Conan had journeyed along the eastern border of his brother Cole's lands. He had never mapped this part of the Torridon Mountains and after trekking the area for hours he had been pleased to find a small loch nestled in the peaks. The surrounding large boulders were easy to climb and gave him a better perspective when it came to mapping the area.

That was his passion. Maps. The idea of converting information to a useful picture inspired how he saw all that was around him. Unfortunately, very few maps depicted such information, and he was not sure any existed that did of Scotland.

Oh, maps were plentiful, but none were accurate, nor were they intended to be. At best, their purpose was to illustrate those with power, and whatever the creator deemed most important was placed in the middle.

Since most scribes were associated with the church, Jerusalem somehow became the center of most countries' maps—something any intelligent being knew could not be true.

Conan intended to create an actual visual depiction of Scotland. Come this spring, nothing was going to stop him from leaving his McTiernay home to spend his life creating maps of real value. They would be accurate. They would show the best routes to travel. His maps would depict probable flashpoints along clan borders and various paths the English might use to re-invade Scotland.

He had already completed several small illustrations of McTiernay lands and those of their ally—the Schelldens. And while he had much of Cole's lands and the majority of the Torridon peninsula sketched out, the eastern region lacked important details, such as the markers the MacCoinnich clan used to denote the border of their land.

Throughout the summer, skirmishes between MacCoinnich and their neighbors had been growing in both number and violence. As of yet, none had involved McTiernays. Both Cole and Conor wanted to keep it this way. It was the reason his brother had gone north despite Laurel's erratic behavior. Conor had called a meeting to discuss the potential reasons behind the increase in activity and whether there was any reason for the McTiernay clan to be concerned. The answer would determine if Conor moved additional soldiers north to support Cole's army. Such a move would not go unnoticed and, in itself, might create tensions where they could still be avoided. So caution was key.

Conan saw the importance of such talks, but he knew he would be no help with them. The best way he could support his brother was not with his sword and certainly not in negotiation, but with information. This surprised some, as he was oftentimes quite vocal with his opinions. Most women of his acquaintance had issue with this character trait, but in his mind, that was their problem. Conan liked who he was and was certainly not going to change just to make a woman feel at ease.

Conan was also well aware that he was *not* the smartest person alive. Not even close. Nor did he have some driving need to *be* the smartest person. The notion was almost as irritating as it was ludicrous.

He had met many monks who were far cleverer and more knowledgeable than he. He welcomed intelligence from anyone—which included women. Anyone who could offer witty and challenging conversations was preferable to someone inane. Unfortunately, his experience had taught him that those women were extremely rare and was why he valued Laurel and Conor's youngest child, Bonny. Despite being only seven years old, she often caused him to pause and think about what she was saying when arguing a point. Bonny's knowledge was only hampered by her limited life experience, but he would not be surprised if his niece grew up to outsmart every living soul she encountered. Conan dreaded saying good-bye to her in the spring and knew he would miss her enormously in the years to come.

Many did not understand the special bond between him and Bonny. Conan knew her parents blamed him for some of her blunt and seemingly offensive comments. Laurel often made it clear that she did not

want her youngest child growing up to be like him—
rude, mean, unsympathetic, and egocentric. Conan
disagreed.

He was an ideal model for his niece.

First, he was not rude. He was honest. Why should
Bonny learn to hold her opinion simply because some
people were incapable of hearing the truth? And just
because they could not accept the truth, that did not
make her mean for stating it. Rarely was there malicious intent behind his words and so calling the
straightforward delivery of his honest opinions brutal
was not only misleading, but incorrect. And aye, sympathy was a quality to be admired, but there were
always countless women around more than willing to
provide a sympathetic ear.

As far as his self-absorptive personality, well, he
knew that to be pure myth. The women he had been
with enjoyed his charms while he was willing to give
them. It was only when he was bored and needed to
refocus his efforts to his future and his freedom that
they suddenly claimed to be wounded by his callous-
ness. So what Laurel viewed as egocentrism, he would
call determination. And in the spring, all that focused
attention was finally going to allow him to travel
the world and never, *ever* be manipulated by Laurel
McTiernay again.

As soon as Conan finished loosening the last knot
in the rope, the dead body dropped to the ground. A
loud crunching sound indicated that several bones
had broken despite the short fall. Conan nudged the
large mass with his foot so the man lay face up. It had
taken almost two days to get from the small loch to

Fàire Creachann, and in that time, the body had gone
from limp to rigid and back to limp again. In a couple
more days, he would no longer be recognizable, but
for right now, he looked much like he had upon his
death, aside from the yellow, somewhat greenish tint
his skin was turning.

"You recognize him?" Conan asked, looking up at
his brother.

"Nay," Cole replied and waved his hand in front of
his face. In the past several hours, the odor had gone
from severely unpleasant to outright nauseating. "*A
shaoghail!* It's like smelling rotten cheese made from
feces. Thank God you stayed outside of the castle walls.
Elle would skin me if she had even a whiff. The stench
is going to linger for days."

"You ever see a young man with really bright red
hair and matching beard. Tall, skinny?"

Again, Cole shook his head. "There are a few red-
heads in the village, but none match that description."

Conan looked down at the dead man and then,
with the tip of his sword, adjusted the man's filthy
tartan so that he could see it better. "I don't recognize
it. Do you?"

Cole's forehead furrowed as he bent over to take a
better look. "Nay, but there are so many small clans
just south of here." He looked over to Dugan, his
commander and second in charge of clan affairs.
"You know more of them than I as you regularly ride
out to our borders. You recognize either him or the
plaid?"

Dugan bent over and studied the face of the man
for several seconds while holding his breath. Satisfied
he had never seen him before, he took several steps
back and exhaled. "I don't know him, and based on

his size, our people would have mentioned something if they saw someone matching his description during my visits."

Conan grimaced. He had really thought that Cole would have at least some insight into who the man was. "What about the plaid?"

Dugan shook his head. "While there are several small clans along the coast, most have aligned themselves with us, the MacLeoid, or MacCoinnich. And you know both their colors. He's not from around here."

Conan nodded. The McTiernay colors of dark greens and blues accented with bright colors of gold, red, and burgundy were well known throughout the Highlands, but so were MacLeoid and MacCoinnich tartans. All three had similar backgrounds, but MacCoinnich had no gold or burgundy lines. Instead, the plaid had a prominent white line outlining each plaid square. MacLeoid lines were bright red and yellow.

The man before them wore a tartan with mostly mustard and brown colors. Few clans strayed beyond green, blue, and red, and he could not recall in all his travels seeing one of this color. *Who are you?* Conan thought to himself.

"Might be Irish," Dugan murmured with a shrug.

Cole nodded in agreement. "Definitely a sword for hire."

Conan crossed his arms. "He recognized both mine and the McTiernay names. However, he was surprised to find that the man he was looking for to be me. I might just have been in the wrong place at the wrong time."

Cole scratched his chin. "We have not had any trouble near Loch Coire Fionnaraich in recent memory, and no one goes there. It's hard to reach, and the waters are uncomfortably cold even in the summer. I can't imagine who he was looking for."

Dugan's head shot up at the mention of the small loch. It had been some time since he had been in that area, but he used to visit it often for personal reasons. He had not returned after discovering he was being betrayed by a certain woman. Had she sent someone to look for him and this was simply an unfortunate case of mistaken identity? Maybe, but Conan and he looked *nothing* alike and the timing was wrong. That was months ago, so why would she send someone to look for him now? And why mercenaries? Conan had said that they had been hired by a man, not a woman. Dugan did not like coincidences, but there was too much to doubt that it was anything but one. It had to be just a random, isolated incident.

"I've smelt enough of this *ablach*," Cole said. "If his friend comes looking for him, we'll question him and then teach him what it means to hold a sword on a McTiernay."

Conan shook his head and crossed his arms. "The man's a coward. He won't show his face."

Dugan grimaced. "I'll go to the loch in the morning. If he shows up again, he won't get away. I'll also ask around and see if our people know or have heard of anything."

Cole nodded and then slapped Conan on the back with a grin. "Let's eat. I'm sure Elle is pacing the floors by now, getting angrier at our delay with each step she takes."

Conan grabbed the reins of his horse and followed Dugan and Cole through what most thought was the sole entrance into the castle. Only known to a few, the second access to Fàire Creachann had been created by Cole from a rocky cove into which a small boat could be brought on the northern side of the cliffs. From there, a steep path wound toward a well-fortified postern gate accessible strictly from the main tower.

The small group walked along the steep path that led up to the gatehouse. Once they were past its gates, the inside of Fàire Creachann could be seen and appreciated not just for its security, but for its dramatic beauty.

The massive castle had been in near ruins when Cole had taken over and established the area as the focal point of his lairdship and the McTiernays of Torridon. Being located on a rocky headland, the inside spanned nearly four acres and was much larger than most castles. It allowed for several buildings, and instead of a garden, it had room for small crops and a few farm animals, enabling Fàire Creachann to be more self-sufficient and protected against sieges.

The large tower house included the great hall and a private chamber for Cole and his family. Next to the tower, a series of ranges had been constructed along the northeastern cliffs, creating large and comfortable living quarters with sea views. On the other side of the tower was the chapel, which had finally been restored, along with a storehouse, a blacksmith's forge, and the kitchens. The stable block ran along the southern edge of the headland.

Before they entered the tower and went into the great hall, the doors opened and Conor stepped outside. Upon seeing Conan, he walked over and waved for Dugan and Cole to continue inside. His face held a pensive expression, and Conan knew what his brother was about to ask. "How's Laurel? It was so unlike her to refuse to come north with me and visit Ellenor, Brighid, and their rambunctious brood."

Conor had practically growled out the description, and Conan suspected that his brother had missed Laurel's presence in more ways than he had anticipated. She usually ran interference with Cole and Donald's children, who were all under the age of five.

Conor considered his words carefully. "She was in high spirits when I left," he offered.

Conan grunted. "I expect you mean *angry* spirits." Conan shrugged, trying to decide what he could say that would not shift his brother's concern to ire that was directed at him.

Conor ran a hand through his hair. "I don't know what is wrong with her. Nothing seems to make her happy, and she avoids things that she always before enjoyed. You have no idea the fights we had when I refused to let her travel with me to Fàire Creachann in the past. For her to refuse . . . it is just more than strange. Something is wrong."

Conan wanted to interrupt and explain that he, along with everyone else who lived at McTiernay Castle, was well aware of the fights between him and Laurel. No McTiernay was good at stifling his emotions, and the angry outbursts between Conor and Laurel were the stuff of legends. If it was not abundantly clear to anyone who ever saw them together how much they loved one another, people might have feared that their explosive interchanges would end in someone's death. But now, for the most part, the couple's fights were ignored and treated by family, castle staff, and clansmen as normal occurrences.

"Have you asked what's wrong?"

Conor issued him a disdainful look. "She only

replies that she is fine, even though it is clear that she is not. I had fully expected her to be eager to come with me to see her youngest nephew." Conan had to agree that it was odd that Laurel had elected not to come and see Cole and Ellenor's new son. "She loves babies. Loves to hold them, be around them. Hell, she even likes how they smell," Conor continued. "I would have thought she would be eager for the chance to be around one now that our children are getting older and more independent."

"Maybe that is what is bothering her."

"How so?"

Conan took in a deep breath and looked upward. In a few minutes, the last bits of sunlight would disappear and it would be a night sky. "I don't know, Conor. What do I know about women and their feelings?"

Conor grabbed Conan's shoulder with a hand and gave it a small shake. "You know nothing about them, but that doesn't mean you don't see what is happening around you. What did you mean?"

Conan twisted his shoulder out of his brother's grasp, annoyed how quickly Conor agreed that he was clueless when it came to women. It was true, but he did not like hearing it. "Only what you were saying. Your children are getting older. They want and need less mothering time. They are—"

The large doors to the great hall unexpectedly opened, cutting Conan off midsentence. A second later, Cole's wife, Ellenor, poked her head out and gave both men a withering stare. "We are all *waiting* for you," she hissed.

Glad for the reprieve, Conan grinned at her and immediately headed for the very full hall. He walked up to the main table, where Cole, his commanders, and their wives were sitting . . . and waiting. He and Conor took a seat, and immediately everyone started to dig into the platters of food before them. The hall was filled with soldiers, and Conan felt a little uncomfortable having made them all wait. He had not expected such a welcome and said as much.

Ellenor rolled her eyes as she started to fill her plate with food. "Only you, Conan, would assume tonight is about *you*. We gather like this every couple of weeks so that all the men get a chance to dine with their laird and enjoy a good meal and the comforts of the castle. You just so happened to arrive on such a night."

Conan grinned. "I don't recall such gatherings during my previous visits. Are you *sure* this isn't all for me? I assure you I appreciate the welcome, but it really isn't necessary."

"I don't think that's it," Conor said contemplatively.

Conan blinked and it took him a second to realize that his eldest brother was continuing the conversation that they had been having outside. Conan sighed. "Then what do you think it could be?"

"I have no idea. We don't even really fight anymore. It is as if someone sapped the energy out of Laurel and all she wants to be is alone."

Laurel *had* spent a lot of time in the Star Tower since Conor had been away. So much so that Conan had noticed and now he felt a little ashamed of feeling glad about her absence when he should have been concerned by it. He considered Laurel an older sister who infuriated him much of the time, but that didn't mean he did not love her. While he hated her meddling in his life, he was not averse to what she had done in his brothers' lives. Laurel had been instrumental in the happiness found by all five of his elder brothers and their wives. If something really was wrong with her, this was not good.

"She has been acting differently, but she seemed healthy when I left. Whatever is bothering her will soon pass, Conor, and she will be back to disagreeing with you, and you will be looking at these days as a brief respite you should have enjoyed."

Conor chewed on a piece of meat. His brows were furrowed, giving the impression that he was not remotely comforted by Conan's words. Conan was not surprised. He was the last person one should go to for encouragement or hope. One came to him for clear absolutes, and on this topic, Conan had only one to give his brother. "Go home and demand she tell you what is going on. Speculating here, with me, is not going to calm your thoughts."

Conor grunted in agreement. "Cole and I have discussed all that we can at this point. He, Dugan, and Donald are going to wait and watch for now. I am not sending any additional troops until we have a better understanding of what is happening between the MacCoinnich clan and their neighbors. So you, I, and Father Lanaghly can leave as soon as we are ready."

Conan pulled off a small piece of bread. "Father Lanaghly is here? I had not seen him and thought he was at the priory or what's left of it."

Conor shook his head. "He arrived about a week ago and, while waiting for you, decided to use the time to prepare the chapel for winter as it is unlikely he will be back until spring."

Conan pushed back the sudden wave of guilt coming over him. If he had left when asked and taken the normal route, he would have arrived about the same time Father Lanaghly had. Instead, his stubbornness had forced the old priest to wait these past several days. "I'll go and let him know that I am here."

"No need. As soon as you were spotted, I let him know that you had arrived. He said he would be ready to leave in the morning."

They finished dinner and Conan rose to his feet. "Should I stay in my old rooms?" he asked Ellenor.

For the past few years, he had come north to stay with Cole and Ellenor for several months at a time. He enjoyed spending time with his elder brother and the soldiers who had elected to leave Conor's guard in an effort to support Cole and what he was trying to build. However, that had never been the main purpose behind his visits. Ellenor had been.

When they had first met, he had been shocked to learn how many languages she not only could speak, but read. With her help, he had been able to decipher several mysterious phrases he had been unable to translate. After a somewhat contentious beginning to their relationship, it had taken a substantial amount of pleading to get Ellenor to agree to teach him what she knew, but eventually she had and was now one of the few women with whom he enjoyed spending time.

They had both been happily surprised to find out how well they worked together. Conan had known Ellenor was intelligent, but he had grown to appreciate her rapier wit and direct approach to things. She also never did anything without reason. So, when she motioned for him to follow her outside, he did so without question.

They left the hall and Conan prepared himself for more questions about Laurel, but instead she pointed to the large, four-wheeled covered cart sitting in front of the stable. "I thought you should be aware that Father Lanaghly convinced Cole to let him take that with you to the priory."

"*Murt!*" Conan muttered. "I thought the church came and got most of the stuff it wanted for the priory."

Ellenor crossed her arms and tilted her head. "They did. Father Lanaghly said they left almost a month ago. But they left someone behind. *That*," she said, pointing at the large cart, "is for her and her items, much of which I understand are mostly documents, books, and scrolls."

"*Her!*" Conan barked. His brain had stopped working right after he'd heard Ellenor tell him that they were not simply retrieving a handful of documents, but rescuing some old nun.

"Aye," Ellenor said. "All I know is she lived at the priory. The church either did not want or could not take her books and things, and she would not leave without them. We would have offered her temporary sanctuary here, but Father Lanaghly thought it might be best for her to be where he was going to be present throughout the winter. Laurel of course agreed, but the herald she sent with the news told us that you were to be told the full aspects of exactly what you were retrieving only *after* you arrived."

Conan was fuming. "My brother knows about this?"

The cold fury in his tone took Ellenor aback. She had known Conan would be mad, which was why she was telling him all that she knew so that he would have time to calm before they left in the morning, but she'd had no idea he would be this mad. Every man hated to be manipulated and Conan was no different, but for some reason Laurel's deceit was cutting him far deeper than Ellenor had anticipated.

"Conor knows, but I don't think he was aware that Laurel kept the full circumstances behind Father Lanaghly's request. Your brother's mind . . . has been a little preoccupied when it comes to his wife, and Cole has tried to minimize anything that might make him more worried about her than he already is."

Conan had been worried about Laurel too, but after this last stunt, any sympathy, concern, or compassion he had been feeling vanished. She had sent him north to get a *nun*! Not only would he be getting things like the writings of Conrad of Saxony and his sermons on the *Speculum Beatæ Mariæ Virginis—The Mirror of the Blessed Virgin Mhàiri*, but a *droch-airidh* nun! Conan was more than half-tempted to refuse. He did not care how many Hail Marys he would have to say. Father Lanaghly would just have to find someone else.

"That's why I'm glad you came. Conor really is worried about Laurel, and Father Lanaghly needs someone who isn't distracted."

Conan gave Ellenor a sideways glance. "You cannot guilt me into agreeing to go."

Ellenor grinned. "I don't need to. You and I both know you won't abandon Father Lanaghly or your brother regardless of how mad you are at Laurel."

Conan pursed his lips together and then pointed at the cart and then toward the gatehouse. "I am *not* driving that thing. Father Lanaghly is. I don't care how old he is."

Ellenor gave his arm a squeeze. "Fine. I'll tell Cole to get one of the stable masters to drive it out to the headland. Now, come see your newest nephew, for it might be some time before you see him again."

Conan turned to follow her toward the keep when he suddenly realized that he had been manipulated yet *again,* just by a different McTiernay wife. "Cole sent you out here to warn me, didn't he?"

Ellenor gave him a wink. "We both knew that surprising you with this in the morning would not be the best way to start the trip."

Conan was not so sure what difference knowing a few hours earlier was going to make. It did not change the facts.

Three men for *one* nun.

Chapter Two

Mhàiri squeezed the knife she held in her hand behind her back as she watched the lone rider slowly come closer. He was not yet close enough for her to see identifying features, but even at a distance, she could see that he was not Father Lanaghly.

Unlike her older sister—who would shock all her fellow nuns if they knew how much Shinae enjoyed wielding a blade—Mhàiri hated to use weapons. Her father had known of her dislike and had not cared. Their nomadic lifestyle had involved a constant, though usually minimal, level of danger; therefore, he had insisted both his daughters learn how to protect themselves. As a result, they had become exceptionally good at being able to handle a dirk. A skill Mhàiri had re-sharpened over the last two weeks while hunting for food. So, if the stranger approaching meant her harm, she could do enough damage to make him regret it.

He was close enough now to make out some details, and Mhàiri was certain she had never before seen the rider. Whoever he was, the man was huge, even for a Highlander—that much Mhàiri could tell. The black beast he rode was similarly massive and would have dwarfed practically every man she had met since she had come to this region, but not him.

He had dark hair and rode with not just confidence but an air of authority. It cloaked him like a second skin. Mhàiri had seen such men when she had lived with her father. They used their stature to intimidate those they encountered, and any show of nervousness signaled either vulnerability or that one had something of value. In her case, both were true. She *was* very vulnerable, *and* she possessed something of enormous value. While many may not recognize the worth of the items inside her small home, it was incalculable to her.

Hoping to give the impression that she neither desired company nor was frightened by his unwanted arrival, Mhàiri took a deep breath and slowly crossed her arms, careful to keep the dirk hidden. The change in stance did nothing to change the stranger's expression, which she could now see was not menacing, or any of the other myriad things she expected to see with such an imposing figure. He looked . . . oddly bored.

The large Highlander tightened the reins and pulled his horse to a stop. Smoke-gray eyes stared down at her for several seconds. The man was much older than her, at least twenty years her senior. Small wrinkles formed across his forehead and under his eyes, and gray hair was slightly visible at his temples, but neither took away from his masculine appeal. Compared to most of the rough-hewn farmers she had encountered in the past couple of years, this man was exceptionally good looking. And refreshingly, he looked to be completely uninterested in her. Too often, her unusual combination of dark hair and pale green eyes pulled to the dark, lustful side of men—especially in this rural part of Scotland. Even married men had a hard time concealing their lust. The large Highlander, however, was definitely not one of them.

"You Mhàiri?" he inquired.

Mhàiri blinked and was about to return his question with one of her own when she saw another rider coming into view. He was approaching more quickly and possibly related to the large Highlander. A much younger, and—if possible—better-looking relation. They were of similar height and build, and both possessed the same shade of dark brown hair as well as chiseled features.

The younger man pulled his horse next to the first man and stared down at her . . . and smiled. Instead of gray eyes, his were a brilliant shade of blue and his smile accentuated deep dimples that should have been appeared feminine, but instead, made him even better looking.

Mentally Mhàiri checked herself and was relieved to know that her jaw had not inadvertently fallen open. Unlike his older friend, the younger Highlander was far from disinterested and was blatantly ogling her as if she were a piece of prized meat.

Mhàiri almost gave him her most withering scowl, but she decided that would be too expected—though she doubted many women had ever spurned this man's advances. She instead opted to assume the look of his older relative and pasted on the most bored look she could muster, coupled with a sigh that only hinted her disgust.

His blue eyes widened with shock. Maybe she had been the first to be unappreciative of his admiration. Mhàiri started to smile triumphantly at the idea, which would have totally ruined the point she had made. Thankfully, at that very moment, she spied the white-haired priest for whom she had been waiting for nearly a week as he rolled into view driving a large cart. She let the grin take over her face and rushed out to greet the one person who had understood her need and vowed to bring back help.

Mhàiri had known Father Lanaghly was a good man the first time she had met him, but when the church had given her no option to continue living with her sister without taking vows, he had become her savior.

No one else had understood or appreciated her predicament. Worse, the leaders of the church had been apathetic that her whole life and plans for the future had been unexpectedly uprooted when the fire burned the small priory to the ground. Her sister, Shinae, had understood but had been powerless to help as she was being ordered to an abbey down south. Mhàiri, who was just shy of twenty years, could have joined them but only if she agreed to take the same vows Shinae was taking. The structured, stifling life of a Catholic nun might have been acceptable for her sister, but not her. Even the offensive idea of marriage would be preferable to a life dictated by the church. Wife and nun were two titles Mhàiri never intended to have.

If marriage had been an option, Mhàiri could have had her choice of local farmers as husbands. Some had been both moderately attractive and quite prosperous, with large stretches of land. But to their shock, she had remained adamant with her refusals. The reason Mhàiri had no desire for a husband was the same reason she had not capitulated to the church's demands to take vows.

Accepting either would mean a loss of the one thing she valued most. Freedom.

One wanted her on her knees praying and doing someone's bidding. The other wanted her on her feet cooking and cleaning until it was time to do her husband's bidding. Both had no appeal, and Mhàiri found it strange that anyone ever intentionally sought out either circumstance.

Before the fire, Mhàiri had been on the verge of regaining the freedom she had relished but had been too naïve to appreciate as a child. The only thing that kept her from losing what little semblance of sanity she retained was that the priory's tiny cottage, which held all her most precious belongings, had been upwind of the flames, escaping the priory's sad destiny.

The priory had been one of the few remaining places in Scotland whose members followed a monastic way of life that focused on helping the local community, not the church. But the Culdees' way of life was disappearing and unless something changed, it would soon all be brought under canonical rule. But it was not other Culdees who had come and emptied the priory.

Priests associated with the Premonstratensian order of the Catholic church had arrived almost a week after the fire. They had been traveling north visiting the Fearn Abbey when they heard about the devastation and came to see if they could offer help. The austere order followed the Rule of St. Augustine as well as several additional statutes that made their life serving God one of great austerity. The life they offered was very different than the one enjoyed by the Culdees at the priory. And it was they who, upon Mhàiri's refusal to join them, had abandoned her to the lonely consequences of her decision.

A decision she might have not been able to make if not for Father Lanaghly.

He had arrived as those of the church were about to leave. He had heard her story, agreed that vows should never be entered into under pressure, and gave her hope. Father Lanaghly promised to send word to the chief of the clan he supported and ask if he would not only keep her things safe, but offer Mhàiri a place to stay until she could get word to the man who could ensure her life of freedom. Her own papa.

That had been nearly two weeks ago.

When Father Lanaghly had left to retrieve a cart and seek out additional help for the journey, Mhàiri had expected him to return within days. She had known deep down that the priest had not forgotten his promise, but she had begun to wonder if the laird Father Lanaghly had sworn would help her was as agreeable to the idea as he had believed. Seeing the kind old priest driving an empty cart immediately restored all the hope he had given her a fortnight ago.

"Father Lanaghly!" Mhàiri cried out and ran out to welcome the priest as he pulled the cart to a halt.

Father Lanaghly smiled down at Mhàiri, glad to see she was in high spirits and still looking healthy after an extended period of being alone. With long, raven-colored hair, an oval face, high cheekbones, and pale green eyes framed by dark lashes, she gave an incorrect impression of being delicate and fragile. Being in the company of five McTiernay wives for the last decade, he had known almost immediately that she was neither. One had only to look into her eyes to see that Mhàiri may be beautiful, but she was not a stranger to challenges. And like some McTiernays he knew, she thrived on them.

"How are you, Mhàiri lass? I was afraid we might find you starving after being gone for so long."

"I told you that I could manage." Mhàiri grinned at him, unable to hide how truly happy she was to see him. She may not like handling weapons, but her accuracy at throwing dirks ensured that she never went without food when game was nearby.

"Indeed," Father Lanaghly responded with a nod. "I assume you are ready to leave? Or should I tell the laird to prepare to camp here tonight?"

"We can leave almost immediately. I only need to pack a few things that I use daily, but it will not take me long. Unless the laird needs to rest?" She looked at Conor with a hint of challenge, intentionally ignoring the younger man at his side.

Conor cracked a smile. "Hope you travel well, for I'll be wanting to make some distance today while there is sunlight and good weather."

Mhàiri arched a brow. "I happen to travel *exceptionally* well."

Father Lanaghly coughed. He gestured at the large empty bed of the wagon he had driven. "Will this suffice?"

Mhàiri enthusiastically bobbed her head up and down. She had feared that she would have to make choices and leave some items behind, but that was no longer a concern. "It should be enough if we also use the small cart that my sister left behind for my use." She pointed to the burned abbey. Peeking out behind some darkened stones was a two-pronged handle that could be attached to a horse's saddle.

Father Lanaghly produced a smile that hinted at mischievous merriment. "'Tis a good thing that I brought assistance then."

The gleam in the larger man's eyes suddenly changed from boredom to one that held mild humor. "Good luck convincing Conan, for that"—Conor pointed to the small, mostly hidden cart—"is not going to be attached to my saddle at any point."

Father Lanaghly just laughed at the threat. "Come and let me introduce you to Laird Conor McTiernay."

Mhàiri noticed out the corner of her eye the younger man had dismounted his horse, but kept her focus on the older Highlander, who remained in his saddle. She wondered if the man was aware he used such intimidation techniques or if it was unintentional. Undaunted, she shaded her eyes from the late morning sun and looked up. "Father Lanaghly, when you promised to bring help, I had no idea that you meant to enlist a laird to help carry my things."

For the first time, the large man smiled. It changed his whole countenance to one that was suspiciously welcoming. Mhàiri felt like a fly being lured into a web. Even more so when he spoke and she heard the rich timbre of his voice. "I respect the father, but no man drags me anywhere I do not want to be. The priest and I just happened to leave at the same time, and I'm not here to help you with your things." Using his thumb, he gestured to the cottage door. "I'm here to help you with *Conan*."

Mhàiri crinkled her brow in confusion and then suddenly realized that the younger Highlander was no longer in sight. Based on where the laird was pointing, the one called Conan was inside her home. She issued a scathing glare at Conor as if he was partly to blame for the invasion and then rushed to the small cottage.

Unperturbed by her hostile glance, Conor threw his leg over his horse's rear end and planted his feet on the ground. Father Lanaghly came to stand beside him and joined his gaze at the cottage's entrance.

Conor crossed his arms and rocked back on his heels. "At least we no longer need to wonder when or how Conan will provoke her to anger." He chuckled. "This time, my brother didn't even have to open his mouth." He glanced at the priest. "I have a feeling things are about to get interesting."

Father Lanaghly returned the smile. "More than you think. She—" The priest paused to point at the woman who came to an abrupt halt at the cottage doorway. "Is the female version of your brother Conan."

Seeing Father Lanaghly was being earnest, Conor raised his brows and took another look at the thin, dark-haired woman. Maybe the slow journey home was not going to be as painful as he had thought. "If you're right, then things are about to get *very* interesting."

Conan picked one of the scrolls out of a bag and carefully started to unfurl it, hoping that it was some type of map despite the unlikelihood any would be kept at a priory. At first glance, it looked to be only an inconsequential sketch of some mountains and he almost put it back. But when he realized what it was, Conan rolled it out completely on the small table to study. It was not just mountains, but a detailed drawing of this region of Scotland and how the land stretched out to the sea from the viewpoint if one were on top of one of the peaks. Scribed on the bottom was *Beinn Eighe*. Conan had never seen anything like it. Drawings were rarely detailed and never accurate. Flat pieces of art, they showed detail, but never any depth. As a result, drawings were symbolic in nature, not very informative. But this . . . this was an *actual* depiction of nearby lands.

Conan pulled out another scroll. It, too, was a drawing, but this one was of Loch Torridon and it even captured Cole's castle, Fàire Creachann, though minutely. Nothing he had ever seen compared to what he was looking at. Artists just did not draw like this.

He wondered how many scrolls held such beauty and eagerly pulled a third scroll out. With a sigh of relief, he found it was what he had originally expected. A common document he had seen in one of any number of abbeys, churches, or places of learning. He put it aside. That was something that could easily be left behind.

The one-room cottage was small, but it was full. Three large chests plus a smaller one that looked as if it had seen better days were in one corner. On a table were several bound documents, and next to them was a crate filled with what looked to be even more bound books. There was also a bag with even more scrolls peeking out. In total, it was too much even for the large cart they had brought. Some things would have to remain. Just because the church had left all this behind did not make it his responsibility. If they wanted what he determined was unimportant, they could come back and retrieve it themselves.

Hearing the rapid patter of light footsteps, Conan kept his eyes on the paper but said out loud, "I'm glad to see not everything here is a religious relic. Some of this might actually be useful beyond an abbey's walls."

Mhàiri immediately had dashed up to the door, afraid of what she might find. While she had been ready for days for the priest's return, she still had a few things that she had been waiting until the last minute to pack. She had feared the large oaf was throwing them into one of the empty crates or, God forbid, a sack. If he had been, she probably would have exploded, potentially saying something that would cause the priest and his laird to decide she was a harpy and not worth the hassle. Instead, the good-looking beast was studying her prized possessions, and while not mishandling them, he was judging them, finding some to be of no value. The idea of being left alone once again was suddenly very appealing.

"Maybe you shouldn't be touching things you know nothing about."

Conan easily ignored the barb, having been on the receiving end of a female's insults for most of his life. However, the lilting quality of her voice caught him off guard. Rather than high-pitched, it was unusually low and therefore compelling. He had not been prepared for it, just like he had not been prepared for what he had seen when he had ridden up to the priory.

When Conan had first spied her, he could tell that she was slender and, while she was much shorter than him, she would be considered almost tall for a woman. However, it was not until he was much closer that he had realized Father Lanaghly's nun was not the old woman he'd assumed she would be. She was young and absolutely not nun-like.

Nuns, even pretty ones, looked severe in their wimples, habits, and overall austere attire. While the garb hinted at their figures, only their eyebrows indicated the color of their hidden hair. But Conan knew this little nun's to be several shades darker than his own, for it had been left free, falling in loose waves down to the middle of her back. Her gown was also not that of a habit, but a simple golden bliaut that was cut rather narrowly around her abdomen with lacing along the sides to create tension. It fit her buxom body perfectly.

When he had ridden up and his blue eyes had locked with hers, Conan had forgotten about where he was, why he was there, and whom he was with. He had seen many beautiful women in his years and charmed a number of them to his bed, but the woman before him was beauty in its purest form.

Immediately he had grown aroused, his body refusing to behave despite the fact that she was a nun. *If she gets offended seeing my desire, then she has only herself to blame*, Conan had thought. What drove a woman like her to the church anyway? With her beauty, she could have any man she wanted. Even he would accept her attentions—if only for a while. That in itself was quite remarkable as he had been abstaining from female company the past several months, having decided they were not worth the eventual headache.

Long-term commitment to a woman had proven impossible, and marriage was a preposterous state meant for men like his brothers. Conan's future was that of a rustic, nomadic life that while appealed to him, made women cringe. In a few months, he would at last be seeking his dreams, never to be in one place long enough to create roots.

However, Conan was not averse to the idea of scratching an itch. And while some in the clergy fully adhered to the concept of abstinence, Conan knew that many did not. Maybe this pretty little nun fell in the latter category.

Instinctively, Conan had tightened his grip on the reins and had grinned down at her. He was quite aware that his dimples had some magical power over the opposite sex. In his youth, he had wondered why, but when one of his brother's elite guards, Hamish, who also had dimples, had pointed out that he should spend less time wondering why they worked and more time using them, Conan had realized his energies had been ill-placed.

For a second, Conan had thought she was going to smile back. But instead, her expression had remained unaffected. In fact, she had looked almost apathetic. It had been as if men like himself rode up to her doorstep daily and he was just one among many. Then, she had broken into a wide, sincere smile that had made her look even *more* beautiful and run to see the priest. Conan had grimaced.

What women thought of him was typically a nonfactor in his life. Once he was done with a woman, he really had no interest in her opinion of him—whether it was good or bad. But this little nun had dismissed him *before* he had given her a good reason. That *never* happened. Women *always* took at least a second, and usually much longer, to look at him. It was so common that he did not even think about it anymore . . . until today. Unfortunately, the obvious snub had happened in front of his observant brother.

Conor had not wasted the opportunity to jibe him either. "You're losing your touch, Conan," he had mumbled, not even trying to conceal his mirth. "Usually you have to at least *talk* to a woman before she decides to ignore you."

It was at that moment Conan had jumped down from his horse to head inside the cottage, uncaring that he had not been invited. He did not need his brother's nonsense and he certainly did not need to be snubbed by a nun who had summoned him for help.

In the cottage, Mhàiri took a step closer. This Conan was either being intentionally rude or daydreaming about something. "Did you hear me?"

Aye, I hear you, Conan answered but not out loud. He held his breath, prepping himself for the memory of what she looked like in hopes of keeping his body from once again reacting in a way he could not control. "Nuns should look like nuns, not women—*especially* if they are beautiful," he mumbled under his breath.

"Excuse me?"

Conan gave up and forced his eyes to open. He put down the document he was holding and then picked up the next one. Almost immediately, he put it down and looked at the next in the stack. "That one you can leave behind," he said, pointing at the scroll he had discarded. "It is fortunate that I didn't send someone else to help you and Father Lanaghly. They wouldn't have been able to help decide what here is worth taking and what can remain behind."

Mhàiri felt her jaw go slack. She had been subjected to the idea that men knew more than women most of her life just because so few females were educated, but it had been a while since she had been around a man so rudely open with his belittling opinions. "You are a presumptuous one."

"Most women simply call me arrogant," Conan murmured, still refusing to look at her. He would never admit it, but he was afraid to do so.

"Then they were wrong."

That made Conan pause, but only momentarily. "How so?" He finished scanning the scroll and then put it down. "It does accurately denote self-assurance." He picked up the next item and inspected its spine.

"Let me clarify then. In your case, I think that arrogant is far too limiting. You are *so* much more."

Mhàiri readied herself for an angry response or at least a scathing but defensive comment, but the Highlander surprised her. He instead glanced over his shoulder and grinned at her before returning his gaze back to the items on the table.

"I must say I am surprised that a woman, let alone a nun, has some of these volumes. Does your abbess know these are in your possession?" He wiggled the small volume that was in his right hand.

Nun? Mhàiri was momentarily stunned and glad that the beast of a man was facing away from her. Did he actually think she was a nun? It was both amusing and idiotic at the same time. The last thing she looked like—or talked like—was a nun. "*Bhreithneachail asal,*" Mhàiri muttered, echoing aloud her own thoughts about him.

Conan turned around abruptly at the insult. It was not the first time someone had called him a judgmental ass, but it was the first time a nun had called him one. "My sister-in-law calls me that from time to time, and while I don't deny being a little judgmental, it's a hard habit to break since I'm right practically all of the time." He paused, looked her in the eye, and then pointed to the items on the table. "Just as I'm right about only some of this stuff being worth the effort of trekking across the Torridon Mountains."

She reached out to grab the volume only for it to be pulled out of her reach. Mhàiri scowled. "It must be nice to be around obviously abundantly patient and tolerant family members who let you live in some fictitious world where they pretend to admire and respect you for your intellect, but I'm not your family. I'm not inclined to indulge your delusions. And though no doubt remarkable to you, I neither need nor want your opinion."

Conan rolled his eyes. It was a surprisingly well-stated insult, if a little wordy. Most women could only muster simple one-word slurs. Nonetheless, she was still a woman, and being a nun did not change a female's natural disposition toward drama. "I doubt there has ever been a female who can humbly accept honesty, but I'll admit that you do seem unusually clever for a *bean rialta feargach.* Maybe you will be the first."

Now the oaf was not only calling her a nun, but an *angry* nun? It was laughable. Almost as much as the idea that she was bothered by honesty. "Honesty is always appreciated from someone worthy of my respect. Something I doubt you'll ever earn."

"I'll earn it, *mo bean rialta go leor beag,* of that I have no doubt."

Mhàiri almost laughed. "*Pretty* little nun? I guess that is better than being an angry one." The man exuded a level of self-confidence that could not be measured, and yet unlike most overly self-important men, this Highlander believed every word he said. There was a lot of bravado to his words, but none of them, in his mind, were false.

"I can't keep calling you that. Too hard. My name is Conan. What is yours?"

Conan. That was what Laird McTiernay called him, Mhàiri thought as she rolled the name around in her head. She liked the sound of it. It fit him. Conan was both elegant and untamed, much like the massive Highlander looked. "Mhàiri."

Conan looked at her then, not a quick glance like he had been giving her, but a long look, as if he was studying her. A version of the name Mhàiri was found in practically every culture and while her pronunciation of it was definitely Gaelic, it gave him no insight as to her origins. She spoke and acted as if she was a Scot, but this nun did not look like any woman born and raised in the Highlands. A very fine and delicate beauty, she looked as if she belonged to another land far away from the harsh one he had always known. Mhàiri was becoming more and more of an enigma. One he did *not* need to figure out. Thank God she was a nun.

Mhàiri arched a brow, reminding him that he was staring. Guilt briefly swept his features. His blue eyes had studied her so intently, she had felt as if she were being stripped of her clothing . . . and by a man who would tempt even the most devout of nuns. And the last thing she was, was a nun. Everything about this Highlander exuded masculinity. Whoever Conan McTiernay was, he was intensely, if not overwhelmingly, male.

"Now it is you who are staring."

Mhàiri squeezed her eyes shut, hating that he was right. "I'm hoping you are not just another brutish soldier who lacks appreciation of anything that cannot be used in battle."

Conan ignored her fiery retort and pointed to the smaller of two stacks on the table. "Mhàiri," he said calmly and with a tone he hoped would elicit compliance, "this pile we should bring. I still need to look at the rest and decide what else should be kept."

Mhàiri looked at the stack a little better and realized that Conan had not been simply looking and putting down the various things he had been going through, but organizing them. "Meaning those other items are going to be just left behind?"

"Aye. We only brought one cart. Either some of *these* remain behind," Conan said, pointing to the crate, the things on the table, and the bag of rolled documents, "or your *personal* things remain behind." He then gestured toward the large chests, and Mhàiri realized he had no idea that those too were full of bound books. The most precious ones she owned. If the church had known they had existed, they would have stolen them from her two weeks ago.

"My chests are *definitely* coming with me," she clarified and, upon seeing him smile, added, "as well as *everything else.*"

Patience gone, Conan picked up one of the thinner documents from the discard pile. "The written word is a wonderful thing but not at the expense of a dead horse trying to haul it for three days across mountains. This is puerile, and it remains."

Mhàiri's father had tried to use the same firm tone when she was a child and it had never worked. "Conan"—this time it was she who used a calm and patient voice—"I think you don't realize why Father Lanaghly asked you to come and help. It was not for this," she smugly replied, jabbing a finger toward his head, "but for these." She pointed to his seriously impressive biceps. "I don't need your opinions. I need only your brute strength. And it is a good thing too, based on these senseless piles you created."

It was not often Conan was taken aback by a woman. And he did not like it. "What's that supposed to mean?"

Mhàiri rolled her eyes and stepped around him, gathering the items on the table and putting them back into a single stack. "Do not take offense, for you are very attractive, Conan, and I'm sure your looks are enough for most women to ignore your nonsensical comments, but you have to know on some level that you are an idiot."

Conan's jaw dropped. Not because Mhàiri had insulted him, but because she *really* thought him to be unintelligent. That was a first, and it rendered him speechless.

"You can go ahead and place those on the large cart while I finish prepping these for travel."

Conan could only think of one thing. He had to prove that *he* was not the idiot—she was for assuming so!

He went to one of the open crates, bent down, and started pulling items out. Conan flashed a small bound volume over his shoulder. "This? *This* is what you absolutely must take with you? Just what does a nun need with the partial recreations of rather lewd French romance poems on the Vulgate Cycle?"

Mhàiri grabbed the book and clutched it to her chest, momentarily mortified that he had recognized what it was. Then she remembered she was not the nun he'd assumed her to be. "So you are not illiterate, just ignorant."

"Do not worry. Most nuns would never admit to it, but I happen to know that several enjoy a good raunchy story and it hurts no one," Conan stated, misunderstanding what she had meant. "Though I must admit they are usually hiding tales about the quest for the Holy Grail or the romance of Lancelot and Guinevere."

Conan pulled out another book and studied it. "Interesting."

Mhàiri tried to grab it, but again Conan moved it out of reach. "What is so interesting?" she asked through clenched teeth.

"That so many of these are not religious-based, but informational." He stood up and flipped through the pages of the medicinal book that would have been a treasure for barber doctors. It was filled with stuff on herbs, plants, and their medicinal effects, as well as sketches of the human anatomy.

He glanced up. Seeing her outstretched hand, he placed the book in it. "That is far from typical reading, especially for a woman, and even more so for a nun. Do you know what that book is about, or were you just charged with its care?"

"My father purchased it before I came to the priory. It was written by an English physician who was concerned about unskilled barbers performing phlebotomies and scarifications." Knowing that he had no idea what she was saying, Mhàiri could not help but add, "And what is your opinion on barber surgeons?"

Conan grimaced and scratched his chin before pointing at the book she now held. "I've heard of Bruno di Longoburgo and recognize some of his sketches, but medicine has never been a keen interest of mine. So I guess I do not know enough about the subject to have an opinion. Not like this," he said, picking up one of her more prized volumes, "if it is what I think it is. *Otia Imperialia*?"

Mhàiri swallowed and nodded. It was the best-known work of Gervase of Tilbury and called the "Book of Marvels" as it focused on three fields—history, geography, and physics.

She had been calling him ignorant for assuming her a nun, but she had made some hugely incorrect assumptions herself. This man was not just literate, or even just educated. He was smart. How smart, she was not sure, but she suspected extremely so. She had spent time around some very bright men in her youth, the most intelligent of which had been her father. But Conan had not only recognized the documents he had pulled out, he had been able to read them . . . and they were each in a different language.

Only old men who spent their lives engrossed in books had such broad knowledge. And Conan was young. Moreover, he did not look like he spent his time indoors. Muscles like the ones he had came about from hours of physical labor. For him to have such knowledge at his age meant that he absorbed material like she did. Rapidly. Considerably faster than most scholars.

"What is your favorite field?" Conan asked, the sincerity of his question unmistakable.

"Um . . . geography," Mhàiri answered. "Though I find some of Gervase's accounts unbelievable."

Conan shrugged and put it down. "Of course they are. It is a hundred years old and created to entertain King Henry II's son. But how does a priory, let alone one of this small size set in the middle of the western Highlands, possess such a copy?"

Mhàiri's back straightened. "The *priory* possessed very little. The Culdees were focused on helping those in the area, not improving their minds."

She was not sure that Conan heard her because he was kneeling down again and looking at what else she had in the crate. He gasped and looked back at her.

"Guido delle Colonne? How did you get the works of an Italian writer?"

Mhàiri blinked. "You can also read Italian?"

He nodded and stood back up. "My brother Cole's wife can read and speak French, Italian, and Latin. She taught me the basics of Latin and from there, the others came quickly. The more I read, the more I understood and could pick up from context. I wouldn't say I could speak it, but I no longer have difficulties reading most things."

Mhàiri took a step forward and placed her hand on his forearm, suddenly feeling as if she had found a kindred spirit. "I also have a mind for languages. My father said it was a gift and that very few find them easy to digest and learn."

Conan looked down at the slender hand on his arm. Need suddenly racked his body, and it was suddenly critical to get some distance between them—physically, mentally, and emotionally. From his experience, the best way to get a woman to go away was to make her angry. "So, since you understand what these are, you can help decide what the church is going to have to come back for and what remains behind. But accept the fact that not all of this is coming with us."

Mhàiri's gaze narrowed and she ripped her hand from his arm. "These are *my* things, not the church's. And because they are mine, every book, scroll, and document you see will be coming with me. Nothing will be left behind, and when we arrive at the end of our journey, everything will *remain* mine."

Conan stood up and waved his hand. "Just where do you plan on putting all *your* things? For we are headed to *my* home, where there is only *one* place where all written material is stored. *My* chambers."

"Then I guess they will become *my* chambers during my stay because, as I said, my things are staying with me!"

"You think you can order a McTiernay out of his castle chambers? Even Conor would say you were mad."

Mhàiri's pale green eyes grew large as she realized what he meant. Conan was not a cousin, nephew, or distant relation to Laird McTiernay. He was his *brother*. And he lived at the very place where the priest had said she and her things would be safe until her father could come get her. Father Lanaghly had told her she would be welcomed by the laird and that all but one of the brothers was married and lived away. All but the one standing right in front of her.

The old priest had further promised that Lady McTiernay was educated and appreciated knowledge and that the castle boasted of one of the largest libraries of information outside of an abbey. Never had Father Lanaghly mentioned that her things would fall into the hands of the unmarried brother.

A loud cough made Mhàiri jump. She turned around and saw Laird McTiernay at her doorway. He had gray eyes and some gray hair, but otherwise their facial features, their build, their air of confidence—they were all almost identical. Mhàiri felt as if she had been physically punched.

The man *was* indeed Conan's older brother.

Laird McTiernay had just heard her spoiled declaration to kick Conan out of his chambers during her stay.

Mhàiri wished she could rewind the day and start all over, beginning with welcoming him and thanking him for helping her. The laird was probably rethinking taking her with him at all, let alone hauling her things and giving her a temporary home until her father was found.

Mhàiri was about to apologize and say as much when she saw two gray eyes sparkling at her. In their smoky depths, she saw not anger, but mirth. "I think Laurel will be delighted at the idea of you taking over the North Tower."

"Over my dead body," came an angry growl behind her. Only four words, but they held much venom. Mhàiri knew that Conan was serious.

"Laurel just might oblige," Conor replied with a chuckle, completely unaffected by his younger brother's threat. "But until then, let's start taking all this out of here. I want to leave as soon as possible."

"It can't all fit in one cart," Conan countered.

The smug tone in his voice rankled Mhàiri once again. "Then it is a good thing that I have another one."

"Aye," Conor confirmed. "Father Lanaghly and I just finished hooking it up to your horse," he said, grinning at Conan so widely Mhàiri thought the laird's face would split. "Only need to load it up so we can go."

Conan glowered first at Conor and then at Mhàiri before stomping outside. "*Murt*," he muttered to himself, seeing that his horse really was hooked up to a second cart. It was smaller, but between the two, there would be enough room to allow Mhàiri to take all her belongings.

Conan marched back in and grabbed a box. Before he exited, he leveled a gaze on Mhàiri. "You may be a nun, but you've got two arms. Use them and help carry *your* things."

Conan walked out and put the box on the smaller

cart. He started to go back and get another load when he heard a truly disconcerting sound. That of a priest in the middle of guffaws. "Mhàiri is no more a nun than you are a monk," Father Lanaghly managed to get out between gasps for breath. "Anyone could tell by looking at her she never took any vows."

"You thought Mhàiri was a *nun*?" he heard Conor ask as he came out with a large stuffed bag of scrolls. "Wait till Laurel hears this. She always said you were not as intelligent as I thought."

Conan was furious. He wanted to say something, anything, to end his humiliation. For a moment, he thought his brother understood and was going to back off, but he should have known that Conor would enjoy this moment for as long as possible.

"I can see you are mad, but even you have to admit that you've never been wrong about so much in such a short period of time."

Mhàiri stared at the night sky and studied the nuances of landscape, trying to decide how to best capture its likeness. It was very late and the mountains' shadows hid most of the details, but the moon was bright, giving her enough light to produce a basic sketch. Normally drawing was the best remedy to a bad day, but tonight, she did not expect it to bring her any measurable level of comfort. How quickly those feelings of smug satisfaction at her cottage had shifted to frustration, regret, and finally complete embarrassment. Thank goodness they were to arrive at McTiernay Castle tomorrow.

They had left her cottage much later in the day than anticipated, mostly because while she had had everything packed, it had not been organized in a way that made efficient use of space. Once they had finally departed, no one had spoken to her except the priest, who had been focused on being hungry and how he had forgotten how uncomfortable it was to travel driving a cart. The next day had been more of the same, although Laird McTiernay had periodically offered her a few words of acknowledgement. The third time the laird had come back, Father Lanaghly had laughed, followed by murmurings that Lady McTiernay would be pleased with her husband's diplomatic efforts, leaving Mhàiri with no doubts that Conor was only talking with her to be nice.

Then there was today. Conan and his brother had ridden way ahead most of the time, leaving her with solely the priest as company. Mhàiri did not mind being alone and could have tolerated silence, but it seemed that Father Lanaghly enjoyed company. He had spoken about anything and everything. So when Conan had mumbled that they were stopping to make camp for the night, Mhàiri had been relieved. She had also decided that she was going to apologize to Conan and hopefully induce him into conversation. She was surprised to find that, looking back at her and Conan's altercation, she had enjoyed it. The last person she had had a worthy debate with was her father—and that had been years ago.

She had barely stepped down off the cart when a dead bird and two small rabbits were laid at her feet. After two nights of doing both the hunting and the cooking, the men had seemed to think she should offer to do the latter.

She had survived for two weeks on her own, so it was not that Mhàiri could not cook; it was that she

could not cook well. Several times, her father, her
sister, or other members of the priory had tried to get
her to learn, but Mhàiri had soundly refused. Such a
skill set was a big step toward a future and life she refused to accept. Standing in a kitchen all day preparing food, only to have to clean up after everyone ate
before seeing to her husband's "other" needs, was how
she defined hell.

After seeing the looks on all three men's faces as
they had bitten into the barely edible piece of charred
meat, she had regretted being so stubborn about
learning *nothing*. Laird McTiernay had looked ill and
the priest's expression had conveyed pity, but Conan's
had been one of utter disgust. It was as if he had somehow *known* that while she had not intended to ruin the
meal, she had intentionally never learned to cook,
which meant someone had served her meals for her
entire life.

Mhàiri felt blessed to have been born from such
wonderful parents whose lifestyle meant continual adventures and seeing new sights. But that did not mean
she did not also know of heartbreak. Her mother had
died when she had been only ten, and by the age of
fourteen, Mhàiri had been sent to join her older sister
at the priory, where her father thought she would be
safe. Aye, Mhàiri had been fortunate in many ways, but
she had never considered herself spoiled. Not until
tonight. And worse, she knew Conan had not been
wrong.

"What are you doing?"

Mhàiri jumped at the sound of his voice. Conan was
surprised. His approach had been loud so she must
have been deep in thought. Then again, she might
have just been surprised he was even talking to her. He

had certainly not enjoyed being humiliated by his many foolish assumptions, but his anger with her had been short-lived. His brother, however, refused to let the matter drop. Conan had had no choice but to stay away lest he encourage another set of witticisms.

Mhàiri turned to look at him. Even in the dim light, her pale green eyes seemed to see through him. "I, um, uh, nothing really. Just sketching the loch and some of the mountains." She then looked around him to see if anyone else was approaching.

"Conor left to visit a nearby farm since we are on the outskirts of McTiernay land."

"I suspect the need for something to eat drove him to that decision," Mhàiri whispered, feeling guilty once again.

"Probably so. My brother does love good food. It's the only reason he and anyone else put up with Fiona."

"Who's Fiona?"

"She runs the kitchens at McTiernay Castle. And when I say Fiona runs the kitchens, that is *exactly* what I mean. Laurel won't admit it, but even she is careful when dealing with the surly beast." Mhàiri furrowed her brows at the slur. Conan waggled his finger at her. "See if that description is not completely accurate after you've met her. And what's more, you won't complain because Fiona's food is that good."

Mhàiri looked around to see who else might hear them. "Where is Father Lanaghly?"

Conan looked behind him and pointed to somewhere in the blackness. "He said it was too warm by the fire and is snoring somewhere way over there." Turning back around, he looked out and said, "It is a pretty view."

He moved to sit down beside her. Mhàiri's eyes grew

large with shock, but she scooted to make room. "Can't sleep?" she finally asked after almost two minutes of silence between them.

Conan shook his head, but offered no explanations.

"My father was sometimes restless at night. Said his brain refused to be quiet. That it was hard to get his thoughts to calm."

Conan stared at her for a second. Was it possible that she understood? That sleeping throughout the night was something he often struggled with and had for his whole life? He picked up a stick and started poking the ground with it. "Then your father and I must be of similar minds."

"My mother called it kindred spirits. My father said talking to her helped," Mhàiri said, hinting that she would be open to him talking to her.

Conan flashed her one of his best smiles. "Talking worked for him, huh? Then, maybe we're *not* kindred spirits." When Mhàiri whipped her head back to face forward, Conan knew that his smile had affected her. It affected most women to some degree, and while he was not above using it as a tool to achieve a goal, that had not been his intention just now. The last thing he wanted was for Mhàiri to get nervous and leave. "Some nights, questions or answers to questions start to spin through my head, making it impossible to fall back asleep. I've tried everything from sitting calmly to being outside, to taking a long ride. Even tried sparring."

Mhàiri quirked a brow. "What about lovemaking?" Immediately, her jaw dropped and she clamped a hand around her mouth, mortified.

Conan just chuckled, glad Mhàiri had not jumped to her feet to run away. But after her so easily ignoring him when they first met, then their heated debate in the cottage, knowing sex was also on her mind was quite comforting. "Of course I've tried it."

And he had. Multiple times and in multiple ways. Not only did it not work, it almost always resulted in less enjoyable consequences. Invariably, within weeks—or days—the woman would seek more than Conan wanted to give, get upset that she was not the "one" who could convince him to give up his bachelor ways, and then cause a scene when she realized she had not changed him in the least. He was still the same opinionated, brutally honest man that everyone had warned her about.

"I can't believe I just asked that!"

"I can," Conan replied. Seeing sparks in her eyes, he added, "What? God did not create the desire for physical intimacy only in men. I happen to know that women enjoy the act just as much."

"I bet you do," she scoffed.

Conan squeezed his eyes shut and mentally chastised himself. If he did not want Mhàiri to order him away, he was certainly talking as if he did. "Now I'm the one shocked by saying my thoughts aloud."

Mhàiri looked at him and shook her head with a small smile. "Aye, but I think that's very rare. God was unfair when he made you, Conan McTiernay. You are far too good looking a man. You snatch a woman's thoughts right out of her head, making her atypically vulnerable to your charms."

Conan had been ready for a caustic comment, but Mhàiri had surprised him. Once again, she had proved to be an enigma he wanted to understand better. "Your own beauty can also be quite disarming."

Mhàiri gave a small, feminine snort. "I doubt the most beautiful woman in the world could 'disarm' you."

Conan turned to look at her directly in the eye. "You underestimate your beauty, Mhàiri, but I must admit that it is your keen wit and disturbingly accurate insight that intrigue me the most."

"So you are not angry anymore with me?"

Conan shrugged. "Conor was right. It's not often I'm wrong, and I hate it when my brother is around when it happens. That it happened repeatedly within the span of an hour was bad enough. But it was Conor who kept reminding me about it that made me ill company. Then, again it's rare anyone considers me decent company even when I'm not riled. Supposedly I'm rude even when I try hard not to be."

A soft smile played on Mhàiri's lips. "It takes more than simple rudeness to upset me."

Conan could tell she truly meant the unusual claim. "Then what does?"

Mhàiri leaned back on her hands and looked upward, thinking. "Oh, the things that would anger most anyone. Deceit. Being unreliable. Excessive whininess or exaggeration. And oh, when I am made to feel like a fool." Seeing him smile, she said, "And condescension. That one really can be very annoying."

"I think I might have touched that last one when we met."

"Maybe a little, but I guess it is understandable you thought I was only the keeper of the books and not their owner. While I hate that it is true, I know that most women have not received the education my father gave me."

"Nor are they blessed with the intelligence you have." His smile got wider, enhancing his dimples.

Mhàiri looked away, thinking that men should not have dimples. It was unfair. "Perhaps. But I would advise you to stop assuming most women have an inherent lack of understanding of anything beyond tending a home. One does not need to be literate and well-read to be sensible and capable of conversation."

"I agree with you on principle, but my experience says otherwise. I've met very few who can hold my interest during a discussion."

Mhàiri nudged his shoulder with her own. "It's your dimples. They get in the way of us females being coherent, let alone witty."

"I was always told it was my eyes." Conan laughed, finding this odd conversation surprisingly enjoyable.

"Oh, they are very nice indeed. So blue a woman could drown in them by staring long enough. But it's your dimples that are the conversation killers. So, in the future, when you want to have a rational conversation with a woman, you know what to do. Simply don't smile."

Conan's grin grew only larger.

"You're doing that on purpose," Mhàiri teased. "But you should know that I'm no longer dazzled by them. Their effect is surprisingly short-lived."

This time Conan laughed out loud. "That explains it! I never could figure out why my track record with women was so astoundingly short."

"I get the feeling that the brevity of your relationships does not really bother you."

Conan shook his head. "Not in the least, though my sister-in-law thinks it should."

"Lady McTiernay?"

"Aye. You will meet Laurel tomorrow." Seeing a look of apprehension invade Mhàiri's eyes, he quickly added, "Don't worry. Not only will she love that you are not vulnerable to either my eyes or dimples, Laurel simply likes everyone. Well, everyone *except* me."

"I doubt that."

Conan shrugged and looked down at what was in Mhàiri's lap. He had known she was drawing something, but he had assumed she was etching on parchment—something he often did before finalizing them in ink. It was a way to enjoy the activity of drawing without incurring the high costs. However, once again, he had been wrong.

Conan could not believe what he was looking at and, without thought, reached over and plucked the drawing off her legs. The feel of it proved the dim light had not confused him. Mhàiri was indeed drawing on hemp.

Hemp paper was much lighter than vellum, was easier to write on and required far less ink. He had only seen it used in the larger abbeys and even then, only in small quantities. The only hemp paper mill he knew of was in Spain, erected a few decades ago, but its product was sought by many. If he had access, he would be one of those many customers.

Such a writing medium would radically change his approach to traveling this spring. Vellum in the quantities he intended to bring was cumbersome. Though the leather was very thin, in large amounts, it was also very heavy. If he ever had a chance to shift to using hemp paper, he would not hesitate.

Conan fingered the material for several seconds and was about to hand it back to Mhàiri when the drawing itself caught his attention. He tilted it toward the moonlight and took a longer look. The unique style was similar to that of the drawings he had found in Mhàiri's cottage. He froze. That unusual artwork had been *hers*.

"This is incredible," he said in a whisper.

"I, uh, thank you."

"No, I am being quite serious," he said more strongly and looked up at her. "Pictures always denote things, but never have I seen something drawn that actually looked like it does in reality. I feel as though I can dip my hand through this and touch what you are drawing."

Mhàiri's face erupted into the largest smile. Conan could not have paid her a higher compliment.

"This almost looks like where we are sitting right . . ." Conan stopped talking and started looking at the paper and then at the landscape. Both were difficult to see in only the moonlight, but Conan could make out differences. Minor to some, but to him, they were significant.

A frisson of anger surged through him. Conan got to his feet and turned to her, doing nothing to disguise his temper. He shook her drawing at her. "This is clearly a drawing of this land, but when I look out I see a river. A *river*, I might add, that clearly denotes just where McTiernay land begins. And yet, in your drawing you changed it to a *loch*."

Mhàiri blinked. "Is *that* why you are suddenly so angry? Because I like to draw lochs more than rivers?" She jumped up and attempted to snatch her drawing out of his grasp but failed.

"No. I'm angry because God gave you a gift. You have the power to put onto paper *exactly* how the world looks but instead you mock him by changing it."

"I do *not* mock God," Mhàiri hissed.

"You do when you misuse your gifts. I don't know how,

but you have hemp—something incredibly precious—and what are you using if for? *Yourself!*" he snarled, shaking the paper in his hand. "Your drawings could have infinite value. You could create not merely the most beautiful maps, but the most accurate ones the world has ever seen. But you draw to amuse only yourself. And *worse*, what you draw is so close to reality that many will actually mistake it for just that."

Conan leaned down so that their noses were a few inches apart. "I would give anything for a gift like yours, but I'd rather not have it at all than misuse it like you do."

Mhàiri stood completely still.

Conan knew he was scaring her and deep down, he also knew he was overreacting, but he had never seen anyone capture the world as it actually looked. Art showed nothing about a country's size, shape, or features. Mhàiri had the ability to capture information that could win wars . . . maybe even stop them. She could save lives by marking safe passageways that even a completely illiterate man could follow. Instead, she drew only for herself.

"My drawing has value to *me*. I draw the world how I wish it to be. I only wish I could do the same for you. For I would capture everything about you just as you are with one exception. Your judgmental soul. For *that* is what needs to be fixed. *That* is why women never want to be with you for very long. It is not your mannerisms or your *honesty* as you would like to think."

"And it is just as clear to me why *you* are not married." Conan marched away before he could hear another word. He hated quarreling with women. It was impossible to reason with someone who countered anything logical with nonsense. But arguing with smart women? They were the absolute worst. They could twist anything to something that sounded logical to them.

Draw someone's soul. Laurel was going to love her.

Spring could not come fast enough.

The next morning, Mhàiri stood staring at the same view that had created such a mixture of strong emotions in her. Hearing someone approach, she glanced to see who it was, relieved to learn that it was Father Lanaghly.

"Good morning, Mhàiri lass. Conan is hitching up the horses now. Conor never returned so he probably rode ahead on his own."

"Thank you." Mhàiri knew her voice was still sorrowful, even though she had tried to mask it.

"I knew after a few minutes of our first meeting that you were special. I knew because I have been fortunate to personally know two others who perceive things like you do—Conan and his niece, Bonny. All three of you see the world differently from anyone else."

"Conan thinks that my seeing the world differently is a crime."

Father Lanaghly chuckled. "Conan is a man who rarely encounters his intellectual equal. Being different has forced him apart from others. Even when he is surrounded by people—including family—he is alone. So do not let Conan or his abrupt ways bother you."

"I grew up with gruff manners and direct words. My father is very smart and has an incredibly direct and forthright personality. It aggravates some, but it is also what made him very successful as a merchant. So while

I might have wished Conan stated his comments very nicely and sweetly, it would not have mattered."

"Some people—usually women—have issues with Conan's approach to things," Father Lanaghly remarked cautiously.

"Not surprising," Mhàiri said with a shrug of her shoulders. "Most would rather have someone lie to them."

Father Lanaghly tipped his head to one side but did not argue. "Even when Conan is completely wrong, he earnestly believes otherwise. I don't think he knows how often he is wrong when it comes to people."

"Not this time," Mhàiri said with a sigh. Father Lanaghly did not know what it was like to see things the way she and Conan did. To observe more in a few seconds than what others did after studying something for an hour. To be able to think through facts and rapidly come to conclusions, which were more often than not correct. Her father used to tell her that someday she would learn to put all that aside and just see the person. To stop viewing people as she did a scene, looking for ways to draw them, but actually get to know them. "Truth is, Conan was telling me things I did not want to hear."

"Well, remember, Mhàiri lass, Conan may have been accurate about one thing, but it was only one of many pieces that make up the whole of you." Seeing that Mhàiri was digesting what he had said, he added, "And keep in mind that you have only seen a limited view of who Conan is well. He, too, is very complex and it takes time to truly understand him—even for the unusually gifted." He winked. "What I do know is that the more I understand Conan, the more I appreciate him for who he is."

* * *

Mhàiri sat in the cart staring straight ahead. Next to her, holding the reins, was Conan, who was just as silent as she was. Shortly after their conversation, Father Lanaghly had decided that he needed some alone time with God. While he had been very nice with his suggestion to exchange carts with Conan, it had also been clear that the request was not so much of a request as a statement. As a result, Mhàiri was now forced to rub shoulders with Conan for the rest of the trip.

It was one thing for Conan to be riding up ahead, but being so silent next to her was going to rob Mhàiri of her sanity. Apologizing, however, was out of the question. He had snatched her work and judged it and her. *He* should be the one to say "I'm sorry." And yet, that was not what was bothering her or what had kept her up the rest of the night.

"Do you really think my drawings could be of value? I mean, to other people?" she blurted out.

Conan's head slightly jerked upright, and then he slowly turned to look at her. "Not as they are, but aye. I have never seen anyone who could do what you can. It is a skill I need to possess, but don't."

"Why?" she asked, truly curious. She tilted her head to one side, causing her hair to fall over one shoulder. "Why would anyone *need* to draw?"

Conan watched as she slid her hand through her hair, pushing it away from her face. Her tongue then touched her lips, moistening the satin finish. Conan felt something twisting deep in his gut. He turned his eyes to the heavens and prayed for help. "This spring, I leave to make maps of Scotland and its clans," he finally answered. "King Robert needs to be able to know all the routes England could use to strike Scotland again and where there is most benefit to fortify against Longshanks's son."

Conan apprehensively stole another glance. Seeing that Mhàiri was interested in what he was saying, he continued. "But mostly I want to make maps for the clans. The constant skirmishes about land and resources need to end. Also, while the major clans are known, there are many out there of which King Robert is unaware. Some are growing and some no longer exist. He needs to know who to seek out if we once again need to fight for our freedom."

"I . . . I, too, was going to embark on my dreams in the spring. And then the priory burnt down." Mhàiri prayed her father would agree to take her with him now that her plans were no more. If he refused to let her come with him, it would not be from lack of love, but too much of it.

"And what were your dreams, Mhàiri?" Conan said her name, and it sent a shiver through her. He sounded as if he truly wanted to know. Maybe the priest was right. She needed to let Conan see more of who she was so that he could understand her better.

"I have an older sister, Shinae. She is incredibly beautiful. Men used to say that her smile could rob them of breath."

Conan chuckled. "We men will say anything if we think it might get us the attention of a pretty woman."

Mhàiri shook her head. "But with Shinae, it's true. She is open and friendly, and has a smile for everyone. When my mother died, she was only fourteen. My father feared that, her being so beautiful, she would attract attention. Knowing he could not always protect her, he sent her to live with his sister, who was a member of the priory's Culdees. When I turned fourteen, he sent me to join them."

"You love your sister."

"I do. Very much. Everyone does," Mhàiri said with a sigh.

"You sound like everyone does not feel similarly about you."

Mhàiri shook her head. "Shinae is outgoing. Friendly. I am not. I'm more comfortable with books or drawing."

"And is she a nun?"

Mhàiri nodded. "Shinae loved the Culdees' way of life, but she knew that I did not. For years, various members of the priory would set up introductions with dozens of men looking for a wife. They were not subtle with their strong hints that I should settle down."

Conan's mouth formed a thin line. He had known last night his comment about understanding why she wasn't married a false one, but the idea that *dozens* of men had been courting Mhàiri did not sit well with him. "So why didn't you . . . um, settle down?" he asked, using her term rather than the word *marry*.

Mhàiri shrugged her shoulders. "No one ever interested me. Oh, most were nice. A few were surprisingly very good looking," she added with a chuckle that sent another shiver down Conan's spine. "And I have no doubt that they would have given me a comfortable life—*if* I desired a home and children. But I can think of nothing worse than the idea of waking every day to the same chores that would only expand as the household grew." Mhàiri shuddered.

Conan felt his shoulders relax and adjusted how he was sitting. There was no man who would be seeking her out. "That's why you don't know how to cook."

Mhàiri faked a grimace but could not hold it and smiled at him. "Probably. Anyway, Shinae knew that I could never be persuaded to settle down and marry— whether it be to the church or a man—and be stuck in one place for the rest of my life."

"So, in the spring, you and your sister were just going to leave the priory and travel?"

Mhàiri could hear the dubious tone of Conan's voice. The concept had appeal, but was also unrealistic. "No. Shinae loved being with the Culdees and working in the community, helping the locals whether it be during sickness or in their gardens."

Conan shifted in his seat again. "Then what was to happen this spring?"

Mhàiri raked her eyes over Conan. He was having trouble sitting still, but he gave her a look that conveyed he earnestly wanted her to continue. "The Culdees' way of life is disappearing. The Catholic church is taking over and slowly displacing them, just like what happened at the priory. So a handful from the priory, including my sister, had decided to leave and travel to various places to start new missions. I was to go with them. But then the priory caught fire and two of the main people who were to come with us died in the flames."

That night had been awful. The community had lost so much. She and her sister had lost their home and dear friends. Shinae had been forced to accept a new way of life, and now Mhàiri had to recreate her own future. At one time, it had looked so promising.

Now, it was not bleak—it was blank. She felt suddenly subject to the decisions of others and no longer had a say in her life.

Conan tried to focus on what Mhàiri was saying, but it was difficult being in the middle of both ecstasy and physical agony. When Father Lanaghly had first proposed that they ride together, Conan had almost refused. Riding in the cart was miserable on the body, but he *had* wanted to talk to Mhàiri.

Last night, he had marched off not realizing that he still had her drawing in his hand. He had stayed up and studied it until exhaustion had taken over. His last thoughts had been that he had to somehow convince Mhàiri to teach him how to draw like she did. If he could learn her technique, even poorly, it would aid him enormously in what he wanted to achieve with his maps. But he had been unable to approach her. Now, he was speaking to her as he had hoped, but sitting next to her was creating a lot of pain in his lower region.

Each bump caused their arms to touch, bringing her even closer. Plus, her hair was driving him to distraction. It kept blowing against him, and the smell of flowers constantly drifted his way. At first, talking had been a welcome distraction. Unfortunately, it was no longer working.

"So what clan do you belong to, Mhàiri?"

"My father's people are the Mayboills. They're in the Lowlands, but it has been many years since he called their land his home."

"He went to your mother's clan then?"

"Nay. She was Romani and felt most at home when free, with no ties to a particular homeland, let alone a clan. She met my father when he was young and went abroad to bring back to Scottish people the treasures of the world. She used to say that my father and she were kindred spirits, always enjoying the place they were at but also just as eager to see what lay ahead."

"And you are like your mother."

Mhàiri sighed softly. "In many ways. But I'm also like my father. I love this wild, harsh but wondrous land, and seeing its beauty has always given me peace."

"You mentioned that your father was a merchant."

"Aye," she answered simply. Then, seeing Conan's frustrated look, Mhàiri realized he wanted her to continue talking. It puzzled her, but she obliged. "He mostly sells goods in the Lowlands and northern England, but he tries to get to Spain at least once a year for hemp paper. He befriended the owner of the paper mill one time and they are now good friends. He always keeps a few blank books ready for Papa."

Conan nodded. That explained a lot. "Your father must have done him a really big favor to have access to hemp." Laurel would be proud. They had been riding for a couple of hours and not a single argument. He had inquired about her family and listened to what Mhàiri had to say. Who knew? Maybe, he was finally learning how to act like a gentleman. "Since you are *not* a nun, what are your plans?"

"Father Lanaghly said that your brother would send word that would reach my father, letting him know to come and get me."

"Conor will, but I'd be careful, otherwise there is a good chance you'll be married before your father ever arrives."

Mhàiri huffed. "I thought I had just made it clear that I absolutely do not want to be married."

Conan put his hand out in retreat. "First, you are not *against* marriage, for I suspect you would find it unacceptable for your father and mother to live together, am I right?"

"Aye, but—"

"*And,*" Conan continued, "I was only trying to warn you about Laurel. Lady McTiernay is very nice and is indeed all the wonderful things you will hear, but she is also incredibly meddlesome. The woman thinks she sees love all around her and enjoys nothing more than putting people together. She has got involved in all of my older brothers' lives and, each time, the result was marriage." Conan decided not to mention that they were happily married and none of them would change a thing about their lives. "I'm the only lucky one. Laurel vows never to help any woman tie herself to the likes of me. So with all my brothers being gone, she is going to see you and get all excited. Just be prepared."

A look of horror overcame Mhàiri's face, and Conan had to bite back a smile. *Ha, Laurel! This is for all the grief you've given me over the years,* he thought to himself as he imagined Laurel failing to persuade Mhàiri into the state of matrimony.

"Lady McTiernay can try, but she will be wasting her time," Mhàiri stated through gritted teeth.

"So you say," Conan returned. "I'm only glad she understands that *I* have no desire or room in my life for a wife."

"Now? Or never?" Mhàiri inquired, suddenly a little sad to think that Conan would be out traveling all alone making maps. She wanted to travel, but with her sister, the Culdees, or her father. Alone with no one to share your thoughts or your discoveries? That sounded as awful as marriage.

Conan opened his mouth to answer and then said, "Let's change the topic. What is the most unusual book you have in these chests?"

He was glad when Mhàiri decided to let the topic go and answered his question, which led to another, and soon he found himself enjoying another heated debate with her. Their conversation rolled easily from one subject to another until a rider leading a horse came into view. At once, all conversation ceased.

The rider was far away, but Conan knew that it was his brother. He called out to Father Lanaghly, who quickly saw Conor and stopped alongside Conan. Both men jumped down off their carts to wait.

When Conor came close, he signaled his horse to a stop and then tossed Conan the reins to the horse he had tethered to his saddle. "I thought, with me gone, that you could use a fresh horse for the cart."

Conan nodded. "I assumed you would be back home with Laurel by now."

Conor frowned. "That was my plan, but someone attacked the homestead I was visiting last night."

That stopped Conan short. "Someone attacked you?"

Conor shook his head. "I don't even think they knew it was me. They hit Wills on the back of the head. He cried out and I came running. They dashed off before they got anything. Wills was out cold for hours, and I needed to make sure he was going to recover before I left him with his wife and two younglings."

"You don't think that it was the same people . . ." Conan's voice trailed off.

"Probably not. Most likely just a normal border skirmish aimed to steal, not maim, but I'm not assuming anything," Conor answered. "I want to get back. Hitch the horse and let's get going. I want to be home while the afternoon sun is still in the sky."

Chapter Three

Mhàiri cringed from her seat on the cart. Conor had ridden with them most of the way, but once they had neared the gatehouse, he had urged his horse ahead. As they were still making their way to the gates, Mhàiri could hear him bellow out Laurel's name, demanding to be told where she was.

Father Lanaghly, who had returned to his cart seat when Conor had rejoined their group, mumbled how it was odd that Laurel was not in the courtyard waiting. "After a lengthy time apart, Lady McTiernay has never not greeted the laird upon his return home. As soon as he is spotted by the watchers on the towers, she goes to the bailey or, if the weather is poor, inside the great hall until he arrives. That she still has not welcomed him home only confirms that something is indeed wrong with her ladyship."

Mhàiri's eyes widened, hearing the priest's concern. She had discerned from the various comments that something was bothering Lady McTiernay. Until now, she had refrained from putting much credence into the supposition that it was serious. When they spoke of her, everything indicated that her ladyship had seemed healthy, but maybe that, too, had been an incorrect assumption. Mhàiri hoped Lady McTiernay was fine, not just because her own temporary well-being and quarters were based on Laurel's generosity, but because she knew, after spending three days with his lairdship, that if something *were* seriously wrong with his wife, he would be crushed—physically, mentally, and emotionally. Her father had loved her mother that way and when she had died, he had been lost for a long time.

As they entered the courtyard, the doors of what looked to be the great hall were flung open and again, Mhàiri heard Conor roar for his wife as he exited into the courtyard headed to what looked like a smaller hall.

Mhàiri looked at Conan, who merely shrugged, showing no concern. "Conor *really* loves his wife," he said with ease. "Don't ask me why. She's pretty to look at, but she's also mean."

Mhàiri could not help herself and laughed. "That's not what Father Lanaghly says."

"He's a priest. He has to lie."

Father Lanaghly narrowed his eyes briefly on Conan and pulled the cart to a stop next to the stables. Conan halted next to him, jumped down, and then helped Mhàiri off the uncomfortable seat.

Mhàiri stretched her limbs, feeling circulation return to them. "So what makes her so mean?" she asked in a hushed but playful tone.

Conan crossed his arms and leaned against the larger cart. "I told you. She is a meddlesome creature who truly enjoys torturing me."

Mhàiri laughed again. Conan was being earnest, and yet she could tell his comments were also coming from a place of love. He thought of Laurel as Shinae was to her—an older sister. "And you think to convince me that none of this supposed torture is deserved?"

Conan scoffed and rolled his eyes. "You haven't even met Laurel and yet you take her side." He raised his brows and pointed to his elder brother, who was exiting the lower hall.

"If someone does not tell me where my wife is in the next five seconds, lives are going to be lost!" Conor roared, and for the first time, the people of the courtyard jumped. If they did not think he had meant it before, they did now. For suddenly they were moving, most of them heading somewhere that would take them out of the laird's sight.

When Mhàiri entered the courtyard, she had expected to see people bustling around, fawning over their laird and attempting to see to his needs, but aside from the stable boy taking his horse, people seemed unfazed by Conor's presence and his bellowing. They smiled and greeted him as if he had just been out for a ride and acted as if he was cheerful and in a good mood. Now, however, they seemed to realize that their laird was truly not happy and his anger was going to shift to them.

Suddenly, a burly man with red and gray hair and matching frizzy beard ran by them from the direction of the gatehouse they had just entered. He was not very tall, but his large chest and biceps hinted at enormous strength. Conor spied him right after Mhàiri had. "Fallon! Where have you been? Where is Laurel?"

Conan leaned down and whispered in Mhàiri's ear, "Fallon is Conor's steward." Mhàiri's eyes grew wide and she nodded.

"Calm yourself, Laird McTiernay," Fallon huffed, trying to catch his breath. He did not look to be out of shape so Mhàiri guessed he had been running some distance to get there. "Lady McTiernay is here and well, and no doubt will be out very soon."

"Something is wrong," Conor stated, his voice cold. Gone was the reserved but pleasant laird who had traveled with them. In his stead was a dangerous man. He was not one to be managed or calmed. He wanted one thing, and Mhàiri prayed Fallon realized that because he looked as if he was about to argue with Conor rather than producing his wife.

Fallon shook his head while waving his hands back and forth. Before he could say anything shouts of *"Athair!"* rang through the air.

Mhàiri swiveled her head to see who was shouting for their father when she spied five people emerging from the massive seven-story tower located on the far side of the courtyard. The first to emerge was a tall, very thin woman with thick, umber-colored hair who looked to be near or about Mhàiri's age. She was holding the hands of two girls, one with pale tresses and the other with deep brown locks. Both girls were eagerly dragging her toward Conor, who was obviously their father from their shouts to him. Behind them were two lanky boys who were not small, but had several years before they would be men. One of them Mhàiri absolutely knew was Conor's son by his looks and mannerisms.

Conor had spun around at their shouts. When he knelt down, the two young girls let the woman's hands go and flew across the courtyard into Conor's outstretched arms.

"Where is your mother?" he asked each of them.

"We missed you!"

"Brenna got in trouble *every day*, Papa," the littlest said.

"You got in trouble too!"

"Not every day," came the quick and huffy retort, her brown curls flouncing.

"Where is your mother?" Conor asked each of them again, this time a little more strongly.

The eldest gave him another big hug. "She's coming."

Mhàiri saw Conor look at the sky as he stood back up. She suspected he was praying. Conor then looked down at the two boys, who had ambled up, refusing to look as eager to say hello as the girls. Their dancing eyes, however, made it clear that they were just as glad to see him.

"Welcome home, Laird," the tawny-haired boy stated.

"*Athair*," said the slightly taller lad with dark brown hair and unusually blue eyes. They were not the bright blue of Conan's, but that of the sea during a storm.

"Son," Conor said gruffly and engulfed him in a bear hug the boy readily returned. The amount of affection between Conor and his children was a reminder of how much Mhàiri missed her own father.

"Braeden, where is your mother?" Conor asked, his tone striving to remain patient, but Mhàiri suspected he had very little left.

"Wet," Braeden replied, laughing, thinking his answer funny. He immediately realized his father was not amused. "Mama, uh, was taking another bath. She told me to tell you that she would be out directly and to, um . . . uh . . . stop all your shouting. That you are scaring everyone, including some visitor."

Mhàiri bit her lip to keep from smiling. The boy was definitely a McTiernay.

"Your mother is well?" Conor pressed.

Braeden's brows shot up, as he was clearly baffled by the question. "I . . . think so. She yelled at Gideon and me earlier and we didn't do *anything* wrong, so she's not in a good mood. Is that what you mean?"

"No." Conor took a deep breath and exhaled. "What visitor? Who is staying here without my knowledge?"

Braeden pulled his head back, and his puzzled look became one of pure confusion. He looked over to the stables and pointed.

Mhàiri's eyes grew wide seeing the finger was pointed in her direction. She felt as if she were being accused of something. "You look scared." Conan chuckled under his breath.

"Why would I be scared?" Mhàiri murmured back, hoping she looked calmer than she felt.

"Don't know. I don't have access to your thoughts, though I suspect if I did, I'd still be confused as to why you look scared."

"He's *still* pointing at me," Mhàiri hissed.

"That's just Braeden. He's probably doing it because he sees that it unnerves you," Conan explained blithely. "He thinks because he is tall for a ten-year-old that he is practically a man."

Conor was about to head toward the tall tower when the sounds of chittering women caught everyone's attention.

"Finally," Conan mumbled. "That one is Laurel, Conor's wife," he said, pointing to the beautiful woman with pale blond hair. "And in tow are her two best friends. Aileen is the fairly pretty one with the light brown hair. She is Gideon's mother." He gestured to the boy who was standing next to Braeden. "And

Finn's wife." He then angled his thumb to a large man who, along with similarly large soldiers, had mysteriously arrived next to Fallon when Mhàiri had not been looking. "He's the commander of Conor's elite guard and someone you *really* should stay clear of. The man never smiles. And I mean never." Mhàiri stole a quick peek at him and confirmed Finn's face completely lacked expression. "I'm serious. The man's lips have never curled in their life."

Mhàiri swallowed. The commander was another person she needed to remain in good graces with or else she might find herself suddenly with nowhere to stay.

She glanced around. With the arrival of Laurel, faces of those who worked around the castle were starting to appear once more. In a few minutes, the courtyard would be bustling once again.

"And who is she?" Mhàiri asked when another woman came from the tower and started waddling out to the group. She was built like a cauldron, round in the middle and made of iron. No effort had been made to tame her wild, slightly graying flame-colored hair. She wore a man's leine underneath her plaid arisaid, which was tied off with a large leather strap. Her expression was a strange combination of a scowl and a smile—something Mhàiri had never seen before and found quite intimidating.

"Is that . . . Fiona?" Mhàiri asked, remembering what Conan had said about the old cook.

"Fiona?" Conan snorted. "At this time of day, she's in the kitchen. Not even the fight that's about to happen could drag her out here."

"You are expecting someone to fight?"

Conan nodded. "Seeing Hagatha here? Absolutely."

He crossed his arms again. "Hagatha's the midwife, and for some inexplicable reason, the old bat is fond of Laurel and she of her. But the eyesore normally lives north of here—Ow!" He yelped in midsentence when Mhàiri's elbow collided with his ribs. He rubbed them and frowned. Mhàiri gave him an unapologetic look. Conan rolled his eyes. Maybe "eyesore" had been a little rude, but it was the truth.

"So if Hagatha is around," he continued, "it almost confirms that things are not as well as Laurel would like them to appear. Conor knows this and will be demanding an explanation. Just wait."

Mhàiri rolled her eyes, but instead of debating the prediction, she turned to watch the couple and see if Conan was right.

Upon seeing Laurel, Conor pulled her into his arms and gave her the kind of kiss that inspired people to write songs and ballads about love. "*A shìorraidh!*" Mhàiri said under her breath. She was shocked and just a little bit jealous.

"Aye." Conan sighed. "Best get used to it. They kiss *a lot.*"

Mhàiri nudged his arm with her shoulder and, with a triumphant smile, said, "They're not fighting."

"Kiss first. Then comes the fight. Then they'll probably kiss again. It's a pattern they follow regularly. Sometimes I think they argue just to have a reason to make up."

Conor and Laurel finally ended their heated embrace and Mhàiri had a good view of Laurel. Beautiful was such a shallow word for the woman. She had long, wavy pale gold hair and fair skin, and her height only made her look ethereal and delicate. She was, in many ways, Mhàiri's opposite. Where Mhàiri was dark, Laurel was fair. Where Laurel had dark eyes like that of a storm, Mhàiri's were light green.

Conor framed Laurel's face in his large hands. "I see circles under your eyes and you are thinner. But what is most disturbing is your presence, Hagatha." He looked up and stared at the frizzy redhead who was not in the least unsettled by his severe look. "I *knew* something was wrong when I left," he said, once again looking at Laurel. "What is it? What don't I know?"

Laurel just went on her tiptoes and gave him a peck on his cheek. She then popped out of his embrace and scanned the crowd. Her eyes stopped when they hit the carts near the stables. "You must be Mhàiri!" she exclaimed and moved with the aim of giving Mhàiri a warm welcome.

However, Laurel got no more than two steps before Conor stopped her. "Answer my question, woman."

Mhàiri watched as Laurel stopped and her blue eyes turned a stormy color before facing Conor. "Woman?" Her voice was sharp and the words were clipped. "I'm going to let that go because you have been on the road and are tired, but you *know* that never ends in success."

"Answer the question, Laurel."

She smoothed her bliaut down in an effort to calm her obviously spiked emotions. "There is nothing wrong. I would tell you if there was, but that is not the case so there is nothing to say." They locked heated gazes for several seconds before she pivoted again toward Mhàiri, her angry face transforming into a welcoming smile.

"Laurel!" Conor shouted so loudly that Mhàiri jumped slightly.

Mhàiri glanced around to see who had noticed, and

that was when she saw that people had indeed emerged and were resuming their duties. No one else was flustered or upset by what was transpiring between the laird and his wife. Most were doing their work as if nothing of interest were occurring in the middle of the courtyard. Even the four children were not paying attention. They were playing tag, totally unfazed by their yelling parents. A strange wave of nostalgia came over Mhàiri.

"Welcome, Mhàiri," Laurel said cheerfully, grasping her hands while ignoring the glares coming from her husband. "We are so glad to have you with us. I love visitors, and we do not have nearly enough of them."

"We have plenty. Our castle is practically the beacon for strays," Conor mumbled.

"Ignore him. He loves them as well for it keeps me occupied and less inclined to meddle in things he is interested in."

Conor's eyes rolled and he tilted his head back and forth, indicating that he somewhat agreed with his wife's statement.

Mhàiri could not help herself. She returned Laurel's smile with a large one of her own. She had forgotten how her parents used to bicker in a similar manner. It was surprising to realize how much she missed this strange dance of love. Many might not understand it, but she did.

"Thank you both for the invitation."

Conor looked Mhàiri straight in the eye. "You are welcome to stay as long as you need." He then swung his gaze to the woman about her age who had walked out with the children. "Maegan, how often have you been needed to look after the twins and Bonny?"

Maegan blinked. Her mouth opened and closed a few times, and though she said nothing, they both knew it was too late to deny what he was implying.

Maegan stuck her chin out, walked over to the cart, hooked her arm with Mhàiri's as if they were lifelong friends, and stated, "Mhàiri and I refuse to be drawn into your argument."

Mhàiri looked down at their hooked elbows and then up and into the prettiest pale blue eyes she had ever seen. Deep set, they were framed with long lashes several shades darker than her umber-colored hair, which was pulled back into simple, but very attractive, plaits.

Seeing Mhàiri's shock, Maegan patted her arm. "Trust me. Being a visitor—even a newly arrived one—won't protect you from getting caught in the fray. But I will." She leaned close, but kept her eyes on Laurel, who was staring at Conor as she approached him. "I'm Maegan by the way," she whispered.

Mhàiri was about to inquire what Maegan had meant by fray when the cold tone of Conor's voice rang out across the ever-quietening courtyard. "I will not be diverted, Laurel. You were out of sorts when I left. Then I return and you are not here to greet me. Next, I find out from my son that you are taking another bath as if you've been requesting them daily, and when you finally do leave the tower, Hagatha is in tow. *Now, what is wrong?*"

Laurel pursed her lips together and Mhàiri could have sworn she also stomped her foot. "Hagatha is my *friend.* And when I say that I am fine, that is became *I am.* Aye, I might have been feeling poorly, but I am not any longer. You and I can discuss it later, but right now I want to see to our guest's needs. Mhàiri—"

"Can wait," Conor clipped. "I cannot believe you were sick and did not tell me! Or send word! I would have come home immediately!"

Laurel rolled her eyes and turned back to Mhàiri. "I had a room prepared for you in the Warden's Tower," she said, pointing to the large stone tower to Mhàiri's right. "There are several rooms in the North Tower, and that is where most of our guests stay, but when Father Lanaghly requested assistance, he also mentioned that you had a great deal of books and scrolls. He made it sound as if you had enough to rival Conan's collection."

Conan scoffed. Laurel leveled a stare at him. "*So*, to ensure that Conan never accidentally mistakes your room for his, I decided a completely different tower was more appropriate."

Conan bent down and whispered in Mhàiri's ear, "That was *not* the reason."

"Hagatha!" Conor shouted and Mhàiri realized just what Maegan had meant about being pulled into the argument. She clutched Maegan's elbow tightly against her side, comforted to know Maegan was doing the same. "I want to know *exactly* what was wrong with my wife, for how long, and if she is in any danger!"

The voice was loud and angry, but, more than anything, Mhàiri heard terror. She guessed Laurel had finally heard it as well. "Conor," she said squeezing his arm to gain his attention. "You are ruining my plans for later," she hissed through tight lips.

"Why later?" Conor pressed. "Why not now?"

"I said I would tell you later! In private!" This time,

it was Laurel who was shouting, and Mhàiri absolutely saw her stomp her foot this time.

"Why? Most of our arguments end up in the courtyard with the world listening to them. Why can't this one?"

"*Because* this was not supposed to be an argument! It was supposed to be special!" Laurel wailed back at him. "It was supposed to be romantic!"

"How is being sick supposed to—"

"A baby, Conor!" Laurel shouted, throwing her hands up in the air. "I'm going to have a *baby*! And God help me, *you* are going to be its father."

Conor took a step back as if someone had punched him in the gut.

Conan took the opportunity to get a little revenge for the ribbing he had been taking the past few days. "Seems someone else has been wrong about more than his share of things as well, huh, brother?"

Laurel shot a finger at him and then pointed at the Warden's Tower. "Take Mhàiri's things to her room, and I better not learn that a *single* thing from either of those carts ended up in your chambers. In fact, you, Seamus," she said to a large guard who exuded masculinity and had snuck in with the commander, "keep Conan from losing his way."

Seamus grimaced and came to stand by Maegan. He had dark blond hair that was a fraction too light to be called brown. His forehead was prominent and tan, his chin was marked with a distinctive cleft, and his hazel eyes were mostly green with chips of gold. Maegan smiled up at him. Then, to Mhàiri, she said, "Seamus, here, is one of the laird's elite guards and one of Scotland's deadliest soldiers. So have no fear. Your things are safe."

"Don't tease," Seamus grumbled, but there was no bite to his words. He twisted his perfectly sculpted lips. "It's bad enough I have to deal with Conan. The least you could do is feel sorry for me."

Maegan just continued smiling before shifting her focus back to Laurel and Conor. "They did not think they could have more children," she explained to Mhàiri.

The youngest girl, who had curly dark brown hair and perceptive gray eyes, came running up to Maegan, bubbling with excitement. "Did you hear? Mama is going to have a baby! Do you know what that means?"

Maegan shook her head. "What, Bonny?"

Bonny sighed as if she thought the answer obvious. "Uncle Conan understands."

Conan bobbed his head up and down. "That I do. I loved the day my brother Clyde was born and I was no longer the baby." Conan reached down and swung the little girl in his arms. It was evident to anyone looking at them that they both adored each other. The warmth in Conan's expression softened all his features and, if possible, made him even more appealing. For a brief second, Mhàiri wondered what it would be like to have him look at her in such a way.

Bonny nodded. "People will *finally* believe I know something. Before, it was only Conan . . . and Mama, but that was only sometimes. I will be so glad not to be the baby." She then assessed Mhàiri. "I'm Bonny."

"Um, I'm Mhàiri."

"I know. I know lots of things." Bonny looked at the carts. "Did you read all of those?"

Mhàiri nodded, but before she could say anything, the word "How?" echoed in the courtyard.

Conor's question recaptured Mhàiri's attention, and she swung back to see what was happening between Laird McTiernay and his wife.

Conan snorted. "After three children, you should know by now." Mhàiri glanced over her shoulder and gave him a cold look and mouthed for him to be quiet. Conan shrugged his shoulders, but seeing her continued glare, he gestured that he would try.

Thank goodness Conor did not appear to have even heard his younger brother. "But I thought . . . we tried for years and *nothing* . . . never . . . not once. You said that we couldn't have any more."

Laurel nodded. Tears starting to emerge. "I thought so too. I thought I would never conceive again. That my childbearing years were over. Then, during the party when Craig and Meriel were visiting, I got so sick. I was not able to keep anything down."

"That was *two months* ago!" Conor roared. "You've been keeping our baby a secret this whole time!"

"Aye!" Laurel shouted back, getting so close that they were nearly touching. "And it was far from easy, but I'd do it again! Guess why? For *you*! That's why!"

That brought several chuckles from the crowd, and unfortunately for Conan and Seamus, theirs were the loudest. "Seamus! Conan!" Laurel barked. Both immediately stopped laughing, but only Seamus had the good sense to look contrite. "I am glad to see that you are in such good moods as you are now also going to help Mhàiri *unpack* all her things."

"You kept silent for me?" Conor asked. "But why?"

Laurel took a deep breath and sighed. "Remember

what happened *after* that party? You had to visit the Schelldens about which soldiers of his you were going to train during the winter months. That took longer than expected. You were gone nearly three weeks. Then, the *very night* you came home, word came that things were happening with Cole that demanded your *immediate* attention. You had to go, but I knew that if you thought for a *moment* that I was sick—especially pregnant and sick—you would refuse to go, even though there was nothing you could do here except drive me crazy with your concern!"

Conor's jaw tightened. Mhàiri did not know either of them, but after watching Conor the past few days and hearing his anger and concern during their fight, she had no doubt that Laurel was right. Conor would not have left no matter how important it was that he meet with his brother.

"I might remind you that I almost lost you twice and *both* times were when you were pregnant."

Hearing that, Mhàiri's eyes widened.

"What I'm experiencing is common for many women. We get sick! Hagatha says that sometimes it lasts until the baby is born. Thankfully, for me, it is getting better. The last couple of days I have felt only tired. Not ill in the least."

Conor softly clutched Laurel's upper arms. "So you really are *fine*."

"Aye. I am well. Crabby due to lack of food, but other than that, I am *very* well." Laurel's voice went soft as her arms slid around Conor's stomach.

"Truly?"

"Completely fine."

Conor grinned. "Not feeling ill at all?"

Laurel's blue eyes twinkled. "Aside from arguing with you, I'm feeling perfectly well."

"Good." Then, with a big grin, Conor swept her into his arms and headed straight for the massive tower across the courtyard. "And remind me to tell you later about when Conan and Mhàiri met."

Laurel's face lit up with anticipation. Then she looked over her husband's shoulder and shouted, "Maegan! You're responsible for Bonny and the twins!"

Maegan uncoupled her and Mhàiri's arms. "Guess that is over! Glad this one ended on a happy note. They usually do, but you can never tell." Maegan's eyes grew wide as saucers as she realized how shocking everything must be to someone who had been living in a priory. "*Oich is oich!* I hope that that didn't alarm you any. I can only imagine how a laird and lady publicly fighting might come across to someone with the church."

Mhàiri sighed with a smile. "My *sister* was with the Culdees, not I. I stayed in a cottage next to the priory and helped them where and when I could." Mhàiri used her chin to point at the spot where the argument had taken place. "As for the laird and lady fighting, I was surprised at first, but truthfully, they reminded me of my own parents. They, too, shared an intense passion for each other. It is something to be envied, not shunned. That is what love was supposed to be. Passionate, intense, and honest. Nothing held in reserve. If I ever fell in love, that is how I would want it to be."

Maegan chuckled. "You will get along fine here then, but you're wrong about the love part. Love doesn't need to be intense. What I have with Clyde is just as strong but thankfully without all the volatile sparks."

"Clyde? Isn't he Conan's younger brother?"

Maegan nodded and got a dreamy look in her eye. "He's my true love, and we are getting married the moment he returns."

"If you two are going to stand around and gab, then I'm leaving. I have other things to do," Seamus grumbled.

Conan snorted. "The sooner you learn to ignore women and their constant nattering about every little thing, the happier you will become."

Mhàiri ignored him.

Maegan whispered, "Conan is not, um, comfortable with people."

"I don't know," Mhàiri countered with a sly smile. "Maybe everyone else is not comfortable with Conan."

Maegan pulled her chin back and looked at Mhàiri strangely. Then after a few seconds, she shrugged her shoulders. "You're both smart and into books. Guess it makes sense that you would like him too. All women do . . . at least for a while."

"Conan and I have discussed his appeal, and he knows that I've become immune to his charms," Mhàiri said, glancing over her shoulder to see both Seamus and Conan shamelessly listening to their conversation. "Unfortunately for him, he is not yet immune to mine."

Conan guffawed. "See? Nattering. Even when you think maybe by chance it just might be something worth listening to—" Conan cut his hand through the air. "It turns out to be nothing."

Maegan closed her eyes and sighed. "The only female who can put up with that one is Bonny."

Fallon clapped his hands and the steward successfully got everyone's attention. "I want these carts out of the courtyard before the sun sets."

Seamus crossed his arms and leveled a steady stare

at Fallon. "I'm not carrying a damn thing. It's Conan's responsibility to get all this up to her room." He gestured to Conan with his thumb. "Not mine. I was just supposed to make sure it all arrived there. And while Conan is many, *many* irritating things, he is *not* a liar or a thief. So my job is done."

Conan looked at Mhàiri and gave her a wicked grin.

Mhàiri took a step closer to him and, jabbing a finger at the large chests in the cart, said, "*Every* scrap that is in these carts will be moved into my chambers." Then she looked at Seamus. "And if it isn't, *you'll* be the one responsible."

Seamus cocked his head to the side and smiled. "Don't worry. Conan won't dare defy Lady McTiernay."

"I just might, knowing you would join me in my misery," Conan warned, hinting that it might be worth the price to see Seamus squirm. "Now help me with these chests."

Seamus clearly thought the threat an empty one. "You hate to wear itchy clothing too much."

"I've got the horses, but I refuse to deal with the carts." Mhàiri searched for the face that went with the gruff voice. A second later, she could see an old, thin man with little hair and a hump on his back yanking on one of the harnesses.

Before Fallon could respond to the old man, Hagatha, the wild-haired friend of Laurel's, approached and said, "Ye heard Lady McTiernay, ye old man. Those two are taking care of it." She waved to Conan and Seamus. "Just unhitch the animals, Neal, and the lads will take care of the cart when they're done. Won't ye, lads?"

Both made a "humph" sound but did not argue as

they finally started to lift things out of the cart. "Which room, Fallon?" Conan grunted.

"Main room on the second floor."

Mhàiri had been to several castles when she had been young, but only briefly and mostly on market days when merchants were selling their goods. She used to envision what it would be like to live in such a grand place, and the McTiernay Castle was definitely one of the grander ones she had seen.

Just passing through the gates would make a person nervous if unsure they had a right to be there. The long and broad entry was guarded by a single well-sized barbican tower fortifying the guard gate. Six round towers and the curtain wall formed a D that housed a substantially large courtyard. Most were three stories, one was four, but the massive tower on the northwest wall had to be seven stories at least.

Only a rich laird of a very large and powerful clan could afford a castle of this size. And with such wealth, Mhàiri would have thought that all the staff would act meek and in fear of those they serve. But that was not the case at McTiernay Castle. Throughout Conor and Laurel's fight, the courtyard had remained busy, giving them no privacy. Even those who had a place to go to like Maegan, Conan, and Laurel's friends Aileen and Hagatha had just stood around and waited until it was over. In Mhàiri's experience, stable masters did not declare what they would and would not do, and midwives did not remind a laird's brother and elite guard what their duties were. It was starting to be too much.

"I can tell you need to sit down and have something to drink," offered the pretty tawny-haired woman named Aileen. "We can probably persuade Fiona into giving us some scraps of food. She seemed to be in a good mood during the midday meal."

Mhàiri furrowed her brow, remembering Conan's alarming comments about the McTiernay cook. She was not sure she wanted to raise the woman's ire.

Hagatha nodded. "Aye, ale sounds good." Then she turned and headed toward two large doors that led to what had to be the castle's great hall. She was the strangest midwife Mhàiri had ever seen. She was large and visually abrasive with wild red hair, but despite that, Mhàiri found the woman comforting. She suspected Hagatha, when riled, could cause the exact opposite feeling, but right now she was offering friendship and Mhàiri was eager to have as many friends as possible during her hopefully short stay at McTiernay Castle.

Aileen called out to the children to behave, avoid the Star Tower until the evening meal, and stay out of trouble lest they suffer her wrath. Mhàiri could not envision Aileen mad, but all four of the children obviously could and immediately nodded their heads. She then rushed to follow Hagatha into the great hall.

Maegan grabbed Mhàiri's arm, forcing her to come along. "Don't worry. Seamus will make sure all your things get to your room." Then she looked back at the cart and murmured, "*A shaoghail!* You *do* have a lot of things."

Mhàiri quickly fell into step. "I . . . uh . . . really don't," she said, feeling awkward for the first time about the substantial load she had insisted come with her. Of course, they probably thought the majority of it was dresses and clothes, although that would have weighed a lot less and wouldn't have been as difficult to transport. Mhàiri was not even sure how her father was going to manage adding the chests to his things when he came for her. He did own a very large wagon that was incredibly sturdy, but just the three large chests were a lot. "I don't really have a lot of personal items, such as clothes and things. Only the small chest has my other dress and undergarments."

They were inside the hall and her words echoed in the empty chamber. The massive hall was a large, open room, and grandly decorated, but it had a warm, inviting feel as well. The ceiling was covered by a high stone vault, and against the east far wall was a canopied fireplace. Behind her, another fireplace was situated to allow for heating on both sides of the room when partitioned. At the far end of the room sat the high table, which was lit by a large window set in the north wall. All sounds were amplified because the floor was made of timber instead of ground earth.

Aileen waved them to come join her near the fire. After everyone was seated, she made introductions. "This is Hagatha, which you probably gathered from Conor's comments outside. She is our midwife and healer. She's crusty and outspoken, but we love her." Hagatha was about to interject, but Aileen cut her off. "I'm Aileen and consider Laurel my closest friend. My husband is Finn, who is the commander of Conor's guard. You cannot miss him. He has a constant scowl on his face that he thinks makes him look fierce. And it looks like you and Maegan are already on the way to becoming friends."

"Did I hear you say you have only *one* spare dress?" Maegan asked, clearly saddened at the concept.

Hagatha huffed and gestured for some food and drink to a servant who was hovering near the timber partition that screened the hall from the service area. "An arisaid and a spare is enough for me and most everyone else. To hear Maegan now, you would never know that she grew up running around this place acting more like a boy than a lass, but no one could make that mistake now. Our Maegan believes no woman can have enough gowns and shoes to go with them. And Laurel indulges such whimsy."

Aileen smiled. "You know that Maegan more than earns those gowns, Hagatha, helping out with Laurel's three children. Even Braeden listens to her, and with the baby coming, Laurel will need Maegan's help even more."

Maegan gave Mhàiri a grin and then shrugged. "I *do* like clothes. They are the secret to happiness."

"I thought Clyde was your secret to happiness," Aileen teased.

"What about baths? Yesterday, a hot bath was your secret to happiness," Hagatha added as she turned to help the servant put the drinks and food on the table. "And . . ."

"Enough! You will make Mhàiri think that I am hopelessly spoiled and ungrateful. Besides, I intend to give some of my gowns to Mhàiri just like her ladyship did for me." She leaned over to Mhàiri and explained, "When my grandmother passed away, Lady Laurel took me in and now I live at the castle. I was here practically all the time anyway, with Clyde and his friend Kam. That was before he left to help King Robert fight the Irish. And since we are getting married when he returns, it only makes sense that I stay here and help with the children."

Aileen laid a soft hand on Mhàiri's arm. "Do you know who Clyde is?"

Mhàiri nodded, pulling off a piece of bread. The

delicious smell made her realize she was famished. "Conan told me all about his brothers."

Hagatha spurted out her ale. "Conan *talked* to you? As in you had an actual conversation during your journey here."

Mhàiri swallowed and then grinned. "Aye. I get the feeling he doesn't get the chance to talk to many people because, once we started, we rarely stopped."

Hagatha put her mug down on the table with a thump. "You're saying you talked *with* Conan and he did not insult you, or make you angry?"

"Of course Conan insulted me," Mhàiri replied with a wave of her hand. "But that only made it more fun to point out when he was in the wrong." She chuckled seeing the three sets of shocked, unblinking eyes staring back at her. "It's been a long time since I had the chance to really debate with someone who could adequately argue his point. Plus, Conan didn't mind when I yelled back and insulted him. It was rather fun," she concluded with a shrug. She did not add that it was only the last day did they get to such a point.

Hagatha, Aileen, and Maegan all shifted their stares from her to one another. "It cannot be *that* shocking," Mhàiri finally stated.

Maegan looked at her and bobbed her head. "Oh, but it is."

"How? I saw everyone's reaction while Laird and Lady McTiernay argued. No one was worried or cared, so why is it so surprising that Conan and I verbally sparred a little as well?"

Aileen's eyes grew even larger. She took a deep breath and exhaled. "Well, uh . . ."

Maegan licked her lips. "It's only that no one *likes* talking to Conan, and I am certain that he does not like talking to us either. And when I say us, I mean us *women.*"

"It's more than that," Hagatha said with her mouth full and jabbed the piece of bread she was holding at Mhàiri. "She *enjoyed* it. Just wait until Laurel hears that!"

Aileen bit her bottom lip. "Aye, but you know what Laurel said last summer. She swore that she would never assist Conan in matters of the heart. She doesn't want to be responsible for the resulting heartache she is certain would eventually come."

Mhàiri wrinkled her nose. "Conan warned me that Laurel was a matchmaker and to be careful of her. That she had sworn off helping him, which meant I was going to be her next target."

Again, all three heads looked at her in astonishment. Mhàiri grimaced. "I told you. We talked."

Aileen shook her head in disbelief. "After Laurel meets you, she just might change her mind about Conan."

Hagatha jogged her head in agreement.

Seeing their eyes grow large with excitement, Mhàiri quickly spoke to halt the speedy direction of their thoughts. "Laurel can change her mind right back then because I have no intentions of getting married. Laird McTiernay promised that he would send runners south to get word to my father of my situation and where I am. As soon as he arrives, I am leaving. I can imagine nothing worse than marrying a man and taking care of him, his home, and his children all my life."

Aileen blinked. Mhàiri had just described her life, which she loved. "If you don't want marriage, then what do you plan to do?"

"My father is a successful merchant and goes everywhere, seeing new sights and meeting interesting people. I cannot wait to travel with him once again. The priory was a safe environment and the Culdees are a wonderful group of people, but there has been no adventure in my life. Nothing exciting to look forward to. The past few years have made me realize I could never settle down, no matter how wonderful the place or the man. And believe it or not, Conan is the first man I have met who understood and supported my desire to remain unmarried."

Aileen was about to say something when the doors swung open and a young girl with pale curly locks and gray eyes who was about the age of ten came running in. "Miss Aileen! It's Gideon! I told him and Braeden not to throw rocks at each other, but they *never* listen. And now he's bleeding *everywhere!*"

Aileen took a deep breath and slowly let it go. Mhàiri guessed this was a common occurrence from her lack of concern. "Go tell him I'm coming, and make sure Braeden knows that I want to speak with him as well." She looked at Hagatha, who was already rising to her feet. "If he's bleeding, then I might need your help. And, Maegan, don't worry about the children tonight. I'll keep them with me and if Finn doesn't like it, he can sleep with the soldiers. It's unlikely we will see Conor or Laurel until the morning."

Hagatha huffed. "Unlikely? It might be noon tomorrow before they emerge based on the look Conor had in his eye when he swept Laurel into his arms."

"So, Maegan, would you help Mhàiri and ensure she is settled? Best tell Fiona about the situation as well. It would not be good if she were surprised."

The doors opened again. This time it was Bonny. "Brenna told me to tell you to hurry. But you don't really have to. He and Braeden are arguing over whose cut is the worst so it can't be *that* bad."

"Braeden is also injured?" Aileen asked crisply, more than a little perturbed.

Bonny nodded. "But it's his arm, not like Gideon's head, so it isn't bleeding as much."

"Good Lord," Aileen muttered and followed the young girl out the door along with Hagatha, leaving Mhàiri and Maegan alone in the huge room.

"Thank goodness the boys got hurt," Maegan murmured and then, realizing what she had said, rushed to explain. "It's just if Aileen and Hagatha were here much longer, there would have been no stopping them. Now that they have decided that you and Conan like each other, those two are about to conspire and take over your lives."

"But . . . but I don't like Conan!"

"Aye, you do," Maegan stated flatly. "But it's understandable. He's good looking, and I've seen him charm many a woman."

"Trust me when I say that Conan was *not* charming."

"I believe you, but you can't argue that he couldn't take his eyes off you outside and you yourself stated that he was *enjoyable* to talk to."

Mhàiri opened and closed her mouth several times before opting for closed. Denying the truth was senseless, just as much as denying that Maegan was one of those few people you met in life that you knew right away that you liked and could trust.

"I *don't* like him, at least not in the way you are implying. Seriously, I don't," Mhàiri reiterated. Then she leaned in close and, in a whisper, added, "But I will admit to wondering what it would be like to kiss him."

Maegan opened her mouth, then closed it into a

thin line. Her eyes narrowed and then, without saying a word, she stood up slowly and then ran to the servants' entrance. A second later, she reemerged, holding the arms of two little girls. "Meet Brenna and Bonny. Lady McTiernay's daughters and our clan's most pervasive eavesdroppers."

Brenna squirmed, but Maegan held fast. "We didn't hear anything, did we, Bonny?" she grumbled.

Bonny shook her head. "Only the part about Mhàiri wanting to kiss Uncle Conan."

Brenna finally wriggled free and rushed to sit right beside Mhàiri. "We want to help. We like Uncle Conan, and it's his turn to fall in love. Mama won't help him so that leaves us," she said proudly, pointing to herself and then her sister.

Mhàiri looked at Brenna and then Bonny, who had come to stand by her older sister. Their wide, innocent eyes looked at her with so much hope and unsuppressed excitement. Mhàiri let her head flop onto her arms that were crossed on the table. She closed her eyes.

"Papa," she whispered, "you cannot get here soon enough."

Conan laid in bed staring at the ceiling. Once again, sleep was evading him, but not for the usual reasons. He had always been attracted to pretty women. The few truly smart females he had encountered had been either married to the church or to one of his brothers. But even the prettiest of women had never created a physical need in him that kept him lying awake at night. But then never could he remember a woman defending him. And that was what Mhàiri had done.

Maybe everyone else just is not comfortable with Conan, she had said.

Did Mhàiri really believe that? He had a feeling she did, for in the last few days he had come to know that she was almost as forthright as he was. Mhàiri was not one to mince words to spare someone's feelings, and she was uncommonly open and honest about her own. She held nothing back and found it insulting when others did. That was probably why she had interpreted Conor and Laurel's fight as romantic.

Very few saw their squabbles as a declaration of love. He always had though, and when Mhàiri had told Maegan that a similar passion-filled relationship was the kind she desired as well, it had shaken him to his core. He could not stop thinking about it long enough to fall asleep.

Simply put, the combination of characteristics and opinions that made up Mhàiri Mayboill was so unusual, so unique, he had not believed someone like her existed.

It would have helped if she had been painful to look at, but Conan could stare at her for hours and then willingly stare at her some more. But it was more than her physical beauty. Her voice soothed something in his soul. Its low pitch drew him in versus the high-pitched sounds many females had, which grated on his nerves. And her scent! God, the woman smelled *phenomenal.* Every time he got even a whiff of her, his body became aroused. His only explanation was that it had been far too long since he had been with a woman. And yet he had no desire to entice someone in his bed. Just the thought of being with another female that way churned his stomach.

The only tresses he wanted to touch were Mhàiri's long dark locks. He wanted to stare into her pale green eyes and see the hazy look of desire come over them from his kiss. He wanted to press her body into his, knowing it would feel like none before her.

Maybe, if he only physically desired her, he could have found another way to relieve his frustrations, but it was not only her body he craved. He yearned to talk with her, argue with her, ask her questions, and answer hers.

He loved how Mhàiri spoke her mind and offered opinions forthrightly and without hesitation. She understood his desire to leave the home he had always known and explore the world. And though she still did not fully agree with him that all art should have value and have an impact on the world, she *did* understand and appreciate that what he wanted to do was of great importance and encouraged him to seek his dreams. *No* woman had ever done that. Not even Laurel. And few men had ever appreciated why he wanted to explore for the rest of his life. But Mhàiri had. She also longed for adventure . . . though of a different type. It enabled her to truly grasp why he was leaving in the spring and how he was not going to let anyone stand in the way of his dreams, for she felt the same about hers.

And that was why he had no choice.

He was going to cut Mhàiri out of his life. She was a distraction. So, much as he could, he would avoid seeing and talking to her until she left.

Thank God her stay would not be long.

Chapter Four

"Mhàiri, it looks like you will be with us for more than a few weeks," Conor announced at dinner three weeks later. "I received word today from my brother Colin who lives in the Lowlands. He asked those nearby about your father and it seems many know him and he is well liked. Unfortunately, Colin also learned that your father has already left for Spain and is not expected back in Scotland until early spring. Even if somehow your message did reach him and he immediately returned, winter would have set in, making it impossible for him to travel north except by foot or horse."

Mhàiri shook her head. "Papa would never leave his wagon behind. It's his life. It holds everything he owns."

"And nor should he," Laurel added and reached over to give Mhàiri's hand a squeeze. "We love having you here with us. Our children adore you, and you and Maegan are becoming good friends. Please say this is not completely unwelcome news."

"I am sorry that Papa could not come sooner, but I

would be dishonest if I said that I was not enjoying being here." In truth, Mhàiri had initially worried about staying in a castle where she knew no one, but after just a few short weeks, she doubted there was a better place in the world to spend a winter. "Thank you very much for the invitation. I know my presence was unexpected, and I promise to leave as soon as Papa arrives in the spring."

"Everyone is leaving in the spring." Brenna pouted. "No one will be left. Why can't we go too?"

Maegan leaned over and tickled her until she squealed. "I will still be here, as will Seamus, Aileen, Gideon, and all your friends. Besides, spring is a long way off. Before then, there will be Christmastide and all the holiday festivities."

"I didn't think of that!" Brenna exclaimed. "Wait until you experience Twelfth Night at our castle, Mhàiri. It is the best!"

Mhàiri returned the little girl's infectious smile. "Sounds exciting. We moved around so much when I was young, I never really got to participate in big feasts and celebrations. This will be a first for me."

"You've never experienced Christmastide and all the feasts that come after?" Laurel asked in astonishment. "Why, I will have to ensure this is the best Epiphany celebration ever had at McTiernay Castle. Tomorrow, I'll send word to Raelynd and Meriel that we will be hosting this year and *a shìorraidh!* It's almost December. We might have to start planning tonight, Aileen," she said to her friend, who bobbed her head in agreement.

"You are *not* going to start planning anything tonight, or tomorrow, or even this week," Conor grumbled. "Christmastide is more than a month from now, and Fallon has other things to think about in prepping for winter."

"Fine, fine," Laurel said in mock agreement. "For the next couple of weeks, whatever planning we do will not affect you or our busy steward. Nor will I subject you to listening to me ramble about it. But I *will* begin preparations, so it would be best to accept that now."

Conor brushed his hand over his face, knowing that arguing would be pointless. "Are you settled in enough for an extended stay?" he asked, turning his attention back to Mhàiri.

Mhàiri loved her chambers and knew that staying in the large space until her father was able to come and get her was not going to be an issue. The room was open and had plenty of light, nothing like the dark, confining cottage she had been living in for years.

The only issue regarding a long-term stay was her books. Despite what Conan thought, she did read them and was actively studying some of the journals her sister had somehow gotten her hands on the past year. Mhàiri wanted them accessible, not locked away in heavy trunks. Mentioning her need, however, was not an option, for she knew what the answer would be— put them in Conan's room, which was littered with shelves specifically made for such items. Or even worse, Conor would ask Conan to build shelves for her room. Neither solution was acceptable. *Anything* involving Conan was completely and in all ways intolerable.

The last couple of weeks, the man had made it abundantly clear he wanted nothing to do with her, and Mhàiri was not going to do anything that forced him even to look in her direction.

He had been ignoring her since the morning after

they arrived. At first, she had thought she was imagining things, but then Brenna had let it escape that she had overheard him talking with Seamus. She had been right. Conan had been intentionally avoiding situations, places, *even meals*, just to keep from being in her company.

It hurt to learn she had been so wrong about him. She had thought that their budding relationship special and that she was one of the few women who had been able to break through his brusque demeanor to see the man beneath. She had been a fool. Thankfully, she had never shared her mistaken beliefs with anyone and had been able to convincingly act as if Conan's disregard were not at all troubling. Instead, Mhàiri had decided that indifference was an excellent idea and pointedly began to ignore him as well.

Most mealtimes, Conan was elsewhere, but on nights when they ate in the lower hall with the soldiers on castle duty, or on nights like this one when Laurel invited her close friends, Conan was forced to join. And each time, Mhàiri acted as if he were not there. She carried on conversations, laughed, and smiled with those who sat on either side of him, but to Conan himself? She never glanced his way. Not once. Which is probably why it had been so noticeable.

But rather than being upset by their silent feud, Laurel had verbally applauded Mhàiri's strength of character. She had said that only a few women could see beyond Conan's charm and dimples to the self-serving man underneath without getting hurt first. Mhàiri had felt like a fraud. She was no different from those other women. Worse, she was jealous of them. At least they had gotten to experience what it was like to kiss Conan *before* mutual disregard took place.

"I think Mhàiri needs shelves, Papa, for her books."

Mhàiri's brows shot up, and she stared at Bonny, who was sitting across from her.

Laurel looked at her daughter and then Mhàiri. "I never thought about that. You are right, Bonny. Mhàiri must have a place to put her things if she is going to be here for several months."

"*And*," Bonny added, this time with a sly, knowing smile, "Uncle Conan is the best one to make them since he was the one who made the shelves in his room."

Conor waved his fork at his daughter. "Great idea, BonBon. What do you think, Mhàiri? Do you need shelves?"

Mhàiri gave Bonny a strong look, but the little girl refused to feel shame. Instead, Bonny winked back, leaving no doubt that she had intentionally created a situation that would force Mhàiri and Conan to interact.

Bonny's older twin siblings could be very amusing, and Brenna was indeed a consummate eavesdropper, but more and more Mhàiri was seeing that Bonny was the most astute of the two, despite being the youngest. Her ability to perceive the truth behind a look or an action was astounding, a skill that would only grow more accurate with age. And she watched anything or anyone associated with Conan.

Mhàiri had little doubt that her and Conan's obvious efforts to ignore each other had led Bonny to believe that there was something far more than disinterest fueling their odd behavior. It certainly did not help that Bonny had overheard Mhàiri admit to wanting to kiss her uncle, and despite her best efforts,

Mhàiri had not convinced Brenna or Bonny that she had only been teasing.

Mhàiri turned to Conan and was surprised to find him not just looking directly at her, but smiling. Not his normal, charming smile that he used to woo women, but a smug one. His blue eyes twinkled as if he knew that Mhàiri would never accept.

A slow smile curved Mhàiri's soft mouth. Conan's twinkle faded and was replaced with discomfort. She raised a single brow and debated about accepting his challenge. Conan held her gaze until she turned to Conor and said, "Thank you for the offer, and I think I will accept. For you are right, Bonny," she said, glancing back to the grinning seven-year-old, "there is no one better to build my shelves than your uncle. Especially as I will be *very* particular about their strength, size, and placement."

Bonny elbowed Brenna, whispering loudly enough for the whole table to hear, "See? I told you it would work."

Brenna then leaned over and cupped her hand over Bonny's ear. "Not yet, but it will."

"Which one are you looking at now?" Mhàiri asked Brenna, who was lying across her bed flipping through one of her bound books.

"A really interesting one," the ten-year-old replied. "Bonny never said these things had pictures. I always thought they were just full of boring words."

That captured Mhàiri's attention, and she put down the newest gown Maegan had left for her so that she could see exactly what Brenna had picked up. Medical texts had been around for more than a thousand years.

Most described plants and their healing qualities, but she had a couple books that went far beyond herbs.

Mhàiri plucked the book out of Brenna's grasp, ignoring her squeal of protest. It was what she had feared. The *Compendium Medicinae* by Gilbertus Anglicus. It had been written by an English physician who had documented a great deal on the practice of medicine, including surgery, with some eye-catching illustrations. She knew because it had caught her eye as a thirteen-year-old. If her father had known exactly what she had convinced him to get for her, he would have exploded. Just as Conor would do if he discovered Mhàiri had allowed his daughter to stare at drawings of naked men—even if most were just of their bones or muscles. "I think not."

"Mama says books expand your mind," Brenna said as she blinked her eyes innocently, but not convincingly.

"Aye, they do, but yours does not need to be expanded in that direction." Mhàiri pointed to some of her favorite manuscripts that contained poems. "Try those."

Brenna shook her head and wrinkled her nose. "Those have no pictures."

"If you want pictures, you should draw some."

Brenna scoffed and flipped over to her back. "Mine wouldn't be nearly so interesting."

Before Mhàiri could respond, there was a knock on her bedroom door. She called out for the person to enter, and Maegan peeked in wearing a large smile. She came in, closed the door, and leaned against it. "Oh, good, you are looking at the dress. It is too long for me, and gold is not my color, but it is *so* pretty and when Laurel said she prefers her other gold gowns to this one, I just couldn't let it sit in a dusty trunk never being appreciated. With your dark hair and green eyes, it would look ravishing on you. More importantly, I happen to know a certain soldier who would *definitely* appreciate it."

Brenna abruptly sat up. "Who?"

Maegan blinked and scanned the room. "Where is Bonny?"

Brenna shrugged. "Where else? With Uncle Conan."

"And why aren't you spying on them?" Maegan asked suspiciously as she went over and poured some water in a mug.

Brenna fell back onto the bed with a bounce. "Bonny will tell me anything interesting later. And Mhàiri needs me."

Mhàiri swiveled her head and narrowed her gaze. Brenna's tone was too playful to be ignored. When Conan had warned Mhàiri about Laurel and her meddlesome matchmaking habits, he had forgotten to mention that her daughters were not only like her— but worse. "And how is it that I need you?"

"I've known Uncle Conan longer than you so I can help you figure out what you can do to thank him for the shelves."

Maegan sputtered and she began to cough. Mhàiri came over to thump her back. When Maegan caught her breath again, she muttered, "Sorry about that. I thought for a moment Brenna said something about *thanking* Conan."

Brenna looked over and nodded, her expression an earnest one. Maegan turned to Mhàiri. "You aren't, are you? I mean that is just begging for . . . well, I don't know what. But it's begging for it all the same."

Mhàiri bit her bottom lip. "I . . . I probably *should* thank him." Then, upon seeing Brenna sit up with an enthusiastic gleam in her eye, she hastily added, "But to *do* something to show my appreciation? I mean, I have no idea what that could be."

Maegan threw up her hands. "Don't look at me! I've never heard of *anyone* thanking Conan for anything before. That's probably because I've never heard of him doing anything for anyone before that was not because of some family obligation. Even then, he complains."

"That's why you will need to thank him," Brenna said with a large smile. "And Bonny and I can help you figure out how."

Maegan arched her brows and collapsed into one of the hearth chairs. "Beware, you are about to be manipulated."

Mhàiri pursed her lips and then let go a large sigh. "Without a doubt, and yet Brenna does have a point. Maybe I can give him something to show my appreciation."

Brenna nodded, bouncing on her knees. "Your paper! Uncle Conan needs a bunch for his maps when he leaves this spring. And you have plenty!"

"I do not have *plenty*," Mhàiri refuted. Although to some it might look like it. She did have several books of blank hemp pages, but there was a reason she had them after so many years. She rationed their use. "It might *look* like a lot, Brenna, but my father bought that paper for me some time ago. The only reason I have any left now is that I have been very careful to make it last."

"Oh," Brenna said, disappointed, for she knew how much her uncle would have really liked having some hemp. She had heard him telling Seamus about it. "How long have you had those books?"

"Two years," Mhàiri quickly answered, glad the young girl seemed to understand how hard it had been to make them last this long. But suddenly Brenna jumped to her feet, excited once anew.

"I thought you said your father was going to be here in the spring."

"He is," Mhàiri confirmed apprehensively.

Brenna began to pace. "*And* he is coming from Spain and that is where Uncle Conan said the hemp paper was made. *So* if all this," she said with great exaggeration, waving her hand at the three large chests, all of which were open, "lasted two years, then you must have enough to share *some*. Especially if you are going to get more in a few months."

Maegan stood up and went over to grab the dizzying Brenna by the shoulders. Using her most authoritarian tone, she asked, "Did Conan tell you to ask for Mhàiri's paper? Or even hint?"

Brenna looked disgusted and pulled free. "If Uncle Conan told me to do that, then how would it be a surprise when Mhàiri gives him the paper?"

Maegan turned around and looked at Mhàiri. She shrugged and went to sit back down. "Well, then what should Mhàiri give Seamus? He is also going to help build them so shouldn't he get something?"

Brenna giggled. "The only thing he wants is . . ." She wiggled her finger in Maegan's direction.

"We are *just* good friends."

"Then you must be *really* good friends from the amount of time you spend together," Brenna chortled and fell back on the bed once again.

Maegan raised her chin defensively. "We are. We have a lot in common, *including* your uncle Clyde, whom I love very much. And guess who else we have in common?" Maegan quickly asked Mhàiri, hoping to change the direction of the conversation. "Loman," she answered and unsuccessfully bit back a smile. "He's the reason I came to see you. Seamus says that he introduced you to him and that Loman has spoken about little else since."

Mhàiri bit the inside of her lip. Loman had light-colored hair and brown eyes and, like all McTiernay elite soldiers, he was incredibly well built. And unlike some of the soldiers, who chose to wear the same austere face as their commander, Finn, Loman was good-humored and easy to talk to. "He did? What did he say?"

Behind her, Brenna gave a soft snort and scooted off the bed. She crossed her arms and her eyes flickered between Maegan and Mhàiri. Something was suddenly bothering her, and she was doing nothing to hide the fact.

"Is something wrong?" Mhàiri finally asked.

Brenna stood staring for several seconds before she shook her head. "I need to find Bonny," she announced, then left without further explanation.

Mhàiri's jaw dropped. "What did I do?"

"Who knows?" Maegan replied, completely unconcerned at the sudden change in the youth's attitude. "But I've seen that look enough to know that, whatever it is, you are part of her plans. So be careful."

Mhàiri swallowed. She wanted to ignore the warning, and told herself that Brenna was only ten years old. A child. But another inner voice reminded her that Brenna was no ordinary little girl.

Mhàiri suspected the havoc Brenna could create was more than most could imagine.

Mhàiri lifted her hand, curled her fingers in preparation to knock, and then paused for the second time. Did she really want to do this? See Conan? Offer him some paper in a show of thanks for making her some shelves? The answer was both yes and no.

She did want to thank him, and offering him some sheets of hemp paper was not really a hardship on her and would be greatly appreciated by him. She knew that. But it was the fact that she *wanted* to see him and talk to him, and was actually excited about having a reason to do so that made Mhàiri think this was not such a good idea.

"*Murt!* Either knock on the damn door and come in or leave. The sound of heavy breathing is not endearing me to be agreeable to whatever brings you here." The curt order came from the other side of the door.

For a second, Mhàiri was mortified, but the feeling was quickly displaced with irritation. She *knew* she had not been breathing loud enough for him to hear. He must have heard her approach. Without waiting for an invitation, she opened the door. "Rumors have it that you happen to like a woman when she is breathing heavily."

Conan's head jerked up as he jumped to his feet. His blue eyes were large as saucers, and suddenly Mhàiri felt a lot better. He had known that *somebody* had been outside his door, but not that it had been her.

Conan's shocked expression quickly morphed into an improper one. "Aye. I do like it, but in my *ear*."

Mhàiri chuckled, not insulted in the least. "Who did you think I was?"

"Seamus," Conan readily answered. "The man is a menace."

Mhàiri knew he was not serious. From what she had seen since her arrival, Seamus was one of the few Conan tolerated. Even more of a miracle, Seamus seemed indifferent to Conan's surly attitude.

Since Conan had not yelled for her to get out, Mhàiri took another tentative step, followed by another. She was eager to see what Conan's chambers looked like. Her head swiveled around, her soft green eyes growing larger the more she saw. Mhàiri had assumed that the area would be something like hers, large with most of the space dedicated as bedchambers, perhaps an area for reading and another a cluttered section full of books, manuscripts, and whatnot. She could not have been more wrong.

First, the room was enormous. Unlike other rooms on the lower floors of the North Tower, or even those in the Warden's Tower she was in, Conan's chamber took up the entire floor. It was separated into three areas, and they were not partitioned off by walls, but by functionality.

Unlike her room, it was not the library portion that was a mess, but the section that functioned as his bedchambers. The rushes were in dire need of replacement. The wood pile next to the hearth—which looked in desperate need of cleaning—had toppled over. His rumpled bed was large, but did not seem so in such a spacious area. Next to it was a massive dark, ornately carved chest with what looked to be a mixture of both clean and dirty clothes draped over it.

Mhàiri looked at him, pointed to the chest, and was surprised to see Conan actually looking a little sheepish.

"Chambermaids," he said with a sigh. "They clean, but they also disrupt. I find the latter more of an issue than wrinkled blankets and sheets."

Mhàiri flashed a coquettish smile. "My guess is that chambermaids only venture here when Laurel forces them and even then you hound their every move."

Conan grinned back, a perfect male smirk. "Lucky guess."

Mhàiri laughed. "You mean *accurate* guess."

She started toward the library section of the room. It was rare that Conan let anyone near his collection of written work. He sometimes allowed Bonny, but only when he was there with her. So that he was letting Mhàiri do so, he really could not explain. But the closer she got, the more her face grew in awe, and knowing that she appreciated what she was seeing made him eager for her to continue.

Unlike his bedroom area, the rest of Conan's room was very orderly—and very crowded. "I should have come up here much sooner," Mhàiri whispered, her eyes darting everywhere. "Then I never would have had any reason to doubt your assurances that you have no interest in my things. You barely have room for what you have." Then she pointed to one of the romance books that he had teased her for owning. "*And* you seem to have your own version already."

Conan nodded and sank back down on the stool he had nearly toppled over upon hearing her voice. "People assume I like any type of manuscript or written word, and while that might have been true at one time, I have had to become a lot more selective in what I keep."

Mhàiri ran her fingers lightly over the wood shelves. They were not simple slats of wood that had been wedged and nailed together, but they had the look and feel of those that would be found in the large abbeys. Four rows of wide open shelves enabled one to access books from either side. Along the far wall, between the two large windows that let in a surprising amount of light, were multiple shelves, specifically built to store scrolls so they could be accessible and yet not rolling about. The whole place was crowded, and yet there was an innate sense of organization to it.

Mhàiri was impressed. "Your room reminds me of a library I once saw when I was young and traveling with my father."

"Remember which one?"

She nodded, still looking, caressing the etchings as she went. "It was one at the Cambuskenneth Abbey. Have you heard of it?"

Conan's jaw twitched. While his room was nothing remotely close to as impressive as the abbey, he *had* modeled his shelving and his room's layout based on his visit to Cambuskenneth. Even Ellenor, who had taught him languages, had not recognized the beauty he had tried to incorporate into his chambers.

Mhàiri had. It once again stirred something in him, heating his already hot blood.

He had spent the past month trying to dismiss Mhàiri from his thoughts. It had been a losing battle as odd tidbits of information about her were relayed to him by Seamus, Bonny, and too often Conor. Her recognizing the library he had patterned his own after was going to be one more thing that would haunt him tonight when he tried to sleep.

Mhàiri scared him.

He had never physically craved a woman like he did her. He had wanted women, sometimes enough to chase them a bit, but never had desire interfered with his ability to concentrate during the day. And what he felt for Mhàiri was not mere desire, but something far stronger—and far more painful.

The moment she had opened the door, the scent of wild flowers had filled the room and turned his insides out. Like she did on most days, Mhàiri had twisted the sides of her hair into loose braids, leaving the rest of her dark tresses to flow down her back. This morning had been windy, causing several strands to become free and frame her face in a way that begged a man to reach out and know their softness.

He was not a man who normally paid attention to what a woman wore, but Mhàiri made that impossible. Maegan and Laurel had been giving her their used clothes, but he did not remember ever seeing either of them in the gowns. Mhàiri was slender, but not wafer thin like Maegan, which must make a large difference, because no man could forget the way Mhàiri was filling out the lavender dress she was currently wearing.

Physically Mhàiri was his dream woman. That was daunting in itself, but what really scared Conan was much greater than that. Mhàiri *understood* him. Every time they spoke, she confirmed it in another unexpected way. And today only compounded his fears. Mhàiri had entered his sanctuary, had seen his untidy bed, and while she commented on it, she did not chide him or tell him to get it cleaned. She had done something far worse.

She had accepted him.

Conan had more than simply believed there was not a woman for him—he had *known* it. His personality did not mind being alone. He had never craved "his other half" like his older brothers had. For him to love a woman like they did their wives would end all his dreams, and eventually, it would eat at him until there was nothing left of him or his love.

Then he had met Mhàiri.

If he was ever going to fall for a woman, it would be her. He was not going to, of course. Not just for his sake, but hers.

Mhàiri wanted nothing of love either. Home, children, *roots*—these were things she did not want almost as much as he did not want them. And while they both longed to see the world, their plans and ways for doing so could not be more different. The life of a traveling merchant was that of constant change, but that change was predictable, consistent . . . expected. He, on the other hand, was venturing into the unknown, where conditions would oftentimes be harsh and uncomfortable.

He had known this all after just a couple of days in her company. So he had made a plan. It was a simple one—ignore Mhàiri. Act as much as possible as if she did not exist until her father came to get her. But that had been when he had thought her father would arrive in a few weeks . . . not months. After weeks of trying to ignore her and the maddening effect of her pretending to ignore him, Conan knew that his simple-but-tormenting plan would not be viable much longer. Certainly not until spring.

Conan shifted uncomfortably in his chair. Maybe he just needed to get her out of his system. His brothers may think he had been with a lot of women, but it was not really true. Conan had *kissed* a lot of women, but when he needed a physical release, he was far more selective. It was rare he ventured outside of those for whom he knew there would be no unexpected claims or children. Laurel would undoubtedly kill him if he pursued Mhàiri to his bed, but what harm would there be in a kiss? He had the benefit of Mhàiri being already interested in him. Normally, her notice would be enough to dampen his desires. Overly eager women were never attractive. However, Mhàiri's interest was less eager and more . . . curious, which was not unappealing.

He smiled at the realization. Perhaps the secret to getting Mhàiri out of his system really was to kiss her. A few poorly executed kisses would definitely solve his problem.

Conan wiggled his brows and pasted on his most charming smile. After a few minutes of sitting there, grinning like a fool, his frustration got to him and he began to scowl. Not *once* had she even glanced his way.

With a sigh, he crossed his arms and leaned back. "Let me guess. You are here about the shelves."

Mhàiri nodded, still keeping her focus on the various volumes Conan owned. Never had she seen a private library so extensive. She had never even heard of one. "What are you going to do with all your things when you leave? You cannot possibly bring all this with you."

Conan coughed at the thought. "Ah, no. I don't really plan on taking hardly any of it. Some maps of course and as much blank vellum as I can carry, but the rest will stay here, in this room, just like it is. Bonny, I'm sure you have come to realize, is very bright—"

"She's brilliant," Mhàiri corrected, her eyes still reading the spines. "I suspect she is smarter than either you or I, and putting humility aside, I don't say that lightly."

Conan's brows arched. He thought similarly. Like him, Bonny was quick to learn languages. Though she was only seven, her mother had already started teaching her how to read both English and Gaelic, and he had focused on making sure she understood the basics of Latin. Her aunt Ellenor could instruct her on Italian and French after he left, whenever she was ready, and he knew someday, Bonny would not only learn to read these other languages, but speak them, mastering them in a way he had never been able to. But Bonny was not only an academic. She had a natural instinct when it came to people. Her sister, Brenna, had it as well, only it manifested itself differently. Bonny was not as obvious with her understanding, which made her, in a way, more dangerous. A good example had been last night and the mention of Mhàiri needing somewhere to put her own manuscripts and books. He still suspected there was far more to Bonny's suggestion than just kindness.

"The shelves?" Conan put forth again.

Mhàiri turned to look at him this time. "Um, oh, the shelves," she stuttered, having forgotten why she had come to visit. "I, uh, first wanted to thank you. I know that Conor put you in an awkward position."

"Conor didn't. I believe we can blame BonBon for that. She and Brenna have unusual influence over their father."

Mhàiri clicked her tongue. "Over everyone. I'm coming to realize that more and more," she said softly without expanding on what she meant. "But I do need them. The shelves, I mean. Nothing fancy like you have. Anything solid would work. And while probably a carpenter could do it . . ."

"You want someone who understands what it will be used for."

Mhàiri nodded, her green eyes looking relieved. "I don't have nearly as much as you, but it still, well, is a *lot*. You saw the bags and the crates, but all three of the large chests are also full of bound books."

Conan leaned forward in shock. "*All* three of the large chests?" Mhàiri nodded. "What about that small chest?"

"That contained my personal things. I know it seems like I have more, but I could not imagine traveling with the number of dresses Maegan has loaned me. I would need a cart just for clothes alone!"

Conan had thought the small chest probably had some of the more precious manuscripts that she had wanted to ensure would not be harmed during their journey. But instead, that was what held all her female garb and stuff. It was difficult to fathom. Every time Crevan's wife, Raelynd, had shown up at McTiernay Castle for an extended stay she had brought mountains of frilly things with her. Craig's wife, Meriel, was not much better.

Conan rocked back, rethinking about the amount of work the project was going to take, for it was much bigger than one small bookcase with two or three shelves. Thank goodness the room Laurel had put her in had the space. Bookshelves the size Mhàiri needed would not fit in one of his brother's old rooms here in the North Tower.

"I know the amount of work is significant and Conor did not know what he was asking of you." Conan's lips twitched. She was right about that. "And if you no longer want to help, I'll understand and work with a carpenter, *but* if you *were* willing to build them, maybe I could offer you something in return for your help."

Conan's brows shot up. Something she could offer him. It was as if the good Lord actually *wanted* him to kiss her. "I can think of something," Conan said huskily.

The change in his voice was unmistakable. Mhàiri scrunched her brows in confusion. "You think I mean to . . . that I was offering to . . . *kiss* you?"

Conan ran his tongue on the inside of his cheek and took in a deep breath. Mhàiri was acting as if she were not interested in him, when he knew that was not the case. "Why not?" he posed. "I know you have longed for a kiss, and I can think of no better way to show thanks."

Mhàiri's mouth opened and closed so many times she felt as if she were a fish out of water. "You *know* I long for a kiss?" she repeated. "Why would you . . . ?" Her eyes grew as large as saucers before rolling into the back of her head. "Bonny," she muttered, throwing her hands in the air. The twinkle in Conan's bright blue eyes confirmed her deduction. Mhàiri wagged a finger at him. "I'll admit that I did want to kiss you *at one time,* but that feeling passed rather quickly the first time you intentionally snubbed me."

Conan flushed at the accusation. "I never snubbed you," he denied, shaking his head as if that made it true.

Mhàiri cocked a single brow. "Really? You are denying that you have been intentionally ignoring me?" Conan stopped moving his head. "As Bonny no doubt disclosed that entire conversation, you also know that I have never been kissed before. So it is less me wanting to kiss *you*, and more like me wanting to kiss *someone* who won't see the act as a commitment or a profession of undying love. And now that you know all this, I *can't* kiss you. It would only place me even deeper in your debt."

Conan feared Mhàiri might actually mean what she had just said. "I promise you that I would not take it that way."

"But I would. Besides, it is no longer necessary. Maegan has introduced me to several of Seamus's friends, and so I am certain my ignorance in that area will not last for much longer."

Conan had the sudden urge to find Seamus and punch him in the jaw. It had never occurred to him before, but Conor allowed an inordinate amount of single men around the castle. No wonder Seamus was constantly fussing about Maegan and all the men around her.

Conan wanted to go to each and every McTiernay clansman and warn him that Mhàiri was his. His alone. That no one was ever to learn what it would be like to touch her soft, warm lips but him. But Conan knew if he did anything like that—even hinted to anyone that those were his feelings—he would be opening Pandora's box, just like the Greek myth from Hesiod's *Works and Days,* which was on one of the shelves in this very room.

Also, there was Laurel's reaction to think about. There was no telling what his sister-in-law would do if he showed signs of possessiveness toward Mhàiri. Laurel might do everything in her power to foster a connection, making him the sixth McTiernay brother subject to her matchmaking schemes. Or—more likely—she would make good on her promise and do everything she could to interfere, ensuring Mhàiri was swept off her feet by someone else.

Unaware of the warring thoughts Conan was having, Mhàiri wandered closer to where he sat on a stool. Nearby was a chair that looked as if it had been stolen from the great hall. She pointed to it. "That is the most surprising thing in this whole room. The great hall hearth chairs are very comfortable and by having one here, you are practically inviting guests to come in and sit and stay for a good . . . long . . . while."

Conan returned her playful smile. "Which is why I discourage visitors. That"—he gestured toward the chair with his thumb—"is a result of my sister-in-law Ellenor, who stayed here at the castle before she married my brother Cole. She is impertinent and stubborn, but also gifted in languages I did not know. She helped me translate some maps and insisted on having a comfortable place to sit while we worked. If I got rid of it now, Bonny would think I didn't love her anymore."

Conan was in the workplace portion of his study, sitting in the middle of an L-shaped table. Multiple papers were all over one half, and on the other, he had one of his more favorite maps uncurled and blocked out. Next to it was the drawing Mhàiri had been working on during their journey from the priory.

"Using Bonny as an excuse is . . ." Her breath caught as she recognized her handiwork. "What is that?"

Conan looked to where her eyes were locked and saw her partially completed landscape. "That is your drawing," he answered, trying to sound matter-of-fact. "You knew I had it."

Actually, she had forgotten about it. "Because you wouldn't give it back to me," she countered. Her eyes darted to his, and their pale green depths were no longer warm and soft, but cold and aloof. "What are you doing with it?"

Conan was not really sure why Mhàiri was suddenly so angry. In his mind, his keeping the drawing was actually the highest form of flattery. "I was trying to figure out how you did it. How you made things look so real, but so far all I've done is wasted a sheet of vellum trying." He handed the picture back to her. "You have a gift I have no hope of ever being able to replicate."

Mhàiri snatched the paper from his hand. "You told me that it was *wrong*. That this was of *no value*. That I was wasting my time. That I had no appreciation of what I could do. And yet, you want to *replicate* it."

Mhàiri turned and walked to the door. She needed to leave. All the memories from that night were crashing back on her. She had felt so angry, so guilty, so lost. For a fleeting moment, she had even considered giving him some of her precious hemp paper. Mhàiri's hand was on the door when she remembered. *Hemp paper. Murt!* That was the reason she was here. To offer Conan some for helping her with the shelves.

Slowly she opened the door and then turned around. Conan was staring at her, clearly searching for something to say but fearing it might make things worse.

"In exchange for the shelves," she said stonily, "I will teach you how to draw like I do."

Mhàiri turned around to exit. Just before she closed

the door, she said, "Lessons begin tomorrow after the noon meal on the hill near the large tree."

"I *told* you that you should have given the drawing back to Mhàiri," Bonny chided as she emerged from her hiding place.

Conan was at the window staring down into the bailey. "Not now, Bonny."

"Girls don't like it when you take their things without their permission."

Conan watched as Mhàiri entered the courtyard and marched toward the Warden's Tower. "I said not now, Bonny." His words were a lot more clipped, and he hoped his niece would take the hint.

"Well, she can't have been *all* that mad at you. She did offer to teach you how to draw," he heard another voice say.

Conan turned around and narrowed his gaze on Bonny, who just shrugged. He had suspected Bonny was nearby hiding, for she had been visiting him when he had heard someone come up the stairs. They had both thought it had been Seamus, and he had sent Bonny into the secret passageway for her to exit the room and the tower. He was not surprised to learn that she had lingered once she had heard Mhàiri's voice. Brenna, however, was a complete surprise.

Bonny walked over to his desk and pulled out the vellum that he had used to try and recreate Mhàiri's landscape. "I don't think drawing is something you learn how to do by looking at it."

Brenna clasped her hands behind her back and swayed up on her toes and then back down. "That's why Mhàiri is going to give him lessons," she said with a smile. "Can we come with you?"

Conan took in a deep breath and strode to his door. He swung it open and pointed to the outside corridor that led to the stairwell. "Out!"

Bonny grabbed her sister's arm and pulled her toward the exit. Just as they went through, she said, "When you go tomorrow, remember you're the one who doesn't know anything about drawing."

"What's that supposed to mean?" he barked.

Bonny looked up and stared him directly in the eye. "It's just that you like telling people what to do, even when you don't know what you are talking about." Then she turned and left to find her sister, who had gone down without her, leaving Conan's mouth agape.

Bonny did not have to go far. A couple of flights down, Brenna sat on one of the narrow winding steps, waiting for her. "Can you believe it?" Brenna giggled and shook with pure joy. "Things are working out perfectly. Just you wait, Bonny. With a little bit of help, Mhàiri and Conan will fall in love and get married. Then, Uncle Conan won't leave and Mhàiri will stay here forever!"

Bonny stared down at her feet. She liked Mhàiri—a lot. She was smart and funny. She was also honest and direct, everything Bonny liked in a person. And she *did* think that Mhàiri was good for her uncle Conan and that they could fall in love. However, she was not sure that Brenna was correct about any of the rest.

While she wanted Uncle Conan to stay and never leave their home, she did not think it was going to happen. Since she could remember, he had been planning to leave and see the world. He wanted it more than anything, and Bonny feared that if he did not get to leave, her uncle would end up very unhappy . . . and being in love was not going to change that. She did not know Mhàiri as well, but from what she had learned, Mhàiri also did not want to stay, even if she did like it here.

The only way for Brenna's plan to truly work was if they somehow convinced Conan and Mhàiri they needed to leave *together*.

That, however, seemed way beyond the ability of a ten-year-old, even a smart one, to mastermind.

At some point, they were going to need their mother.

Chapter Five

The next day, Conan trudged up the hill toward the large tree where Mhàiri sat. He had known exactly which one she had been referring to when she had told him where to meet her. There were several trees in the area, but one was an enormous oak that stood out amongst the rest. It had been huge when he was a lad, and his father had told him that it had been just as big when he was a small boy. Conan had no idea how old the tree was, but it had to be the oldest tree in the area. And everyone knew of it. If someone said, "Meet me by the tree," one knew exactly what and where they were talking about.

Conan gritted his teeth. Mhàiri's back was to him. She was sitting on a blanket drawing, completely unaware of his approach and completely unaware that he was deeply conflicted about meeting her.

He had been in a foul mood all morning. It had begun during the first meal, when Mhàiri had barely acknowledged him. It had not been anger that greeted him but indifference. It had been as if she had forgotten yesterday and had reverted back to ignoring him.

Then, an hour before they were to meet, his mood

had gone from sour to irate when Conor had requested his presence in the lower hall. He had barely taken a step in the room when he saw the scrawny piece of red-headed filth that had held a sword on him just over a month ago.

Upon seeing him, Conan had charged in, immediately demanding to know what the maggot was doing on McTiernay lands, and why Conor had not yet removed his head. The answer had startled him to his core. Anger had flooded through every fiber of his being so fiercely that it had taken everything not to pummel the man to unconsciousness. Even now if he closed his eyes, he could see every movement, hear every word.

"What did you say?" Conan asked slowly, his icy tone enough to send shivers through not only the weakling, but his brother.

The redhead narrowed his dark, beady eyes and arrogantly leaned forward. "You McTiernays," he spat, and Conan could see the man's rotten teeth despite his young age. "You got my sister pregnant this summer. My father demands you marry her and pledge yourself and the McTiernay armies to him and our family."

Conor did not say a word, but it was not necessary. Conan knew that it never happened. Even if he had done what the *sùibhealtan* claimed, his brother would never pledge even a dull blade to a man such as the one before him. "Your sister lies," Conan snarled.

Fury filled the redhead's gaze, causing him to start to quiver and sputter. "Do you know who I am?" he finally got out. "My father is the laird of—"

Conan cut him off. "*I don't care!*" he roared, slamming his fist on the table, making the thin man jump in fear. "Go home and tell your sister that she should not have named a man who would never allow himself to be a pawn."

"Honor demands that—"

"You know nothing about honor, or you wouldn't be trying to blackmail me into accepting your sister's bastard bairn. Hard to believe I'm her lover as the first time I journeyed north of the River Carron was around the time I saw you running away from a fight like a *bleidire*."

"And why should I believe a McTiernay?" the irksome man snorted, his deep-seated hatred showing.

Conan did not know this man nor did he have even the remotest clue why the man hated McTiernays, but he was beyond caring.

Conor tapped his finger on the table, getting the attention of both Conan and the unwanted visitor. "Perhaps you would trust the word of our priest, Father Lanaghly?" His question sounded calm, but the man was a fool not to understand what that meant. He had no idea how close he was to meeting his death. For that last insult had been lobbed not just at Conan, but at Conor and every McTiernay clansman.

Conan, however, was done. He slammed his fists down on the table and leaned over it, his heated glare enough to make the man hold his breath. "Nay," he said, removing the option. "We don't need to bother the priest. This conversation is over, and the only reason you are leaving here alive is to deliver a message. Go tell your father, *the laird,* that nothing in this world or in the heavens above could persuade, let alone force, me into marriage with *anyone*—pregnant or not. My future does not include a wife, and your sister's future is one of her own making. She should have kept her legs closed."

Refusing to endure any more lies or insults, Conan had stomped out of the hall and gone directly to his rooms. There, he had found Bonny and shooed her out, making it clear that Brenna best not come near him either. Unable to sit or think, he had paced back and forth, waiting until Conor stopped by. Finally, after what felt like an interminable amount of time, his brother had arrived.

"Did you find out who he was?"

Conor shook his head. "I did not want him to have the satisfaction of telling me. Plus, like you, I didn't care. I only told him that if he takes a step onto *any* McTiernay lands, it will mean his painful death." He glanced out the window. "Finn's escorting him to our borders with instructions to muzzle him if he utters a single word."

"That man is full of rage and is a fool. He'll be back."

"And if he does, he will die, but I doubt he will return. His sister probably named you because you are the only unwed McTiernay left still in the Highlands."

"I meant what I said. I don't care what anyone says or believes. I'll never take a wife."

"And I think of all the things that he heard, *that* is the one he believed. You are not a man who could be coerced into marriage. Hopefully, he can convince his father." Conor clapped him on the back. "Gather your wits. BonBon told me to remind you that you have a drawing lesson with Mhàiri."

"Your *daughter*—"

"Is delightful and, for some reason, adores you!" Conor laughed and paused just as he exited the room to growl, "Don't cancel or I'll tell Laurel."

It was lucky Conor had been across the room when

he had made the threat, or Conan might have decked him. But the warning had been enough to get him to leave the tower. Now that he was here, he began to care less and less what Laurel knew or thought.

The oak loomed ahead. Conan took a deep breath and then let it escape slowly. But before he could decide whether or not he was too angry to be fit company, Mhàiri turned and saw him. Her mouth broke out into a large smile as she waved him over. How he wanted to kiss that mouth. He knew with one touch she could make all that had happened today disappear, if only for a while. If only she wanted a kiss too.

He approached cautiously. Mhàiri had not changed since lunch and was still wearing a forest green gown that highlighted and hugged every morsel of her perfect body. The woman was exceptionally pretty. So much so that even if he weren't in a bad mood, the outing was destined to be a waste of time. He was going to be incapable of learning anything. Each time he saw her, she only looked more desirable and his thoughts grew more lascivious. Even now, a part of his mind was still wondering how Mhàiri would taste if he were to kiss her.

"You *are* here," Conan said as he squatted down beside her, hoping to deflect any of his own misgivings onto her. He took a deep breath, closed his eyes, and savored her scent. It both calmed him and excited him. Surprisingly, the dual effect was exactly what he needed to let go of the previous hour completely and just concentrate on her.

Conan looked over her shoulder. Mhàiri had obviously been there for a little while, for she had already

sketched out the basics of the view all the way down to
the loch and the mountains beyond.

Mhàiri tilted her head and gave him a questioning
look. "Of course I am here," she said, somewhat offended. "Just as I said I would be. Oh, this morning,"
she whispered, suddenly realizing why he might have
thought she would not have come. Mhàiri closed her
eyes for a brief moment and then looked at him, winc-
ing. "I did not want anyone to know or suspect we were
meeting, so I thought it would be best to continue
acting the way we have been."

Conan gave her a crooked smile and shook his head.
"Good idea, but it won't work. Bonny and Brenna overheard our whole conversation yesterday afternoon. It
was a chore just to keep them from tagging along
today."

Mhàiri's jaw dropped open. *The* whole *conversation*,
she mouthed.

He nodded. "Don't worry. Brenna loves to know all
that is going on, but for someone so young, she is
surprisingly circumspect about revealing what she
knows. Neither she nor Bonny lean toward gossip."

Mhàiri pressed her lips together and prayed Conan
was correct. Then she rolled her eyes and sighed. "I
don't know why I care. They learned I want to kiss you
weeks ago and the one person I wouldn't want to know
that is *you*, and you, of course, are the one person she
went directly to and told."

Conan bit back the large smile that was invading his
soul. *Want to kiss you*, she had said. Not *wanted* to kiss
you. Mhàiri still desired him.

For that tidbit alone, he was definitely glad he had
come. Her claim that she desired him no more had
needled him and kept him awake most of the night.

He wanted her, but even more, he wanted Mhàiri to want him back.

Conan reached over to pull a wax tablet out of the small bag he had brought with him. Mhàiri looked at what he was holding and cackled. The sound was not a feminine one, and it certainly was not a high-pitched giggle. Seeing his frustrated look, only made Mhàiri laugh harder. Gasping for breath, she clutched at her stomach with one hand and his shoulder for support with her other. He gave her a perturbed look, which did not help. Her laughter renewed and tears began to fall.

After several deep, calming breaths, she finally got out, "What is that?" while only letting go a few chuckles.

"A wax tablet," he said impatiently, waving it in his hand for her to see.

"I *know* that, but what are *you* doing with it?"

"Well, I'm not going to waste more vellum. The stuff is hard and expensive to make, and I need every scrap of it for my journey. Not all of us have access to a private supply of hemp paper," he said with a hint of a sneer, using his chin to point at the drawing in her hand.

Mhàiri wiped away her tears, then took the wax tablet out of his hand and put it on the ground. "If that is what you practice drawing on, then no wonder you are having difficulties."

A wax tablet was a reusable and portable writing surface. A piece of flat wood was coated with black or green wax that people could use and then erase by heating the wax through vigorous rubbing. But to make a mark, one had to push hard, and it was impossible to change the direction of a line without lifting the stylus and starting again.

Mhàiri lifted her bag and pulled out a large, flat board. Stretched across was a rectangular piece of off-white linen cloth. "This was something my father made for me when I was young and wanted to draw on everything. I did not have access to a private supply of hemp paper then," she said with a quick wink, "though even if I *had*, it would have been too expensive on which to practice. And as you made clear, vellum is costly and not easily come by. So, my father made me this to use over and over again," Mhàiri said, proudly showing it to him.

Conan just stared at it. "Cloth?" The only thing that would mark it was the ink he used on the vellum, which would stain the material. Linen seemed even less practical a medium than wax. "Maybe we should stick to sticks and dirt," he grumbled.

Undeterred, Mhàiri laid the cloth board in her lap. She pulled out a small leather bag and then opened it wide. Inside was a dark, wet substance. "I made this from the ash in my fireplace. You just add a little water until you get the right consistency. Now, you can take your stylus, dip it in, and look." Mhàiri outlined the petals to a flower in the lower right-hand corner. "At night, you untie it, wash it, and let it dry. Then you can start all over again the next day."

Mhàiri beamed him a smile and handed the board to him. For a second, Conan thought he was going to drown in the crystal-clear pools of her green eyes. Then he forced himself to look down at the board. He studied it with renewed appreciation. Bonny had been right. He had already forgotten her reminder that he knew nothing about drawing.

Conan picked up the stylus and looked at Mhàiri. Her excitement ran through him, and he told himself to focus on what she was about to show him. If Mhàiri really could teach him even some of the fundamentals of her style of drawing, it could revolutionize his approach to making maps. They would be more detailed, more readable, and most importantly, more usable than he had ever imagined.

"So where do we begin?"

"We begin with perspective. First, look and study our view. Do you see the tree right in front of us and the snow-topped mountain beyond the loch?" Conan nodded. "Now I want you to draw them on this corner. Just like you see them."

Conan did so, and when finished, he was both pleased and frustrated with his work. He thought all three well done considering he was not an artist, but they were nothing like Mhàiri's.

"Each is good, but I did not ask you to draw me a tree and a mountain. I asked you to draw me what you *see*. You made the mountain as big as the tree."

Seeing his mistake, Conan grunted and tried again.

"Interesting," Mhàiri hummed. "It must look different from where you sit because your mountain is bigger than the tree," Mhàiri said.

"But it is," Conan argued.

"A mountain may be larger than a tree in life, but I asked you to draw me what you see." Mhàiri then showed him what she had drawn. "When I look out, the tree is really close. I see so much more of it than I do the mountain. It is actually *bigger* because of my perspective."

Conan studied her drawing and then looked back up. The tree *was* bigger than the mountain. It was even bigger than the loch and the forest beyond, and he said so.

"That's right! That is the first thing you need to understand about perspective. It is not about how things actually are, but how they are perceived. To truly provide an understanding of something through a drawing, one should consider the object's size and position in relation to others *from a particular point*. You still can tell my mountain is larger in life than this tree, but because it is smaller, you also know how *far* it is from the tree."

Conan twisted his lips. "It seems so simple an idea. I don't think I have ever felt more like an idiot."

Mhàiri jerked back her chin. "Why? Every picture I have ever seen is depicted like what you first drew. Visual depth is never depicted." She pointed to the canvas. "Now it's time for you to practice and *really* start to feel like an idiot. Because nothing is more frustrating to me than knowing what I want to do but not having the skills to do it." Mhàiri reached into her bag and pulled out three more canvas boards. "For you. When you fill that one, go to these. Just note that you will have to disassemble them and get one of the chambermaids to wash the cloths tonight so that they will be dry tomorrow."

"You and I are coming back out tomorrow?"

Mhàiri held his gaze. "You think by the end of the day you will be proficient at drawing?"

He scoffed. "Hardly."

"Then, aye, we should plan to meet each afternoon we can until it turns too cold."

Afraid that his voice would show his happiness at the suggestion, Conan said nothing but instead picked up his stylus and began sketching the view. After what felt like only a handful of minutes, Mhàiri stretched her arms and then arched her back. She then pushed herself up to her feet and looked down where he stared up at her with a puzzled expression. "I think I'm done for the day, so I'm going to head back to the castle. But don't let my absence stop you."

Conan blinked and looked around. The sun had sunk low and was nearing the horizon. The fourth canvas board was in his hands, half full of marginal sketches and the other three were next to him full of ashy markings. He could not believe it. They had been drawing for hours.

When Conan had first sat down, he had thought it was going to be impossible to focus on anything with Mhàiri nearby. Every time the wind caught her hair, a piece would drift over his arm, teasing him. And her wildflower scent wreaked havoc with his ability to focus on anything but her. Knowing this, he had planned to convince her to put her own drawing aside and entertain his first notion of thanking him by means of a kiss.

But that had not happened. What had was akin to a miracle—at least for him.

Never had he been able to work with a pretty woman nearby. Usually, he found the sound of their constant jabbering annoying, but even the silent ones affected his ability to focus, for invariably his mind drifted to lustful thoughts. But, amazingly, he had spent an entire afternoon with Mhàiri and actually *worked*. And it was not that he did not desire Mhàiri. Just thinking of her created waves of lust inside him. He dreamed about how she would taste and how she would come alive in his arms. He longed to experience her hidden passion exploding in his embrace. And yet, somehow, he had become completely fixated on learning what she had shown him.

A sense of eagerness engulfed him. It had been a long time since he had felt so impatient, but tomorrow afternoon could not arrive fast enough.

Four days later, Conan paced by the oak tree waiting for Mhàiri to arrive. He had come early in hopes of releasing some of his tension before they met.

When he was around her, he felt incredibly alive, like anything was possible—even more so than he did when he was engrossed in a new map. Unfortunately, his mind was not the only thing that was more alive. Being around her every day was also making it very difficult to keep his desires under control and images of Mhàiri in his arms, passionate and wanting, was invading too many of his thoughts. He knew if his imagination could be put to rest and he could actually just *kiss* her, much of his angst would disappear. Aye, there would probably be an excellent chance he would want another kiss, but he would at least then *know,* thereby ending his torment.

However, events like that of the previous night did not help.

On their second outing, Bonny, Brenna, and Maegan had tagged along and the following day the weather had not cooperated. Yesterday had started similarly to their first. Mhàiri had shown him a couple of tricks about how to mentally measure each component before trying to capture it on the cloth. Conan had had every intention on practicing them per her instruction, but he had also intended to take a break at some point and pursue other, more physically pleasurable things. The one thing critical to his plan, however, was the one thing he did not have—Mhàiri's presence.

Right after she had given her advice, she had instructed him to continue practicing. Then she had risen to her feet, dusted off her gown, grabbed her bag, and begun to head back to the castle.

Conan had jumped up and chased after her. "You are just leaving me here? Alone?"

Amusement had filled Mhàiri's green eyes as she reached out and squeezed his bicep. "You seem capable enough to handle anything scary that might come along."

Conan had swallowed. Mhàiri had only briefly touched him, and the lower part of his body had gone hard. Any movement to hide the fact would have only shifted her gaze downward. He should have said goodbye and let her leave, but he had already appeared desperate. And yet, when he had opened his mouth to tell her to be careful, what had actually come out was, "How will I know if I did it right and if I am ready for the next lesson?"

"You can show me tomorrow."

"But I have to wash the cloths at night."

"So, you can draw something for me tomorrow."

"How about tonight?" Conan had pressed, acting completely unlike himself. And yet, part of him had not cared. It had been nearly a week since he had ended his ill-conceived plan to ignore her, and other than their first outing, he had yet to spend any quality time alone with her—and only her.

Mhàiri had sighed and given him a long look. "How about after dinner?" she had suggested. "In the great hall?"

Conan had nodded and waited for her to turn and leave before returning to the blanket and his sketches.

All that afternoon, throughout the entire meal, and right up until the doors opened, he had looked forward to their meeting. He had planned not only to show her the drawings, but what they could have been doing if she had not left their lesson early. Then again, there were several benefits of meeting at night in the great hall—no wind, unexpected passersby, or setting sun forcing an inconvenient end to their time together.

The night should have ended only after Mhàiri had thoroughly and repeatedly been kissed. But when it was finally time for them to meet in the great hall, nothing had gone according to plan.

He had arrived first and his heart had started to pound hearing Mhàiri enter and seeing her wear a huge, welcoming smile. He returned her smile but only briefly for tailing right behind her had been Bonny and Brenna. Upon seeing him, both screeched and ran forward, jabbering about wanting to see what their uncle Conan was learning to do.

Conan could not remember a time either of his nieces had been so chatty or critical. They had pointed out all the flaws in his sketches and what they thought he needed to practice more. Then they'd asked Mhàiri question after question about her drawings. Bonny, who had never been interested in art or maps before, had constantly poked him, telling him to pay attention, which he had pointedly refused to do. Instead, he had sat there, stretched out, moping as he downed several mugs of ale. He had not cared that he was being rude and immature. He had not cared about Bonny or Brenna either.

It had not been until this morning, when he had

awoken to a huge headache and the memories of his boorish behavior, that he'd had a few pangs of regret that resulted in an illuminating conclusion. He needed to end his pointless pursuit of kissing Mhàiri. If it happened, it happened, but the effort of trying to *make* it happen was—if possible—driving him even more insane.

Conan had missed the morning meal and had persuaded Fiona to let him take some food to his room. He had remained there through the noon meal so he had yet to see anyone. He had no idea of just how mad Mhàiri was. Any other woman, Conan would not have had to wonder. He would already know. She would have reamed him out that night before retiring, and most likely he would have woken up to something just as bitter being shouted from the bailey. But that was not Mhàiri's style. All he could remember was her whispering to the girls that the next time they all decided to meet with Uncle Conan, they should warn him first. That they were lucky he had stayed with them and had not left, especially when he was not having any fun.

Had she meant it? Or had Mhàiri only offered the words to comfort his two nieces?

Conan spotted Mhàiri approaching and stopped his pacing. He shielded his eyes from the bright overhead sun and tried to detect her mood from her expression, but he could not tell anything other than she was not smiling.

He swallowed. "You angry about last night?"

Mhàiri tilted her head slightly and looked at him quizzically. "I thought *you* were mad at *me*," she said, fanning herself with her hand. "Laurel insisted Brenna and Bonny come with me, and I *know* you don't like surprises."

She was right. He didn't. And Laurel knew it as well.

He had wondered what his sister-in-law's reaction would be if she suspected his desire for Mhàiri. Now he had his answer. Unlike with his brothers, Laurel was not going to ease his path toward true love. Which was good, because he did not want true love or any of the burdens that came with it. He only wanted a kiss. Laurel must have realized it, and unfortunately, she saw kissing him as a woman's first step to heartache.

"I was still kind of a *thòin* last night."

"You were." Mhàiri laughed at the memory. "That was why annoying you was so much fun. You only got grumpier. We took score at who could get you to growl the loudest."

Conan pursed his lips. Once again, Mhàiri was discombobulating him to the point where he lacked for words. "Who won?" he finally asked.

Mhàiri bit her lower lip in an effort to hide her smile. "We promised each other not to tell." She then fanned herself again. "It is strangely hot for this time of year. If it continues, we may need to meet after first meal before the sun is blazing overhead."

Conan shook his head. "I can't then. I train in the mornings."

"Do you have to train then? Couldn't you, um, take a break for a few weeks?"

Conan flexed the muscle in his arm that she had touched the prior day. "If I didn't, I would be a twig like Maegan. And wielding a sword is a skill that must be regularly practiced to be maintained."

"Then what are you going to do when you leave in

the spring? The image of you waving a sword around in the air each morning is not very flattering."

Conan chortled at the idea. "There will be plenty of opportunities for me to keep up my skills. It's not like I'm going to be sleeping outside under the stars all the time. I'm traveling and mapping the land at the request of King Robert. So, most nights, I will be staying as guest to a laird, much like you are to my brother. While I'm there, I'll train with their men as I can. Once I'm done, I'll move to the next clan and map their lands."

Mhàiri stared at him for several seconds in disbelief. She knew that Conan thought when they left in the spring and went their separate ways that his travels were going to be far more severe and uncomfortable. He had intimated as much several times. And she had believed him, thinking him hunting each night for his food, sleeping on the ground with only a blanket to shield him from the cold or the rain. Now she just wanted to laugh.

Aye, Conan was going to have to forage for his food *periodically*. But from what he described, most nights he would be served a delicious meal that consisted of a wide variety of foods. Merchants rarely experienced such luxuries, even wealthy ones like her father. Unlike her, Conan was going to be nestled on a mattress in a cozy bed with a large hearth fire to warm him. Her blanket-cushioned bed was going to be inside their wagon and was going to be put together and dismantled each night.

If their two futures were reversed, Conan would have a much harder time surviving hers. An opinion she decided was best kept to herself. Still, she could not help but say, "Based on last night and today, you have a lot of work to do on perspective. Yours is definitely skewed."

Conan looked down at the canvas in his hands and realized it was blank from being cleaned. He sighed heavily. He had thought he had been improving.

"You can practice trees and mountains later," Mhàiri said, gesturing for him to bring everything and follow her. "Today we are going to learn how to draw an object that is both near and far."

Mhàiri started walking, coming to a stop about half way down a sloping hill. She pointed to a thick rock wall that was about waist high. She sat down and said, "Try drawing the rock wall."

Conan sat next to her and attempted to sketch the wall. The result was a wall, but it looked nothing like the rock wall in front of them. It no longer bothered him that it was wrong. He actually liked Mhàiri's style of instruction. Instead of teaching as she, herself, drew things, Mhàiri preferred to use his efforts as a starting point. "That's good, but remember to draw what you *see*, not what you know. Aye, the wall is the same height and width its whole length, but it doesn't look that way from here. It starts out very small and narrow and then gets wider and taller the closer it gets."

Conan stared at the scene she wanted him to capture and realized that the wall did look like it was "shrinking" as it stretched into the distance. He tried again to draw it and with a frustrated grunt, handed the stylus to Mhàiri. She scrunched her nose and he almost thought she was going to refuse his non-verbal request.

"Fine," Mhàiri playfully grumbled. "One time, but I have my own drawing to focus on."

Mhàiri quickly sketched it. Conan watched carefully

how she started, using basic shapes to outline the primary features. "Next you add features in layers, beginning with the most distant thing and ending with the closest."

When Mhàiri leaned over to grab her bag, Conan panicked. "You leaving me again?"

"Not today," she answered with a brief shake of her head. "I love Brenna and Bonny, even Maegan, but I'm not used to having noise around me all the time. I like to have quiet when I read or draw. Normally, I would come out here by myself, but during your first lesson, I realized we had something else in common. When we get started on a project, our focus consumes us to the point an army could be marching by and we would never know."

Mhàiri was right, but the idea that she would come this far away from the castle by herself was disturbing. There were wild animals in the area, some of them vicious. In the colder months when prey was less easy to find, it was not unthinkable for a wildcat to attack a lone female. "Promise me you will never come out here without someone, preferably skilled in weaponry, accompanying you."

"Why?" Mhàiri asked, nudging his arm with her shoulder. "Worried about me?"

With a serious look, he answered, "Aye. Promise me, Mhàiri."

"I'll have you know that I can take care of myself and am not scared of wild animals. You need not worry about me. I did survive alone for nearly two weeks in my cottage before you arrived."

"Promise me, Mhàiri, or I'll order the guards at the gate not to let you pass."

Mhàiri blinked. Conan was being deadly serious.

She had been earnest about being capable of taking care of herself, but she was not sure how to convince Conan of that without killing and skinning a wildcat to prove it. "I already promised Laurel that I would not venture out alone, so you do not have to worry so."

Conan swallowed and nodded, relief relaxing his tense features. "Good. Make sure you keep that promise."

For the next couple of weeks, they kept to their routine. They would meet for a few hours in the afternoon before Conan returned to help Conor with clan needs or work on things in preparation for his journey. Mhàiri was certain that Conan had either forgotten or was delaying building her shelves, but she found herself to be caring less and less each day. She was getting used to dealing with the cluttered mess in her room, and Mhàiri truly enjoyed spending time with Conan. Though she would never admit it; she preferred his company more than anyone else's.

That did not mean she did not enjoy being around others. Mhàiri liked Maegan enormously and felt fortunate to have found in her an unexpected friend. They could and did talk about almost anything. Even discussing clothes with Maegan could be entertaining. She had the most hilarious stories about Bonny and Brenna as well as Gideon and Braeden, but mostly they would chatter about the soldiers and the silly things men did for attention. Maegan teased her about Conan, and Mhàiri teased her back about Seamus, for Mhàiri was positive Maegan liked the large soldier despite her constant assurances that she was in love with the absent Clyde. And while they got along very well, there was still only so much time the two of them could spend together before they ran out of things to say. Luckily, both had become fairly good at recognizing the precursors to such awkward moments and would go their separate ways before only silence was between them.

Mhàiri would have thought she would experience the same desire for space after several hours in Conan's company, and yet she didn't.

Sometimes they congenially talked almost the entire time they were together. Other times, their conversation ended up in a heated debate with voices raised. But just as often, they found themselves laughing together at a story one remembered, a funny thought, or something random one of them saw. And then were the times that neither said anything at all. Never before had she been able to sit with someone quietly without her silence being questioned. Even her father had had trouble with that one.

Spending time with Conan had felt so natural that Mhàiri had not realized just how unusual their relationship had become. At least not until Maegan had commented that some of the soldiers were betting on who was going to break first—her or Conan. That was when Mhàiri had learned that she held the record for the most days a woman had spent in Conan's company without some kind of public eruption. Most did not even make it a week before they accosted him in the courtyard, calling him heartless, selfish, and other unflattering things at the top of their lungs.

When Mhàiri had mentioned it to Conan, he had asked her what she had thought, and her answer had been the same as what she had told Maegan. "It's not your fault they lost their hearts to you. You probably even warned them against doing so."

Conan had flashed her a grin. "You know, I actually did."

"Then again, those dimples are an unfair advantage. I told you that they are lethal to a woman's good sense."

"Good thing they do not work on you," he said with a chortle as he continued practicing the lesson of the day.

That was when Mhàiri had known that it was not going to happen. Conan was never going to kiss her. He may have thought about it at one time, but that desire had been replaced with simple friendship.

Deep down, Mhàiri knew it was a good thing. She most likely was going to be staying at McTiernay Castle for another four months and that time would be far more pleasant if she and Conan continued as they were. While she truly believed she could keep the emotional aspect of kissing away from her heart, it was a risk to test that belief.

"How's it going?" Mhàiri asked, leaning over to see how Conan was progressing. They had moved on to how to draw lochs, rivers, and they'd even figured out a way to make it small enough to be depicted on a map. It was clear Conan understood the concepts she was teaching him, but skilled execution of them would take time and a lot of practice.

"I'm still trying to figure out how to capture the right amount of detail to show the features of an area but capture enough land mass to make the map of value. I don't expect King Robert to piece together hundreds of these things on his hall wall just to see all of Scotland. It needs to be smaller. Something that could be bound in a book and transported."

Mhàiri sighed and put her own stylus down. She

leaned back on her hands and closed her eyes, soaking in the warmth of the sun. "We should enjoy these warm afternoons. Did you feel how cold it got last night?"

"Aye," he murmured, concentrating on his drawing. The temperature was not truly warm like it was in the summer, but the sun was bright and the wind was slight, making the day enjoyable when dressed in warm clothes. "I think I understand this enough for now. Let's work on castles tomorrow. I know that there is not a large call for it on maps, but it might be useful and I want to learn all I can while I have the chance."

Mhàiri took in a deep breath and exhaled, completely relaxed. "I can show you castles next if you want, but not tomorrow. I promised to go on an afternoon picnic with Loman while the warm weather still permitted."

Conan froze, glad that Mhàiri's eyes were still closed.

He knew several of the soldiers liked Mhàiri. It was to be expected. She was beautiful and aggravatingly friendly. Of course, she had admirers. But he had not thought Mhàiri returned their regard. And Loman was the worst. Practically the day after Seamus had introduced them, he had taken every opportunity to say some overly sweet hello, trap her into talking with him, or compel her to laugh at some story that was, in essence, boring and trite. Conan had thought Mhàiri felt the same.

They were so alike in their attitudes and opinions . . . about so many things, he had just assumed that she viewed Loman's machinations the same way he did. Contrived and unwanted. But if she was going on an afternoon picnic with Loman, he had been wrong. Very wrong. And about a lot.

A whole afternoon together. If Loman's attraction to Mhàiri was anything similar to Conan's, the honey-haired soldier was not going to return to the castle with only a full belly and some conversation to get him through the night.

"You know Loman is going to try and kiss you," he gritted out.

"Probably," Mhàiri answered, eyes still closed, unperturbed at the idea.

"And are you going to let him?"

Conan's clipped tone caused Mhàiri to open her eyes. She held his gaze steady and answered, "Of course, I am. I told you that I wanted to know what it was like to kiss a man. All the farmers I met while at the priory wanted to marry me. To kiss them would have been like accepting a marriage proposal. Now I finally have the chance, and I am going to take it."

Conan could feel his jaw clench. The logic was there. Mhàiri did not sound as if she desired Loman, and yet the idea of that man's lips against hers was turning his stomach into knots. "And you don't think that Loman wants to marry you?"

Mhàiri thought for a moment and then, with a shrug, shook her head. She leaned back again, closed her eyes, and continued enjoying the sun. "He knows I plan to leave McTiernay Castle and travel with my father. And I don't see Loman suddenly wanting to become a merchant. So no, I don't think he has any thoughts toward marriage and a kiss certainly isn't going to create them. We just enjoy each other's company."

Conan stood up abruptly. Mhàiri reopened her eyes to see that he was packing his things. "We're leaving?" she asked, rising to her feet as well.

"Aye," he said, clearly disgruntled.

"I promise we will get together again in two days and I will show you how to draw buildings, castles, or whatever you want."

Conan dropped his things to the ground. "You think that's what I care about right now?" He reached out and his hands gripped her arms, not painfully, but with enough force Mhàiri could feel the tension raging in his body. "If you wanted to know what a kiss was like so damn bad, you should have asked me."

The desire Conan had worked so hard to suppress suddenly erupted and was beyond his control. His mouth came down on hers before Mhàiri could even think of moving. He caught her face between his hands, pulled her close, and kissed her—hard and deliberately—letting her feel the frustration and temper she had aroused in him.

Mhàiri was not sure what was happening until the moment she felt Conan's mouth close roughly over hers, searing their lips together. Surprised, she at first clutched his forearms and resisted, but Conan did not lessen his hold. The pressure against her mouth was deep and persuasive and undeniable. And before she realized what she was doing, her mouth opened and welcomed him in.

Her first real kiss. It was more than Mhàiri had ever dreamed it could be. She knew there were different types of kisses—those with closed lips and those with an open mouth. And when she had thought about what her first kiss should be, she had always envisioned something soft and sweet, where two pairs of lips met together. The exchange was supposed to be pleasurable—nothing like what she was feeling with Conan. Her body was on fire. She felt as if she were melting and hungry at the same time.

Conan moaned. Mhàiri's initial resistance was gone, and she was starting to respond. When she finally reached out and tasted him with her tongue, a shudder of need racked him. Something told him to let her go and maybe he would have found the will if Mhàiri's slim fingers had not slid up his arms and clutched at his shoulders. Ending the kiss now was not a possibility.

A sharp groan escaped his throat and Conan pulled her in closer. His whole body was tight with desire. The full force of his own hunger burned inside him, and he refused to suffer alone. He would fan her own growing desire to such levels that she would never consider kissing another man.

Mhàiri whimpered as Conan invaded the vulnerable warmth behind her lips with an intimate aggression that seared her senses. She had been completely unprepared for the flood of sensations his tongue would create, boldly stroking the inside of her mouth. His arms and body were taut with muscle. He was broader and, excitingly, harder than she. Mhàiri knew she should do something to stop Conan's passionate assault upon her senses, but she couldn't muster the will to push him away. Not yet.

If anything, she wanted to be closer to him and leaned into him, unable to rationalize why or what she was doing. His musky scent filled her nostrils and caused an unfamiliar stir in her belly. Her hands ran down over his chest of their own accord and then back up around his neck. He matched her need and pulled her tightly to him, causing her to groan.

Conan reveled in the way her lips moved against his. Mhàiri tasted as good as he had known she would, but instead of quenching his desire for her, her taste only inflamed it. He wanted her more than he had ever thought it possible to want any woman.

Conan's hands became as undisciplined as his mouth, taming and exciting as he stroked a warm path from her shoulders to the base of her spine.

Mhàiri trembled under his touch. It hardly seemed possible, but his fierce kiss had turned even more wild and ravenous. A shiver rolled through her and she suspected that what she was feeling could not be experienced in the arms of any other man. Conan was masterful, demanding, and all consuming. The hot, sensuous kiss went on and on, suffusing her body with an aching need for more. He was kissing her as though she were a drink of water and he were a man dying of thirst, and part of her hoped he would never be quenched. She moaned and felt her legs begin to quiver.

Conan held her tight so that she did not fall, but he did break off the kiss, giving them a chance to suck in much-needed air.

"Conan," Mhàiri whispered just before she rocked against him and went up on her tiptoes to seek his mouth again.

He cursed, "*Murt,*" and then bent his head to kiss her once more, his tongue penetrating, stroking, taking. His body hard and hot with wanting her.

Over and over again, he slanted his mouth over Mhàiri's. He curved his hand around the nape of her neck, keeping her in place, enjoying the silken feel of her skin while his body raged for something more.

Mhàiri let go another moan, and Conan knew he was at the brink of insanity. He had never shared an embrace that had turned so hot, so consuming, as to be in danger of losing control. But that was where he was at with Mhàiri.

With the last of his strength, he lifted his mouth from hers and looked down into her pale emerald eyes. She stared back at him with a mixture of confusion and vulnerability, but he steeled himself against it. Her chest heaved with the effort it took to breathe. He had never before experienced a need so deep, and it felt . . . threatening.

Suddenly, he needed to protect himself, his heart, and his future. He needed to get away. Now, before it was too late.

Conan held her face in his hands and looked down into the shining depths of her passion-filled eyes.

"There. Now you have something to compare Loman's kiss to."

Then he let her go and walked away, knowing those words, when they finally penetrated, would keep her from running after him.

Chapter Six

"Hold it there," Conan said to Seamus as he shifted the heavy shelf into place.

"So where's Mhàiri?" Seamus grunted.

"Out on a picnic with Loman."

Seamus leaned back to look at Conan. His eyebrows were arched high, and a slight smile formed on his lips. "Interesting."

Conan gave Seamus a quick glare and then went back to focus on securing the board in the panel's groove. Neither would ever admit they considered each other friends. Both told others they stomached the other's company, but in truth Conan respected the quiet soldier, and in the past year a surprising, but strong, bond of friendship had grown between them.

And all because of a woman.

Conan never had been attracted to Maegan, though he could see her appeal when he considered the idea objectively. But to him, Maegan would always be the skinny spitfire who had chased after his younger brother for years. He had seen the mutual attachment start to grow between them before Clyde had left. Clyde, in actions more than words, had claimed the girl as his own and probably this more than anything else kept Conan from truly seeing the soft beauty she had become. Her bony arms and body had filled out in the last few years, and her large eyes, the color of a clear winter sky, had begun to mesmerize many a soldier in Clyde's absence. One of them was Seamus.

With Hamish gone and living in the north, Seamus had taken the man's place next to Finn as Conor's second in command. As such, he had been around the castle a lot more than most and routinely crossed paths with Maegan. And each time they had spoken, the more Seamus had grown to like her. And soon he had begun to search for ways to be in her company whenever he was not on duty. Since Maegan was usually watching over Bonny and the little girl preferred to spend time with her uncle, Seamus had found himself in a situation he had never predicted to be in— seeking out Conan's company.

At first, Conan had thought of Seamus just as another nuisance who clearly was using him to spend time with a woman—something Conan might have respected more if Seamus liked someone other than Maegan. But when Bonny had mentioned how much the soldier had been helping him while he was there in prepping for his travels, Conan had realized she was right. After that, he no longer cared about Seamus's ulterior motives. Not only did he respect the soldier, but he liked the man. Conan also hoped that Maegan would realize before it was too late that Clyde was never coming back and that she could do no better than a good man who was inexplicably in love with her.

"What's so *interesting* about it?" Conan grumbled as he fought with the board. He knew it fit; the frustrating piece of wood just did not know it yet.

"Only that building all these shelves was a lot of work. One typically does not spend a lot of time on a project when there is no personal benefit. *You* certainly don't."

"I was ordered to do it if you recall. I did not have much of a choice." Finally, the board slid all the way into the groove. Conan put downward pressure on it, testing its strength. Pleased, he went to grab the next shelf. "Why do you care, anyway?"

"I don't necessarily, but there are several men I know who are very interested in your relationship with Mhàiri."

Conan felt his jaw tighten. He should have anticipated something like this. Fighting men, especially the unmarried ones, bet all the time and on anything. Mhàiri was something new to wager on. But *their* relationship? Making bets on that was senseless when he and Mhàiri did not have one. "What kind of wagers are you talking about?"

Seamus grunted when Conan began to push against the panel he was holding in an effort to wedge the next shelf into place. "Just what you would expect. Everyone knows you two are friends and go out each afternoon, so there are wagers on whether you two are going to pair up. But most just bet on when you are going to infuriate Mhàiri to the point that she yells at you like all your other past women. I wonder who won today?"

"She didn't yell at me today, and if she hasn't already, I doubt she will."

Seamus peeked around, and when he caught Conan's eye, he grinned largely. "I was talking about the bet on Loman being the *first* to successfully ask Mhàiri out."

Conan scowled at the hint.

"There will be others."

"What if there are?" Conan grumbled, frustrated with both the board he was fighting and the revelations Seamus was sharing.

"Why haven't you tried your charms with Mhàiri? I know it's been a while since you've actually pursued a woman, but I have never seen anyone get a female as quickly as you when you are of the mind to have one."

"Right now I have more important things to think about. And it's been a while because I've learned that women are the definition of trouble." Conan heard the popping sound of the second shelf sliding into place. He slapped his hands together. Curiosity forced him to ask, "So which way did you bet?"

"Who says I did?"

"I do."

Seamus scoffed. "Believe it or not, I bet on you."

"Bad bet, my friend," Conan replied, picking up the third and final shelf. Unfortunately, they had two more bookcases to put together.

"Why? Of all the women you have ever encountered— or are likely to encounter—Mhàiri is by far the best suited for someone with your temperament. Her wit, for example. You both have a strange sense of humor, although hers is one others tend to enjoy." This time it was Conan who peeked around to give Seamus an annoyed look. "What? People laugh when they're around her. Even you on occasion. She likes pictures just like you do *and* she also wants to see the world." Hearing no response from Conan, Seamus added, "And there is the fact that Mhàiri is unquestionably beautiful. I don't see how even you can resist that combination."

"You're resisting it."

"That's because my heart has already been claimed and so will Mhàiri's be if you do not stop pretending you are not interested in her."

Conan did not like hearing that other men thought Mhàiri beautiful, but to hear Seamus say it really rankled. And Conan had not realized others thought she was so funny. He put the board in place and gave it a forceful shove. "She'd be happier with someone else."

"Not in the long run. The woman is *really* smart. She is a female version of yourself," Seamus continued, waving his hand at all the books and manuscripts scattered around the room. "I've seen her challenge you a few times. And want to know what I saw? You *liked* it."

"Are you going to talk nonsense the whole afternoon?" Conan asked as he went to start putting together the second bookcase.

Seamus ignored him. "And what is really crazy is that Mhàiri, after spending hours in your company, doesn't seem to be repelled by you. Hell, I bet if you try, you could convince her to fall in love with you."

The pit that had been in Conan's stomach since he and Mhàiri kissed turned over. Love was not a notion he wanted to entertain. And what they had shared yesterday had been more than simple desire.

Kissing women was an act of lust driven by a basic, primal need to mate. But kissing Mhàiri had been different. Once their lips met, Conan had craved her in a way that he could not explain. Such physical desires wane once parted, but with Mhàiri, he did not just want her in his bed, he wanted to be around her. He actually *enjoyed* her company. Wanting her physically and emotionally—*that* was a dangerous combination.

"Your five older brothers seem happy to have found someone and be married. Maybe it's your turn."

Conan paused to look at Seamus to see if he was serious. "What are you really asking? Because it sounds like you are sizing me up for another bet. If that's true, I'll save everyone some money. It is *not* going to happen. Trust me when I say that Mhàiri is just as much against the idea of being tied down as I am."

Seamus shrugged disbelievingly and took the side panel Conan handed him. "I'll remind you that all your brothers said the same thing until Lady McTiernay got involved."

"Well, then lucky for me my sister-in-law has sworn never to help a woman ruin her life by attaching herself to me. Laurel discourages them from even talking to me, let alone falling in love and all that other nonsense."

"Then you *really* don't mind that a lot of other men are looking at Mhàiri? Wanting to know if she is available?"

Conan kept his focus on the panel in front of him. The first shelf was the hardest, for it secured the vertical panels. Once he was sure his expression was under control, Conan looked at Seamus. The damn man was smiling again. Seamus *never* smiled, but all afternoon he had had one plastered on his face. His grin was really becoming irritating.

"Listen closely," Conan said through gritted teeth. "I might like to hear Mhàiri laugh as much as the next man. And I won't deny I enjoy looking at her, but *nothing* is going to keep me from leaving in the spring. Alone."

Conan almost added that if other men wanted her, they were welcome to chase her, but he could not compel himself to say the words. He knew without doubt that come spring, just like him, Mhàiri would be leaving the Highlands happily unwed. Her reasons were as deeply rooted as his. And if she wanted to enjoy herself while she was here, he was not going to act like a lovesick puppy and stop it.

Loman's hand brushed Mhàiri's cheek, and her breath hitched in her throat knowing what was about to happen. Loman tipped her chin up, and his kind eyes stared down at her before narrowing on her lips. Then he leaned forward, cradled her face in his strong hands, and brushed his lips against hers.

Soft and gentle, it was nothing like Conan's demanding kiss from yesterday. Loman was sweet, smooth, and tender. So different from Conan. Loman's lips may not be passion-filled, but they were soft and warm and while molded to hers, they were surprisingly pleasant. The long, gradual kiss was not meant to create intense waves of need, but instead was a sweet mixture of patience and hope—quite different from the scorching, primal embrace she had shared with Conan. Today, she was not being branded or seduced. She was being asked.

After Conan had left, it had taken Mhàiri hours to calm her racing heart enough to recall what he had said. His parting words had practically been a dare, and Mhàiri had wondered if it would be possible to enjoy another man's kiss. Now she knew.

She did like it.

She was kissing Loman and not cringing at his touch, but enjoying the feeling of being desirable. However, Mhàiri knew there was only one mouth she would ever crave. One man who could make her lose all thought and control. And while Loman's lips were soft, warm, and sweet, they lacked the aggressive passion that made her feel alive and fully as a woman.

Loman pulled away slowly from her lips and smiled. "That was nice."

Mhàiri stroked his cheek and then leaned back. "It was nice. But I don't think we should do it again."

Loman reached out to caress her chin with his thumb. "Why not if we both enjoyed it?"

Mhàiri pulled back further. She licked her lips and held his gaze so that he knew she was not playing games. "Because, Loman, I think if we continued kissing you would eventually believe it would lead to other things." She swallowed. "And I'm not wanting those . . . things."

"You could, if you let yourself," Loman encouraged.

Mhàiri shook her head. "Another kiss is not going to change my mind."

"What about Conan?" he asked. "Is that why you are with him so much? Because he makes no demands?"

Mhàiri rolled her eyes, hoping to hide any feelings she might have for Conan. "He has nothing to do with what I want. My sister and I made plans to travel throughout Scotland long before I came here, and now I am planning to do so with my father."

"But plans change," Loman countered, his lips curled in a boyish smile. "Yours did. They could again." His tone was light, good-humoredly hopeful, despite knowing that they were not meant to be.

Mhàiri bit her bottom lip to keep from laughing. "Fine, persistent one. Let's say we kissed again."

"And again," Loman added with a cheeky smile that was aimed to wear her down.

"And even again," Mhàiri capitulated. "Then what is going to happen this spring when my father comes? Because no matter how much I was in love, there is one thing that will *never* change. I could never live in one place for the rest of my life. The idea of a small home to care for is beyond unappealing." She shuddered. "Cooking and cleaning every day would make me miserable and then I would make *you* miserable." Seeing she had his attention, she did not stop. "And knowing this, are you saying that you would agree to leave with my father and me? Live a merchant's way of life? Travel on the road all the time, meeting new people? The daily challenge would not be wielding a sword but outthinking the buyer, trying to convince him to give up some of his hard-earned coin for some quality goods."

Loman swallowed and straightened his shoulders, his smile gone. Though he did not say anything, but Mhàiri knew his answer. "You and I both know you would never be happy as a merchant."

"No," Loman agreed. "I have no desire to be anything like a merchant. I don't mind periodically visiting other places, but I have a home here. And the idea of coming home to a welcoming family is what I want. I just haven't found anyone who wants to have it with me."

Mhàiri found that hard to believe, but then Loman was not simply looking for a wife. He wanted a woman to love and who would love him in return. "She will come. Give her time," she encouraged.

Loman took a deep breath and exhaled. "Still friends?"

Mhàiri laughed. "Of course we are! One little kiss doesn't have the power to end a friendship." But she knew that was a lie. One little kiss just might have done that very thing with her and Conan, and their bond had been much stronger, far more compelling. Yet the power of a single kiss might have snapped it.

Mhàiri shifted and began to look around at the remnants of the lovely meal they had enjoyed. "Shall I start to pack up?"

Loman laid back and crossed his feet at the ankles. He hooked his hands behind his head and said, "Why? Finn gave me the whole afternoon to do what I please, and what pleases me most right now is spending time with you. Mostly because I know that every moment you and I are out here together is another moment I'm making Conan squirm."

Mhàiri looked to the heavens and shook her head. "You are awful," she said, chuckling, hoping that Loman was right. "Well, until the wind grows too cold."

Loman let go a loud laugh and slapped his thighs. "It's settled then. We let Conan squirm for as long as we can."

"Say that again," Maegan demanded.

"I kissed Loman," Mhàiri repeated, lying on Maegan's bed, staring at the ceiling. "Well, I guess he kissed me, but I let him."

Maegan got up and went to the large window that looked outside the castle walls. Below was a large ravine, but beyond that were rolling hills. It was still a couple of hours before sunset, but dark clouds were coming in, making it seem later than it was. It did not help that her bedroom was on the first floor of the Star Tower and did not allow for some of the great views on the upper floors. McTiernay Castle was large, but there were several that were bigger in Scotland. What made it notable was its great hall and the Star Tower. Seven stories tall, it was one of the biggest in the country.

The tower was where the laird and his family lived. Maegan knew she was fortunate that Conor and Laurel felt she was part of theirs. They considered her family and she considered them hers.

"Did you *want* to kiss Loman?"

Mhàiri shrugged noncommittedly. "I was curious to know if it would be different from Conan's."

"You did *what*?" Maegan screeched in shock as she spun around from her bedroom window.

"You heard me."

"You actually *kissed* Conan."

Mhàiri sighed. "I did not want to kiss him, and I'm not sure he wanted to kiss me either. He and I were arguing and then suddenly we were grasping onto each other as if some force were preventing us from letting go. That was why I kissed Loman."

Maegan shook her head. "I am not following."

"To see if it would be different. Until yesterday I had never kissed anyone before. I was not sure if they were all the same. But they aren't."

"They aren't?"

Realizing what Maegan was implying, Mhàiri got up on her elbows. "Are you saying that in your twenty years, you've never kissed *anyone*?"

"You're twenty too!"

"But I lived in a priory," Mhàiri protested. "Even then I had opportunities. What about Clyde?"

"I was not really old enough for kissing before he left," Maegan whispered, somewhat embarrassed by the admission. It was easy to say that you loved someone and that they loved you. She had repeated it enough that everyone believed her, but if she let it be known that she and Clyde had never even kissed, her assertions of love would not be taken as seriously.

"You know you can kiss a man without being in love with them. I've done it twice this week."

"I know, but . . ."

"But what?" Mhàiri pressed. "What about Seamus? The man is completely besotted. Don't you find him good looking?"

Maegan flopped down on the bed beside Mhàiri and sighed. "Seamus is more than good looking. I watch him train with the men for hours and never get bored looking at him. But looking is one thing. Kissing? I couldn't do that to Clyde."

Mhàiri studied the rafters on the ceiling of the room. She had not had very many female friends in her life, living on the road and then in a priory. She treasured her friendship with Maegan and did not want to say anything that might jeopardize theirs, which meant she couldn't tell her what she thought about Clyde.

Mhàiri knew Maegan earnestly believed she was in love with the youngest McTiernay brother, but she also used that belief as a way to protect herself. Mhàiri suspected that on some level Maegan knew it as well. She was scared of love just like everyone else. Maegan had found a way of shielding her heart from pain, and Mhàiri was not going to strip it from her. But that did not mean she wouldn't from time to time try to nudge it a little.

"So are you going to kiss him again?" Maegan asked.

"Loman? No. He knows that I am not the one for him."

"I was talking about Conan," Maegan said with an exasperated sigh.

Mhàiri bit the inside of her cheek. She had asked herself that very question multiple times. "I don't think so."

"Do you want to kiss anyone else?"

Mhàiri scrunched up her nose at the idea. "I don't know. Why?"

Maegan rolled over and looked at Mhàiri. "Because Christmastide is almost here and there will be a *lot* of opportunities. Laurel has already invited the Schelldens so Callum will be coming, and though I still think Seamus is better looking, Callum does come close."

Mhàiri pursed her lips at the idea. "Maybe I don't want to kiss anyone else," she admitted.

Maegan looked at Mhàiri and began to shake her head. She sat up and crossed her arms. "Do not fall for Conan."

"Don't be ridiculous," Mhàiri said and went to roll off the bed and look out the window.

"I'm not. I know love. I'm an expert on it, and it starts just this way."

Mhàiri's back stiffened. "I am—"

The sudden opening of the bedchamber door stopped her from finishing her thought. "Brenna! I thought you were with your mother."

"I was. The baby was moving, but only Bonny got to feel it. It must be a boy. Boys never do what I want to," Brenna grumbled.

"Where's Bonny? She still with your mother?"

Brenna shook her head. "She left to go check on Seamus and Uncle Conan. They are in Mhàiri's room putting together her shelves."

Mhàiri turned around abruptly. She had gone straight

to see Maegan when she had returned. She'd had no idea that Conan had been installing her shelves.

Maegan gleefully clapped her hands together. "Are they still there?"

Brenna bobbed her shoulders. "I think so. Why?"

"Because I'm curious to know what they are doing and saying."

Brenna twirled around in a circle, a smile erupting on her face. "I know the best way to learn what people are thinking. Follow me!"

Fifteen minutes later, Mhàiri was scrunched down, sitting on a cold floor next to Maegan and Brenna. The back passageway was narrow, and she could only see a little through the slits in the stone to the activities taking place in her room, but she could hear everything that was said perfectly.

"That's it. The last shelf is in," Conan said, glad he was almost done.

Seamus wiped his brow. The air had turned humid, foretelling that storms were on the way. Though it was not hot, it still made indoor physical labor uncomfortable. "Great. Time for some ale."

Conan snorted and then pointed to all the manuscripts. "Laurel told me that we must also unpack everything."

"*We?*" Seamus challenged.

"Aye, *we*," Conan replied. In fact, Laurel had included Seamus in the request, but only after Conan had twisted things to ensure she did so.

Seamus studied Conan, who just returned his stare

with an arched brow. "Fine. I'll help," Seamus groused, "but I don't know where to put anything."

"Anywhere it won't roll or fall off. Mhàiri can figure out how she wants things arranged later when we are gone." Conan moved to the first of the three large chests. "I'll unpack these. Once we are done, ale it is."

Seamus picked up the medical book that Mhàiri had taken away from Brenna. "I may not know how to read, but I can look at pictures just fine. And these"—he opened the book to show Conan pictures of the male anatomy—"are not what I would expect to see in a young woman's library. I now see why you find abbeys so interesting."

Conan grabbed the book to see what Seamus was waving about. "It's a medical book about surgery." He handed it back. "There are drawings of the female body in there as well."

Seamus pulled in his chin, furrowed his brow with increased curiosity, and skimmed through the book again. Stopping at a page, he turned it to view at different angles. "I'm starting to understand the appeal of being a scholar."

Conan ignored him and opened the first large chest. He pulled out several books and manuscripts and put them on the shelves.

Seamus sighed and placed the medical book on the nearest bookcase. He then went to the smaller chest and lifted the lid. He stood up holding a blue gown with small seed pearls along the hem up to his chest. "What do you think?"

Conan glanced at him. "I think it just might be what you need to get Maegan to finally take notice of you."

"*Go n-ithe an cat thú is go n-ithe an diabhal an cat,*"

Seamus growled. He hastily rolled up the dress and put it back down to see what else was in the trunk. "Do you think that women like wearing all these things?"

Conan shrugged and shoved some scrolled manuscripts on the top shelf. "If they didn't, then I suspect they wouldn't wear them." Then he realized what Seamus was doing. "Close that up. Mhàiri wouldn't be dumb enough to pack gowns with her books."

Seamus closed the lid with a *thunk*. "How was I to know? I've been around you brilliant people enough to see you do an awful lot of dumb things."

Conan ignored his friend and pulled out one very large volume with a thin leather cover. The binding was not a permanent one. Instead, lace pulled the front and back slats of wood tightly together. When it was loosened, someone could take sheets out individually and then bind them again to keep them protected. He did not need to open it to see that it was not vellum within the leather bindings, but hemp paper.

Conan placed the book on the shelf and then went to see if there was another. There was. Exactly the same. Wondering how many more hemp books there were, Conan began opening the lids to the second and third chests. There were twelve large hemp books in total.

"What has you so enamored?" Seamus asked, looking over Conan's shoulder, watching him stroke the cover.

Slowly Conan opened the book and was not surprised by what he saw. Mhàiri's drawings. He flipped through the pages and saw lochs, flowers, buildings, people—the last few years of her life was staring back at him.

Conan put the book down and reached out for another. This time, only blank pages stared back at him.

Conan swallowed and began going through all the books, his breathing becoming more rapid as he began to realize exactly what he was seeing—and why Mhàiri had kept it hidden within the heavy chests. Nearly half of the books were blank. She had literally *hundreds* of sheets of blank hemp paper. And she had kept it a secret.

"I cannot believe it," Conan whispered. "All this paper."

Seamus looked at it. "What of it? It's blank."

"Touch it," Conan ordered.

Seamus complied. "What is it?" he asked, realizing that it was different.

"This is hemp." Conan pointed at all the large bound volumes. "*All* of this hemp. Probably the best thing to write on. And it's *here*. Can you imagine the maps I could make using this?"

Seamus might have spent a good deal of time with Conan over the past year, but he did not know anything about making maps. Mostly because he did not want to know about them. What little he did know was that it required vellum, the making of which was tedious. He knew that because Conan had roped him to helping with the chore often enough.

"I expect Mhàiri looks at this and imagines all the *pictures* she could create."

Conan lightly touched the smooth surface. "It's so light. I bet I could carry a dozen sheets for every one of vellum. Using hemp would increase my output tenfold," he said, more to himself than to Seamus. He knew it was impossible, but it was hard not to imagine, seeing so much blank hemp within reach.

"Too bad it's not yours," Seamus reiterated, taking the book from Conan's hands. Seeing his friend's crushed expression, he added, "But maybe it could be. I mean, her father is the one who got it for her and Mhàiri will be with him again this spring. She might give you them if you asked."

Conan squeezed his eyes shut. "Maybe two days ago it would have been a possibility, but after yesterday, I do not see it happening."

Seamus grimaced and wagged his finger at him before grabbing a set of rolls. "That's right. The kiss," he said with a shake of his head.

"We already agreed it wasn't my best idea," Conan muttered.

"Hey! You could buy them from her. Her father is a merchant, and she wants to live that life. Mhàiri might be willing to trade or accept coin for the paper."

Conan sighed. It was clear Seamus did not understand the value of what he was looking at. And Mhàiri was using the hemp paper herself. She used it all the time. It was just as important and valuable to her as it would be to him. "I don't think that is an option either."

"Well, there has to be a way," Seamus said under his breath, trying to think. "Is it stealing if you charm Mhàiri into giving them to you?"

Conan furrowed his brow. "What do you mean?"

"It's like I was saying earlier. I haven't seen a woman yet who could resist you when you aim to have her. And we already know that Mhàiri is susceptible to your kisses. . . ."

Conan stroked his chin. Seamus was right. It might

be possible to gain Mhàiri's affections. She might deny wanting him, but he could use that to his advantage. He would never consider fully seducing Mhàiri—that crossed a line. Just the idea of *any* man taking such advantage of her sent a surge of anger through him. If it ever actually happened, he would not be responsible for his actions. But wooing her enough so that she would be willing to share a hemp book or two? That he could do.

It wouldn't be a lie either, for he actually liked Mhàiri. And it was not like he would be teasing her with the possibility of a future that was never going to happen, for she, too, was soundly against the idea of marriage.

Seamus tapped the bookcase's panel, looking at all the filigree Conan had carved into the wood. That was what had taken him so long. "You and I know that you could have built bookshelves that would have been sufficient in a day or two, but instead you spent weeks making this furniture fancy."

"I had my reasons."

"Aye," Seamus said dismissively. "But think about this. Most women, when they get gifts, they want to give something in return."

Conan grinned, seeing where Seamus was heading. "And the nicer the gift, the more they want to reciprocate."

"Aye," Seamus said, nodding his head. "And these bookshelves? They are a *very* nice gift. Don't you agree?"

Conan crossed his arms and assessed his work. He proudly bobbed his head. "I certainly do." Hopefully Mhàiri thought they were nice enough for a book, maybe even two as well. "Help me put all these books back in the chests."

"*Back* in the chests? We just got them out."

"Aye. But I don't want Mhàiri to realize I know about the hemp paper. She needs to tell me about them. That way, when she offers them to me, she'll believe it is all her idea."

Mhàiri stomped to the hearth in Maegan's bedchambers, turned, and then headed to the window. Reaching it, she turned around and made the round again . . . and again. Pacing was the only thing that was keeping her from screaming the anger raging through her body.

To think that at one time she had considered giving Conan one of her prized hemp books as a surprise gift for his journey. She had known it would be too much of a burden on her father to bring all her manuscripts, scrolls, and things with them on their travels. She had already planned to offer what was to remain behind to Laurel or Father Lanaghly and the church. But her hemp paper? That had been coming with her.

"And he *knew*," Mhàiri hissed. "Conan *knew* they were a gift from my father!"

Maegan bit her bottom lip and winced. "That does make it worse somehow."

"What a *buthaigir duine*."

Maegan's eyes grew wide. She glanced at Brenna, who played with a loose thread on the bed's blanket and then back at Mhàiri. The term was not a nice one, but Maegan could not disagree. What Conan was planning *did* make him a complete and total bastard. It also made Seamus one. "I guess it was a good thing I was wrong and that you weren't falling for him."

Mhàiri groaned. She may not have fallen in love

with Conan, but she had liked him. A lot. And she had thought he had liked her as well, and more than just as some female who amused him, but as someone he respected. How could she have been so wrong?

"Conan is exactly what you first said he was. A menace to women."

Maegan was not sure she had actually said those words, but she was not about to argue with Mhàiri right now. Especially as she was just as angry as her friend. Maegan could not believe Seamus—a man she had thought so honorable and genuinely *nice*—could devise such a plan. And it was *his* plan. Conan might have agreed to it, but it was Seamus's diabolical idea.

"We should go tell Laurel," Maegan put forth, tapping her foot. "If she knew . . . oh . . . no one is better at making men miserable when they deserve it. Let's go."

Mhàiri put up her hand, halting Maegan before she reached the door. "No. I'm going to handle this. Conan thought he could outsmart *me*. He has no idea what I am capable of, but he is going to learn. I'm not some simple village *baoit* he was trying to take advantage of. I am Iain Mayboill's daughter, and Conan McTiernay is about to find out exactly what that means."

"What are you going to do?" asked Brenna, who had been discreetly listening to every word spoken. Earlier, she had told Mhàiri that she knew the best way to learn what people were thinking, but she had forgotten to warn her that she might not like what she heard.

Mhàiri tapped her chin and then said, "First, I'm not going to let Conan know that I know about his little plan."

"You're going to let Conan charm you into giving away your books?" Maegan asked, shocked.

"That is *never* going to happen," Mhàiri stated. "But he won't know that. I'll even pretend to resist his charms at first so that he has to work even harder to win me over."

Maegan let go a sinister giggle. "I like it."

"And then, when Conan thinks he has me so mesmerized that I would give him anything, I'll . . ."

"You'll what?"

Mhàiri waved her hand. "Oh, I don't know, but I can decide that later."

Maegan took in a deep breath. "That might work, but only if you don't fall for Conan's appeal, because if you do, you'll end up giving him everything."

Mhàiri woke up and stretched, studying the three large bookcases that lined the walls of her room. They were beautiful pieces of art, and if she was not so mad at Conan, they *would* have been enough for her to hand over one or two of her books. That was why it was so hurtful that he planned to cheat them from her. After all the time they had spent together, she had thought he knew her. And she had thought she knew him.

Mhàiri's stomach growled. She rolled out of bed and began to dress. Last night, she and Maegan had decided to eat in her bedchambers and were grateful that Laurel had not pressed them too much for explanations. But if she missed this morning, there would be questions.

Conan sat across the table and returned Mhàiri's glare. She knew she needed to put aside her anger because there was no way he was going to pursue her when she was shooting him full of daggers with her eyes, but she could not seem to make her eyes cooperate.

Finally, giving up, she put her fork down and made a quick excuse to leave the hall and put some space between her and Conan. It was obviously going to take more than a single night of sleep for her to calm down. Until then, she needed to stay away from him.

Mhàiri was halfway across the courtyard when strong fingers gripped her arm, startling her out of her mental dialogue. "What?" she snapped, not meaning it to sound as harsh as it came out. Then, discovering it was Conan, she no longer felt guilty.

"I *asked* if you liked the shelves," Conan said through clenched teeth, clearly frustrated.

"Aye. They work well. I'm glad I was able to spend the afternoon with Loman so you could finally put them together." Mhàiri knew the comment was unworthy of her, but she could not bring herself to apologize. Not when Conan was planning on using those very shelves as a "gift" to persuade her to give him one in return.

Conan's eyes narrowed. "And how was your little outing?" His voice increased in volume as his anger grew in intensity.

"Quite pleasurable," Mhàiri answered, matching his volume.

"What does that mean?"

"Only that I had a *lovely* time," she shouted. "I like Loman, and he made it very clear that he likes me."

Conan towered over her, his blue eyes shooting sparks. "Did Loman kiss you? Did you let him?" he jeered.

"You knew he would, and I must say, I was surprised to enjoy it as much as I did." It was true. She had enjoyed the kiss more than she had expected, for she had not thought to like it at all. But that did not mean she wanted to kiss Loman again. However, that Conan did not need to know.

Conan clenched his fists as the sudden need to punch something—like Loman's jaw—coursed through him. He had been a fool to think the passionate embrace they'd shared would deter Mhàiri from seeking attention from other men. Whatever it was he had felt had been an illusion. "So first me, then Loman. I guess we should warn all the other single men that you will be seeking out their attentions. I wonder who will be next? Buzz, Fergus, Gil? Too bad Jaime Ruadh is at Cole's. He was quite the ladies' man when he lived here."

Mhàiri crossed her arms and stuck out her chin. "I was thinking about Callum Schellden. I understand that he is *very* good looking and will be here in a couple of weeks for the celebrations."

Conan bent over her and stared down into her eyes. She just glared back. "Don't you even *think* about kissing Callum," he growled loudly. "If I find out that you even talked to that *bladaire . . .*"

"You'll what? *Yell* at me?" Mhàiri bellowed back.

Conan took a step back and fought to lower his voice. "I don't *yell* at women. I'm an intellect and don't need to resort to such means to win a fight. My brothers' dispositions are to holler, not mine."

"Really?" Mhàiri countered, uncaring that her voice could still clearly be heard by anyone in the courtyard. "Because I think you are exactly like your brothers. *You've just never met a woman who will yell back.*" She took a finger and poked his chest. "Now you have."

Conan grabbed the finger and squeezed it. Not

enough to cause her pain, but enough so that she could not free it until he let go. "I already have one Laurel in my life. I don't need two."

"And I don't need another arrogant man who thinks he's always right. But at least my father is an honorable man."

"Are you saying I'm not an honorable man?"

"How would I know? You could tell me anything and a silly little female like me would probably believe you."

Conan let go of her finger. "Then believe this. I would never lie to you."

Without another word, Conan turned and headed for the North Tower, leaving Mhàiri standing in the courtyard with her mouth open.

She wanted to believe him. But then she remembered what he had said when he had not known she was listening.

I would never lie to you.

A false promise made toward an end goal. How Mhàiri wished it were a real one.

Chapter Seven

Laurel stood outside the great hall along with Hagatha, and Aileen, staring at the arguing couple causing all the commotion in the courtyard.

Ever since she had gotten so ill with her pregnancy, it had become a morning ritual for Hagatha and Aileen to pay her a visit. Now that she could eat food again, most mornings they convened in the great hall. Laurel had tried to encourage Hagatha to return to her home, knowing her crotchety friend did not enjoy the bustle of castle life and preferred her solitude, but the old midwife had put her foot down. She was staying until the babe was born, and nothing was going to convince her otherwise.

Laurel had even less luck with keeping her best friend, Aileen, away. Even her husband, Finn, who was the commander of Conor's elite guard, would not help, stating that his wife knew her own mind and that he enjoyed having all his body parts where they were and in working order. And while Aileen had been a godsend during the worst of her morning sickness, Laurel knew it had to be hard on her.

For years, the two of them had so many things in

common, but their inability to have another child had bonded them even more tightly together. While Laurel and Conor had tried repeatedly to get pregnant, Aileen had not had that difficulty. Hers had been far more painful as she never made it to full term. Soon after she realized she was with child, Aileen would lose the baby. And each time, her friend gained another heartbreak at the devastating loss of a child. It was something they rarely spoke of, but each understood the other's desire for another baby and the aching sadness of its absence.

And then Laurel had discovered she was pregnant.

She knew it was hard on her friend, but Aileen refused to discuss it. She just pasted on a happy face that Laurel knew was sincere, but also masked the pain of jealousy. She knew because that was how she would have felt.

Hagatha took a step closer to Laurel and whispered, "What are those two going on about?"

Laurel pursed her lips together and shook her head. Normally she was a lot more aware of the activities and personal relationships around the castle, and that definitely included Conan. For when he was interested in a woman, it never ended well. Today was reminiscent of those times, but while before, all the emotions and outbursts had come solely from whomever Conan had injured, that had not been the case today.

The hum of people starting to move about their day had returned quickly, but just a few minutes ago the courtyard had been filled with a swirl of strong emotions. The anger, passion, and chemistry between Conan and Mhàiri were unmistakable.

Laurel was not surprised.

She had watched them over dinner over the past few weeks. Both had been excessively friendly, which Laurel knew was a sign that more was going on between them than it seemed. Then, there were the afternoon outings. Suspicious, Laurel had sent spies to watch them for the first week to see if she should intervene and protect the young woman. But they had come back each time assuring her that Mhàiri and Conan appeared to be just friends. She was teaching him how to draw, and nothing untoward was happening between them.

When Laurel had heard Loman had asked Mhàiri on a picnic, she wondered if she might have been wrong to assume Mhàiri and Conan were drawn toward each other. But watching Conan and Mhàiri now, Laurel knew her initial assessment had been right. Their feelings went way beyond that of friendship.

"I already have one Laurel in my life. I don't need two." Conan's angry declaration was heard by all.

"I'm sure he meant that as a compliment," Aileen said, biting back a smile.

Laurel dismissed the insult, for even Conor did not want two of her, and her husband loved her more than anyone. "What I am more interested in is what came before."

Hagatha nodded. "Aye. All that nonsense about kissing. Just friends my arse."

Laurel watched as Conan made a final comment, pivoted, and headed to his rooms in the North Tower. Immediately, Aileen's son, Gideon, and Laurel's son, Braeden, started jumping up and down, whooping and hollering with glee.

"I *told* you," Gideon shouted with a triumphant grin

as he pushed his dark hair out of the way. "They were sure to fight today after Mhàiri went out with Loman."

Seeing the gleam in her son's hazel eyes, Aileen asked, "Just what are you so happy about?"

"We just won the bet," Braeden answered for his friend. "And Gilroy better not think he doesn't owe us. We won it fair and he lost."

Gideon waved his hand. "Come on. We better go find him before he suddenly forgets our deal."

Brenna grabbed Bonny. "We should go too!"

Laurel reached out and placed a tight grip on the shoulders of both her daughters. "First, why don't you tell me what all that was about?"

Bonny shrugged. "I don't know what their bet was with Gilroy," she said innocently, pretending not to know what her mother meant.

"Brenna?"

The ten-year-old sighed, for she knew trying to keep a secret from her mother was pointless. "Seamus told Conan to try and charm Mhàiri into liking him so he can take her hemp paper. He's pretending not to know about the paper, but he doesn't know that Mhàiri caught him looking at it. So she is pretending to let him try and charm her so that she can trick him into thinking what he's doing is working. Then she and Maegan are going to teach him and Seamus an embarrassing lesson, but they don't know what it is yet."

Aileen shifted her gaze from Brenna to Laurel. "Did you follow any of that?"

Laurel gave a small shake to her head. "Not nearly enough." Then, to Bonny and Brenna, she said, "Both of you. Back in the hall. I think you need to tell me everything that has been going on."

* * *

Aileen stared in awe as Brenna explained all that she knew about Conan and Mhàiri. Once again, it was staggering just how much the child knew. Aileen leaned over and whispered to Hagatha, "I wonder if Brenna knows details on everyone, including Finn."

Brenna stopped her explanation of Conan and Mhàiri midsentence. "Commander Finn is boring. He does the same thing every day."

Aileen smiled, relieved—but only for a second, because Brenna kept talking. "He really hates it when people are late and at least one person has been late to morning training every day this week. So, when Donnan was late again yesterday, Commander Finn yelled at them for a *long* time. I know when he is yelling because his voice actually gets softer, not louder. And he never smiles. It's kind of scary. Loman must have thought so too, because he said to Seamus that the commander had forgotten how to smile a long time ago and if he wasn't careful, Seamus was going to become just like him." Brenna paused and grinned at Aileen. "A while ago, I heard Commander Finn tell Papa about it, saying that the only thing that made him ever want to smile was you and since you were never on the training fields, the men were going to have to just deal with his expression the way it was."

Aileen sat there, feeling her mouth slowly drop. Her husband was not one to vocalize his feelings for her. She knew Finn loved her, but he showed it more through his actions than his words. What Brenna had just told her touched her soul. She couldn't wait until Finn got home that night, for the man was going to get very lucky.

"But other than that, Commander Finn doesn't talk much. Even the stuff he tells Papa is boring."

Laurel clucked her tongue. "I thought you promised your father that you would stop listening to his conversations."

"I have!" Brenna said vehemently, sitting up straight in her chair to emphasize her assertion. "I can't help it if I'm already there listening to other people when he comes in!"

Laurel bit her tongue. She could not lecture her daughter on the evils of eavesdropping right as she was asking Brenna to reveal all that she knew from that very act. "And so is that all you know about Conan and Mhàiri?"

Brenna shook her head and then picked up from where she had left off with Mhàiri, her, and Maegan listening as Conan and Seamus put in the shelves. "And so," Brenna said with a long sigh, indicating she was almost done, "even though it might *sound* like a bad thing that they are trying to trick each other, it isn't. For the more time Mhàiri and Conan spend together, the better chance they have at falling in love."

Laurel was not surprised that her daughter's romantic heart and mind hoped for such a thing. Tapping her finger on the small table by her hearth chair, she asked Bonny, "And what do you think?"

Her youngest was only seven and was still very naïve to the ways of women and men, and yet sometimes that allowed her keen mind to see things in a clearer way than most adults. To think that Bonny did not understand people and situations because of her youth was a mistake many made. But Laurel was not among them.

Bonny squirmed in the big chair. They had elected

not to sit at the table, but in the semi-circle of chairs placed around the main large hearth. "I guess I hope that Uncle Conan wins," she finally said. "It's his turn to be happy. All my other uncles have found someone so he should get to find someone, too. And I think Mhàiri would make him happy. I'm just afraid that won't happen if he finds out that she has been tricking him, even though he started it."

Brenna lightly kicked Bonny's leg with her own. "What about Uncle Clyde?"

Bonny kicked her back. "He has Maegan. Uncle Conan doesn't have anyone."

Laurel snapped her fingers to get their attention. "I think that is enough gossip for a long while. You understand me, Brenna?" The blonde bobbed her head way too readily. "Bonny?" Her youngest was at least more honest and reluctantly gave her a nod. "Then out with you."

Bonny turned to follow Brenna, who was almost at the hall doors, but then she stopped and asked, "Mama, are you going to help Conan find happiness?"

Laurel pointed her finger to the door. "Now, Bonny." She waited until the door was completely closed again before turning to her friends. "It scares me how much Brenna learns and retains."

Hagatha nodded and took a large gulp of ale. "I fear her little habit is going to get her into great trouble someday."

"Undoubtedly," Laurel agreed, clearly unhappy at the prospect. "I've warned her, tried to stop her, but it does no good. And today, though I hate to admit it, what she told us revealed a lot."

Hagatha put down her mug. "Maybe it wasn't such

a good idea not to interfere with those two. Now they're fighting and ye know what that leads to."

"I have no idea," Laurel said, with an impish grin.

"Aye, ye do or ye wouldn't fight with yer man like ye do."

"So what are you going to do?" Aileen asked. "You did not respond to Bonny's question, but Hagatha and I know the answer. It's obvious Conan and Mhàiri are perfect for each other, so how do you propose we help get those two together?"

Laurel drummed her fingers on the arm of her chair. Aileen was right in that Conan and Mhàiri *could* be right for each other, but they could also be very wrong. Based on what had happened in the courtyard, it was not help getting together the couple needed. That was the path they were already on, for it was clear they both had emotions for the other that ran very deep. But that same path could also end in a way that would only bring them both misery.

Laurel glanced at Hagatha and then at Aileen as a wide, mischievous smile took over her face. "I don't think we do. Nay. I'm thinking sabotage is what is needed." Both her friends looked surprised, but at the same time, eager. "And not just Conan's plans. We need to sabotage Mhàiri's as well."

Mhàiri sat at the dinner table, thankful that tonight was a family dinner. Eating in the lower hall with all the soldiers was usually entertaining, but it was also loud and nearly impossible to carry on a conversation. Here, in the great hall, when it was only close friends and family, talking was possible. Unfortunately, conversations could also be heard by all.

Their small group sat in the same order they always
did, with Conor at the head, then Laurel, Hagatha,
Conan, and Seamus on his right and Finn, Aileen,
Mhàiri, and Maegan on his left. After that, the seating
fluctuated, depending on who from the elite guard
was not on duty and near the castle and whether
Aileen and Laurel's children ate in their rooms or with
the family. Tonight, only the children were added to
the ensemble, sitting next to Maegan, who put forth
no more than half-hearted efforts to keep them quiet
in order to talk to Seamus. Maegan would never admit
it, but she enjoyed talking with him at dinner as much
as Seamus enjoyed talking with her.

Normally, Mhàiri was similarly engaged with Conan,
matching wits, launching harmless barbs, or sharing
stories about their childhood. Tonight, however, was
reminiscent of her first days at the castle when both
had refused to look, let alone speak, to the other. And
as difficult as she was going to find it, she needed to
engage with the man, which started with an apology.
It was the only way to convince him to pursue her
once more.

It was Maegan who had pointed out her folly. She
had sympathized with Mhàiri, stating that pretending
to like someone she was angry with would be difficult
for anyone, but that Mhàiri and Conan's fight was
probably going to result in him ending his plans to
trick Mhàiri out of her hemp paper. And that meant
Mhàiri would lose her chance to teach him a humiliating lesson. Realizing her friend was probably right,
Mhàiri decided to make amends. She needed Conan
to re-embrace his lunatic idea that he could beguile
her into giving up her most precious possession.

"You said today that you would never lie to me."

Conan's head whipped around at the lilting sound of Mhàiri's voice. She had hardly spoken all night, and he had not really blamed her. He had been serious about yelling being more of his brothers' habits than his. Then Finn had mentioned during their training that Conor had not been prone to hollering, nor had Cole or Colin or any of his brothers, until they had met their wives. That all McTiernay men had that trait and it just took the right woman to bring it out of them.

The implication that Mhàiri was the right woman and that he would follow in the same path as his brothers had been unmistakable. But it would take a lot more than one public fight to make Conan accept Mhàiri could be anything other than an enjoyable diversion.

Conan's blue eyes bored into Mhàiri's for several seconds. "And I never will," he finally answered.

How Mhàiri wanted to believe him. Her heart said he was telling the truth. And if she had not heard for herself that he was intending to be duplicitous, she would not have thought it possible. Conan argued any point when he thought she was wrong, but had consistently conceded when she had adequately debated her opinion. He was a man who enjoyed being right and flaunted it when he won an argument, but he did not *need* to be right. He had never twisted facts to suit his case, and when his logic failed—which was rare—he accepted it. In all the weeks she had gotten to know Conan, *he had not lied.*

But that did not mean he would not play her for the fool. Mhàiri decided his promise of honesty would also be her weapon against him.

Mhàiri licked her lips and mentally braced herself. "About our earlier conversation," she began.

"You mean our *heated* conversation," Conan corrected, then sat back and crossed his arms. "You were angry long before that conversation started. I just don't know why."

Mhàiri swallowed. Conan had a point, but she was not about to explain why she had been angry. However, she was also determined not to lie to him either. When the truth was eventually revealed, he was not going to be able to say that she was no better. "I was angry. I had not known you were even working on the shelves. I was surprised and, well, I don't like the kind of surprises I got that day."

Conan narrowed his gaze. "Don't worry. It will not happen again."

Mhàiri took in a deep breath and rallied her courage. "I should have said thank you. They are beautiful."

"You should thank him as well," Conan replied snidely, gesturing with his thumb toward Seamus. "He helped."

"Thank you, Seamus," Mhàiri said, hoping she sounded sincere. But she had not forgotten his role in suggesting the farce. "I appreciate all that you did, but I am sure it was Conan who designed them. For everything about them is perfect."

Conan twisted his lips. "So you really do like them."

"Aye, and I was wondering if you could help me organize them. I liked the way you did yours, and I was hoping that you would help me do something similar."

Mhàiri watched as Seamus nudged Conan with his elbow and gave him a wink of encouragement. She almost sighed aloud with relief. Her apology was working.

"I could probably help if you want," Conan murmured, not yet totally convinced.

"I would like that."

"But wouldn't Loman mind?"

"Why would he?" she asked with mock innocence. "Books, manuscripts, and drawings don't interest him. And in return there is something I want to show you. Something *very* special."

Conan leaned forward, forming a steeple with his fingers. "Helping you would give me a chance to make up for this morning."

Mhàiri blushed. This time, it was in earnest, but before she could say another word, Laurel muttered, "This is about to get embarrassing and it needs to be stopped."

Mhàiri did not know what Laurel meant, but assumed it was about something at their end of the table. Mhàiri was about to ask Conan once more to clarify his feelings of guilt when Laurel coughed loudly into her hand. It was not the kind to clear one's throat, but to gain everyone's attention.

When Mhàiri looked in her direction, Laurel spoke, this time clearly and without any ambiguity. "Stop feigning interest where you have none, Mhàiri. Conan may act like a fool, but that doesn't make him one. He would have seen through your act long before you had the chance to teach him your lesson."

Conan looked puzzled.

Mhàiri looked horrified.

Laurel knew then that she was not incorrect and all that Brenna had told them had been true. "Mhàiri knows, Conan," she stated with exasperation. "*Ó dhìol, everyone* is aware that Mhàiri knows of your ill-gotten plans to seduce her for her paper . . . well, except

Seamus," Laurel said, waving her hand at the suddenly stupefied soldier. "You may be incredibly smart, brother, but you are also incredibly simple-minded when it comes to women."

Mhàiri's jaw went slack. *Seduce?* Conan had actually planned to go that far to get her books? And how had Laurel learned of everything? It had only happened yesterday. Mhàiri glanced back down the table to where Brenna was seated, staring at the ceiling, refusing to make eye contact with anyone.

Conan's gaze followed Mhàiri's, and he realized whom she was looking at. McTiernay Castle's infamous little eavesdropper. Suddenly, everything made sense. Why Mhàiri had not shown up for dinner the previous night, her anger this morning, her lack of appreciation for the shelves that he had *known,* with her knowledge of libraries, she would absolutely love.

He should have put it all together this morning, but the mental image of Loman kissing her had sent him spiraling. They had eaten in the lower hall the previous night and the entire elite guard had been chattering about Loman and his outing, making plans to be the next in line. The idea of all those men pursuing Mhàiri had infuriated Conan. He knew none of them deserved her or would understand her the way he did. He had been so focused on keeping his own swirling emotions in check that he had not even thought to wonder why Mhàiri had been missing.

His two blue eyes bore holes into the green ones across from him. "You knew?" Conan said in a quiet voice, so full of fury that several sucked in their breaths. "You *knew* I had discovered the hemp?" he asked again.

Mhàiri glared back at Conan, feeling no remorse.

"Aye. I also learned that its value meant more to you than your honor."

Conan's mind was racing, putting things together, including her sudden change in attitude from this morning to tonight. "So tonight's gratitude for the shelves . . . that was a lie."

"I did not lie. I do appreciate the shelves. I just did not enjoy learning that someone I trusted and respected was using me to attain what he wanted."

Conan jumped out of his chair at the accusation. Seething anger poured out through every cell as he punched his fists on the table and leaned forward. "I was going to try and persuade you to be generous. There is nothing dishonorable in that."

Mhàiri jumped up to her feet. She too leaned in and said, "*Persuade?* Is that what you call your scheme to try and swindle me out of my books?"

"And what about your scheme? What did you plan on doing? Pretending to like me, knowing my attraction to you was earnest, only to throw it back in my face in the most humiliating and public way? To lead me on, let me believe that you would share something that could make my travels infinitely better, only to dash my hopes at the last moment? To be able to carry out such a plan . . . *that* borders on malicious."

"Nay. What is malicious is using a woman's emotions for your own gain. Something I understand you have been doing for years, just this time instead of my body, you wanted my goods. How does it feel to realize that you were the one who was going to be used without a single care of the injury being inflicted?"

"At least I was never dishonest. Every woman who was ever supposedly 'hurt' by my actions knew that I would never return their emotions and yet they *still pursued me.*"

"And that justifies your intentions?" Mhàiri gritted out. "You know what that paper means to me and yet you still planned to trick me out of it."

"I can see that whatever I say is meaningless to you. Consider your lesson well taught and your precious paper safe from my shameful hands." Then his cold gaze swung to Laurel. "You may be Conor's wife and you may be pregnant, but that does not give you the right to do what you did tonight." And without waiting to hear anyone's response or asking for his leave, Conan spun on his heel and marched out the doors of the great hall.

Mhàiri swallowed. She was shaking. She was furious, for she knew she was in the right, and yet something about how Conan had looked at her, as if he was deeply wounded, was causing her to tremble. Mhàiri felt a soft hand clasp hers, urging her to sit down.

Aileen let go of a long breath that she had been holding, and Hagatha let go a sharp *hrmph.*

Conor's commander simply sighed. "Well, I hope you know what you're doing," Finn said to Laurel disapprovingly and then turned to his wife. "Let us leave now." Aileen gave a wary look to Laurel, but quickly said her good-byes and followed her husband and son out of the hall.

Undaunted, Laurel stood up and, with a satisfying look, said, "I think I, too, will be saying good night now that all is right again." Conor grimaced and made to stand up and follow her when she shooed him back down. "No need. Stay and finish your meal. Come join me when you are done. I look forward to it," she added with a wink and a quick peck on the cheek, knowing both the action and her words would perplex him enormously. A half a minute later, Laurel, too, was gone from the dinner table.

Maegan looked wide-eyed at Seamus, who had a similar expression of shock on his face. Both had expected quite a different ending to the cat-and-mouse game that Conan and Mhàiri had embarked on only yesterday. Each had privately planned to be amused by their friends' antics for at least a few weeks before it came down to a fiery explosion. It was not as if either of them wanted Conan or Mhàiri to fight, but rather they thought the journey to that emotional conclusion would give the two time to bond, not just as friends, but as potential lovers. For anyone could see Conan and Mhàiri were perfect for each other.

A *thunk* from the end of the table disrupted everyone's thoughts. Brenna's forehead was on the table, rocking back and forth. "Because of Mama, now *no one* is going to win," she lamented. And then, sitting back up, she looked at Seamus and said, "And Bonny and I wanted Uncle Conan to win."

Conor swirled the ale in his mouth around. He wished events like tonight at his dinner table were so rare that they were unheard of, but unfortunately, while not common, they were no longer shocking. What was even less surprising was that his wife was at the center of the commotion.

Laurel had been very wrong earlier. Not *everyone* knew what was going on. She had more or less told him that he would receive answers to what had just happened when he came to their bedchambers, but to leave now would mean that he would only learn what Laurel decided to reveal.

Conor generally preferred being ill-informed of the

emotional comings and goings of those around him—
for the less he knew, the less he was involved. But
Laurel was going to have to learn that there was a time
and place to inform her husband *and laird* of certain
happenings. One of which was *before,* not *after,* she
launched melodramatic events like she had tonight.

"Brenna," Conor began, trying to keep calm. "What
do you mean that you wanted Conan to win? Win
what, *leanbh*?"

Brenna looked to her father and told him what she
had told her mother earlier. "Uncle Conan was pretending to court Mhàiri so that she would give him all
of her paper, only Mhàiri knew because we overheard
him and Seamus planning the whole thing. She was
going to trick him into thinking it was working, but we
told Mama so that she would *help* Uncle Conan. But
now they will never kiss and they *need* to if Conan is
ever going to win like you, and Uncle Cole, and Uncle
Crevan."

Bonny nodded in agreement, her gray eyes large as
she stared at her plate. "Mama even helped Uncle
Craig, and he seemed impossible."

Brenna looked at her sister and shook her head as a
tear began to roll down her cheek. "I don't think Mama
wants Uncle Conan to ever win somebody's heart."

Conor inhaled and then slowly exhaled. He was
beginning to understand what his daughter was talking about. "You want your mother to help Conan fall
in love?"

Brenna scrunched up her face and shook her head.
"I wanted *his* plan to win. To get Mhàiri to like him
enough to give him the books."

Mhàiri, unable to listen any longer as people talked
about her, said, "But Brenna, why would you want him

to have my things? I thought you and I were friends and you would want me to . . . uh, win," she finished, unable to think of a better word.

Brenna looked at Mhàiri with wide eyes. "We are friends!" she promised. "But if Uncle Conan wins, you'll be happy too. Trust me. Bonny and I have seen a lot. For the girl to win, the boy *always* has to think they are the one winning." She then looked at her father for confirmation.

Bonny sighed, her small shoulders slumped with disappointment. "I don't think Uncle Conan is ever going to seduce Mhàiri now."

Conor put his mug down on the table with more force than he had intended and caught the eye of his youngest daughter. "What do you mean . . . *seduce*?"

Mhàiri covered her face with her hands. That humiliating word again.

"What Mama said." Bonny looked at Brenna, and then they both said simultaneously, "They kiss."

A loud groan suddenly came from their brother Braeden. His arm was on the table, propping up his head as if it weighed a hundred pounds. "You are talking about kissing again? That's *all* girls ever talk about."

"It is not!" Brenna denied.

Braeden rolled his eyes. "Well, if Mama really didn't want Uncle Conan to win, she should have just let them kiss. After that happens, no one likes him anymore." Everyone stared at him for a moment. He shrugged his shoulders. "It's true."

"You three!" Conor barked, getting his children's attention. "Go prepare for bed while I go find your mother." Hearing the sharp tone, the trio immediately jumped out of their seats and dashed out of the room.

Conor then stood up, pushed his chair back with his knees, and mumbled, "I must have been insane to want to add to this brood." As he walked by Seamus's seat, he paused. "You better find Conan and you," he said, pointing to Mhàiri, "be careful." Then, realizing he had been through this four times with his other brothers, he added, "Though I probably should be warning Conan and not you."

Conor closed the solar door with a *thump* behind him, comforted to see Laurel was already in his chambers and nearly ready for bed. They each had a room to dress and another for private meetings, but the solar—the highest room of the Star Tower—was where the McTiernay laird had slept in the castle since it was erected. And here was where he held Laurel at night, regardless of the day's events and fights, whenever they were home.

Laurel smiled at him but continued to brush her hair. Conor loved it when it was down, free of its plaits, pins, and ribbons. The fire caught the strawberry highlights, making the pale-gold tresses shimmer with each stroke. It was enough to make him want to forget about dinner and the discussion waiting before them, and go and claim her in a kiss that would lead to activities that needed no words. And he might have, if Laurel was not wearing her robe. That robe had become a sign from early on in their marriage that she intended for them to talk before they slept. And tonight was one of the rare times he was not going to try and persuade her to think of other, more carnal things.

"How are you feeling?" Conor asked before leaning down to give Laurel a soft but loving peck on her cheek.

"Remarkably well." Laurel laid her brush on the table and turned to give him a more thorough kiss.

Conor obliged and claimed Laurel's mouth, tangling his tongue with hers as he clasped the back of her head, holding her immobile. Kissing her never got old and never failed to make him instantly crave her body. And he knew Laurel felt the same as she succumbed to his embrace. She wrapped her arms around his neck and let his tongue probe the warmth of her mouth, moaning as he deepened the kiss.

They clung to each other for several minutes before Conor slowly pulled away. "I would say you do feel well."

"I have not been sick in days, and my energy is finally returning. Hagatha thinks the worst has finally passed."

Conor gave her a quick kiss on her nose before breaking away to undress. It was early and he was not remotely sleepy. Neither was his wife, it seemed. He barred the door to make sure they would not be interrupted and then began to free his belt, hoping to make this conversation even quicker than he had planned. "So dinner," he prompted. "What was all that nonsense? Were Brenna and Bonny right about Conan, Mhàiri, and all that stuff about tricking the other?"

Laurel stood up and went over to her side of their bed. "As I was not there, I cannot say for certain, but we have very bright daughters, so you can probably assume what they told you was correct."

Belt off, Conor grabbed his loose kilt and flung it so

that it draped over a hearth chair. "So then tonight's goal was to interfere with whatever might be growing between Conan and Mhàiri."

Laurel reached for the cover to pull it down and paused. "You noticed?"

"You interfering?" He looked up and gave her a roguish grin. "Aye. I noticed."

Laurel was tempted to throw a pillow at him, but she yanked on the belt of her robe. "I meant about Conan and Mhàiri."

Conor came to the bed. "Men don't talk only about weapons and war. We sometimes take time to discuss the mysteries of women," he said with a mischievous wink as he got under the covers. He leaned back against the headboard and tapped the blanket beside him. "Finn tells me that Conan has spent many an afternoon with Mhàiri, and according to his spies, they have not fought once, that is until this morning."

Laurel's brows furrowed as she shimmied out of her robe to crawl into bed next to Conor. "*Finn's* spies?" she asked, placing her cheek on her husband's chest. "Seems a lot of people have been interested in those two."

"Finn and I were less interested and more wary. Word is that Mhàiri's father is not just a merchant, but according to Colin, a very wealthy and well-respected man in the Lowlands. He may not have an army, but it would not be good for him to arrive to a sticky situation. While I love Conan, his past relationships with women have never ended well."

"Nay, they have not," Laurel agreed, playing with his chest hairs.

"And yet the first woman Conan not only gets along with but respects, you don't like."

Laurel pushed herself up at the accusation and looked down into Conor's smoky gray eyes. "That is not true. I like Mhàiri a lot."

"Then why are you not doing what you always do?" he asked, gently caressing her cheek. "Meddling in their affairs and being a matchmaker, instead of the other way around."

Laurel let go a soft *hrmph* and laid back down. "Right now, the last thing those two need is a matchmaker."

"So is it that you do not think my brother is good enough for Mhàiri?"

Laurel blew out a breath. "I would not say that exactly."

"Then what would you say—*exactly*?"

Laurel gave him a playful tap. "You make it sound sinister when it is just the opposite. Those two were going down a path that would lead to heartache. They needed someone to stop them from making an enduring mistake."

"Why would it be a mistake? Mhàiri must be very smart, for I cannot see him willingly spending hours with someone who was merely pretty. And, by some miracle, they get along. With the exception of Bonny, Conan is not overly fond of your gender, my love. Even you wear on his nerves at times."

Laurel let go a soft snort. "He wears on mine as well."

"That's my point. Both of them sought each other's company time and time again. And I think Mhàiri is good for Conan. I can't remember the last time I heard his tongue wag about the trials of being forced to deal with tedious servants, witless clanswomen, or ignorant soldiers. And there was this morning," Conor said, tapping her arm to emphasize his point. "He actually *argued* back instead of walking away. And from what I heard, Mhàiri was not in the least afraid when he began to yell. She supposedly shouted back. Now you know what happens when couples fight like that, love."

Laurel slowly began to draw circles, forgetting what that always led to. "They make up, but Conan and Mhàiri are not a couple. And what's more, they do not see themselves as a couple, not now or in the future. And you and I might have denied saying our feelings aloud, but deep down we both wanted to be with each other almost from the moment we met."

"I would have thought spending more time together would fix that. Not create a fight."

"Mhàiri is young and inexperienced, and Conan has been focused for so long on only one thing— leaving." She took a deep breath and sighed once more. "Both think they see their futures clearly, and neither have considered including the other in them. And I have no doubt that Mhàiri will get hurt if she falls for him first."

Conor pulled back and waited until Laurel tilted her head to look at him. "First?"

Laurel nodded. "I don't know if they are destined for each other, at least not like your brothers. But I do know that if I had not stopped their foolish plans to trick the other before it really got started, they would not have one." She laid her head back down. "Neither of them knows what they want when it comes to love.

They've never considered the idea of falling in love, and now that they have met someone who might indeed be their soul mate, neither seems to realize they may need to change their vision of the future, let alone being willing to do it."

"How do you know that? Perhaps given more time together they would. It took me time to adjust, same as it did for Colin, and look at Craig. Remember, he resisted Meriel for quite a long while."

"Now look who is trying to play the matchmaker."

Conor did not deny it. "I worry about Conan going off alone. Not physically, but I've already lost Clyde, I fear. I do not want to lose Conan as well. He may be comfortable being by himself, but that doesn't mean he does not need someone."

"We all do," Laurel agreed. "And if Mhàiri and Conan are right for each other, then they will find their way. Now they at least have a chance."

"A good fight can help clear misunderstandings. I only hope it wasn't betrayal I saw on both Conan and Mhàiri's faces. That is not easily overcome."

Laurel rolled over on top of Conor. Her tummy was seriously starting to show, and soon she would not be able to do so. She gazed into his gray eyes. "You know that love is not the only necessary ingredient to a happy marriage. Honesty is just as important. And now Mhàiri and Conan are no longer pretending."

"Pretending to like each other?"

"Pretending they only felt friendship—her pretending to be interested in others and him pretending not to be jealous. Those two treasure brutal honesty, and both were being dishonest, not just with each other but themselves."

Conor gave her a quick kiss. "So tonight was about forcing them to be honest with each other. That's a good thing."

Laurel nodded and returned his kiss with a sweet one of her own. "And once they are, it's possible they will fall in love," she said, her voice low and dubious.

Conor sighed and flopped his head back on the pillows. "You are confusing me again, woman. I thought we just agreed that it would be better if Conan was not alone and, to do that, they needed to be honest and fall in love."

"Aye, but is love going to be enough for Conan to include Mhàiri into his future?"

Conor gave her a light squeeze. "Then it will be his loss because if he knew how good it feels to have a woman who loves him in his arms every night, Father Lanaghly would be preparing for a wedding."

Laurel splayed her fingers across Conor's chest and lifted her face, offering him her mouth. He kissed her slowly, lingeringly, and with a deep, tender possessiveness. "He still might." Laurel grinned.

"On second thought, I don't think you should resume your role of matchmaker, Laurel. Especially in your condition. Conan can make even the most patient person furious at times, and you should not get riled. Besides, he is so furious with you, I don't think he is going to listen to anything you have to say."

"I have no intention of directly taking on that role," she said, with a mischievous smile. "I have no need to. Conan already has a female in his life to whom he listens. He just doesn't realize it."

Then Laurel kissed him thoroughly, ending any possibility of continuing the conversation.

* * *

Brenna and Bonny raced into their room right after their father ordered them to leave the great hall. He had told them to prepare for bed, but it was still early and it would be at least an hour or two before Maegan or a servant came to ensure they were settled for the night.

Bonny went to sit by the hearth and looked for one of the Latin books that Conor had given her to practice. She expected Brenna to undress and put on a robe per her normal routine, but her sister was instead quickly running a brush through her blond hair.

Bonny stood up, put the book down, and went over to where Brenna was splashing water on her face. "What are you planning?" she asked, crossing her arms, imitating what Conan did when he suspected her sister of something.

Brenna dabbed a cloth on her face to dry it and said, "I'm leaving." She gave the towel to Bonny and pointed to the bowl. "And so are you."

Bonny took the towel and said, "But Papa said—"

"Papa only said to come to the room and prepare for bed. I've brushed my hair and washed my face. I did what he said. Now it is your turn."

Bonny began to splash water on her face. "I don't think he meant for us to leave again," she mumbled, as she began to dry her face off.

"Then stay," Brenna replied in superior tone, "but I'm going to find out what is happening with Mhàiri and Uncle Conan." She then headed for the secret door in their room. Their castle was full of them. Her great-grandfather had insisted that there be multiple ways to escape any room in case McTiernay Castle was ever attacked. Brenna had never known anyone to need the passageways for safety reasons, but she thought them marvelous things for discovering bits and pieces of information. And the best conversations were the ones everyone thought her too young to know.

Bonny narrowed her eyes. Most knew about Brenna and her continual propensity to eavesdrop, but it was not as well-known just how often Bonny went with her. If Brenna was about to take the risk and sneak back out, it was not very hard to figure out who her sister wanted to spy on. Besides, Brenna was right. Things were happening, and it was certain that Conan and Mhàiri were not going to tell them anything. Bonny had discovered a few years ago that while she did not share her older sister's passion for the thrill of not being caught, she did learn a lot more about people by eavesdropping than she did by asking grownups questions.

"I'm coming," Bonny announced.

Brenna stopped and turned around. "Fine, but hurry. Braeden is going to get bored and come here any minute."

Bonny ran two quick swipes of a brush through her hair and rushed after her older sister into the dark corridor. Minutes later, they emerged from the stairwell into the storage room on the bottom floor of the tower. After years of practice, both were adept at hearing approaching footsteps and knowing where to duck out of sight until they passed.

Bonny whispered, "Where are we going first? Mhàiri's or Conan's?"

Brenna bit her bottom lip. "Both could be talking right now. So you go find out what Uncle Conan is saying to Seamus, and I'll go listen to Mhàiri and Maegan."

"How do you know they are not alone?"

Brenna rolled her eyes in an exaggerated fashion that Bonny hated. "If Maegan wasn't talking to Mhàiri, she would have been checking on us. And if she is speaking to Mhàiri, then she told Seamus to check on Uncle Conan."

Bonny was not sure, but it did not matter. "We meet back at the room?" she asked.

Brenna nodded and began to rub her hands together as if she were about to start an exciting game. "You tell me everything Uncle Conan said, and I will tell you everything I heard Mhàiri say."

"And then what?" Bonny asked, seeing that her sister was up to more than just discovering what was going on.

"*Then* we figure out what we are going to do, because if Mama won't help Uncle Conan win, then *we will.*"

Now that was the first idea Brenna had had that Bonny fully supported. With a smile and a nod, she followed her sister into the shadows of the courtyard before splitting off to the North Tower as Brenna headed for Mhàiri's room.

Chapter Eight

Seamus slowly opened the door to Conan's chambers and peeked in. Conan was inside, pacing in the work area of his chambers. Seamus hesitated and then thought better of it. He had been outside for over a half hour getting reamed by Maegan, who seemed to think everything that was happening was *his* fault as it had been *his* idea for Conan to deceive Mhàiri.

At first, he had been so shocked by Maegan's tirade that he had not responded well at all. Seamus had felt his honor was being attacked and had immediately gone on both the defensive and offensive, making it clear that *she* was the one who should be ashamed of her actions, not him. That it was one thing for a child to eavesdrop on a private conversation, but for an adult woman to take what she had overheard and use it to embarrass and belittle a man whose family had taken her in when she had no one was inexcusable.

Almost as soon as the words had left his mouth, Seamus had wished he could take them back, but it was too late. At least then he had done the smart thing and stuck with apologies and explanations, which Maegan had ignored while peppering him with more words on the delicacy of the human heart. In the end, he wondered if Maegan was going to ever talk to him again and felt his heart break when she walked away with a good-bye that felt all too final.

Knowing sleep was not possible, Seamus had sought the one other man he knew was as miserable as he was. Conan. But by the looks of things, Conan was not miserable at all. He was furious. And it was going to take a lot longer than an hour to cool the anger visibly writhing through his friend.

There was minimal room for walking, so Conan could only take a handful of steps before being forced to turn, and then a couple of seconds later he was turning once more. It was making Seamus dizzy, but asking Conan to sit or slow his pacing was not an option at the moment.

"Damn woman," Conan growled with significant bite upon seeing Seamus, continuing his fast back-and-forth walk.

"Which one?" Seamus asked, hoping that a little levity might at least get Conan to stop and sit down. Seamus could only recall being as furious as Conan was right now a couple of times, and both of them had been over a woman. The first time it had happened, his response had been to pace as well, which had only fueled his ire, not helped it. With every step, he had repeated the words that had driven him to a fury, which eventually resulted in him punching a wooden door and nearly breaking his hand. Seamus could still remember the pain and the weeks it had taken before he could properly grip a sword with any authority again. Conan was on that same path.

"Laurel," Conan answered. "*And* Mhàiri. *And* Maegan."

He took a few steps and stopped to glare at Seamus. "Damn them all." He began to pace again.

"Might want to damn me as well," Seamus said, leaning against one of the bookcases. "I encouraged you to try that bad idea to charm Mhàiri."

"Ha! According to Laurel, I was trying to *seduce* Mhàiri, as if I could. Men should be warned about her. How dare she accuse *me* of using someone emotionally when every day she is teasing another man, toying with him, kissing him, making him believe she feels more than she does. I wish Loman the best of luck getting anything real from that woman."

Seamus shifted his stance and began to wonder how deep Conan's feelings were for Mhàiri. The man had refused to admit that he even liked her, but based on what Seamus was seeing and hearing, Conan did a lot more than like the woman. For his normal reaction to an angry woman was complete indifference.

"I don't think Loman is interested in Mhàiri, nor she him."

Conan snorted. "Then I wonder who will be next. Sean seemed eager enough when I saw him the other day."

"Do you know what your real problem is?" Seamus posed. "You like Mhàiri. In fact, I would say you're fascinated by her. Just admit it. You've never met anyone like her, and that's why what she did has you so upset."

Conan turned his back on Seamus and stared into the dark courtyard below. He could see shadows moving, but the world had quieted.

"It's understandable," Seamus continued. "Mhàiri is beautiful and smart and sweet. It's impossible not to like her."

Conan continued to stare down into the inky darkness.

"Mhàiri is not sweet in the least. She is calculating and, as I discovered tonight, quite devious."

"Aye, that *was* surprising, to learn she had over-heard us plotting."

Conan stopped short. "You think Laurel was right? That I was trying to *swindle* Mhàiri out of her things?"

Seamus shook his head and kept his expression neutral. "I don't think so, but I can see how Mhàiri might see it that way."

Conan narrowed his gaze and took a couple of threatening steps toward Seamus. "She got to you, didn't she?" he asked rhetorically before waving a hand and resuming his pacing. "Maegan. I should have known she would blame you and make you feel guilty for something *you* didn't even do! *Murt!* You like her so much you can't even have an opinion that she won't approve of anymore."

Seamus pushed himself off the bookcase and was about to remind Conan with his fists that, while he could ignore most of Conan's barbs, his tolerance did not extend to insulting Maegan. But before he could take a step, the door opened again.

Bonny entered, waved at him as she moved by, and then plopped down in the chair she always sat on when she came to visit her uncle.

Bonny sat and looked at Seamus and Uncle Conan, who were both staring at her. She wondered if she had made a mistake about joining Conan versus listening in on him like Brenna had wanted. The problem with eavesdropping was that while it was an effective way to learn what was going on, it never allowed for asking questions. And Bonny had several. She decided to start with what she thought was the easiest.

"Why are you so mad, Uncle Conan?"

"Because," he sputtered, "your friend Mhàiri wanted to make me look like a fool."

Bonny was still confused and pursed her lips together and nodded. "Girls don't like it when you try to take their stuff. Maybe you should apologize," she suggested.

"*I* apologize?" he repeated. "*I* should apologize?" he said once more, this time to Seamus, who gave a half-hearted shrug in agreement.

"What about Mhàiri?" Conan asked. "What about *her* listening in on my conversation? Even you," he said, pointing to Bonny in the chair, "have more honesty about you coming in here and not hiding behind some door misinterpreting everything you hear."

Bonny crossed her arms and thought for a second. "But it was her room she was listening to. I don't think she would do that anywhere else." Conan's jaw dropped. "I mean, if she was in here with Maegan, wouldn't you have wanted to know what was going on?"

"Were you with them, Bonny?"

She shook her head. "Only Brenna, Mhàiri, and Maegan were there. I thought you were building shelves, not trying to take all her books."

Conan threw his hands up into the air. "I *wasn't* trying to take all her books! *Murt!* I was really hoping for some pages or maybe, by some miracle, *one* book if her father brought some new ones to sell when he arrived. I know what those books mean to Mhàiri, and she should know that!" he shouted angrily.

Bonny was surprised to hear her uncle shout. It was very unlike him. Unlike the rest of the family, when he was annoyed, he did not yell. He just grumbled—a lot. Which was good, Bonny thought, because he was annoyed a lot. And yet, hearing her uncle shout right now did not bother her. In fact, she thought Brenna would think it a good thing because whenever their parents fought, it always ended up with them together.

"I don't think Mhàiri knows that," Bonny said. "If you told me that you weren't really trying to take my stuff, it would make me feel better."

"I should not have to. Mhàiri knows I plan on using vellum. Paper may be lighter and so I could carry more of it and capture more information, but eventually it would not matter. The vellum I'm preparing is much larger and, more importantly, easier to stitch together into a single large map."

Bonny rolled her eyes upward and thought for a minute. "I think she might have forgotten that. I still think maybe," she said, tapping her chin like her mama did when she was thinking, "you should tell her. Mhàiri cried when she thought you wanted all her stuff. Brenna says that girls only get mad at boys when they like them, and Mhàiri was *really* mad at you. She said that she thought you were different, but that she was wrong and you were like all the rest. I'm not sure what that means. Do you?"

Conan stared at Bonny for several long seconds before answering. "I do. It means that I need to talk to Mhàiri right now." And then he was gone.

Bonny blinked. She was not sure that going to see Mhàiri while she was still so angry was such a good idea. Bonny had been thinking that Conan would seek Mhàiri out in the morning or tell her he was sorry over the morning meal. Regardless, Brenna was going to be very excited about this.

Thinking about her sister reminded Bonny that Brenna was actively eavesdropping on Mhàiri and would soon be listening to Conan as well. It was one thing for Brenna to tell her about what Mhàiri was saying to Maegan, but Bonny did not want to learn what Conan said to Mhàiri secondhand. It was she who had sent him there so it should be she who got to listen to how it went.

Bonny looked at Seamus, who was staring where Conan had been standing, still looking a little befuddled. "I have to go," she announced, and then she, too, disappeared out the door. Bonny took the shortcut, glad she knew where Brenna liked to hide in the Warden's Tower when it was only her.

Mhàiri took a deep breath when she heard the sharp knock on the door. She wanted to shout at her friend that she had meant what she had said, that she was done talking for the evening and wanted to hear no more advice.

When Maegan had joined her earlier, Mhàiri had been happy to see her nearly as angry as she was. She had been even happier to hear that Maegan had ambushed Seamus, telling him how disgusted she was with his part in all that had happened. *Then* Maegan had done the unthinkable and begun to defend the man. It was as if Conan were there himself, trying to minimize what he had done.

Maybe they had jumped to the wrong conclusions about what Seamus and Conan were trying to do.

Maybe it was not really as bad as they'd first thought.

Maybe they should believe Seamus and Conan, for they had looked truly shocked and betrayed by their accusations.

Maybe they should have thought things through before wanting revenge.

Maybe it was somewhat underhanded to entrap someone with only one goal—to humiliate them.

Mhàiri had finally had enough and practically shoved Maegan out her door, proclaiming she needed time to think. Unfortunately, the ceaseless knock on her door proved Maegan was not so easily gotten rid of.

Mhàiri was almost resolved to let her friend knock all night when it occurred to her that Maegan might be trying to apologize.

Ready to listen to an apology or, once again, send her friend away as politely but firmly as possible, Mhàiri opened the door. The moment she saw who was on the other side, her jaw literally dropped.

She was still in shock when Conan moved around her and entered her room without even asking. Her wits were just returning, and she was about to order him to leave when he pressed one index finger against her lips and one against his own. Then he tiptoed over to the large tapestry that hung from ceiling to floor next to the hearth. With a grand gesture, he pulled back the heavy drape and then rammed his foot on the half-sized wooden door it hid. The planks gave way and the semi-door creaked open to reveal a dark, narrow passageway.

Mhàiri realized she was looking at the very place she, Maegan, and Brenna had sat huddled together, listening to Conan as he planned to *persuade* her to give him all her hemp paper.

Conan closed the door and let the tapestry fall back into place. "Good," he announced. "We are alone. Now we can talk."

Mhàiri crossed her arms and tilted her chin up. "I have nothing to say."

Conan's gaze burned into Mhàiri's. "Aye. You do.

You are going to answer my questions," he said without equivocation.

His directness shook her, but Mhàiri did not want Conan to know he affected her at all, so she shrugged her shoulders in mock resignation. "I will never lie to you," she said, echoing what he had told her.

"I only want to know if you *really* thought that I would try and take your things away from you."

Mhàiri blinked her peridot-like eyes. She was going to declare that she did, but seeing Conan, with his blue eyes smoldering with indignation, she wondered if she had been wrong. "But I heard you," she finally said, for it was true.

"Then let me ask you this. Before overhearing Seamus and my conversation yesterday, would you have *ever* thought that I would try and take your things away from you?"

Mhàiri swallowed with difficulty, but after a couple of seconds, she found her voice and once again answered honestly. "I would have thought the opposite, probably even come to your defense if somebody had accused you of such an act. But then *I heard what you said*," she finished, emphasizing that it was not a simple misunderstanding, and that Conan had damned himself with his own words.

Fury began to build within Conan once again. "So all the hours we spent together, talking, sharing, and getting to know one another were just what—a lie? A waste of time?"

Mhàiri's brow furrowed. "Of course not."

"They must be! Because if you truly believe that I would stoop so low to steal *paper*, you must believe everything else we shared was a falsehood. I cannot be both your friend who would do serious bodily injury to anyone who did what you accused me of and your enemy at the same time."

Nervously, Mhàiri bit her lip. She hated to admit it, but Conan had a point. "Then why?" she whispered, the pain she felt coming through. "*Why* would you say all those things about me being susceptible to your kisses? And that I should give a gift in return for these shelves? Or that it should be all my idea to give you all my paper?"

Conan reached out and gripped her arms tightly. "First, I never wanted all your paper but only what you were willing to give me. I was hoping for some pages and, in my dreams, perhaps a book. But I realized not even an hour later that your father was coming and I could probably buy as much paper as I wanted from him. But as for *why* I said all those things, haven't you mused something aloud? Some fantasy that if someone overheard they could misconstrue into thinking you actually believed what you were saying?"

Tears began to roll down Mhàiri's cheeks as she finally understood. "I didn't want to believe what I heard. I'm sorry. I just was so hurt."

Conan pulled her into his arms and held her close. "*Shhhh,*" he whispered into her hair. "I wished you had come to me. Confronted me directly. Why didn't you?"

Mhàiri clung to Conan, reveling the feeling of being in his arms. For the past twenty-four hours, she had felt alone and bereft, and now all she felt was safe. A part of her wanted to stay there forever. Another part wanted to run and protect her heart. She batted the painful thought away into a recess of her mind and, instead, pressed even closer to his warmth.

There was something about his physical presence—Mhàiri never wanted him to stop holding her, plain and simple.

The feel of his hand on her face caused her lashes to flutter open and look up in the bluest of eyes. She had no idea how he could channel so much intensity through them, but the look he was giving her made her heart race.

Conan pushed Mhàiri's soft, thick hair off her shoulders, wishing he could hear what she was thinking. He knew he should step away. His control was already on a knife's edge, inflamed by her anger, her tears, and now the desire shimmering beneath the apprehension in her green eyes. But he couldn't. Mhàiri was the most stunning woman he had ever seen. Everything from her satin skin and silky tresses to her tempting lips and unusual green eyes fringed with long lashes called to him on a primal level. Not a detail escaped him.

Mhàiri's breath caught in her throat. Conan's fingers traced the planes of her face with a feather-light touch, tipped with heat. She felt herself melt under his scrutiny, aching for him to speak, to touch her, to do something other than stare into her eyes.

Conan lightly caressed her cheek. "You are so beautiful," he whispered in a thick, gruff voice that sent an ache racing through her. He bent his dark head and his warm breath sent a shiver of heat through the pit of her stomach. "Kiss me, Mhàiri," he demanded hoarsely.

Needing no more coaxing, Mhàiri met his lips and opened her mouth, allowing Conan to make slow love to her with his tongue.

Mhàiri closed her eyes and let herself fall into the embrace, sinking into his strong arms. Unlike their previous kiss, which had been powerful, claiming, and aggressive, Conan was kissing her slowly, lingeringly, and with deep, tender possessiveness. Her heart slammed in her chest as Conan was creating an irresistible desire to become his, and only his, in every way.

Conan captured her sigh and deepened their embrace, kissing her over and over again. Her mouth was warm and welcoming, exactly like he had remembered.

He cradled her face in his hands and drank hungrily from her lips, delighting in the feel of her wild pulse underneath his thumb telling him that she desired him just as much. Soon, need would overtake them both. Conan was about to pull away when he felt Mhàiri's hands press against his back. The soft, hesitant caress caused him to growl and delve once again into the sweetness of her mouth.

Her fingers traveled up his back and plunged into his hair. The impassioned touch sent a new heat curling through his blood. Mhàiri's mouth responded to each stroke of his tongue, hot, wet, and clinging. Her body moved against his, each touch innocent, and erotic.

God, she was soft, inviting. Conan knew he would never get enough of her. No caress, no kiss, no touch would ever be enough. He wanted to consume the essence of her vibrant spirit.

Mhàiri felt herself quivering. Conan's sheer masculinity was overpowering. With each kiss, she wanted more, but he refused to give in and it was making her senseless with a growing need she did not understand.

His kisses were soft but consuming, filled with so much tenderness it felt as if her heart was swelling in her chest, nearly choking her. But the longer his lips caressed her, the less will she had.

From deep within him, she heard the rumblings of a satisfied groan. Mhàiri twisted her fingers in his hair and held on for dear life. Nothing had prepared her for what she was feeling. She could feel the warmth of his hands splayed over her back through the material of her gown. A strange heat burned low in her stomach as a rush of shivers ran from the top of her neck down her spine, his kiss feeding both of those glorious feelings at once. Soon, hot ripples of pleasure slid down her thighs, and a moan of despair and desire, escaped her throat. Mhàiri was not sure what she was asking for, but it was flooding her with an aching demand.

Mhàiri's earnest and open response to each caress shocked Conan. His pulse raced as she surged against him. His lips left hers and found the soft, sensitive spot beneath her ear, then slid down her neck. "God, you're everything a man could want," he whispered against her skin. "Smart, fiery, and uncommonly sensuous."

Conan's mouth was soft and wet and firm, and the feel of his lips roaming her skin made her dizzy. When he nibbled at her earlobe, Mhàiri forgot to breathe. Her knees suddenly gave out, and if Conan's arms hadn't been around her, she would have dissolved into a little puddle of desire at his feet.

"I don't know what's happening to me," Mhàiri heard herself mumble, surprised she could talk at all, for every fiber of her being was on fire, aroused into a bright burning flame. But still she wanted more.

Mhàiri's soft confession was enough to remind Conan that he needed to regain his diminishing control. They were in her bedchambers, alone, and moments away from doing something that would change their lives forever. Self-perseverance forced him to release her lips.

He kept his arms circled about her, breathing in her scent. "Can you speak?" he murmured.

His face was buried in the side of Mhàiri's neck as he struggled for control over his rampant, covetous emotions. He wasn't sure what would have happened if Mhàiri had asked him to stay with her. A whole night with Mhàiri in his arms? He feared he would be lost . . . addicted. And that he might never be able to let her go.

"You robbed me of words." Her voice was muffled, her face buried against his chest as she inhaled his musky scent.

With all the women before, he had easily kept himself detached, using them for what he needed and then leaving soon after. He had become careful to bed only those who would not cling or ask for more, because he knew he would never commit himself to a woman. With Mhàiri, that still did not change.

Yet, a slowly growing voice deep inside him disagreed.

Conan lifted his hand, moving one of the dark wisps of hair from her forehead. With only the tips of his fingers, he tenderly traced every hollow, every curve of her face he so longed to kiss and know more intimately, but knew he never would. He stared down into her passion-filled eyes. "I think I like the idea of being able to make you speechless."

Mhàiri smiled. "I think I like that idea as well." Then she placed her cheek back on his chest, basking in his warmth. "Good thing it is your turn to do all the talking."

Conan lightly kissed the top of her head, unwilling to let her go just yet. "How so?"

Mhàiri giggled. "Well, I apologized. Now, it is your turn."

Conan stiffened. "Apologize for what?"

Mhàiri leaned back to look up at him. Her brows arched in surprise. "Why, for all those things that you said."

Conan was sorry. He had even planned on apologizing for them . . . at some time . . . in his own way. But demanding contrition was too reminiscent of how his brothers' wives acted after a fight. Conan had always thought it manipulative and conniving, but had been even more disgusted that his brothers had always so easily fallen for the trap. Now he understood, for he had almost become that very person.

Conan's jaw tightened. He took a step back and let his gaze sweep over Mhàiri, taking her in from head to toe in one swift, heated glance. "Do not turn a simple kiss into some imaginative love story where you suddenly feel emboldened with power to compel me to do your bidding just to make you happy."

If Conan had reached out and slapped her, Mhàiri could not have been more shocked or hurt, but it did not matter, for that pain began to morph into white-hot anger.

"How dare you!" she hissed, pushing him away. "The whole world knows no one compels the great Conan McTiernay to do anyone's bidding but his own. I was not *demanding* an apology, but assuming you felt some regret for your role in what happened. And while I will not deny being attracted to you, it is not like I am alone. Any sane woman would find you physically tempting. But enjoying a *simple* kiss is a far cry from a love story. My heart could only be stolen by someone who is honorable, honest, kind and . . . and heroic."

Mhàiri marched to her bedchamber door and swung it open, gesturing for him to leave. "And you most certainly are none of those things."

Bonny and Brenna listened in misery as Mhàiri and Conan broke away followed by the clunk of her bedroom door. Knowing there was nothing left to hear, Brenna tugged on Bonny's sleeve, indicating that she was leaving.

Bonny followed Brenna all the way back to their chambers in silence, waiting until they were inside and alone before she spoke. "I think Conan just lost for good this time."

Brenna used her toes to pull off her slippers and then slumped into one of the two chairs that were by the fireplace in their room. It was nothing as nice and grand as the great hall chairs everyone liked to steal for their rooms, but they were padded and comfortable and no one ever got mad when she sat in her preferred position of sideways. "I wonder what made Uncle Conan say that?"

Bonny flopped into the chair next to Brenna. "Probably fear. I heard Mama say that about Uncle Craig once. Or maybe it was Uncle Crevan," she mused. "She said he was afraid of love and that was why he pushed it away."

Brenna swung her legs back and forth over the chair's sidearm. "You're right. Uncle Conan loves Mhàiri, but I'm not sure she loves him anymore."

"Why?" Bonny asked. "Uncle Conan *is* all those things she said."

Brenna grimaced. "Well, he's honest, but I'm not sure about kind. And did you notice how he refused to apologize?" She took a deep breath and sighed as she dropped her head back to let her blond hair swing over the other sidearm. "Boys are so silly. Why is 'I'm sorry' so hard to say?"

Bonny shrugged. "I don't know. We say it all the time."

Brenna nodded upside down. "I think it's because we're girls. Braeden and Gideon won't apologize, not even to each other."

Bonny nodded. "But Uncle Conan *is* honorable. Papa says that's when someone is honest, trustworthy, and loyal, and keeps his word. So Uncle Conan definitely is honorable."

"Maybe," Brenna acknowledged. "But what about kind?"

"Uncle Conan is when he wants to be," Bonny refuted, stretching to pick up the brush on the table next to her where she had left it in her mad rush earlier. "He's always nice to me."

"True," Brenna said, drawing out the word as she thought over all the qualifications Mhàiri had listed for the person with whom she could fall in love. *Honorable, honest, kind and . . . and heroic.* She lifted her head and looked at her younger sister. "So let's say we were able to show Mhàiri that Uncle Conan's honorable, honest, and kind. What about the last one? How are we going to prove he's a hero?"

Bonny began to toss her brush in the air and catch it. "That is the easiest one. Uncle Conan is a hero practically every day."

Brenna snorted and let her head flop back down. "I don't think anyone but you thinks so."

"What about making those shelves?"

"That's not heroic."

"Would be to me. And Mhàiri thinks so as well. Did you see her touching the design he carved in them?" Bonny threw the brush up, but this time missed catching it.

Brenna sat up and retrieved the brush. "A hero is someone who saves someone. Like when Papa saved Mama from the ice storm," she asserted, using the brush to gesture and emphasize her point. "Or when Uncle Cole saved Aunt Ellenor from the bad men."

Bonny snatched her brush back. "You think Uncle Conan needs to save Mhàiri?"

Brenna pursed her lips together and arched her brows. "If he is going to win, he will."

Bonny studied her sister, trying to see if she was being serious. "Do you still think he can?"

Brenna nodded. "He just needs help."

Bonny's eyes widened. "Mama won't help, and I don't think Maegan will because she is Mhàiri's friend."

"Uncle Conan needs someone who *wants* him to win." A large smile grew across Brenna's face. "He needs us."

Chapter Nine

Mhàiri smiled sweetly as she took the small cloth being handed to her. The large piece of bread nestled inside was still warm. She held on to it and waited as each person in the large circle was served their morsel and their beverage.

She stole a quick glance at Conan, who sat across from her, as he swallowed the contents from the cup, learning that it was not ale, not even mead, but water. She had to admit that she was impressed. His only sign of dissatisfaction was the brief moment of realization. Then he crinkled his eyes and pasted on a smile that almost looked sincere.

It had been four days since their fight, and Mhàiri would have never dreamed that this setting would be their first encounter. She was still not even sure how she had been hoodwinked into coming. This was Maegan's weekly thing, enduring the widows' social circle.

Maegan was not a widow, but her grandmother had been a faithful member of the circle since before Maegan had been born. And after Maegan's parents had died and she had come to live with her grandmother, Maegan had dutifully joined her each week to listen to the older clanswomen talk as they sewed. She loved it and had continued to come after her grandmother had passed. Until this week, Mhàiri had always found a way to escape, but yesterday, she had finally succumbed to the pressure of her friend. And then Maegan had the nerve to not even show up.

Conan lifted his bread as a sign of acknowledgement, his empty smile frozen in place. Mhàiri curled her lips into a similar expression.

"We are so glad you two joined us this week," the lady on her left said, her voice warm and kind.

"Aye," came a rickety voice from someone on her right.

"We normally just sew, but today, as we have special guests, we decided to have a treat first," said another woman a couple of chairs down. She had gray hair that was pulled back into a single plait. Her face was wrinkled, but Mhàiri could tell it was due to excessive smiling. The woman pointed to her bread. "Try it," she said with a nod. "It's Almeda's. No one's bread is more delicious."

Mhàiri took a bite and had to agree it was very good.

The woman beaming with pride, who must have been Almeda, sat next to Conan on his left. She was large set with round cheeks and small, bright blue eyes that, despite her years, still looked young and bright.

Mhàiri's gaze landed on Conan and narrowed. What was he doing here? She could not imagine he did this sort of thing often. She had never heard Maegan mention his attendance at the circle, and it was just not in his nature to sit patiently and listen as old women prattled about things in which he had no interest.

Seeing her inquisitive look, Conan arched a brow

and then took a large bite. A second later, he turned and said, "Excellent, Almeda. Even Fiona would be envious of your skill." This brought on giggles by several of the women.

"Please excuse us, Mhàiri, dear," came from the woman on her left, "but we are so excited to have Conan with us." And as if she knew Mhàiri needed further explanation, she added, "We have been asking him to come for years, but until today he has refused."

Conan took a drink of water. "Seems my little niece thought it time I came as well, Gavina."

Mhàiri pulled off a small piece of bread and popped it into her mouth, glad to have something to help mask her shocked expression. She wondered how Bonny had convinced him to come today. She could ask, but for a seven-year-old, Bonny was incredibly smart and evasive when she wanted to be. She would be more successful asking Maegan, which she planned on doing right after she finished scolding her for leaving her alone with a bunch of strangers.

"We are so sad to hear you will be leaving us in the spring. Whatever will we do?" The question came from a thin woman who looked incredibly frail. Mhàiri feared a good wind would knock her over and wondered how the old woman was able to survive the cold winters.

"Now, Leane, you do not have to worry," Conan answered. "I will make sure someone from Conor's guard steps forward and continues when I leave."

The woman sitting to her left leaned closer and said in a loud whisper, "A few years ago, us widows started finding meat at our door. Nothing very big, usually a bird or a rabbit, but the perfect size for us to prepare and eat without leaving anything to spoil. For months, we tried to figure out who it was, but it was not until Conan here"—a long finger pointed to him—"left several times over the course of a summer to visit some abbeys with Father Lanaghly that we discovered his secret. You see, each time he left, the meat ceased to appear." Realizing that Conan was listening to her, as was everyone else, she spoke louder. "And that is when we knew who our angel was."

Mhàiri's jaw had been dropping farther and farther as the story had been told. When it was finished, she raised her astonished gaze to Conan, but he was looking elsewhere.

Two hours later, Mhàiri was surprised to realize she was enjoying herself. Each woman had regaled them with her own personal story of love, and when finished, they had wished for Conan to also find someone who would cherish him, like his brothers had. Some shared tales of their children, most of whom were grown but lived near.

Once the bread was consumed, Mhàiri watched as the women brought out their sewing and was glad that Maegan had suggested she bring the drawing she had started sketching to give her something to do. Only two women were working on the same piece, combining two pieces of fabric together to make a thicker, warmer blanket. Most were doing mending, and another was fashioning a new leine for her son to wear during the upcoming festivities.

"Conan, young man, could you help me thread this needle?" Almeda asked, handing him some thread. He took the needle and thread in hand and deftly pushed the fiber through the small hole. "*Tapadh leat*," she said when Conan handed it back. "I was hoping you could help me with one last favor."

Mhàiri watched him arch a brow as he turned in Almeda's direction. He looked as if he was agreeing, but Mhàiri noticed he had yet to actually commit himself. "Your brother Crevan found me the sweetest puppy when he lived here."

"He was such a sweet man," Gavina sighed, then tapped Mhàiri's hand with a soft finger. "Not as sweet as our Conan though."

"Piegi just passed," Almeda continued, "and I was hoping you could find me another."

Finally, Conan glanced Mhàiri's way, catching her staring at him. He gave her a triumphant wink and then said, "Of course. I would be delighted."

Mhàiri almost scoffed aloud, swallowing it just in time. Conan, delighted to find a puppy. Conan, eager to thread needles. Conan, feeding widows. The man sitting across from her might look like Conan. He might even have his name and his voice, but he certainly was *not* Conan.

"You are *so* kind." Almeda gave his hand a little squeeze.

Conan coughed into his other hand, causing Mhàiri to look up. As soon as she did, he caught her gaze, and that was when she knew. Aye, some of his deeds proved he was charitable, but everything he had said and done that afternoon had been to prove her wrong. "Some may disagree with you, I think," he said. "Why, just this week I was told that one of the very things I was not capable of was kindness."

This brought about chuckles from the group, as they assumed he was just teasing them. "What nonsense," Leane said, plunging her needle through the thick material with more force than it seemed possible from her feeble form. "Why, it was just yesterday that a wee lad—you know, Rona's boy—was pestering you about learning how to sword fight. I've heard him ask other soldiers, but they said they didn't have time."

"Or that he was too small," another remarked.

"Aye, but our Conan stopped and showed him a few ways to stop the teases of another child who was bigger and stronger. Made that lad's day."

"My granddaughter is your chambermaid and thinks you are the kindest man she knows," Almeda commented, her plump cheeks turning pink.

Conan's head jerked back, and Mhàiri could tell even he was surprised at that one. She had seen his room, and it was in a state of disarray. And while she did not know for certain, her gut said that was its normal state. "I, uh, must say I'm surprised," Conan finally got out.

"Whenever you see her hauling a basket of clothes and linens, you always stop and carry it the rest of the way. You never yell for her to clean the stairwell, and you only ask her to help with your chambers a couple times a month. She considers it a blessing to work for you and will be sad to see you go."

Conan licked his lips, and a large grin came over his face. He leaned back, crossed his legs at the ankles, and sent Mhàiri a large "so there" grin.

"And then there is little Bonny," the woman who sat on Conan's right said, finally joining the conversation. Minna's perfect posture clashed with the chaos of her white hair, which fought its braided constraints. "Pretty little thing is as smart as they come, but I've noticed she doesn't play with the other children much. Don't think just because we don't live in the castle that we don't know you have befriended the little lass."

"Aye," Leane piped in again. "Maegan says you are

never impatient with her, teaching her things, making time for her even when you are busy preparing for your trip."

Mhàiri licked her lips. *Our Conan.* It was too much. To think that his most ardent admirers were old *women.* "I must say, ladies, your view of Conan is much different from the one a lot of women have." Hearing Mhàiri's voice, Conan's gaze immediately shifted to lock with hers once again. "I understand that he is a regular insulter of our gender and incapable of apologizing, *even when he is in the wrong.*"

Gavina clucked her tongue. "Of course we've heard how our Conan is quite fond of the ladies," she began, "but do not be fooled by idle gossip."

"Aye," Leane interjected. "Those women who caused a stir were just silly enough to believe they could turn his head. It is their fault they gave their heart away before our Conan was ready to ask for it."

A single brow formed a perfect arch on his forehead. How Mhàiri wanted to erase that smirk.

"Maybe he can teach the rest of Conor's soldiers to be like him, for I recently had a horrid experience," Mhàiri stated.

Gavina perked up. "Really? Please tell us, my dear. What happened? Did he say something unpleasant?"

"Did he try to kiss you?" Almeda asked. She had laid her sewing in her lap and leaned forward, her blue eyes twinkling with interest.

Mhàiri nodded. "He did, but I learned that he was doing it just so that he could trick me out of the paper I use to draw on."

"Well, that is strange," Minna acknowledged. "Why would a man want your drawings?"

"Maybe he wanted it to prove to you that he was

interested in what you do," Almeda chimed in. "Men have a hard time expressing themselves. Did you know that it took nearly three years before my man would even look at me? I thought he didn't like me at all when all the while the reason he wouldn't speak to me was because he didn't think that I would ever like him back."

Gavina nodded. "Perhaps he likes you, Mhàiri. Conan, dear, maybe you can help Maegan's friend Mhàiri find out just what this man is thinking and then explain it to her."

Mhàiri smiled and squeezed the old woman's hand. "Why, I would appreciate that very much. And if you could find out why he refuses to apologize for his behavior even though he knows he was in the wrong, that, too, would be very helpful."

Conan sat up and placed his hands on his knees. "I can answer that last one for you now. Some men don't mind saying and doing anything to make a woman happy. Men like me do."

Mhàiri gritted her teeth and then forced herself to smile. "I'll be sure to mention that to Laird McTiernay next time we speak. I wonder what category he will think you put him in."

Brenna twirled around in the bedchambers, encouraged by the feeling of success. "You know, Bonny, kindness was not nearly as hard as I thought it was going to be. And I don't think we need to prove he's honest. Everyone knows Uncle Conan never lies, even to save a person's feelings."

Bonny toed off her slippers and began to yank on

the ties on the left side of her gown. "You think today worked?"

"Absolutely! They had to have called Uncle Conan kind at least a dozen times!"

"But he and Mhàiri didn't seem very happy in the end."

Brenna stopped spinning. She began to sway from being dizzy. "That's because she doesn't believe Uncle Conan's being honorable. We just need to prove he is not going to hurt her."

Bonny attacked the other side of her bliaut. "Well, I thought of what to do for kindness. You have to do honorable," she said and shimmied out of her bliaut before diving under the covers of her bed. It would be another hour before evening dinner would be ready, but Bonny was freezing. Two days ago, the weather had turned and while it had not been raining, there had been no sun for warmth. It had been very cold outside listening to the old women talk, but it had been worth it. Brenna was right. Mhàiri might not love Uncle Conan yet, but she could no longer say he wasn't kind. "I think we should wait for proving he's heroic."

Brenna moved to stand close to the fire. "Maybe we can do something at Christmastide for that one."

Another shiver went through Bonny, and she wondered why her sister was not as cold as she was from their escapade. "That's next week. So how are we going to show that he is honorable before then?"

Brenna shook her head, thinking. "We need something to show that Uncle Conan is trustworthy and loyal." She swayed back and forth on her toes with her back to the fire. Her hands were behind her, absorbing the warmth, when suddenly, she snapped her fingers. Her gray eyes, huge with excitement, locked onto Bonny's smoky ones. "I know what to do," she said giddily. "We need to learn how to draw."

"Draw?" Bonny asked dubiously.

"It will be perfect. You will be out with Conan learning how to make maps . . ."

"But I don't want to know how to make maps."

"Shh! Listen. You will be out with him, and at the same time I will be with Mhàiri on an outing. Then, we will just happen to run into each other."

Bonny shuddered just thinking of going back outside again. "It's cold outside. I don't think Mhàiri is going to want to go if it is going to be outside. I know Uncle Conan won't."

Brenna waved her hand dismissively. "We'll wait for a sunny day, and then she will want to go. Everyone is preparing for Christmastide and getting all the rooms ready for guests to arrive. Uncle Conan will want a reason to escape, and Mhàiri is always happy to draw."

"That's because she's like you and doesn't get cold," Bonny groused. "And I'm not sure how this is going to prove Uncle Conan's honorable."

Brenna's eyes were sparkling. "Don't worry. It will."

Bonny lifted the blanket and covered her head. "Let me guess. You have an idea."

Brenna's laughter reached under the covers. "And it's a good one, Bonny! You are going to *love* it!"

Conan knelt down beside Bonny and leaned back against the large boulder his niece had selected as the perfect place to practice drawing. He looked over Bonny's shoulder to see what she was creating. It looked to be a hill with a sun shining over it.

Next to her was Nairne, another little girl about

Bonny's age whom he had seen periodically while walking through the village. Her curly bright red hair made her hard to miss. She was the spitting image of her mother, who often helped Laurel design some of her more intricate tapestries. Nairne had inherited both her mother's hair and her soft freckles, which were scattered all over her face, but her large dark brown eyes and unusual height she got from her father, who was one of the McTiernay clan's more successful farmers.

"How are you doing, Nairne?" he asked.

"I'm well," she said, concentrating.

Conan could see why both girls got along so well. Neither was a great talker, and it was not in Nairne's nature to accept another's opinion as her own. She did not care if Bonny knew more or was considered very smart; she had her own thoughts and ideas and was going to keep them until she decided otherwise.

Conan stared at what Nairne was sketching. It was surprisingly detailed for being created in dirt using a stick. "What are you drawing?" he asked.

"Today," she replied, and with that answer, the image started to make sense. The left side indicated daylight, but it quickly morphed into what was night-time, which was the majority of the picture. It did indeed represent the winter solstice, the shortest day and longest night of the year.

"Well, let me know if you get cold," he said. The day was bright and sunny, which kept the cold wind from being unbearable.

Nairne never looked up, but answered, "Bonny gets cold. Not me. You should ask her."

"I'm fine," Bonny replied, half-heartedly stabbing at

her sketch. Conan wondered what was going on, for it was clear his niece was not there to learn about maps as she had said.

For days, Bonny had been hounding him to take her out and show her what he would be doing when he left. At first, the weather had not cooperated and he had been busy helping with gathering the necessary logs for the many bonfires that would be erected over the next several days. But Conan had made a promise to Bonny and would chop off his arm before he let her down. So today, when he had seen the sun was high in the sky without a cloud in sight, bringing much warmer temperatures, he had told his eldest brother that he was busy and would not be available. Thankfully, Conor had been too occupied to give more than just a *hrmph*, forgoing his lecture on familial responsibilities.

Conan had been looking forward to spending time with his niece. It was the first time Bonny had shown interest in what he would be doing come this spring. He had only a few months left with her and he would cherish every memory they shared. So, when he had announced that today was the day of their outing and learned that they would be taking one of her new friends, Nairne, with them, he had been highly disappointed. Now, he was glad the little girl had come, for she was the only one actually interested in drawing anything.

Bonny tossed her stick on the ground. She pulled up her knees with her arms and rested her chin upon them. "I really don't like to draw," she admitted.

Nairne stopped working on her dirt picture and studied it, obviously not happy with how it had turned out. She picked up the stick to erase the evidence of her inability to execute what was in her mind but was stopped before she could.

Conan took Nairne's stick from her hand. "Why would you want to wipe all your hard work when it is so good?"

Bonny leaned over and nodded. "You draw like Mhàiri."

Nairne took the stick back and used it to smudge part of her work and try again. "It's just a silly drawing," she answered.

"She does draw like Mhàiri, doesn't she?" Conan acknowledged. "And being able to draw like you do, Nairne, isn't silly. You should never stop as long as you like to do it."

"My papa says I should be busy doing other things."

Conan nodded. "Those other things I'm sure are very important, and you should learn to do them and make your papa proud. But you should also know that there is something special about people who can draw what they see."

Bonny tossed her stick as far as she could. "You should draw maps so people know where clans are and how to get to places."

"Aye, she could, but it is also important to be able to just draw pictures that people enjoy and make them smile."

"Like our mamas' tapestries," Bonny offered.

"Do you draw?" Nairne asked.

"In a way," Conan answered. "I draw the maps Bonny was talking about. Do you want to see?"

The little girl bobbed her red head. Conan smoothed a section of dirt with his hand and then, taking Nairne's stick, quickly drew a small map on the ground of McTiernay Castle, its village and the main features surrounding them—the loch, the forest and the mountains.

Nairne looked up at him, her brown eyes large with awe. Then she looked at Bonny, who just shrugged. "I told you he was a good drawer."

Conan shook his head and gave the stick back to Nairne. "Not yet, but I try all the time to get better."

"How?" The question had come from Nairne, who was clearly curious at how one became better at being an artist.

Conan pushed up from the ground to stand up. He leaned against the boulder and looked down. "By asking for help from someone."

"Like Mhàiri," Bonny stated.

"Like Mhàiri," Conan agreed.

Bonny tilted her head to look up at her uncle. She had been curious about something for a while. "Mhàiri used to help you with your drawing all the time. She doesn't anymore. Is that because of what you said when you and Seamus were building her those fancy bookshelves?"

"Aye, she heard some things that she didn't like, *but*," Conan cautioned, "as you know she was *eavesdropping* at the time."

Nairne pushed the stick around his drawing, adding small details here and there. "Do you not want any more lessons?"

Conan took a deep breath. Both girls were young and he could tell them anything to end this line of questioning, but he had never once treated Bonny that way. It was one of the reasons she loved him so much. And her direct, though often child-like, honesty was one of the reasons he enjoyed her company when he tolerated that of so few others.

"Aye. I would like more lessons," he answered honestly. "But that is very unlikely to happen."

Bonny looked up, squinting into the sun. "Why don't you just tell her you're sorry?" she asked innocently. "Brenna always forgives Braeden for coming into our room and making a mess, but not until he says sorry. I don't know why he doesn't just say it right away, but he never does. Why?" Conan could hear the inquisitive tone in her voice and knew that she was being sincere. "Why would Braeden rather be miserable dealing with Brenna being mad at him than just say he was sorry right away?"

Conan sighed and crossed his arms. This seemed to be a reoccurring theme in his life these days. He had told Mhàiri and said as much again at the widows' circle, and she had had mixed feelings about his response. So, if Bonny wanted to know, he was going to tell her what he had told everyone else. "Braeden probably refuses to apologize because Brenna is making him say it."

"But I thought you were supposed to say I'm sorry when you felt bad. I always do."

"That's because you are a girl," Nairne explained. "Boys don't like it when you make them do anything. Whenever I try to make my little brothers do something, they hate it and cause a fit." Nairne moved to stand up.

Bonny joined her wiping the dirt off her hands using her gown. "Is that what happened with you and Mhàiri?"

Conan nodded.

"Then maybe it's a good thing you didn't apologize

to Mhàiri. It would be like saying a lie if you said I'm sorry when you weren't. Just like it would be a lie to let her think you weren't sorry when you really were."

Conan stood still, regarding his beloved niece, digesting the simple truth behind what she had just said. "You know what, Bonny? I'm going to miss you when I leave. More than you will ever know."

Bonny leaned in and hugged him around his middle. "I'll miss you too, Uncle Conan."

Mhàiri and Maegan had sat frozen, eyes wide, barely breathing the entire time Conan, Bonny, and Nairne had been talking.

Brenna had coaxed them away from the warmth of the fire to the outdoors, professing it would be their last chance before the cold winter winds came. That alone had been enough to get Mhàiri to agree. Eventually, Maegan had capitulated, and the three had ventured outside.

Mhàiri had wanted to head to the loch, for she had started a sketch she had yet to finish there. Maegan had wanted to stay close to the castle in case the wind picked up and it became too cold, but it was Brenna who had finally decided where they were to go. Mostly because she would not take no for an answer.

Soon after they had settled down on a large blanket, Brenna had jumped up, saying that she had forgotten something, and then run off to fetch it. Mhàiri had already gotten out her paper and stylus, and Maegan, not wanting to walk all the way to the castle and back again, had decided to remain with Mhàiri.

Mhàiri had been teasing Maegan about Seamus and whether he was finally going to make his feelings known during the festivities when Bonny and Conan's voices could be heard just on the other side of the large rock. The boulder was enormous and no one knew exactly how it got there. There were a few massive rocks randomly found in the area. The most prominent one was by the loch. The boulders, like the big oak, were common meeting points, so Mhàiri had thought nothing of it when Brenna had suggested they sit there that afternoon.

But the moment she had heard Conan's deep baritone sounds she had known that Brenna had laid a trap. It was not until she had seen the shock in Maegan's face that she had believed her friend had not been involved. But she, too, had come to the same conclusion.

Recovering from the jolt, Mhàiri had been about to plop her things down on the ground, stand up, and make her presence known when she heard Conan start to talk about Nairne's ability to draw and how it was a special gift. When he mentioned that it was just as important to create something for people to enjoy as it was to produce a map, tears had formed in her eyes. But it had been the end, the discussion between him and Bonny about why men sometimes don't like to apologize, that had made her finally understand what Conan had been trying to say to her. It wasn't that he was not sorry. He was. But like any normal man, he did not want to be told what to feel or say.

Mhàiri quietly stood up and smoothed out her gown. "Perhaps you and I should stop eavesdropping."

Maegan nodded, and both women stepped around the boulder into Conan's line of sight. He was leaning against the large rock with both his ankles and arms crossed, looking more handsome than any man should.

When he only cocked a brow, she took a deep breath and exhaled. "How long did you know we were there?"

"Not long," he assured her. "I only knew when I heard you stand up. I thought you might be trying to sneak away."

"I thought about it," Mhàiri acknowledged.

Maegan appeared, grumbling. "I was *not* an accomplice to this"—she swirled her finger to include everyone—"supposedly impromptu get-together. Not only is it too cold, but its purpose eludes me."

Conan glanced at Bonny, who quickly looked away, and said, "I think we all know who was behind today's scheme."

Mhàiri looked down to see what the redheaded girl was drawing. And, indeed, a representation of the winter solstice was staring up at her. She wondered what Nairne would be able to accomplish with an actual stylus and decided that she would have to seek her out to show her how to build a cloth board. "So is this what brought you out today?"

Nairne looked up, shaking her head. She pointed a finger at Conan. "He was telling us about maps."

"Very interesting." A bemused smile formed on Mhàiri's lips as she glanced back at Conan. "Do you know in all the times we came out here, you never once told me about your maps or showed me what it is to be a mapmaker? It was always me showing you what I did. Never the reverse."

"Are you asking now?"

"I suppose I am."

Conan studied her for a moment, assessing whether or not she was serious. He must have decided she was, for he pushed himself erect. "First, most scholars do not call those who draw maps mapmakers, but map painters. That is because most have no interest in creating actual maps, but in creating art. Their fabricated symmetry holds little accuracy and certainly nothing that shows where bodies of land and water are. Instead, they illustrate concepts, and almost always religious ones."

Mhàiri was already fascinated. She loved learning anything new and moved to get more comfortable by leaning on the boulder, in the very space he had just vacated.

"Those that aren't religious still are not very useful, for no measurements are used to demonstrate scale. Almost every one I have ever seen does not make use of longitudes and latitudes but instead uses methods that predate Ptolemy and Anaximander."

"Who's Anaximander?"

"He was a Greek philosopher who lived more than two thousand years ago. He was the headmaster of a school and drew what many believe is the first accurate map of the known world. Unfortunately, one of his students, Anaximenes, thought his ideas wrong and put forth that the world was of a rectangular form, instead of round."

Bonny, who had sat back down and was watching Nairne doodle in the dirt, had also been paying attention to what Conan was saying. "What does the world look like?"

"Round," Conan answered. "Maybe like a potato, but it is definitely not flat."

"But how do you know?" Bonny pressed, skepticism lining her voice.

"I've seen proof." He knelt down and found a large, mostly round rock and handed it to Bonny. "Now hold it out from you. Do you see the edge of the rock and how it curves?" She nodded, "Well, the world does the same thing."

"It does?" Mhàiri asked, holding out a rock for herself, mimicking what Conan was showing Bonny.

"Aye. If you ever get a chance to go to the sea, look out at the horizon, and right where the water's edge meets the sky, you will see a line just like you do with the rock. If the world was flat, the line would be straight. But it's not. It bends," Conan explained. He stood back up and went to stand next to Mhàiri. "Now, some think that the bend means the world is just shaped like a flat disk, but Aristotle ended that argument not long after Anaximander."

Mhàiri frowned. She took a few steps and threw her rock, silently impressed with how far it went. She then swiped her hands together to get the dirt off. "I'm not sure how math proves the world is round."

"He didn't just use math, but logic. The lunar eclipse, for example."

"Aye, but that is the moon."

"Then what about the stars?" Conan reached down and picked up the rock that Bonny had discarded and gave it to Mhàiri. He then picked up a small pebble and held it high above the rock. "Think about the stars when you travel. They are not in the same place." He pointed to a place on the rock. "Let's say this is the world and you were standing here. You look straight up and there are the stars." He wiggled the pebble. "But if you go to a different spot, when you look up, they would be in a different place. And if you go far enough"—he moved his finger to the other side— "you would not be able to see them at all, but new ones." Mhàiri's mouth parted with understanding.

"And *that* is why ships always seem to sink as they move away out of view."

"Amazing," Mhàiri said with heartfelt wonder.

Conan chucked the pebble and then took the rock from her palm, sending it far past the one Mhàiri had thrown earlier. "And it is not only Aristotle who thinks the world is round. I haven't read it, but a man named Elucidarius wrote a book that is supposed to have evidence that we live on a sphere. And Johannes de Sacrobosco's work was based on Ptolemy."

"Who's Ptolemy?"

Conan began to walk to where he'd thrown the rocks. Mhàiri grabbed one of the tartans, threw it across her shoulders, and fell in beside him. "It's his discoveries that are going to enable me to create the maps I want. Because the world is round and drawings are flat, it is intrinsically very difficult to capture land accurately."

"That might be one of the reasons people stopped trying."

"Aye," Conan agreed, kicking one of the smaller stones farther away. "It is much easier to put Jerusalem in the middle of everything and place things randomly around it. But representing the world *is* possible."

"Let me guess. Ptolemy."

A grin lit up Conan's face. "Aye. Ptolemy developed precise methods for identifying exactly where something is on the world. He came up with a coordinate system made up of latitudes and longitudes." Using a stick, he drew a straight line. "If you knew the coordinates . . ." He paused to draw a second line intersecting the first. "You could go to a specific spot anywhere in the world, even if you had never before been there."

Mhàiri stared at the spot where the two lines met and then back up at Conan, her eyes wide with astonishment. "Is that really true?"

Conan nodded. "Ptolemy assigned coordinates to more than eight thousand locations and put them into a book, *Geographia*."

"And you plan to do the same thing, but for Scotland."

Conan bobbed his head again. "That is my dream."

"I now see what you meant about drawings needing to have real value. If you really could create such maps, they would be very powerful pieces of information."

"I was wrong to say that. The world also needs more beauty in it. Not everything has to have a tangible benefit."

Mhàiri gasped. She stopped short and grabbed his forearm. "Did I hear you right?"

It took a second for him to comprehend Mhàiri's question. With a smirk, he answered, "You heard me say I was wrong, *not* that I was sorry."

Mhàiri shrugged as a smile tipped the corners of her mouth and grew from there. "I know. And I think hearing you admit you were wrong sounds sweeter than an apology."

Conan chuckled. "You'll never know."

He stared down into her eyes, and Mhàiri's body responded to his seductive gaze. She could feel herself start to sway closer and forced herself to step back. "Um, uh, how did you become so interested in maps?"

Conan stared at her with mixed feelings. "Father Lanaghly, seeing that I've always been interested in books and learning, usually brought me with him when he went to visit other priests. About nine or ten years ago, we went to one abbey where there was a visiting scholar from Italy who was similarly fascinated with the idea of capturing the world on paper. He told me of the travels of Marco Polo and the faraway places to which he had been, and at that moment I knew what I wanted to do. So I stayed there and learned everything he had to teach me about maps, their origin, and history. Since then, I continued my studies, especially anything that was associated with Ptolemy and how to calculate coordinates."

They continued walking and talking, and Conan answered all her questions about how he intended to capture the various topography he might encounter. They were still debating certain difficulties when a strong breeze came up and Mhàiri began to rub her arms. "I think the wind is getting colder."

Conan nodded and went to tell Bonny and Nairne to pack things up, that they were returning to the castle, but no one was in sight. "When did they leave?"

Mhàiri smiled. "Some time ago. Maegan was not in the mood for an outing in the first place. They said good-bye, but you were telling me about how Aristotle proved the world was round."

Now that Mhàiri mentioned it, Conan did faintly recall Bonny saying something to him. Another gust of wind swept across them. "We should head in."

Mhàiri nodded and tried to tuck wisps of her hair back. "I hope this breeze doesn't mean rain is coming. I've never been to a bonfire, and I don't want it to be canceled."

Conan looked up and sniffed. "I detect no moisture, just the cold." Mhàiri shivered, emphasizing his point. "Come on, let's get you back to the castle and indoors."

Mhàiri fell in beside him, her own long strides easily

keeping up with his. Her mind was spinning on all that Conan had said, going back to even their first conversations on their ride from the priory. "I was wondering something about your maps."

Conan was rubbing his hands together and blowing into them for warmth. "And that was?" he prompted.

"You mentioned that you wanted to include enough detail so that someone could use them to know what the land looked like at that very spot."

"Aye, that is why I asked you to give me lessons."

"But the map I saw in your chambers was of a large area. It would be impossible to capture the overall shape of the land, *and* include that level of detail."

Conan sighed. "I know. I'm still trying to figure out a way to address that issue. Symbols might work, but I might just have to accept that I won't be able to capture as much as I would like on a single sheet of vellum."

"Have you ever considered including a symbol where you want to show more detail? That symbol could be related to a specific drawing. Then, if someone wanted to see more of that area, they could flip to a particular drawing. Then, the main map would not be cluttered with information some may not be interested in."

Conan began to rub his hands together vigorously. Excitement coursed through him, for it was the perfect solution. "You know what this means." He gave her his most dazzling smile. "I need more lessons."

Mhàiri lifted her lashes and found herself looking up into laughing eyes. The happy glint in the bright blue pools was enough to make her racing heart to skip a beat. "We'll begin again after Christmastide," she promised.

Chapter Ten

Bonny flopped onto her bed and groaned. "It's *never* going to work."

"Of course it will," Brenna said dismissively as she pulled the thick tartan around her shoulders tightly and sat down in front of the fire. "I told you what happened. Today was a complete success."

Bonny grabbed her pillow and started tossing it in the air and then catching it. "You said they didn't kiss."

"I said they *almost* kissed," Brenna clarified, trying to keep her teeth from chattering.

Normally the cold did not bother her, but she had been outside a long time spying on everything that had happened after she had exited Maegan and Mhàiri's company before they realized what she had done. And based on what she had witnessed, Mhàiri was not going to be mad at her either.

"Seeing them *almost* kiss proves that our plan is working, Bonny."

"Well, Mama *almost* figured it out today. She came looking for you."

Brenna jumped to her feet and went to stand over Bonny. "What did you say?"

Unfazed by her sister's malevolent stare, Bonny said, "I told her the truth. That you were with Uncle Conan and Mhàiri."

"Why did you do that? Now Mama will be suspicious and start asking questions! If she learns that Uncle Conan and Mhàiri are about to get together, she will do something to ruin things again!"

Bonny threw the pillow in her older sister's face to get her to back away. "What should I have said?" Bonny yelped, seeing Brenna prepare for revenge. "She would have found out the truth if I said something else! This way, Mama knew you were safe and didn't keep looking for you."

Brenna considered that rationalization and then threw the pillow back down forcefully before returning to her blanket and the fire.

"Well, all we have to do now is make Uncle Conan heroic."

"Everyone already knows he's brave."

Brenna shook her head. "He needs to do a heroic act to be a hero."

Bonny grunted. "That's going to be impossible."

"Why?" Brenna challenged.

"How are we going to create a situation where Uncle Conan can be a hero? Do you know how hard it was to get him to go outside the castle today? And now that he knows I tricked him, he's going to suspect everything I say." Bonny turned on her side and propped her head up with her hand. "And both Mhàiri and Maegan are going to be worse."

Brenna tapped her chin. "I've thought about that," she said with a smile. "And you're right. *We*"—she pointed to Bonny and then herself—"can't do it."

Bonny's eyes grew wide. "Not Mama."

Brenna shook her head in agreement. "I was thinking about someone Mhàiri and Conan would never suspect," she said as her impish grin grew even larger.

"You want me to do *what?*" Maegan gasped. "You cannot be serious."

Brenna gave what she hoped to be her newest ally her most infectious grin and bobbed her head. "Will you do it?"

Maegan's head pulled back as if she were trying to avoid someone's fist. "Of *course* I won't do it."

She had come up to the girls' bedchambers to talk to them about their antics that afternoon, not get drawn into another one of their schemes. All their eavesdropping and plotting was stirring up trouble, and if it did not stop, someone was going to get hurt. Maegan had intended to give them one last warning with a promise that if they instigated any more surprises their father was going to be told. Maegan normally would have gone to Laurel about the situation, but Conor had made it very clear that no one, and he meant *no one*, was to unduly stress his wife. And Maegan had no idea whether Laurel would be angry, or secretly delighted that her daughters were following in her matchmaking footsteps.

She had barely taken two steps inside the room when Brenna had squealed with excitement upon seeing her. Unable to utter even a single word of her lecture, Maegan had been guided to one of the chairs and forced to listen to the craziest matchmaking plan ever concocted.

"Brenna," Maegan began, trying to ignore the little

girl's hopeful look. "I think it is sweet that you want to bring Mhàiri and Conan together, but it will never work."

Brenna giggled. "But it *is* working." Seeing the continued doubt in Maegan's eyes, she gave her best evidence to prove she was right. "Mhàiri and Conan almost *kissed* today. Their mouths were that far apart." She created an inch of space between her index finger and her thumb. "And they would have if Mhàiri had not taken a step back."

Maegan licked her lips. Mhàiri had forgotten to include *that* little detail in her summary of what had transpired after she, Bonny, and Nairne had left for the warmth of the castle's fires. "How do you know?"

Brenna raised her shoulders along with her hands. "I was there," she answered with an impish grin.

Maegan closed her eyes and looked upward, praying silently for both patience and guidance. Someday, Brenna was going to hear something she should not and get into serious trouble. Her only hope to avoid that fate was to break this awful habit of hers.

"Brenna, you were out there that *entire* time?" When she nodded, Maegan sought for calm and said, "It's too cold to be outside for so long, and you could have gotten very ill. But more importantly, your uncle would have been furious to learn that you had been spying on him out there."

"It's not like I wanted to be there," Brenna announced in her defense. "But there was no other way to know if our plan was working or if we had to do honorable all over again. But it *did* work." Brenna got to her feet and held out four fingers. "Mhàiri wanted someone who was honest"—Brenna pulled

down one finger, "kind"—a second finger disappeared—
"honorable"—down came a third—"and a hero." She
waved her remaining index finger at Maegan. "That's
the only one we still need to do to prove to Mhàiri that
she can fall in love with Uncle Conan."

Maegan slunk back into her chair. With her elbow
on the sidearm, she rested her forehead in her hand.
If only love were that easy to turn off and on. Sometimes she wished she could simply dismiss what she felt
for Clyde and find happiness and love with someone
else . . . maybe even Seamus. But it was not that easy.

Peeking out from her hand, she asked, "Why do you
want them together so badly?"

Brenna breathed in deeply and exhaled. "I want
Uncle Conan to be happy before he leaves. It is his
turn to fall in love and get married. Until Mhàiri, I
didn't think it possible, but she liked him when no one
else ever did. She just needs to fall in love with him."

"But how do you know that Conan loves her?"

"He keeps kissing her," Bonny answered.

Maegan swung around. "What does that prove? Lots
of men kiss women, and while you may want it to mean
love, it often doesn't . . . especially in the case of your
uncle."

Bonny, who was lying on her stomach with her head
on the heels of her palms, shook her head. "They all
kissed *him*. He never kissed them. The only women he
ever kissed were the two widows that live outside the
village."

Maegan's jaw dropped an inch. "How . . . how do
you know them?" she asked even though she knew the
answer.

"I heard him tell Seamus once," Bonny replied.

"Uncle Conan was mad that Seamus believed all the soldiers' chatter about him being with lots of women just because lots of women had chased him."

Maegan was shocked. She had been one of those people, and she was sure that Laurel was among them as well. "Why did Conan never say anything?"

"He didn't want to," Bonny answered. "He thought the rumors would help keep women away and he *especially* didn't want Mama to find him a wife."

Maegan felt her jaw tighten. Once again, she had been played. It did not matter that she understood Conan's reasons, but that he had successfully fooled all of them about his nonexistent exploits was rankling. "So you think because Mhàiri is the first one he has kissed—"

"More than once," Brenna chimed in.

"—more than once, that Conan is in love with her."

Brenna nodded. Maegan looked back at Bonny, who was also nodding. "I don't think he knows it though," the seven-year-old added. "Or if he even wants to be, but he looks exactly like Uncle Craig and Uncle Crevan did when they were in love."

A disturbing thought came to Maegan. "How do you know they kissed before?"

"Mhàiri told you about the one that happened just before she went on a picnic and I saw the last one. If you had seen them, you would want them together, too. They kiss like Mama and Papa do."

Maegan swallowed at the idea that Brenna, whom she loved like a little sister, had secretly witnessed what sounded to be a very heated embrace. "You were there? Because Mhàiri told me she had opened the passageway and made sure *you* were not around."

Brenna bit her bottom lip, realizing her mistake.

"There is more than one secret area in a lot of rooms. I don't know where they all are either. She won't tell even me," Bonny chimed in, hoping to make Maegan feel better for not knowing about the second secret hiding spot. "Why don't you want Mhàiri and Uncle Conan to be together?"

Maegan's eyebrows rose as she searched for an adequate answer. Finding none, she finally said, "It's not that I don't want them together. I just think they would get mad if they found out that people were trying to trick them into falling in love. Love should find its own way."

Brenna scoffed and crossed her arms. "Then it will never happen. They don't have years, like Craig and Meriel did, to figure out that they should be more than friends. Mhàiri and Conan are leaving in the spring! That's why they need our help."

"Uncle Conan won't be mad if Mhàiri and he get together. He's nicer when he's around her. And Mhàiri would be happier if she were with Conan. She doesn't really want to go with her father."

Now that was something Maegan knew for certain was incorrect. "Aye, she does. Mhàiri has told me several times how she never wanted to marry."

Bonny looked unconcerned. "She just doesn't want to live in a house and never go anywhere. Uncle Conan is never going to live in one place and is going to travel all the time. He could make her happy, but she won't believe it unless we can finish her list."

Maegan realized she was nodding her head and immediately stopped. She could not believe she was being sucked into their logic.

"And that's why we need your help. All we have left is hero, and we can't prove Uncle Conan is one without you."

Maegan rose to her feet and wagged her finger. "But it's not me you really want. You think I can get Seamus to agree, but he won't. It will be a waste of time even asking. I can promise you there is no way he would agree to any part of your plan."

Brenna would not be daunted. "He would if you asked him."

Maegan pursed her lips together. She believed Brenna was wrong, but part of her wondered if she really did have that kind of power over Seamus.

Since she could remember, she had loved Clyde. And she still did. But lately, it had been very hard to keep from also falling for Seamus. The man was kind, handsome, funny, and most importantly, *here*. And something deep inside her knew that he would always be there for her. Whereas Clyde had proven that he would not. She refused to let Clyde go, yet she did not want to even entertain the notion of seeing Seamus woo another woman. Even if it was all part of Brenna's crazy plan.

"Maybe, but I'm not going to put him in a position of saying no." Even though that was what she would want to hear, he might say yes if only to keep from disappointing her. It was truly a no-win situation for both her and him.

Brenna's expression hardened, and her normally clear gray eyes turned into dark storm clouds as frustration sank in. She had to find something to convince Maegan to help Mhàiri, and as that thought entered her mind, another did as well. Something she remembered her mama telling her friend Aileen. The easiest way to persuade someone to do something was to show them why it was in their best interest.

Brenna began to pace, thinking of all the things Maegan wanted that were in her power to give or make happen. Problem was she was only ten years old. She had no power . . . only information.

Brenna stopped in front of Maegan and looked her dead in the eye. "What if I promised not to listen to you again while Mhàiri and Conan are still here?"

Maegan opened her mouth to dismiss the bribe, but then closed it again when she was struck with the possibilities. This potential compromise had enormous merit. "Promise me forever."

Brenna's eyes got huge. "*Forever?*" she wailed softly in pain. "That's a very long time."

Maegan nodded. "It's forever. As in never again." Just the sound of it was making Maegan excited. Privacy. She had not realized until tonight how little of it she had if Brenna had a mind to spy on her. She suddenly wanted this deal quite badly. "If I ask Seamus to help, you promise to not spy on me for the rest of your life, *even* if he refuses."

Brenna's shoulders slumped even more. "But you have to *really* try and convince him."

Maegan smiled an evil smile. "I think I could if you are willing to make the same promise to him. If Seamus agrees to do his part in your little plan, you have to promise never to eavesdrop on him either."

Brenna threw her head back as if she was struck. "That's not fair. After Mhàiri and Conan leave, you and Seamus will be the only interesting people around here."

Maegan licked her lips, worried that her harsh stipulations might be too onerous for someone who thrived on listening to gossip. But the idea of Brenna never eavesdropping on her again was a prize she desperately wanted. "If you find yourself too bored, you could always ask to visit your uncle Cole. Fàire Creachann is a huge castle, and you know a lot of people there— Jaime, Donald, Brighid, and your aunt Ellenor. Just imagine what fun you could have visiting them."

Maegan felt a twinge of remorse because she had no doubt that because of her suggestion, Brenna would somehow find her way north to her uncle's home for an extended visit.

Brenna's head snapped back up as if the weight of the world was no longer on her shoulders. Her gray eyes were twinkling, and Maegan's guilt melted away when she heard two words.

"I agree."

"You want me to do *what?*" Seamus sneered in disbelief. "You must be mad." He blinked and shook his head as the dozens of reasons why her suggestion was inconceivable ran through his mind.

Maegan waved her hands back and forth in denial. "*I* don't want you to do anything. Brenna and Bonny do."

"But you must want me to agree to be asking."

"That's not true," Maegan strongly denied and reached out to clutch his forearm so he could feel the truth. "I think their plan is as outrageous as you do. I refused to get involved, but then Brenna promised me that she would *never eavesdrop on me again.*" Her sky-blue eyes were large with delight at the concept. "How could I refuse just for asking you a question?"

"That I can understand, but there is no way I am going to seek out Mhàiri and pretend to be interested in her during the festivities in order to make Conan jealous."

Maegan winced. "It's a *little* more than that. You have to try and kiss her. Brenna has some notion that if Conan witnessed this, that he would step in and become the 'hero' they believe Mhàiri wants."

Seamus stood frozen with his arms crossed, unblinking, for several long seconds at Maegan. "You cannot be serious."

Maegan bit her bottom lip. "They believe Mhàiri loves him but will only admit it once they prove Conan is honest, kind, honorable, and a hero. They say they've done the first three, and all they need now is to show that he is indeed a hero. Hence, Mhàiri needs to be 'saved' from your advances."

Seamus tilted his head upward and studied the ceiling rafters of the lower hall. It was the one place Conor had made sure there were no secret passageways, hidden rooms, or obscure places for Brenna to hide in. This was where he held his meetings with his commanders and other lairds when they were visiting and the discussion was serious. He had not barred the hidden spots in the Star Tower. It was rare, but if a fire broke out and the stairwell was blocked—or if, God forbid, the castle was attacked and somehow invaded— Conor wanted a way to get his family out of the tower, from any room, to safety.

"I doubt they've proven he's kind," Seamus mumbled. "And as far as jealousy? I don't think Conan is capable of the emotion."

"Simply because someone has not been jealous over someone before does not mean he wouldn't be."

Seamus looked back down. "Are you talking about

you or Conan?" A piece of him hoped Maegan would admit that she would not like seeing him seek the attentions of another woman.

Maegan lifted her chin. "Conan of course." She may not think Brenna's idea would work, but she did believe Conan felt something a lot more than friendship for Mhàiri based on his reactions both during and after their fights. "Why would I be jealous when I know it is all a ruse?"

Seamus lifted a single brow. "You really think Conan is going to stop me from kissing Mhàiri when he didn't with Loman."

Maegan took a step back and threw up her hands. "What do we care if it works? Brenna's promise is not based on success. We simply need to try. The only reason I am doing this is for privacy. I would think you might want that too."

Seamus looked back down and studied Maegan as if he was trying to discern whether he should read more meaning into her last comment. Agreeing would mean they would *both* have privacy. Something he would definitely want and be willing to do almost anything to get, with Brenna seemingly everywhere. But only if Maegan was seriously considering letting go of the possibility of Clyde ever returning.

"And why would I want privacy, Maegan? Right now, I'm not doing anything Brenna would care to listen to, so are you saying that might change?"

"I don't know," she answered honestly. "But all this talk about Mhàiri and Conan deserving to be happy is making me think that I deserve that too."

Seamus took a step forward and leaned down until

his face neared hers. "Assuming that's true, I'll do it. But when this is all over, be prepared, Maegan."

Maegan stared into his eyes and swallowed. She did not need to ask what he meant.

She knew.

Chapter Eleven

"The sword dance is next," Callum said with a wink, handing Mhàiri a mug of ale. "Dance with me?"

Mhàiri laughed and her eyes began to gleam with anticipation. "You mean dance *against* you!" she said, taking the cup. "I think the only reason you like to dance next to me is that I make you look good."

"I *am* good, and that is not the only reason I like to dance next to you. It's because I am the envy of every man in the room when I do."

"You're incorrigible."

Callum winked. "I'm going to get the swords."

He disappeared into the crowd. Mhàiri leaned back against the wall of the great hall and took a sip of the cool ale. Tomorrow was Epiphany and the last day of the Christmastide festivities. She did not want to think about all the merriment coming to an end. The holiday season could last another week, and she would still not want it to be over. Never had she had so much fun, and it saddened her to think that this might be her only chance to enjoy the twelve days of Christmas as they were meant to be experienced. Traveling merchants did not have celebrations with large bonfires, dancing, and feasts like those held by clans.

Long-time McTiernay ally Rae Schellden, his two daughters who had married twin McTiernay brothers, and his grandson Shaun had arrived the night the celebrations started. Unfortunately, their stay was not going to be an extended one. Though Mhàiri had only met Raelynd and Meriel—Crevan and Craig's wives—a few days ago, she already considered them friends. Both women were not just lovely, but also highly spirited and mischievous. Nothing was more comical than watching them interact with their husbands.

They had the kind of relationship she would want—if she ever were inclined to make a marital commitment. Neither wife nor husband capitulated to the other when riled, and one could not help but see the great love and respect the two couples had for each other. They gave and supported, but when provoked, they also stood up to the other. Craig and Crevan did not dictate to their wives—though they periodically tried—and Meriel and Raelynd did not harangue their husbands, though they were not above various forms of persuasion.

The most joyful of the four was Raelynd. She was pregnant with her first child, which was due in late spring. It had been quite a massive effort for Raelynd to convince Crevan to let her come. She had been pregnant before and lost the child, and that fear never really quite left either of their minds. So Raelynd did not argue when Crevan announced that they would be leaving the day after Epiphany. But, like Mhàiri, Raelynd did not want to think about the days after the merriment was over; she only wished to focus on enjoying the little time there was left.

Raelynd had sat with the similarly pregnant Laurel in the great hall much of the time, each keeping the other company, watching everyone as they drank and danced. Mhàiri found watching them amusing, especially Laurel. Lady McTiernay, despite growing large with child, practically danced from her chair. Her light blond hair swung about, for she could not keep her feet still when the music played. But it was when the swords began to appear that a much greater level of excitement shone in her normally storm-colored eyes.

The sword dance had grown into something of a unique rivalry between the Schellden and McTiernay clans, having evolved into a challenge of endurance. The music would start and members of each clan would pound the floor to an ever-increasing tempo, deftly hopping among the quarters made by crossing two broadswords. The music would continue until only one person was left and declared the champion. The clan that claimed the winner also claimed bragging rights that they exercised whenever possible until the next festivity and sword dance.

For years, only men had participated, but one night Laurel had decided to join them, having failed to understand why women had been excluded from even trying. Honestly believing she did not have a chance at lasting very long, let alone winning the challenge, the men from both the McTiernay and Schellden clans had allowed her to join the competition, mostly to prove their assumptions true. To everyone's surprise—except Laurel's—she had won. Ever since then, clanswomen had participated in the sword dance.

Maegan, who had never won but had come close a few times, had warned Mhàiri ahead of time about what was to come. For days leading up to Christmastide, the two women had practiced the steps. After ten nights of hopping around for a quarter of an hour, she was getting better, but she would have to more than double that time to ever have a chance at winning. It would take months to build up a level of endurance to be anything close to competitive. But it did not matter. Mhàiri loved the dance.

During her first sword dance, Callum came up and introduced himself. Mhàiri recognized the name and knew immediately he was the Schellden guard whom Maegan kept mentioning—and for good reason.

Callum was startlingly handsome for a Highland soldier. Several of the McTiernay men were very good looking, but Callum attracted the eye of every woman around him, Mhàiri included. Possessing a classic rugged bone structure, unusual turquoise-colored eyes, and thick dark auburn hair, Callum was almost too handsome. But it was more than his looks that drew women to his side. One could tell just by looking at him—how he walked, stood, and spoke with soft authority—that he could take care of himself and anyone he cared for.

So, when Callum had begun to flirt with her, Mhàiri could not help but be flattered. But she was surprised to discover that there was much more to the man than an attractive smile and gorgeous body. Callum was honest, fair, and extremely witty. She was always entertained when he was around and therefore never felt compelled to avoid his company. And since Conan had been in a disagreeable mood since practically the festivities had begun, she had been in Callum's company a lot.

Mhàiri had tried a few times to pull Conan out of his surly mindset and get him to join her in some of the diversions, but he had made it clear that he would rather be left alone to sulk. So she had honored his unsaid request. This Christmastide was her first with festivities, and she had refused to let them be ruined by his churlish attitude. There was too much fun to be had, and she was determined to relish every second.

By the third night of revelry, however, Mhàiri began to realize Conan was not alone in his strange behavior. Bonny and Brenna, who had been her two shadows for weeks, were suddenly never around. Mhàiri only saw them here and there, and each time only briefly. At first, she was concerned they were up to a new scheme, but after a couple of nights of dancing, drinking and laughing, she no longer cared. If the two girls were hatching a plan, it would soon be known. And if that plan included Conan, it was sure to fail. So, Mhàiri stopped worrying about them.

She could not say the same for Seamus and Maegan, however. Those two were almost always together, which at first was encouraging until Mhàiri realized they were rarely smiling. What was really bothersome was their frowns were usually aimed in her direction, as if they were anxious about something.

Thinking it was Callum's attention that had them concerned, Mhàiri had tried to assure them that the handsome soldier and she were simply enjoying each other's company. That while Callum might be a bit over-the-top with his flattery, it was all in fun. They both knew he would be returning with the Schelldens when Christmastide was over. Unfortunately, her reassurances seemed to do very little to relieve the apprehensive looks on either Maegan or Seamus's faces. So, again, Mhàiri had decided to put her concerns aside as much as possible, and focus on having fun.

* * *

Maegan pulled the blanket up and tucked it around Bonny's sweet face. She looked so tired, but also determined. After eleven nights of festivities, Laurel was getting tired earlier in the night. Being pregnant, she was not running around like she normally did and therefore had been able to keep a much closer eye on her daughters. This year, they had not been able to wander about like they had in the past. So, when Laurel had wanted to leave hours before the feast would be drawing to a close, both girls had begged to stay with Maegan.

Maegan had agreed despite knowing that they would confront her later. For Seamus had yet to corner Mhàiri for that ill-fated kiss, and Brenna and Bonny wanted to know why.

"Seamus isn't going to do it, is he?" Bonny asked, with a yawn.

Brenna grabbed a blanket, wrapped it around her shoulders, and sat on Bonny's bed, waiting for Maegan to answer.

Maegan did not like to disappoint them, especially as she and Seamus had told them that they would try, but in this case, she just could not fault Seamus for deciding that he couldn't fulfill his promise.

Each night, she and Seamus had huddled together and talked about the best way to approach Mhàiri, what he could say, and how to best entice her away from the crowd. Once he approached Mhàiri, Maegan was to give a signal to Brenna, who would be responsible for convincing Conan to come out and intervene. But there had never been a perfect time, and tonight, Seamus had admitted that he just could not do it.

"I can't, Maegan. I know I said I would, but it feels wrong. It's a lie. I cannot do that to either Conan or Mhàiri. You and she are close, but I also like her and don't want to lose our friendship, not to mention Conan's. There are other ways to deal with Brenna."

Maegan had leaned into Seamus and buried her face in his chest with his admission, relief flooding her every limb. She had pushed those same feelings aside, trying to stay focused on the positives, but that first night, when they had looked at Mhàiri with the intention of trying to deceive her, she had known deep down it was wrong.

Seamus had wrapped his arms around her, and it had felt so good and surprisingly right. Maegan had not wanted to move, to ever leave their haven, and would not have if Seamus had not gently separated them. "But I do have an idea." Using his chin, he had pointed to Callum, who was once again talking and laughing with Mhàiri. "What about Callum?"

Maegan had leaned back. "Callum?"

"Aye, he wouldn't be pretending to have an interest in Mhàiri. It's real, and it would not be a surprise either. I bet if an opportunity arose, he would take advantage. I know I would."

That had really got Maegan's attention, and she had stepped totally out of his embrace. "You would?"

He had reached out and clutched her hand and said, "If it were the right woman and I thought for a moment that it would be welcomed."

Maegan had not known what to say and only swallowed. Then, with a brief glance at Callum and Mhàiri, she had asked, "So what do you propose?"

Maegan briefly explained Seamus's idea to Brenna and Bonny and waited as the two girls mulled it over.

If Brenna agreed Callum was a suitable substitute, she was still going to hold the ten-year-old to her promise of privacy.

Brenna finally nodded. It was probably more from lack of options, but she agreed. "Use the same signal to let us know when we need to get Uncle Conan."

Conan stood impassively as Mhàiri sashayed up to him, her luscious pink lips wearing a large smile. Once again, she was more beautiful than any woman had a right to look, in his opinion.

A natural blush shaded her high cheekbones, made only more attractive with her olive complexion. Pale green eyes framed with dark lashes were full of mirth as she looked at him. Then the smell of sunshine and grass, mixed with the sweetness of flowers, washed over him, and he felt his lower body grow painfully hard as the feeling of her in his arms flooded his memory. Mhàiri had not even said a word, and yet once again he was trying to quash the rush of sexual desire that stirred in him whenever she was near.

Could one kiss really ruin a person's life? Conan feared that was what had happened to him. Never had he thought it possible to desire a woman so much. Beautiful women were dangerous creatures, and this time it was he who had fallen prey to Mhàiri's charms. It was getting so he dreaded going to sleep. Not a night went by that he did not dream of her. And during the day, it was no better.

The very first night of Christmastide, when Mhàiri had arrived with Maegan, his stomach had turned completely sour. She had worn a deep blue ankle-length chainse with a rich gold-colored bliaut over it.

A band of intricate needlework circled the long sleeves, hem, and belt of the tunic. The ensemble clung to her breasts like honey. The gold intensified her exotic features and brought out the rich dark brown of her hair, which was styled mostly in a soft updo, with the rest hanging in a single curl off to one side.

When Mhàiri had entered the hall, he had seen all the heads swivel to see who was causing a stir. But Schellden's guard, whom women had declared the ideal man for years, had been the most enamored and taken with her beauty. Mhàiri, however, had not immediately returned his admiration, which had only fueled Callum's efforts to get her attention.

Conan had told himself that he did not care. Mhàiri was not his to claim. She was not even his to court. There was no room for a woman in his future. So he had rebuffed her encouragement to join the fun, electing instead to stand and watch as men drooled all over themselves to spend some time with her.

How he wished he could just forgo attending, but this was the last Christmastide he would spend at his home with his brothers for probably several years. If he was to disappear, they would find him, drag him back, and pepper him with questions until he admitted being troubled because of a woman.

Tonight was Epiphany and marked the end of his suffering, thank God. Watching Mhàiri and Callum together had been torture. As the supposed definition of perfection, Callum could have any woman he wanted . . . and he wanted Mhàiri. Tonight was no different.

She wore an emerald-colored bliaut that once again hugged her figure, leaving little to the imagination.

Strings of tiny crystals crisscrossed along the neckline. She was mesmerizing in it, and from across the room, Conan could see the look of blatant desire on Callum's face.

The man's appreciation had grown into something much more potent. One only had to look at him to discern what he was thinking and whom he wanted. It was enough to cause Conan to have doubts about facts he knew were true.

Had Mhàiri changed her mind about leaving in the spring? Did she still wish to remain free of commitment? If so, had she told Callum that? Conan believed he knew the answers. Nothing had changed. Mhàiri was still just as determined to avoid the trappings of a home and marriage as he was.

He hoped.

"It's the last dance," Mhàiri pleaded. "Come, Conan. Join us for the sword dance. Craig claims you are awkward and always one of the first to drop out. I know him to be wrong. Prove me right."

Conan was on the verge of agreeing when Callum approached her side and whispered in her ear that he had their swords ready.

"Thank you," Mhàiri whispered back. "I'll be there in a minute." Callum, taking the hint, left, but he kept his gaze on Mhàiri. She, however, was looking at Conan expectantly. "You coming?"

"Nay. You go entertain your latest beau. I wouldn't want to interfere with your plans to conquer and discard the hopes of yet another unsuspecting soldier."

Mhàiri swallowed, clearly hurt by the slight and knowing that it had been intentional. Conan saw the tears filling her eyes and immediately felt guilty. He had just wanted her to leave. To take her enticing floral scent and alluring flesh that beckoned him to abandon his dreams, and just go. But he had done more than that.

He had hurt her.

And there was nothing he could do about it now.

The music started, and suddenly the last thing Mhàiri wanted to do was dance. She just wanted to seek out a place that Conan was not.

Mhàiri cut through the crowd and headed to the Warden's Tower and her bedchambers—the one place that was not infested with people and their levity.

She knew Conan had said those things not because he actually believed them, but because he had wanted to hurt her. Wanted her to leave. Maybe even wanted her to cry. But what she could not fathom was why.

Mhàiri reached the tower, entered the bottom floor, and was about to head up the stairwell when strong fingers curled around her upper arm. She stopped and turned around. She was surprised to see Callum there looking concerned.

"I heard what Conan said, Mhàiri. He was a *thòin* to cause you pain when you have done nothing wrong."

"But I have if I made you think that I wanted something more than friendship."

Callum took a step closer so that he stood in front of her. If she took in a deep breath, her chest would touch his. "Is it Conan?" he asked, tucking away a stray lock of her hair. "Sounds as if he might have designs on marrying you himself, even though I know at one time he was against the idea of permanently tying himself to anyone. But a woman like you can make a man change his mind."

Mhàiri stared up into Callum's sea-colored eyes. "You're wrong," she whispered.

Callum cupped her cheek. "You are so beautiful."

Mhàiri swallowed. "Thank you."

"I want to kiss you, Mhàiri, and make you happy again."

"Callum, I like you and I've enjoyed our time together, but I'm not looking for a husband."

His thumb moved along her cheekbone. The soft caress was so tender she could barely find her breath. "That's fine, Mhàiri. I'm not ready for a wife. But your lips have been tempting me since the first moment I saw you, and I can think of no more pleasurable way to end Christmastide."

Mhàiri had known Callum had been waiting for such an opportunity for the last few nights, and she had intentionally made sure to avoid circumstances that would give him one. Conan's kisses had left her with absolutely zero interest in another man's touch. But after his cutting remark, she needed kindness. She needed to feel desired, and Callum was offering both without the pressure of something more.

So when he put his hands to her cheeks, held her face, and drew her mouth to his, she let him.

The kiss, like Loman's, was pleasant, but that was all. Once again, it stirred nothing in her, and Mhàiri knew she would not long for another. For the moment their lips touched, she knew. She had not been certain before, but she knew now.

She loved Conan.

And there would never be another man for her.

Chapter Twelve

Mhàiri was about to ask Callum to stop for the second time when suddenly there was a grunt and Callum was no longer there.

He had been kissing her and using his tongue to open her mouth. Mhàiri, however, had wanted the kiss to end. She had put her hands to his chest and mumbled his name, followed by a "Please don't." She had not thought Callum had heard or understood because instead of breaking away, he was pulling her closer.

Unexpectedly free, Mhàiri stumbled back, her eyes darting around to see where Callum had gone. A groan coming from the ground caught her attention, and she realized that it had come from Callum.

"She told you to stop."

Mhàiri's breath hitched in her throat at the deadly tone in Conan's voice. She knew then that Conan must have followed her and, seeing her struggle, punched Callum so hard in the jaw that the man had fallen.

Callum was very good looking, but he was also large and muscular, more so than even Conan. The man was unused to finding himself on the floor and was not taking the idea that he had been pummeled without warning very well. He was furious. His eyes flashed, and Mhàiri could see Callum cock his fists even though he was still on the ground. When he got up, he was going to attack.

Conan knew it too. "Move, Mhàiri," he ordered and got ready.

Mhàiri instinctively did what she was told, but said, "Conan, don't."

He did not look at her. "You said to stop, and Callum is going to learn to do so when a woman says no, especially if that woman is you."

"*You* insult her and then have the audacity to think you can teach *me* on how to treat a woman?" Callum taunted back, now on his feet. "If anyone has ever deserved to be taught a lesson about sensitivity to a woman's feelings, it is you. You've had this coming for a long time, Conan. I'm just delighted to be the one to give it to you."

To Mhàiri's horror, the fight started. Callum was wider and stronger, but Conan was slightly taller and had speed and accuracy. Each blow seemed to land, and both men were ignoring her cries to stop.

Then she saw Seamus leap into the middle, forcing the two men to take a step back or gain a third man in the mix. Thankfully, they did not seem inclined to hit Seamus.

While landing several hits seemed to have calmed Callum's furor, it had done nothing to lessen Conan's. Fury still rolled off him in waves, but instead of restarting the fight, Conan pivoted, gave Mhàiri a long, hard stare filled with betrayal and anguish, and then exited the tower.

Callum wiped the blood off his chin and then said, "This ended a little differently than I had planned, *àluinn*, but thank you for the kiss. I enjoyed it and will remember it with much pleasure." Then he, too, was gone.

Mhàiri felt Maegan's arms go around her frozen frame as she hugged her close. "I'm so, so sorry. That wasn't supposed to happen. If Seamus and I had known . . . oh, I'm so sorry, Mhàiri."

Mhàiri stood there being held by Maegan for several minutes in silence as she slowly processed all that had happened and all that had been said. It was almost too much.

She loved Conan.

Conan had been jealous.

Conan had witnessed her kiss another man and had been enraged.

Any feelings he might have had for her had just been consumed in a flame of his fury.

And somehow Maegan and Seamus were implying they had orchestrated all the events to bring about this result.

"What do you mean, you are sorry, that you never meant for this to happen?" Mhàiri asked in a stilted voice.

Maegan pulled back and tried to explain about Brenna and Bonny. "But there can be no doubt. Conan loves you. He does. He would not have reacted that way if he did not."

"Whatever feelings he has for me, they are gone or

they will be. I know him. He lost control, and he will make sure that never happens again."

Maegan shook her head. "No, he loves you. He wants you."

Mhàiri looked at her friend then, her voice cold and penetrating. "It does not matter. We have no future. Now more than ever."

Maegan's hand flew to her mouth.

Seamus, seeing Maegan begin to tremble because of the pain she thought she had caused Mhàiri, pulled her back against his chest for support. Then, to Mhàiri, he said, "Maegan's right. I wasn't sure until tonight, but I am now. You love Conan, and there can be no doubt that he loves you. He may not want to admit it. He has his whole life planned and never once considered including anyone in those dreams, especially not a wife. But if you love him, find a way to make it work. Find a way to be together and create new dreams that you can share. Find a way or you will both be miserable always knowing that you had met the one you were supposed to be with, but never had the courage to compromise to include them in your life. Because you *will* compromise eventually. We all do in some ways. I just don't want you to look back with regret."

Mhàiri told herself to breathe. She could feel her heart beating rapidly and did not know whether it was from anger or hope. Slowly, she looked at Seamus and then Maegan. "You may be right, but you were wrong to have interfered. Conan and I were in a good place before tonight. Spring is months away, and we had time. We may have figured it out on our own. Right now, things are not better, but far worse. Next time, meddle in your own love affairs and stay out of mine."

* * *

Maegan watched as Mhàiri disappeared up the stairwell. Her heart was breaking for what had happened. She had known Conan might get upset, but not to that extent. He had looked as if he wanted to kill Callum, and Callum's instincts had recognized that and had responded in kind.

"Seamus, what have we done?"

"It doesn't matter. It's done, and now it is up to Mhàiri."

Maegan spun around in his arms. "Why Mhàiri? Why not Conan?"

"Because he can't. He has so many walls around his heart, he is unable to see the truth for himself. Hopefully, Mhàiri saw the truth tonight and will try to find a way to make it work. I know I saw it."

Maegan looked up. "What do you mean?"

Seamus bent his head and took her mouth, answering her question in the way he had dreamed of for months. He kissed her long and hot, hoping to reach the very depths of her soul.

As soon as their lips made contact, the connection between them ran straight through their bodies. Every nerve was awakened by low, inviting passion that took Maegan's breath away.

Seamus felt her shiver in his arms, but she did not pull away. Encouraged, he brushed his mouth persuasively across hers. Maegan was as sweet as honey. Slowly, he swept his tongue along the crest of her lips. He almost groaned aloud when she opened her mouth for his entrance.

Maegan could feel the urgency in Seamus, the

tension in the arms, the rigidity of his shoulders, back, and neck beneath her hands. The power of his mouth on hers ran through her frame to her very fingertips. Unconsciously, she pressed herself against him and followed her instincts to slide her tongue into his mouth. Her fingers mimicked the movement in his hair.

When Maegan leaned into him and kissed him back with growing eagerness, a dam of need broke in Seamus. The kiss quickly changed from a gentle caress to one of wild passion. Soon, their tongues were mating again and again. He was almost mindless with wanting more.

Maegan's heart pounded and her legs trembled. Her stomach was in knots. When Seamus deepened the kiss, the heat of it melted away the last rational thought she had. The feel of his tongue invading her mouth, touching every corner, tasting her, overwhelmed her completely. It felt so incredibly *right*. Like it was a missing piece in her life that she had been denying for way too long. All she could do was cling to him helplessly, letting the sensations take over her mind and soul.

Seamus had meant only to give Maegan a gentle kiss, but what they were sharing was so much more. It was the most incredible kiss he had ever experienced, and he would not have stopped if she had not started trembling.

When he released her, Maegan stood dumbfounded, staring at him with misty eyes filled with passion, and her lips, red and swollen, beckoned him to taste her again. Somehow, he resisted.

"Just like Mhàiri and Conan, you have this set idea for your future, but is it going to make you happy? Or is it time to change those plans and make room for someone who would love you as deeply as any other man ever did or could."

He kissed her forehead, brushing his lips softly against her skin before placing one last soft, tender kiss on her lips. "I love you, Maegan. You've known that, and I've given you time. Now, you need to decide whether that means anything to you."

Seamus left, his heart pounding. He knew that Mhàiri and Conan were both confused and hurting, but if he had to do tonight all over again, he would not change a thing.

Mhàiri stood looking down at the revelry taking place in the courtyard. It would go on for several more hours. Last night, she had been among them. Tonight, the last thing she felt like doing was dancing and making merry. She did not want to be with people, forced to talk and make conversation, but neither did she want to be alone. She felt like a rudderless ship, moving about with no direction or purpose.

A soft knock interrupted her thoughts. Mhàiri sighed. She knew Maegan's heart and that her friend had never intended for tonight to go the way it had, but that did not mean she was ready to talk to her just yet. The knock persisted, and Mhàiri turned from the window to go answer the door, assure Maegan she would be fine, and return to her silent examination of her heart.

But it was not Maegan who was at the door.

"Lady McTiernay!" Mhàiri gasped in surprise. "I . . . I was not aware that you knew I had left."

Laurel offered her an apologetic smile and entered

the room when Mhàiri stepped aside and held open the door. "I saw you leave after speaking with Conan. He has been in a foul mood lately, and seeing your face, I knew he had taken his sullenness out on you, for which I apologize. I should have made him disappear until he could be of good humor, but I had thought the entertainment would pull him from his gloominess and into good cheer. It seems I was wrong."

"I hope I did not alarm you, but I am well," Mhàiri replied, closing the door and reluctantly letting go of the handle. She hoped Laurel was not planning to stay and keep her company. "Conan did say something unpleasant, but I promise that is not the reason I decided to retire early. It was . . . other events that took place this evening that proved to be a little overwhelming. Perhaps I am not used to so many of these types of celebrations."

"Then it is good I came to see you for another reason. One that is sure to bring you some needed cheer to end this Epiphany. News came this evening about your father. He knows you are here and will arrive as soon as the weather permits safe travel. Until then, he has been invited to stay with Conor's brother Colin, who is a laird in the Lowlands."

The message itself was not startling as it changed nothing from what had been anticipated, and yet Mhàiri felt her chest tighten. She loved her father, but deep down she did not want the life of a merchant. It was still limiting. They traveled, but to familiar markets or places where his goods could be bought and sold, never to some of the more isolated, wild, and stunning parts of Scotland. And yet, it was her only alternative outside of becoming a wife and settling down.

Laurel clutched her hands together. "I can tell that

you are tired and would like to rest." She maneuvered around Mhàiri and pulled on the handle to open the door.

Mhàiri jumped a little, realizing that she had been preoccupied with her thoughts. "I, uh, thank you for coming and telling me about my father. And, I wanted to thank you again for letting me stay here for so long. I'm not sure what I would have done if you hadn't."

Laurel turned in the doorway and smiled at Mhàiri. "You would have stayed in your cottage next to the priory until your father could come to you there. It would have been hard, but you are a survivor, Mhàiri. That is why the idea of traveling the world is adventurous to you, whereas to others it would be a terrifying notion."

"Well, I'm glad staying here and not the priory was my fate."

Laurel was about to turn around and leave, when she stopped. "Don't judge Conan too harshly, Mhàiri. Despite what he thinks, I love him very much and only want to see him happy. Unfortunately, he has not a clue what that is."

"I think he does."

"I know the look of true fulfillment, and he has never once experienced that feeling. Oh, he loves his maps and is invigorated by the challenge his plans for his future hold, but they will only bring him partial satisfaction. He does not realize that a person needs to seek out what their heart desires—there is more to life than only avoiding what makes one unhappy. Don't you agree?"

Mhàiri furrowed her brow, puzzled by the unexpected question. Realizing that Laurel was waiting for an answer, she said, "I never really thought about it."

"Unhappiness is an odd thing when you think about it. If you are not happy, then you are in fact unhappy. It is impossible to avoid unless you know what it is that fills your soul and makes you truly content. What I fear most for Conan is that he is so fixated on his idea for a future that he won't seize happiness when he gets the chance because it will mean making a change—one that he promised never to consider." Then, pulling the door closed behind her, Laurel said, "Good night, Mhàiri. See you on the morrow."

Mhàiri did not know how long she stood staring at the door through which Laurel had disappeared. Only her eyes moved, blinking as Laurel's thoughts on unhappiness churned in her mind.

"Laurel is right," she breathed aloud. "She's right."

Mhàiri yanked open the door to her bedchambers and ran out and then down the stairwell. Not caring who saw her, she headed to the North Tower. She raced up four flights of stairs only to stop and catch her breath once she reached Conan's door.

Able to breathe again, she knocked. There was no answer to her second knock as well, but Mhàiri knew he was in there. She had sought sanctuary in her chambers; she knew Conan had gone to his. Mhàiri started banging on the door with the outside of her fist, refusing to stop until Conan let her in.

A few seconds later, Conan yanked the door open. Seeing Mhàiri, he choked back the string of curse words he had almost laid on whom he had thought was Seamus. Recovering from his shock, Conan narrowed his gaze. "What do you want?"

Mhàiri did not wait for an invitation to come in, mostly because she was fairly certain that Conan was never going to issue one. "I think it is clear that I want to talk to you," she replied and went back to his workspace and began to look around.

Conan followed her. "What the hell are you looking for?"

"Bonny? Is she with you? Or even Brenna? Where do they like to hide?"

Conan shook his head. "They are under strict orders to either be in the line of sight of their mother or Aileen until they fall asleep. Brenna may be overly curious, but she won't openly defy her father."

Mhàiri closed her eyes and took a deep breath, for she had dashed over without really having a plan. Coming here and visiting a man alone in his bedchambers at night was definitely not wise, and yet she did not care. She had made a decision to seize not just her happiness, but Conan's.

"You need to leave, Mhàiri. Now." Conan pointed to the door.

Mhàiri did not move. "We need to talk."

"Nay, we don't. If Callum no longer fancies you, then find someone else," he said, hoping his biting remark would get Mhàiri to leave. He had lost control tonight, and if she stayed much longer, he was in danger of losing it again. Her presence was just too much. He needed to distance himself from her and somehow extinguish his feelings. And there was no way he could do that with her standing twenty feet away from his bed. "You do not lack for admirers, only time to spend with all of them."

Mhàiri looked at him but refused to flinch under his icy glare. She knew the truth, and all the coldness rolling off him proved he knew it too. "This is now the third time you have tried to get me to pursue another, and I know that isn't what you want."

Conan took a step closer. A fury of emotions was swirling in his blue eyes. "Why are you here, Mhàiri?"

"Because I don't want to go to anyone but you either."

Conan's heart was beating so hard he could hear it pound in his ears. Mhàiri was in his room, alone, telling him that she wanted him. She was not a fool. She knew what would happen upon such a declaration, and she also knew that in the end it would change nothing. Conan knew he should send her away, but his eyes could not break away from her mouth. She had a great mouth. Perfect. Inviting. *Murt*, he wanted her mouth.

He made an inarticulate sound, and his hands reached out and pulled at her waist, yanking her to him. The moment she was within reach, his lips were on hers. Without hesitation, Mhàiri wrapped her arms around his neck and kissed him fervently back.

Conan slanted his mouth across hers, wanting to cease any thought of whether or not she should or should not be in his arms. She was there. Her arms were holding him close as if they never wanted to let him go.

Conan devoured her lips in a desperate claiming to which she submitted willingly, eagerly. Her fingers explored his hair, and it would not be long before he could not stop at only a kiss. This was leading down a path of commitment, and he had to make sure Mhàiri understood that fate would not be waiting for her when they woke tomorrow.

He bore the sweet torture for another moment before he stepped away. "Leave now, or I won't be responsible for the consequences."

"I'm not leaving."

Conan's eyes searched her face, trying to reach into her thoughts. "You're tempting the devil, and you will get burned. You know how this will end."

"I'm not leaving."

Their eyes held, and he saw the truth of her words right there in the depths of her magnificent green pools. "Damn you! I will not feel guilty on the morrow."

"Neither will I," Mhàiri declared.

Conan's eyes blazed. "Then so be it, for you are going to learn what it means to be mine."

Because that was what Mhàiri was. His.

She would never be his wife, his companion, his *sonuachar*. But nevertheless she was still his. He would claim her in such a way that she would never belong to anyone else.

His control snapped. Jerking her to him, he slammed his mouth down on hers, taking her lips with an intensity that stunned him. Hot and wet, his tongue found hers. He needed to touch her, all of her, and make her writhe with need for the same.

His kisses moved from her lips to her neck. One hand held her head, preventing her from ending their embrace and what was to come. With the fingers of his free hand, he found the ties to her bliaut and freed them. He then eased the gown down her shoulders and let it pool about her waist. Next, he reached for the bow securing her chemise and, with one tug, it broke free. His lips followed, leaving a trail of fiery-hot kisses along her collarbone.

Mhàiri let out a soft, feminine sound. She was not sure what she wanted, but with each kiss, each touch, something stirred inside of her, flooding her with aching demand. She turned and arched toward him, a wordless invitation.

Need slammed into him, hard and painful, but Conan took a deep breath, fought, and won. He wanted to take things slow, but he was already having trouble holding on to his control. His shaft was hard and throbbing to the point of pain, but he wanted to make this good for her. He needed to make this special.

He could see the worry in her beautiful green eyes as she watched him. She bit at her lower lip in a nervous gesture, and his gaze dropped. Mesmerized by the sight, he wanted to bite that lush lip and soothe the sting away with his tongue. Instead, he gently cupped her face, and his thumbs rubbed her cheeks slowly. Conan was overcome by a surge of possessiveness. He would be her first. And he wanted tonight to be so good that he would be her last.

Mhàiri was sheer perfection. His mouth watered at the sight of her full breasts. He wanted to taste them until she cried out, and he would, but first he simply wanted to know the silky feel of her skin. He brushed the backs of his hands against the swell of her breasts and smiled when she shivered in response.

He bent his head and glided his mouth over hers. A hungry sound escaped him as he demanded entry. Her arms latched around his neck, and she willingly gave in, opening for him as she pushed her body deeper into his.

That small action was his undoing. There was no way he could stop now. Conan wanted to devour her, consume her. He was drowning in a desperate need to have her, and he wanted to take her deep into the dark depths so she would never be free of him.

He went to work, undoing the rest of the laces of her dress, stripping her from her gown, letting it and the chemise underneath fall to the floor. His mouth descended. The feel of her skin caused every muscle in his body to become tight with sexual tension. Never breaking the kiss, Conan swept her up into his arms and entered his private chambers, heading directly to his bed.

Breaking off the kiss, he laid her down. He eased back and simply stared at her quivering body laid out before him. He had wanted her since he had first seen her standing in that small cottage doorway. She had a body made for loving. Her waist was small, but her hips curved out slightly, creating a sexy contour to her body. His gaze lowered to her dark mound and saw proof of her desire. He couldn't wait to touch every inch of her and slowly drifted a finger down her neck through the valley of her breasts.

Mhàiri instinctively arched herself against him as his hand moved across her stomach to the curve of her hip. He heard himself utter a thick, husky groan. "You are so beautiful," he muttered, awed.

Mhàiri felt her whole body respond to the heavy, sensual weight of his eyes on her. She wanted to live in this moment forever. Conan wanted her. He had not yet promised her marriage and commitment. But that was something she would worry about later. Right now, she was solely focused on the massive male doing his best to make her breathless. She moaned as her body heated to his touch, and the sound of his answering groan filled her with ecstasy.

He needed to claim her now. Unable to bear not

touching her skin to skin, he stood up and removed his clothes.

Mhàiri had a few seconds to collect herself while he was in the process of removing his shirt. She was beginning to comprehend that she was naked in Conan's bed when he whipped off his leine and the sight of his muscular chest distracted her thoughts once again. Massively built, with thick, corded muscles, Conan was impressive. She wondered if the rest of him matched his size and girth.

He jerked his tartan off, baring all to her, and her light green eyes watched him with rapt fascination. Kneeling on the bed, Conan braced a massive arm on either side of her head, pausing before he sank down for another passionate kiss.

Mhàiri reached up as if to trace the hard lines of the muscles on his abdomen, hesitating before she made contact.

"Touch me, Mhàiri," he said, part command, part plea. He had to hold back a groan when her hands softly began to stroke over his skin. His body felt hot, tight with tension. He was so hard, he feared he might burst.

Reaching out, Conan cupped one of her breasts in his hand so her nipple poked at the very center of his palm. "You are lovely, Mhàiri. You are so much more than I even dreamed."

He was determined to make Mhàiri his. To seal her to him with passion and so much pleasure that thoughts of any other man would be impossible. Slamming his lips down on hers, he ravaged her mouth. He kept kissing her until he could not hold back any longer.

Mhàiri's heart fluttered as she felt Conan stretch out beside her, his larger, heavier frame dwarfing hers.

His lips felt so good she could barely think of anything else. She wanted to touch, to taste, to feel every inch of him, but she didn't know what to do. She tried to grab on to him, and he took both of her hands in one of his and raised them over her head.

Conan pulled away from her lips, his hot mouth trailing down to her neck. A whimper of need escaped her parted lips as he nipped at her earlobe, so he immediately repeated the action.

With his free hand, he ran one finger along the swell of one breast. "So soft," he murmured as his fingers stroked over her skin.

Mhàiri jerked in surprise, but he caught her gasp in his mouth as he kissed her again.

Mhàiri's heart thudded in her chest, and her blood roared in her ears as his eyes met hers, blazing with a hunger that made it hard for her to breathe. Shifting lower, he captured the nipple of her right breast in his mouth, tugging lightly at the peak with his teeth.

"Oh my God, that feels so good," she moaned.

He hummed as he curled his tongue and drew her nipple into his mouth, suckling deeper. When Mhàiri shuddered, Conan moved to the other breast, kissing a soft line to the pink nub, flicking it carefully with his hot, wet tongue, pulling it fully into his mouth.

Mhàiri was on fire; she had never felt like this. Her entire life, logic had ruled her actions. Everything was thought out and calculated. Sensation had never superseded control. But Conan's touch was overwhelming. She was not a master of her reactions. She needed more, and Conan was the only one who could give it to her. She arched into his touch, desperate to feel his lips glide further down her body.

Conan switched to the other nipple, freeing her hands so he could slowly work his fingers down to her core and stroke her silken folds.

He trailed a single finger softly over her slit and then moved his finger inside her ever so slightly while stroking her outer flesh with a careful thumb, watching her melt. He could not remember wanting anything more than this. Mhàiri was giving herself to him, body and soul, in this one timely siege.

Mhàiri began undulating her hips to his rocking finger. His lips returned to her breast as his fingers made slow, maddening movements. The pressure began to build. Then he delved another finger inside her. She cried out as it overwhelmed her, making her breaths short and fast, and her heart pound against the wall of her chest. She squeaked out a moan and opened wider for him. The power he had over her was amazing. Her brain was usually a constant haze of thoughts and ideas, but when Conan touched her, there was nothing but him.

Tremors began in her belly, her muscles tightening, and then, without warning, her body shattered into a million tiny pieces. The only thing holding her together was him.

Conan let out a low growl as he watched sheer pleasure wash over her as her tight sheath clenched around him. He wanted her to scream his name, to tell him that she was his. He needed her to be as desperate for him as he was for her, and he damn well wouldn't stop until he got what he wanted. The sounds of her moans were like the sweetest music, making him determined to drive her up again.

Hooking his hands beneath her knees, he slid her body down to the end of the bed, then knelt between her parted thighs. Hungry for her, he leaned forward and used his tongue to lick at her juices. He heard her cry out in shock, but didn't stop. He pushed one of his fingers into her and found her warm and slick. He groaned while she sucked in a sharp breath. He loved her reactions. He parted her tender folds with two of his fingers, once again stretching her to be ready for him, for she was so tight he knew he would lose his mind as soon as he was inside her.

Mhàiri arched off the bed, her back bowed as he drove her to another climax.

"It's too much!" He drank down her passionate cry and felt her nails score his back.

Conan wanted to say that she was wrong, but he was past the ability to speak. He had already waited too long to have her. He was throbbing painfully. Pulling his fingers from her, he rose to his feet. He reached for her waist and moved her back on the bed so she was lying in the center. He moved over her, covering her perfect body with his.

Entering her, he found she was even smaller and tighter than he had thought, but oh so hot and so wet. His massive arms started to quiver. He did not want to hurt her.

Mhàiri groaned. Her eyes had darkened to emeralds and were glazing over. Her hips circled, wanting more.

"Easy," Conan groaned, sweat beginning to slick his chest from the strain of holding back. "We need to go slow. I don't want to hurt you."

But Mhàiri was past all thought; only need ruled. She had felt what his fingers could give her, but she needed more. "Conan," she whispered and pulled him down into a blinding kiss that had her tongue devouring his.

Conan's hips jerked, thrusting deep. He closed his eyes as her tightness surrounded his thick shaft. Mhàiri threw her head back with a stunned cry. "Conan!"

Freezing, he held her still. "Did I hurt you?"

Her parted lips were swollen from their kisses, and her eyes were glazed with passion as she shook her head. "No, it's . . . I feel full."

He closed his eyes as he fought the need to pull out and thrust again. "Tight. You feel tight."

"It's so good. You feel so good. I never—"

Watching her face, he let himself sink deeper, sliding the full length of him into her. She gasped and instinctively raised her legs up to wrap around him. Then, without warning, she screamed, "More! Oh, God, please more!"

He let out a groan against her mouth as he pulled back, then started thrusting inside her using a slow, steady rhythm. Mhàiri's nails dug into his shoulders. Her soft moans were driving him crazy. He lost control when she tilted her hips up to meet his, grinding against him, building the tension to an unbearable level. He pulled back, then slammed into her, repeating the motion over and over again, lost in the pleasure of feeling her wrapped around him.

"Conan!" she cried out again.

He could hear the fear in her voice and understood, for he too was frightened by what he was feeling. His own release was building with an intensity that he had never experienced before, and there was nothing he could do to stop it. And he wouldn't even if he could.

"Come, Mhàiri. Come and take me with you."

He didn't give her a choice. Pounding into her, he

pushed her further toward the edge, needing her to find her release before he gave in to his own pleasure.

Mhàiri held on to him, her arms wrapped around his neck tightly. She let out a wild cry as the unbearable tension finally snapped. Shudders racked her body as she came, and he couldn't stop himself from coming when she clenched down around him. His muscles tensed as his own release tore through him. He let out a loud roar as he exploded inside her.

He rested his forehead on hers as he tried to regain his breath. He had never experienced a release like that and feared his lack of control had harmed her.

Conan held her close. He didn't want to leave the haven of her body, but he worried that he might be crushing her. Wanting to ask if she was okay, he lifted his head, but when he saw her face, he just smiled.

Mhàiri knew she was right where she belonged, safe and secure in his arms. And she was determined to stay there . . . forever.

"I love you, Conan. There will never be another man for me but you."

Love. It occurred to him he did not like the word. It was too vague, too imprecise, too shallow to capture what he felt. Mhàiri was his soul mate. *A ghrà mo chroì.* Never had another occupied his heart, and another never would. His heart was Mhàiri's and hers alone.

But he could not tell her. Tonight was what they had, and it was all that they would have. So he did the only thing he could. He brought her pleasure over and over again, and each time her responses became more impetuous, more fevered, loosening his own tightly held reins. He made love to her as if consumed by a ravenous need, for tonight had to be enough to quench his thirst for her for life.

Mhàiri snuggled against him as their legs intertwined. "Are you happy?"

Conan nuzzled her hair. Training would start soon and he needed to get out to the fields, but after last night's revelry, he knew that he would not be the only one arriving late. So, instead, he held Mhàiri tight as though he never wanted to let go. "Aye, more than I have a right to be."

He knew he should regret what had happened between them. But he never would. He could live forever and he knew there would never be another woman for him.

Mhàiri placed her hands on his chest as his arms wound their way around her back of their own accord. "That's not true, Conan. You have a right to happiness, and so do I. That's what I realized. Why I came here to you." She rose up on an elbow and looked down at him. "Traveling with my father was a way to avoid the misery of maintaining a home, but it would not have made me happy. I want more than not being miserable. Nor is it enough to be merely satisfied when you just showed me more pleasure than I ever knew possible. So why is it wrong for us to want to continue to know and experience that joy?"

The fingers stroking her back stilled. Tonight had been beyond words, but they both knew that their coming together changed nothing. "It is not wrong to seek happiness as long as that doesn't include me."

Mhàiri's gaze grew in intensity. "But it does. I know you and I together are not what either of us had planned, but we could be happy together. Surely you see that. I'm willing to change and—"

"But I am not. I will not give up what I have worked for all my life."

Mhàiri pushed herself up to a sitting position. "And I'm not asking you to. I'm only asking you to include me in your dreams. I can draw the detailed sketches, and you can focus on all the math and measuring to ensure what is captured is accurate. We will go where you wish, but we will be together."

Conan did not want to have this conversation, especially with her sitting in front of him, exposing her perfect breasts to his touch. Forcing himself to turn away, he threw his legs to the side of the bed and sat up. "You might be happy at first, but I eventually sour the fondest woman's feelings. Even my own brothers would attest to that. Out there is someone who would nourish your love. Find him and the happiness you deserve. The best thing I can give you is to leave immediately. It would make it easier on you." *Make it easier on him.*

Mhàiri sat still, unable to move. Conan was not just denying her, but denying her of a future she now very much wanted. He had given her a passion for drawing things of meaning and value. And with Conan, she would have both love and a life—a combination she had always secretly wanted but never thought possible.

"I did find him and the happiness I deserve. It is *you*," Mhàiri said to his back. She would not let his fear of change rob them both of what they could have. "And you deserve happiness too, which is why *we* are going to wait until spring to marry so my father can be there."

"Mhàiri . . ." he said, twisting around.

"Nay, Conan!" Mhàiri said, standing up. She went and found her chemise and bliaut and started yanking them on. "You tell me that I would be miserable, but you cannot speak for me. We could be married for thirty years and you would still not be able to read my heart and mind enough to tell me what to feel and think."

Conan had to admit that, based on some of the fights Conor and Laurel had, Mhàiri was probably right, for Conor was still clueless about his wife.

"So, unless you can give me a real reason why we cannot be together, we are leaving in the spring *and we are leaving together.*"

Conan jabbed a finger in her direction. "That's one problem right there. Everything you stated included the word *we*," he said, grabbing his leine. "Not only would we wear on each other's nerves, when I did have to leave your side from time to time, you would be left unprotected. I will not be bringing soldiers or guards. You would be alone."

"If that is your objection, let me put your fears aside. I can protect myself, Conan." He arched a brow in disbelief. "I did for two weeks until you and Father Lanaghly arrived," she reminded him and began to tie one side of her bliaut. "My father feared the same thing and made sure that my sister and I were able to handle any situation that might arise."

"And what about bathing? Your father has a large wagon in which to tote his belongings as well as his goods. I will be living off the land, bathing in rivers, hunting for dinner each night, eating over a fire, and sleeping on ground that is often cold and wet."

"I love to bathe in the river. I enjoy the feel of the water as it goes over my skin. And I think campfires are romantic. Besides, you and I both know that the majority of your nights will be spent in a bed just like this one. You are traveling on orders of your king. Doors will open to you for however long you need. For those nights that we are in between shelter, we will sleep in a cart, like merchants do, when it is too cold and wet to sleep on the ground."

"But I'm not bringing a cart," Conan countered.

"Of course we are," Mhàiri replied, tossing his plaid at him. "How else do you plan on keeping everything protected? I agree it shouldn't be a large one, just one big enough to tote our belongings and carry all my books of hemp paper."

"Now you are trying to bribe me," he huffed and began to fold the plaid around his waist.

"I already did that when I threw myself into your arms this evening. And lucky for us both, you accepted it." She held on to the side of a bookcase and pulled on one slipper. "I need to speak to Maegan. I spoke somewhat harshly to her and need to apologize since she is going to help me prepare for a wedding!"

Conan dropped his sword. Snatching it up again, he jammed it into the sheath on his belt. He took ten deep breaths. How had a fantastic night and morning making memories he would treasure turned into this nightmare? "You can say all the nonsense you want, but it will not work."

Mhàiri went over to stand right in front of him. "You love me."

"I do not recall ever telling you that."

Mhàiri smiled, still sure that this would end with them together. She knew he loved her. Of that, she had no doubt. "Good thing I don't need all the flowery and passion-filled words then, isn't it? Besides, you not saying it doesn't make it less true."

Conan stepped around her. "What if I do love you?" he asked, whipping around now that she was no longer in kissing distance. "You knew since we met that my future plans did not include a wife, and I have never wavered on the idea of going alone. You attempting to change that is the same as you trying to change me. And I am not changing for anyone!" he decreed, stabbing his thumb into his chest.

Mhàiri fought the compulsion to roll her eyes. "What a ridiculous thing to say. Of course change is happening. Life happens and we change because of it. You and I had plans. Then we met. The moment that happened, things began to change. It just took a few months, several fights, and last night to figure out how, but now that we have, to pretend otherwise . . . is . . . well, it's ridiculous!"

"Ridiculous or not, I'm not changing."

"I don't believe you. You are too smart to mean what you are saying. That you would rather go alone, with a fraction of the resources, and novice abilities to draw. That you would forgo potential happiness rather than travel with me at your side, when I would help you conquer all your dreams and so much more. Together, we would be the ultimate team, and deep down you know it."

Conan faced her without expression, without moving a muscle. "What about children? What happens to this ultimate team you are envisioning when you get pregnant and we have to suddenly settle down into the static life you and I both dread."

Mhàiri threw up her arms in exasperation. "Why would having a child affect our lifestyle? My parents raised my sister and me on the road, and we turned out fairly well."

"Ha! She became a nun."

"And I became like you!"

"You can't cook!"

"So I'll learn! We aren't leaving for a couple of months. I have time. Fiona will teach me, and you will be the best-fed man in Scotland."

Conan was breathing hard. Fiona was not a kind woman and did not like anyone to interfere in her kitchen. Ever. But somehow he suspected Mhàiri would be the exception.

"You aren't listening and you need to, Mhàiri. It doesn't matter whether you can cook, are willing to sleep outside, or are the bravest woman in the world. I. Don't. Want. You. With. Me."

That got her to pause. She took a step back as if he had struck her physically. "Why?" she choked out.

Conan took a breath and slowly exhaled. He ran a hand through his hair. "Because," he began, searching for the words to explain what he felt. "Because it is not what I planned."

"You never planned to have a wife so you don't want one?" she said, the sound barely a whisper. "Even one willing to do everything you want, doesn't even consider it a compromise, but an opportunity, one you love . . . only because it is not what you had *planned*?" Her voice gained strength. "Because if that's true, Conan, you are right. There is nothing I can do to prove that we can be happy, living a life that is so wonderful, so incredible, neither of us could have envisioned it."

Mhàiri marched to his chamber door and yanked it

open. She spun around. "You may go on your trip, make your maps, but years from now, when you still are puzzled as to why it doesn't bring you the satisfaction you thought it would, you think back on today. This conversation. For until you realize that only by giving up on your old dreams can you embrace the one that God is offering, you won't be truly happy. And I've decided that is what I want. I don't want to just avoid being unhappy. I want it all. And I intend to have it all."

Chapter Thirteen

Laurel rubbed her stomach as she studied Mhàiri. The last couple of months since Epiphany, she had started to grow large, and Conor feared she was carrying twins again. Laurel knew she wasn't. The babe was large, but Hagatha suspected it was because this was her fourth child.

She had forgotten what pregnancy was like. She had remembered it as wonderful, but now that she was in her last couple of months, she realized that it was the *baby* that made it wonderful. In reality, being pregnant was anything but.

Last week, Aileen revealed that she, too, was pregnant and a happier expectant mother could not be found. Laurel had been waiting for the announcement for weeks. Finn had been grinning far too regularly for someone who preferred to frown. But Laurel had not asked because she knew Aileen was intentionally waiting. Her best friend had conceived several times over the years, but always lost her children early in her pregnancy. Aileen no doubt feared it would happen again. But the weeks passed and she was still carrying. So on Epiphany she had told Finn, who could not have been more surprised . . . or thrilled. Now that another two months had gone by, the fear had been replaced with anticipation. The babes would be only a few months apart, but essentially the same age.

"I asked you to come here today so that I could make a request. I want you to stop bathing in the river."

Mhàiri's eyes widened. She had hoped Laurel had seen all that she had been doing for the past several weeks and was finally going to offer her help. It was Laurel who had made her realize what she wanted and she did not think that had been an accident, but now it seemed Lady McTiernay had changed her mind.

"I don't mind it, and I have my reasons."

Laurel inhaled and then sighed. "You are going to get sick. Whatever point you were trying to make has been made."

Mhàiri's jaw clenched. Laurel did not understand the situation, for she had never told anyone what had happened between her and Conan—not even Maegan. And she was certain he, too, had kept what happened on Epiphany and their argument afterwards to himself.

For two months, Mhàiri had been trying to prove to Conan that she would not be a burden during their travels, reminding him in whatever ways possible that she wanted to be with him. However, his ability to avoid her had made it more than just a little difficult. She was mostly relying on rumors about her accomplishments getting to him, because they had yet to talk since that fateful night.

"I am not sure it has."

"Well, trekking all the way back to the castle is not

the same as immediately sitting by a campfire to get warm, so please stop."

Mhàiri pursed her lips and rose to her feet. "Fine. Is there anything else you would like me to cease doing?" she challenged.

It had been difficult, but Mhàiri had finally gotten Fiona to agree to a truce, of sorts. The old cook was a gray-haired, stoutly built woman, and her dark brown eyes were always aware of everything going on in her kitchen. She loved to cook, but she did not love people. And she especially did not like anyone coming into the kitchens to bother her, help, or even pinch some of her food before she was ready to serve it. She had a wicked tongue, and Mhàiri had been frightened by it until she had realized that was all the woman had. So Mhàiri kept coming in. Every day, she would come and talk to the help and move things around. Not much, but just enough to be annoying. Fiona would rant and rave, but it had done no good. And that was when Mhàiri had offered Fiona a bargain. Teach her how to cook and she would leave her kitchens.

So Fiona had reluctantly agreed, but refused to do so in her kitchens. The crotchety woman made it clear that if Mhàiri wanted to learn how to cook over a campfire, then that was where she was going to learn. So Mhàiri had been yelled at, insulted, criticized, and even injured. But she had also learned.

Mhàiri could now quickly pluck a bird, clean it, and skin a rabbit. She now recognized what grew wild that could be used to make food tastier. She was becoming an expert at telling when meat was done and how to keep it from becoming too dry. Her repertoire of recipes included soup, dried meat, and bread, which she had learned how to bake in a pot over a fire. And Mhàiri knew for a fact that Conan had eaten and enjoyed a couple of her meals because Fiona had surprised everyone when she came out near the end of one of the dinners and announced to all that Mhàiri had been the one to prepare most of what had been served. But Mhàiri was not done learning. Fiona still had to teach her about fish, certain pies, and many other things. Mhàiri did not want Laurel stripping those from her as well.

Laurel shrugged her shoulders. "That you convinced Fiona to teach you how to cook is a miracle and I won't interfere with it. But if that was going to change anything between you and Conan, it already would have."

The shock that Laurel had seen and recognized what she was doing rocketed through Mhàiri. She collapsed by Laurel's feet. "Please help me. Please help me make him see what he is giving up."

Laurel swept Mhàiri's hair from her face and cupped her cheek. "I cannot. For two reasons. First, despite what people think, all I have ever done for anyone is given a little bit of advice. A few words spoken at just the right time often can put things into motion, but all the pieces have to be in place first. I cannot create what isn't there."

Mhàiri still did not understand. "But it *is* there."

"And what words would I say that you have not already spoken? When words no longer work, the only thing left is action, and that is the one thing I cannot do for you."

Alarm overtook Mhàiri's expression, and Laurel immediately doused the flames that she could see growing. "I do not know what transpired between you and Conan. I only know something did."

Mhàiri sat back. "Then how do you know I spoke the right words?"

"Because of the second reason I cannot help you." Laurel paused and waited until Mhàiri was looking at her again. "Conan asked me not to."

Mhàiri would have fallen if she had not already been sitting on the floor.

Conan knew. He had known at some point she would be desperate enough to seek out Laurel's help. And he had feared she would give it to her because he had feared it would work. That should have given her hope, for it meant that he was struggling with his feelings, warring with them, and yet it did just the opposite. Mhàiri felt all her confidence dissipate until she had none left at all. If Conan was this adamant, she was at a loss. He feared her changing him, but he was the one who had changed her. And for what? An impossible dream.

Mhàiri rose to her feet and was about to say her good-byes when Bonny came running into the room. "Guess who is here!" she cried. "Your papa! Fallon says you are to come right away!"

Mhàiri swallowed. How did God know? The one person she needed more than ever was her beloved father. He would wrap her in his arms and take her away. Away from the pain and the loss and the heartbreak.

With a cry, she ran past Bonny and down the stairwell. Entering the courtyard, she spied him and his massive cart. How he had gotten that thing this far north when winter was only now easing, she did not know. Nor did she care. All Mhàiri knew was her father was here and somehow he was going to make it all better.

"*Athair!*" she yelled.

A large man who had been talking to Fallon turned to the voice. Iain Mayboill had the craggy look of an unfinished sculpture and yet women found him deliciously appealing. He had a massive, self-confident presence that was so striking, it caused those around him to turn and stare. Wings of gray hair fanned out at his temples, adding drama and distinction. With bright green eyes and dark hair, he had a smile that she had heard could cut a man like a knife. But to Mhàiri, he was just her father. A man who loved her without question.

Upon seeing her, pleasure softened his granite-like face. He opened his arms wide as she collided into his embrace. "Ah, *inghean*, it is so good to see you so well and bonnie. I have missed you, lass."

Mhàiri hugged him close and felt a shadow over her shoulder. She glanced back to see Laurel and Conor. "Father, please let me introduce Laird and Lady Mc-Tiernay."

"I'm Iain Mayboill. A great privilege it is to meet you. Not only is your clan's name well known throughout Scotland, but you took care of my Mhàiri, here, and that means more to me than I can express."

Laurel gave him her warmest, most welcoming smile. "She was a pleasure."

Iain wagged his finger at Laurel. "Quite a weapon she has there," he said to Conor, who was about to take exception to this man pointing at his wife. "Those stormy eyes, that smile, her beauty. That combination renders you powerless most days, I bet. My wife could do the same to me when she was alive."

Conor blinked. The man spoke the truth, and Laurel was practically giggling with the idea that she had power over him that she already *knew* she had. "We were not expecting you so soon. The snow just began to thaw here."

"It wasn't so bad, though the last day got to be a little bit of fun in parts. Your brother Colin encouraged me to stay longer, but his three wee ones are a bit like his wife—wild and rambunctious. And before I forget, I was supposed to tell you that they have another on the way."

Laurel's fingers rose to her lips. Aislinn was seven, about to turn eight, Machara was almost four, and Connor was not even two yet. Thinking of stoic Colin chasing all those children around was enough to bring her to laughter. "Aye," Iain said to her unspoken words, "I think your brother Colin is actually scared, especially when his wife says that she still plans on having at least six. The man will have to learn how to relax or go stark raving mad, I expect."

At that, Conor laughed. "Come and tell us of your travels."

"Where would you like me to put my cart? The man wasn't pleased I insisted on bringing it inside, but this is my home, my livelihood."

Laurel wiped the tears from her eyes. "Your livelihood is in no jeopardy outside the walls, and you can stay in the North Tower while you are here. I'll have Glynis prepare you a room."

Iain folded his arms and stared down at Laurel and then finally laughed. "I would argue with you, but I think I would lose. You have that look about you my

Mhàiri gets, which she got from her mother. It says the argument would be a long and bloody battle, but you're willing to wage it and do whatever it takes to come out the victor. So I shall concede now." Then he gave a wink to Mhàiri, and nudged her side with his elbow. "You see that, lass? I'm finally learning to listen. If only your mother were here to see it."

"She still wouldn't believe it," Mhàiri said, smiling up at him. "And she enjoyed arguing with you as much as you enjoyed arguing with her."

"Much like the laird and his lady, I suspect."

Laurel closed her eyes and shook her head, trying not to grin and failing. "Colin has been talking about me and Conor, I see."

"Nay!" Iain denied. "I would never listen to such gossip. I just sees what I see. And what I'm seeing is that *you* need a longer pillow at night to sleep so that you won't wake with your back hurting."

Laurel's mouth dropped in shock. Her back *did* hurt and she was not sleeping well. "You think a longer pillow is all I need?"

Iain walked to his cart and pulled out a large pillow packed with feathers. "Aye. Leave the one you have for your head and use this to curl up to. This beast here," he said, gesturing to Conor, "is all meat and hardness. No doubt a lot of fun and the reason you have a bairn on the way, but for the next couple of months, snuggle up to this here pillow and you will wake refreshed and with more energy."

Conor was about to strongly object. He liked his wife at his side and most definitely did not want to be replaced by a pillow. But when he saw the look of sheer excitement in Laurel's face, he knew he could not deny her.

Mhàiri bit her bottom lip. "That's Father," she said timidly. "He is very friendly and always seems to know what you need."

Conor pursed his lips. "Your father is exceptionally shrewd." He had met men like Iain before. Laird MacInnes was one of them. He was his father's best friend who had moved to the south when he had married a woman who'd turned out to be Laurel's grandmother. He, too, could within minutes understand those around him as though he had spent a lifetime in their company. It enabled him to draw one in quickly so they trusted him.

Bonny stood by Mhàiri. She had followed her outside and had been carefully watching the newcomer. "I've decided I like you," she announced, surprising everyone around her.

Iain knelt down to her level. "And why is that?"

"Because you are smart like me."

Iain peered into Bonny's gray eyes and what he saw was his own soul staring back at him. Brilliance, with a natural understanding of people. "Why, you are quite smart, aren't you?" he said and swung her up in his arms. "Do your mama and papa know this?"

Bonny shook her head, to the surprise of both her parents. "Only Uncle Conan," she replied.

"Come, let us go and get some ale. I'm sure you are parched after your journey," Conor encouraged Iain.

"Aye, but first let me get a present from my cart before it is sent rolling out of reach." He went over and shifted some things around before pulling out a large crate. He pried it open and there inside was a treasure. Books of hemp paper. "I thought, on your travels, you would need some more. So this is for you."

Mhàiri gasped, and knelt down to see. At least five books were inside. "Travels? How did you—?"

"Shinae," her father answered.

"I went to see your sister and she mentioned what you and she had planned to do before the priory had burned down. She explained that you want to see the world and if I know my sweet Mhàiri, she has found a way to do that besides traveling with an old merchant like me."

Tears filled Mhàiri's eyes. How right her father was. And how wrong. "How is Shinae? You know she was forced to take her vows."

"No one can force another to do anything. Shinae is living with that decision, but you know your sister. She always finds a way to locate the sun in every rain cloud."

Mhàiri nodded. Her sister could do that. She was the kindest of souls, but also the most stubborn, and could be a force unlike any other when pressed.

"Now, let's go have this drink and you can tell me all about that man hovering over there with a scowl and how he is troubling you, lass. I'm guessing he's wee Bonny's Uncle Conan."

The fire crackled in the great hall, and Mhàiri studied the flames. They had gone to enjoy some ale, and soon word had spread of Iain Mayboill's arrival. The group grew as Hagatha, then Aileen and Finn, followed by Seamus and Maegan joined them. Their laughter created curiosity, and soon every nearby soldier not on duty and anyone who was not busy with time-sensitive chores were in the great hall, listening and laughing as Iain regaled them with one story followed by another. Some Mhàiri knew, some Mhàiri had participated in, and some she had never heard because they had taken place after she had left for the priory.

Now it was quiet. They had all left, letting father and daughter get reacquainted.

"So, *inghean*, what keeps your heart from smiling? Your lips curl, but there is no light in your eyes. Not even for your old father who traveled all this way to see you. Could it be that I should be arriving to news of a wedding, but I'm not?"

Mhàiri should have known her father would have accurately guessed. Conan had joined them, but only briefly. Her father had asked pointed questions about his plans and Conan had answered them, just as directly. Nothing had been odd about his comments or demeanor, and yet her father had known.

"I wish there to be one. I do. But you heard Conan. He will not change his plans despite all that I've done." Iain listened quietly as Mhàiri described all of Conan's arguments and her efforts to thwart them. "But he cares not. He refuses to change the dreams he has held on to for the chance at something better."

"And nor should he. I don't think I would either. You don't know if you want that life. You've never done it, day after day. In three days, you might be so bored and dirty you'll never want to see Conan again."

"But I wouldn't!" Mhàiri insisted.

"Words," her father said with a shrug. "To ask a man to give up his life for a new one based on only mere words, now *that* is a lot to ask."

Anger began to boil once again in Mhàiri. She could not believe it. First Laurel and now her own father. No one believed she could be happy with Conan.

That what they shared was not just about love and physical passion—though that was definitely a major incentive—it was much more. This was her life that she was fighting for. A life that she very much wanted. To travel and draw with a purpose. To meet people and see places. To have complete autonomy over where she lived and went. She would do anything, adjust to anything, and endure anything to have it. It was no wonder that Conan did not believe her. No one did.

Iain reached over and tapped her knee. "I can tell you are upset and have been for a while. What you need is a way to release some of that aggression." He rose to his feet. "I heard Finn mention that his men train every morning in some fields outside the castle walls."

"I know them. I've gone to watch a few times."

"But have you joined them?"

Mhàiri scoffed. "I think Finn would have more than a few words at that idea."

Iain grinned at his daughter. "Aye. He will be shocked. You should remember his expression on the morrow and sketch it later. Then give it to his wife." That got Mhàiri to smile. "But I bet I could convince him to let you join for a while, if only to see what would happen."

Mhàiri bit the inside of her cheek and then shook her head. "I'm not in the mood to spar, Papa."

A hard glint entered his eyes. "You're angry. You're frustrated. That means you're in the mood. So tomorrow morning?"

Knowing it would do little good to argue, Mhàiri nodded in agreement. For somehow, someway, she would be there anyway.

* * *

Finn held his hands up, and immediately all the activity halted. Conan looked to see why they'd stopped and spied Iain and Mhàiri. "What brings you here?" Finn asked with impatience.

Iain gripped Mhàiri's shoulder in one of his large hands and said with a smile, "Mhàiri tells me that she has not trained all winter. I'm a merchant and sometimes that means I encounter people who are not so honest. And Mhàiri is pretty. I need to make sure she still knows how to protect herself before we leave your lands and are back on our own."

Finn looked at Mhàiri, arched a brow, and then coughed into his hand in an effort to hide his laughter. Mhàiri narrowed her gaze. "For that, Finn, your wife is going to get a present from me later today," she hissed.

Finn had no idea what Mhàiri meant, but he did detect the sharp tone and realized Iain had been serious. Suddenly he remembered Laurel's unusual ability with a bow and thought perhaps he had been too hasty with his assumptions. "Well, what skills do you have then that need practice?"

Iain rubbed his chin. "Do you have a target?"

"Tell her to go where the women train." The sharp comment had come from one of Finn's largest men, who was leaning forward against his sword, tip in the ground. Buzz was a good-natured but mouthy soldier. He had shown interest in Mhàiri after Loman and was not pleased when she had made it clear that she was not interested. After that, she had received at least one jeering remark from the man a week. Mhàiri had had enough.

With incredible speed, Mhàiri whipped out the knives she had strapped on this morning and sent them zinging through the air. The first hit his sword out of his hand. The next three landed right in front of him, all in the same spot so that they fanned out, making it clear that each one had landed exactly where she had aimed.

Iain slapped his hands together. "Not bad. He was a little close, but I think we can say that you still can throw, daughter." He then turned to Finn, whose mouth was hanging open. "Mhàiri," Iain said, using his thumb to gesture toward Finn, "you might want to remember that expression as well."

Mhàiri nodded. "I think I just might."

"You've proven your aim is still good, but what about the rest?"

Mhàiri scanned the men. Her eyes landed on Conan. His expression was inscrutable. "Will anyone spar with me?" she asked.

Conan continued to stare at her, but his countenance did not change. He did not move. Nothing to be misconstrued as volunteering.

"I will," Seamus said, stepping forward.

Finn nodded, knowing that Seamus was good enough to give her a challenge without accidentally pushing too far and hurting her. Mhàiri's father might be watching, even encouraging, this crazy pursuit, but Conor would have all of them for dinner if Mhàiri got hurt. And that was only after Laurel made them all miserable.

Five minutes later, Seamus found himself on his back staring at the sky. His side was stinging something awful. He had totally underestimated Mhàiri and had ended up looking like a fool because of it. The only upside was that maybe Maegan would take pity on him and talk to him. He had scared her at Epiphany, pushed her too far. He only hoped with enough time she would see that they were good together. He could make her happy. But first she had to let go of Clyde, and he wondered if she was ever going to be able to do that.

"I am *so* sorry, Seamus," Mhàiri said, clearly upset. "I think you are going to need a thread and needle."

Seamus tried to sit up and winced. "Aye, I think you are right."

Mhàiri closed her eyes. "Father is right. I should have kept up with my skills. I leaned in way too far on that last spin when we were just sparring."

Seamus looked at his side. "Just sparring. You are deadly, Mhàiri."

Iain took a look. "Aye, that's a nasty cut." He offered Seamus an arm. "Come on. Let's go get you cleaned up." Then, with a wave, they left and headed back to the castle. "You have someone good with a needle?"

Seamus nodded. "Hagatha and Laurel."

Iain chuckled. "I thought you might be wanting that pretty little lass Maegan to be tending to you."

"I'm, uh, not sure she would want to."

Iain grinned. "She would, and afterwards, she'll be talking to you again and you'll be thanking my Mhàiri here for giving you such a scar."

Seamus hobbled another couple of steps before he realized exactly what Iain had said. Based on all the stuff he had witnessed last night, he had no doubt that Iain Mayboill had an ability to see into someone like he had never witnessed before. He looked at the older man and then grinned. "I think I will."

Mhàiri watched as Seamus's hobble turned into a near sprint, leaving her and her father to walk back alone.

She looked at her father. "Did you see what you came to see?"

"Aye. Your knives are still good. You are slow with your left hand, and your Conan definitely loves you. So why aren't you doing anything about it?"

Mhàiri's hands curled into fists. "I know you were listening when I told you all that I had been doing to convince him. You said my actions had no more influence to change his mind than words."

"Your promises are just words and knowing how to cook over a campfire doesn't mean you will want to do so every meal."

"Then what do you mean? What else can I do?"

"Only you know that. I do know that the man is scared. I felt that way when I met your mother. I knew she was willing to come with me, but I had trouble believing she could really be happy as a merchant's wife. Good thing she was more determined than you. Otherwise, I might have left her village alone."

"How did she convince you?"

Iain laughed. "That woman did the most insane thing I had ever seen in my life," he replied. "She became a merchant! And what's more, she loved it! When I saw her smile after her first sale, I knew she was hooked and I knew then that I had to have her."

Mhàiri suddenly realized what Laurel had meant. *When words no longer work, the only thing left is action.* Words were not enough. That's what Laurel and her father were trying to tell her. She had come to them for some way to reach Conan, but that was something she could only do.

Mhàiri reached up on her tiptoes and gave her father a kiss on the cheek. "Thank you, *Athair*. I have something I have to do, so don't worry about me if you don't see me for a few days."

Conan entered the great hall and shook the water out of his hair. It had been cold and raining for the last two days, and the wind was getting worse. The warm spell they had been experiencing had left with a vengeance. Winter wanted one more storm before it left for the year, and it was going to be a bad one. By tomorrow, everything would be frozen under a thick layer of ice.

He moved to sit in his normal spot at the dinner table, surprised to find that he was nearly the last one to arrive. It had been more than a week since he had joined the family for dinner, and he had half expected Laurel to have chased him down, ordering his return by now. She just smiled and waved at him, continuing to listen to something Iain Mayboill was saying. Everyone was tuned in with rapt attention. Laurel and Aileen's pregnancies were stirring up the old merchant's memories of when Shinae and Mhàiri had been born, and the adventures of bringing them into the world while on the road were the ones he cherished the most.

Conan could listen no more. Every time he heard Iain's voice, he remembered the last time he had seen him . . . and Mhàiri.

She had said she could protect herself, but he had had no idea exactly what that had meant. It had needled at him for days before he had figured out why. She *could* protect herself. Her vulnerability had been one of the main reasons he had been so reluctant to even consider the idea of her coming with him. But she had been right. Mhàiri could protect herself better than most men.

Conan decided to risk catching her eye and glanced around the table to see where she was sitting. He looked again. She was not there, nor was there a hole as if her arrival was anticipated.

"Maegan," he clipped, finally getting her attention from Seamus. She was smiling, and his friend, who had been almost intolerable the last two months, seemed himself again. "Where's Mhàiri?"

Maegan finished swallowing her food and then took a sip of ale. She licked her lips. Conan wondered if she was delaying telling him on purpose. Was this some lame scheme she and Mhàiri had hatched to prove he still cared about her? "I don't know," Maegan finally replied with a shrug of her shoulders.

Conan gripped his mug tightly in his hand and prayed for patience. "No games, Maegan. Where is she?"

Maegan put her own mug down and leveled her sky-blue eyes on him. "I do not know," she repeated. "I have not seen her for days. Her father told us not to worry, so I haven't."

Days? Conan thought in shock. Had Mhàiri been trying to avoid him, like he had her? Or was she ill? If so, why had he not been told? But Conan knew the answer. He had not been around and had made it clear to Laurel that when it came to Mhàiri, he wanted to hear nothing. But he had meant no advice, not that he wouldn't want to know if she was not well.

"Is someone taking Mhàiri food?" he asked Brenna, knowing the ten-year-old would be well aware of where Mhàiri was, her status, and why she was not at dinner.

Brenna imitated Maegan and shrugged her shoulders.

"Well, at least tell me where she is," he hissed.

Brenna's gray eyes grew large. "I don't know, Uncle Conan."

Conan sat quietly fuming for the rest of the dinner. When everyone stood to leave, he waited for Iain and carefully cornered him. He intended to get some answers, and if Iain thought he could play his mind and word games with him, he was about to learn very differently.

"Where is Mhàiri?"

Iain crossed his arms and rocked back on his heels. "I don't know. Last I saw her, she kissed my cheek and told me not to worry about her and that I wouldn't be seeing her for a few days. Last time that happened, I had made her a cloth drawing board. The girl barely stopped to eat, but she slowed down soon enough. If I had tried to make Mhàiri stop before she was ready, she would have resented me and kept drawing, but only for longer."

Conan spun on his heel and headed for the Warden's Tower. He ran up the stairs and began to bang on Mhàiri's door, shouting at her to open up. When she did not answer, he considered barging in. If he had to, he would, but he knew there was someone to whom she would respond.

An hour later, he had found Maegan, who was in the Star Tower, ensuring his nieces were getting ready for bed. He waved for her to meet him in the hallway right outside the room. "I need you to do something," he stated without preamble or pleasantries.

Maegan huffed. "I am done scheming. For Brenna. For Bonny. For everyone, which includes you."

Conan's face grew hard. "I am not asking you to scheme," he snarled. "I'm asking you to check on your friend, whom it seems that *no one* has seen for the past week."

"That's impossible," Maegan said.

"Then why haven't you seen her at dinner?"

"I assumed she was avoiding Seamus. She did cut him very badly. He could have gotten a fever and died." Maegan's voice had grown cold, and her anger could not be missed.

"She was not avoiding Seamus. You know Mhàiri—she doesn't run from problems. Ever. It's actually more surprising that she has not checked on him every day, which proves that something is not right."

Maegan blinked. She had been rather busy, and after seeing what Mhàiri had done to Seamus, she had been angry with her friend and not really in the mood to see or talk to her. Just the thought of losing Seamus had scared her enormously, but Conan was right. Maegan *should* have at least seen her in passing. It had been over a week now, and it was clear Seamus was going to recover. "Mhàiri must be with her father. They will be leaving soon, so she is probably just making preparations." She snapped her fingers, and relief flooded her countenance. "I know. In addition to more paper, her father had brought her a couple of books that she was very excited about. I am sure she is simply completely engrossed in them, like you are when you get new scrolls and whatnot."

Maegan opened the door to finish checking on the

girls. Conan took a deep breath and exhaled. That had to be it. He knew what it was like to get absorbed in a new activity to the exclusion of all else. Mhàiri was the same way. She had probably told her father not to worry and was having servants run her up food.

He stepped into the room and said, "I'm sure you are right, but I need to know for sure."

Maegan had just started to comb Bonny's hair. "You know, only a man in love would be asking this when even Mhàiri's own father is not concerned."

"I don't deny loving Mhàiri, but loving someone does not mean we would be happy together."

Maegan looked at him then and swallowed. "I'll check on her right after I finish here."

"Thank you."

Maegan was shocked. That was the first time Conan had ever voiced his appreciation to her that she could recall. She was about to say something to that effect when Bonny tugged on her sleeve.

"You won't find Mhàiri in her room," she whispered, but it was loud enough for Conan to hear her.

He marched up beside her. "What do you mean, Bonny?"

"She left the castle the day she hurt Seamus. I saw her."

Terror twisted his stomach. "Left how?"

"Neal gave her a horse and a small cart. She put a couple blankets and some books in it and left. I asked Neal yesterday when she was coming back, and he said that he didn't know. That Mhàiri had only told him that she needed an animal that wouldn't be missed for a while. He had assumed she would only be gone that afternoon because she didn't take any food, but as far as he knew, Mhàiri had still not returned."

Conan felt his heart turn to stone and the sweat chill on his body. An ice storm was upon them. The rain that had been falling down would turn to ice now that it was dark, and it would be coming down hard and painfully. People died in weather like this. Did her father not know this? Did he and Laurel and everyone else assume what he had? That Mhàiri was in her room, drawing or studying a new book?

Panic began to take hold, and he fought the urge to race off madly, blindly.

Conan looked at Maegan, who was beginning to shake with fear for her friend. "This storm is getting worse, and if Mhàiri is out in it, she won't survive to the morning. Go find Conor and Laurel and tell them that I'm going out now to find and bring her back, but if I don't return by the morning to form a search party."

Tears filled Maegan's eyes to the brim and began to fall down her cheeks. "Find her, Conan."

"I will. And she will be alive."

She will be alive, he repeated to himself.

For Mhàiri was his. She had his heart, and now it was time to claim hers.

She will be alive.

Chapter Fourteen

"Thank you, Maegan, but don't look so alarmed!" Iain chided, his laughter filling the great hall.

Maegan was shocked that he, Laurel, and Conor did not move. All three just remained sitting by the hearth, prepared to continue talking and smiling without any concerns.

"My daughter knows how to stay warm and dry in an ice storm. We've lived through many. She knows what to do."

Maegan stared at him incredulously. "You knew?" she asked. "You knew Mhàiri has been living out there on her own for *days*?"

"Well, how else is she supposed to know if she is going to like it? And after the past few hellacious days, I suppose she does, otherwise she would have been back by now."

Laurel grinned. "I think we will be preparing for a wedding when those two return."

"You better hope so," Conor snorted. "After listening to you two applaud your devious ways, I would not let you forget it if you are wrong."

Laurel patted his hand. "Oh, we're right. You know it, too."

Conor looked at Maegan. "You would have thought they had known each other for months, planning this whole thing between Conan and Mhàiri." He pointed at Iain. "You need to go, my friend. You and my wife enjoy each other's company too much. It's dangerous. Better run, Maegan, while you can."

Conan had been out for a few hours, searching each of the places they had been to during their outings, when he realized where Mhàiri had gone. The day Bonny had told him she wanted to learn about maps, but he had taught Mhàiri instead, she had identified a half dozen spots she thought would be ideal places to draw in detail, for they included all aspects of this area of Scotland.

When she was not at the fourth area, he began to get worried. The final two were the farthest from McTiernay Castle, and if she were not at either of those, he would have to stop and find shelter. He had come prepared to deal with the brutal cold and ice, but based on what Bonny had said, Mhàiri had very little and nothing to keep her safe and protected.

He hoped his brother had waited to send out a search party. It was almost impossible to see, and if he had not known every knot and hole in these parts, he would have injured himself or his horse as soon as he had left the main path. As it was, the fifth place was set atop a rocky cliff that would have been the coldest and least protected from the wind and the elements. Conan feared he might lame his horse and slid off the saddle to guide the animal along the rocky path to a small canyon-like stretch. There were no caves in the area, but at least the rock wall would shield his horse from the worst of the storm.

He rounded one massive boulder that had at one time jutted out from the cliff above. Without warning, a knife flew by his face and clinked on the rock face behind him. He jumped back out of sight.

"Know that I missed on purpose and have more knives, two of which are in my hands. So speak your name, stranger, and pray I recognize it."

Conan could hear the stark alarm in Mhàiri's voice. She was scared. Genuinely, thoroughly, deep-down scared. "Then your aim better be damn good," he said, stepping back into view once more. "Mhàiri, I've come to—"

Before he could finish his sentence and say that he was there to rescue her, Mhàiri had launched herself into his arms. "Oh, Conan! What are you doing out here! You have to be freezing!"

"I was looking for you. I didn't know—not until tonight—that you were out here all alone. God, if anything had happened to you," he mumbled into her hair, squeezing her close. "Why did you go? Why did you not return when the weather got bad? Why did you leave me?"

Mhàiri pulled back to answer, but before she could say a word, his mouth crushed hers with animal-like fury. His tongue thrust into her mouth, then withdrew, then thrust again, engulfing her with unleashed need, fear, and lust.

Mhàiri clung to him in confusion and desire. Conan held her close and showered her face with hungry kisses, groaning with intense yearning as he frantically sought out new places for his lips.

For hours, he had told himself that he would find her. And when he did, he would scold her for hours on the dangers of adventuring out alone without anyone knowing where she was. Then he would make love to her until she was limp followed by another lecture on the dangers of scaring him to death. But with his lips upon hers, all he could think was that she was safe. She was alive and he never wanted to let her go.

Slowly, he released her. He cupped her face and asked again, "Why, Mhàiri? Why?"

She put her warm hand around his freezing one and said, "Come. Come back where it's warm and dry, and then you can tell me why you are here."

Conan followed. Just past the fallen boulder, she had made a makeshift camp. She had leaned the cart over on its side, and between the cliff wall, the boulder, and the cart, she was completely protected from the wind. She must have known the weather had been turning foul, for she had collected branches and stacked them to make a thick, temporary roof. A fire crackled next to blankets that were laid out. A large stack of sticks, which included some sizeable logs, were in one corner to keep the fire going, and a plate was on the ground with what looked to be a half-eaten rabbit.

"Do you live here now?" he choked in surprise.

Mhàiri laughed and went to sit down on the blanket, patting the spot next to her. "It does look like it, but I've been here only a couple of days. I would have returned to the castle today, but I feared it might turn worse and it did. I knew that at least here I would be safe and dry."

Conan unhooked his sword and laid it down before

sitting next to her on the blankets she was using as a bed. "And warm. How did you get dry wood?"

"Some of it isn't so I have to be careful not to add too many of the wet ones on at a time, but those old broken logs were here already. I think someone else must have used this area for shelter as well."

Conan pointed to the roof. "Since when did you know to do that?"

Mhàiri grinned. "Since I was a child. We had to build protected places for us to sleep when traveling. It was Shinae's and my job to build the shelter, which included a roof most of the time. It did not take very many wet nights for us to figure out not only how to build them quickly but how to lay the branches so that the wind won't blow it away and keep everything warm and dry underneath, no matter how harsh the weather. Though I must say, I am glad to be surrounded by these big rocks in this wind."

"You truly were not exaggerating when you said that you could take care of yourself."

Mhàiri shook her head. "Everything I said that night was true, except for one thing."

Conan leaned in and put his hands near the fire to get warm. "And what was that?"

"I promised you that I would be happy living out here, day after day, drawing with only the quiet of my thoughts. That was unfair, for I had no right to make such a promise when I did not know if that was true."

Tension ran through every one of Conan's limbs. Fate was cruel. Just as he had realized he could not live without her, she had realized she could not live with him.

"But now I can," she said, looking up into his eyes. Fear lingered there and she longed to remove it. She reached up and caressed his chapped cheek. "I've been out here for days now. Did you know that I have never done anything like this? Just out drawing, traveling, alone with only my thoughts to keep me company?" Conan shook his head. "I mean, at times, it was lonely and I wished you were here so we could talk, but most of the time, I reveled in the peace. It was colder than I'd thought, more uncomfortable than I had anticipated, and one night food was hard to find, but despite all of those things, I discovered something."

"And what's that?" he asked, watching her every emotion as it flittered across her face.

"That I love it. I love the feeling of freedom. I love living by my rules and schedules and yet still serving a greater purpose through my drawings. I know who I am now, Conan. I am my mother's child, born to roam and never be tied down. That's what makes me happy. And even if you can never understand that and still believe this life would make me miserable, it doesn't matter anymore, because I know what I want now."

"It does matter, Mhàiri." Lowering his head, he pressed her back onto the tartan-padded ground and covered her with his massive body, pushing himself between her legs.

He was a love-maddened dolt and he did not care. His mouth came down on hers in a searing kiss. A hungry sound escaped him as he demanded entry. She willingly gave in, opening for him. Hot and wet, his tongue found hers. He held her in place by the back of her neck as his lips devoured hers in a desperate need to claim her body and soul.

Needing to kiss and taste her everywhere, his lips trailed down her throat and suckled the warm pulse, uncaring that it would leave a mark on her. His hands were gliding along her hips and sides, taking everything in.

Mhàiri's body screamed for more of him. To give him anything he wanted. To give him all of her. Conan was her every dream. A strong, confident, yet tender lover. Someone who believed in her. Who would let her be herself. A man who could show her things she had never seen before and, at night, unleash her passion, matching it with his own.

Mhàiri loved him so much, but did he love her?

Conan felt the change in her and cupped her cheeks gently in his large hands. "Mhàiri." Her name on his tongue was thick with lust. Grabbing her hips, he pulled her against him, creating a wild need for him to plunge his hardness into her. "I want you, *àluinn*."

"But do you love me?"

"Aye, but you already knew that. I want you to be mine. Every day. Forever." He threaded his fingers through her hair as if it were precious silk. "You are mine, *a chuisle*," he whispered, sounding hoarse. "I claimed you before, but this time I'm never letting you go."

With a carnal sound, he pulled her lips to his and scorched her with his kiss.

Mhàiri groaned and leaned her weight against him. This was not like any kiss before. This was a branding, primal, and possessive kiss.

When she brushed her hard nipples against his chest, she was rewarded with a callused hand coming up to press her breast with one hand. Her eyes rolled and her head fell back, body arching to his touch. He smiled. Mhàiri wanted him as well.

As quickly as possible, he eased off her and removed all her clothing. She lay there before him, the firelight flickering over her body. He marveled at her beauty.

Her body throbbed under his stare. Her skin grew hot and sensitive. Mhàiri loved his touch, but longed for more. She reached up and pulled his mouth to her waiting lips. She let out a soft needy moan, and he went wild.

He covered her with his massive body, pushing himself between her legs. His hands flowed over her skin, cupping the tightest, most luscious breast that was ever captured by five fingers. She moaned again, and he took her mouth with his as she pressed her core against his painfully hard shaft.

She rubbed herself against him, driving him mad with lust. If she continued, he would lose the bare tendrils of control he still had, and he refused to let their coming together be that quick.

Pulling away, he grabbed another log and tossed it on the fire, preventing any touch of the cold winter's storm. Then he unhooked his belt, dropping his tartan, and tore his leine over his head, removing the last bit of hindrance between them.

He basked in the feel of her soft naked skin against his own as he climbed over her. Immersing himself in the feel of her soft, warm body beneath him, he leaned down and seared her mouth to his. Her arms came around his neck to lock him in place, as if he had anywhere to go when he had her right where he wanted her.

He almost thought it was more than he could bear, and then Mhàiri began to stroke his back and buttocks with roaming fingertips. His shaft strained for her body. He needed to be inside her, but as bad as he needed her tight core clutching his shaft, he had to know she was absolutely ready for him.

Mhàiri made an aggravated sound when he removed his mouth from hers and raised an eyebrow at him. But she caught the gleam in his eye, a wicked look burning with promises of things to come.

In the next instant, her hard, little nipple was in his mouth. Conan twirled his tongue over the first peak, then the next, suckling, deeper and deeper. Arching into his touch, Mhàiri cried out from pleasure. The sensation was better than she remembered. It stole her breath.

But Conan had only just begun.

He continued flicking and teasing her breast with his tongue, letting his hand trail down her stomach and through the soft curls until he met with her core.

She gasped once more, mindless with an overload of sensation.

"Is this where you need me?" His voice sounded rough and on the verge of losing control.

"Please!" Mhàiri cried out and began rocking her hips in search of relief.

Conan's lips returned to her breast as his finger made slow, maddening circles along her opening. Then he delved one finger inside her.

Mhàiri's breath hitched and she opened wider for him. A second finger entered, increasing her pleasure. "*A chiall beannaich mise!* Conan!" she cried out. The sensations he was creating overwhelmed her, making her heart pound against the wall of her chest as pressure began to build.

Her nipple was in his mouth, his tongue swirling over the peak, teasing and stroking her. Mhàiri did not know what to do with the double onslaught of sensations.

Conan could feel coiled tension condense about her. Mhàiri opened her knees wider to take him even deeper. She was on the brink.

Conan watched her intently, waiting, as the world started to coalesce into a potent point of pleasure. He smiled possessively as the first jolting spasms echoed deep within her, the sound of her panting scream muffled by the storm raging around them.

Shifting, he gripped her thighs and opened her legs to him. Her eyes went wide, and her heart began to hammer. He groaned.

Mhàiri was just coming back to earth when she realized what Conan had planned. She shuddered in anticipation. When his hot tongue met her liquid core, she could not prevent the scream of pleasure that came from somewhere deep inside her. She writhed, thrashing her head on the blanket, and then another scream tore out of her as she climaxed once more. The waves of pleasure seemed never-ending, and all the while, he continued his relentless licking and sucking.

When Mhàiri finally went limp, Conan rose above her and eased himself between her legs. Slowly he pushed himself against her, rubbing their slickness together.

In a rough voice, he asked, "Do you love me?"

Heart drumming, she gazed back at him and challenged him with a question of her own. "Do you want me?"

His answer came quick. "Forever," he replied and then they came together with the strength of a McTiernay Highlander who had found his *sonuachar* at last.

He relished the exquisite feel of her soft flesh

around him and dipped his head to take one of her beckoning nipples into his mouth.

Forcing himself into a slow rhythm, he eased in and out of her, trying to keep himself from bucking too hard. He watched her breasts rise and fall with her heavy breathing. Her nails dug into his back, and soon she was writhing beneath him. Her legs widened for him, and her back arched, causing her breasts to press against him.

"More . . ." she begged, her voice a strained whisper.

Mhàiri was the most beautiful creature he had ever beheld.

Lifting her hips off the ground, Conan obliged. He thrust into her again and again, filling her full of more pleasure than she thought her body could contain.

Ecstasy was a word she had only thought she understood. Her body quaked at the unbelievable feel of him inside her. It was almost too much to bear. She had never felt so connected to anyone, and she wanted the sensation to last forever.

Mhàiri heard someone screaming and realized it was her. Bowing her back, her body convulsed around his shaft so that Conan soon followed her. On and on it went for both of them, until they were both drained and fatigued from the onslaught of pleasure.

Conan slumped on top of her, holding himself up by his elbows so as not to crush her. Mhàiri nuzzled her face into the crook of his neck. Her legs were still wrapped around him, her hands rubbing his arms, his chest, his back, as if she could not get enough of touching him.

Conan rolled to lie beside her and pulled her against him as they slowly were able to catch their breaths. Mhàiri sighed with satisfaction, burrowing deeper into his chest, and Conan knew there was no better feeling than having her in his arms. If he had realized every one of his prior dreams, none of them could compare to being with Mhàiri.

They lay there like that, basking in each other for a long while. Not speaking, just touching, kissing, loving each other.

Mhàiri awoke to a heavy need. Wetness was pooling between her legs and she soon began to move. Conan's fingers were touching her, building desire. Her nipples were already hard. Her body wanted him again. She could not get enough.

She cracked open her eyes and smiled. The flickering firelight heightened the shadows on Conan's face and illuminated his rich, blue eyes.

Conan gave her a wicked grin. "I cannot get my fill of you." His voice was husky. "Imagine a lifetime . . . a lifetime of this . . ."

Mhàiri responded by grinding her hips against his turgid arousal. Never had she thought she would be so insatiable.

Wearing a luxurious half smile, she demanded, "I want more."

"I'm at your service," he said and then kissed a path down her breastbone to her navel to lave her with his warm tongue.

A hard, masculine groan vibrated through her core, and Mhàiri shook with sheer pleasure. What Conan was doing to her was nothing short of amazing. He continued to stroke and caress her until he had her panting, chest heaving, body aching. Fisting the blankets, her head thrashed back and forth until there was an explosion of ecstasy. Riding her through it, he dipped a finger inside, heightening her pleasure.

"I think I'm addicted to you," he said as he kissed his way up her body, stopping to pay close attention to each breast. Then, Conan was inside her. Not hard as the night before, but gentle. It flooded her mind with bliss.

Cupping her backside as he thrust into her, Conan watched her with sapphire eyes. She wanted him harder, deeper. He quickened his movements.

Taking her mouth with his, he swallowed her cries of satisfaction and followed her with his own release.

Mhàiri snuggled against him as their legs intertwined. "I guess we should dress and get ready to return."

"Aye, since there is a search party looking for you." Conan kissed the top of her head but did not move otherwise.

Mhàiri tried to move to look at him, but Conan held her in place. "Why? My father knew I was capable of building a shelter to outlast the storm."

"Maybe, but I did not know that."

Mhàiri giggled. "We should probably return soon then to let them know they don't have to send a search party out for you."

Conan tickled her side. Mhàiri screamed and began to thrash. By the time she begged for mercy, he was atop her and she was breathing heavily. He had to fight the urge to take her once more.

"Maybe we should return because you need to plan a wedding."

Mhàiri's soft green eyes sparkled with love and excitement. "A wedding?"

"Aye, a wedding."

"By chance whose wedding would I be planning?"

Conan leaned down and kissed the top of her nose. "It just so happens, you will be the bride and I will be the groom."

Mhàiri bit her bottom lip, her grin large and full of joy. "And when is this wedding to take place?"

"Tomorrow. Right at sunset."

Chapter Fifteen

"Tomorrow afternoon! I think not!" Laurel choked out, the sound echoing in the great hall. "That is not nearly enough time!"

"For what?" Conan asked, mystified, as he snuggled Mhàiri closer on his lap. He was wondering how he was going to last tonight without her in his arms and if they had enough time to marry today. Sunset—when all the McTiernays wed—was a little more than an hour away. It was possible.

"There is a *considerable* amount to do," Laurel stated in her most authoritative voice.

"I agree with Conan," Conor chimed in. "Tomorrow is good. The sooner you are wed, the sooner calm reenters my life."

Laurel took his hand and rubbed her round stomach. "You, my love, are about to have another child. Calm is not something you are going to see again for a long, long time." Conor grunted. "And as far as a wedding, Conan, yours will not be taking place next week, let alone tomorrow."

"Next week!" Conan shouted.

"I said *not* next week. I would guess three weeks. At the very least."

Hagatha nodded. "And that is only if Conor sends the runners out today. People will need time to prepare."

Conan stilled. "What people?"

Aileen waved a finger over Mhàiri's form. "And you need a gown."

Excited with the idea of a new outfit that was not a hand-me-down, Mhàiri slid off Conan's lap. "A *new* dress?"

"Oh, it will be the most beautiful dress ever created," Maegan sighed. "I've some ideas that I want to share with you. And your hair . . . we need to wait a few weeks for the spring flowers to bloom."

Seamus elbowed Conan. "Looks like your marriage is waiting on flowers, my friend."

"People?" Conan repeated, this time with a little more force.

"All of us have been looking forward to this happy event for months and *nothing*"—Laurel paused to look at Conan and then her husband, Conor—"is going to ruin our plans."

"*Just what do you mean by people?*" Conan croaked.

"Well, did you think that we are the only ones who are going to want to witness this event?" Laurel huffed. "Because you could not be more mistaken. I have a feeling when word spreads that you, Conan McTiernay, are not only *wanting* to get married, but have found a woman who also *wants* to marry you, our home is going to draw quite a crowd."

"Then we will marry today. I am *not* someone people need to come and ogle at."

Laurel scrunched her nose at the idea. "They won't

be coming to see *you* . . . they will be coming to see Mhàiri. And when we are done," she said to her soon-to-be sister-in-law, "you will be the envy of every woman in Scotland."

Mhàiri's eyes grew large with excitement. She looked at Conan, who was scowling. She grinned at him and shrugged her shoulders. "We're waiting," she said with such happiness he could not say no. "It isn't every day a girl gets to be the envy of every woman in Scotland."

Conan sat brooding in the great hall, drinking ale that was too damn weak. Ale was always brewing, and too many were working in the buttery that never had before. When Conor had said they were going to have to ration the ale to only dinner, thank God Rae Schellden—the McTiernays' closest friend, ally, and neighbor—had not been happy with the decision. He had ordered his people to begin making ale as well, and after a week they'd begun getting a delivery every day.

Conor maneuvered through the crowd of men who had come in out of the rain and slid into a chair next to Conan. Immediately, a servant handed him a mug, which was another thing that had run out. It was fortunate that people brought their own utensils to use on their journeys; otherwise many of them would not have anything to eat on.

Conor took a swig and wrinkled his nose at the weak flavor. It needed less water and more time. They were just lucky that the last few harvests had been extremely good and there were enough oats for the crush of people who had seized McTiernay Castle and its lands for the last few weeks. He looked at his brother. "You look in a fouler mood than normal."

"I've decided I hate your wife."

Conor took another gulp. "That's not news. You've disliked her for various reasons over the years, but the last one, I think, resulted in you getting married."

"You can seriously say that to me? It's because of her that I'm *not* married. I'm ready, Mhàiri is ready, Father Lanaghly is ready, even the damn dress is ready. The only one who isn't is Laurel. She is now insisting we wait for MacInnes to arrive."

"He was our father's best friend. He wants to see you wed."

"Then he should have gotten his arse up here with the rest of Scotland." Conan looked at Conor. "It's been almost *six weeks*," he snarled. "That's long enough, and it's time you tell Laurel."

"Tell Laurel what?" The question came from behind Conan. He glanced momentarily over his shoulder. Hamish and Colin, his second-oldest brother from the Lowlands, had come to join them.

"That I don't care to wait for stragglers like yourself any longer."

Hamish nodded to Conor, Colin, and Cole, who were sitting at the table, enjoying the frustration of their younger brother. "It's your fault. We honestly thought the first missive an error. And we were not alone in that assumption either."

Conan snorted. No one had believed it. *No one.* Even Rae Schellden, their neighbor and close ally, had doubted the news.

Cole, who had been sitting drinking quietly beside his brother, agreed with Hamish, especially as he too had had doubts the first time he had heard the news. "I mean would *you* have believed a herald claiming the great Conan McTiernay had fallen madly in love with a beautiful woman who adored him in return, and was to marry imminently?"

The missive had been more than that. Laurel's message had also said that all were welcome to come join and witness the event. They just needed to bring tents, their own servants, and significant contributions to the food and drink. So, like everyone else, Colin had sent a runner back with a statement asking if the real reason Laurel wanted them to visit was to say good-bye to Conan. For that, he and Makenna would have liked to have come, but would never have left their homes for such a reason, especially as they were expecting their fourth child. And because most heralds were not sent to only one clan, but had to make multiple stops, it had taken almost two weeks for the heralds to return to Laurel with words of disbelief, some teasing comments about the insanity of the alleged bride, and requests for proof.

The runners had been dispatched out again. It had not been until Hamish received a message from Rae Schellden stating that the news was earnest that he had believed it. Conan was indeed getting married. Then the heralds had returned, all with variations on one theme—the ceremony could not take place until they arrived. Conan getting married was something that needed to be seen to be believed.

Colin winked at Conan, which rankled him further. "I think he just misses his woman," he said playfully, with a massive grin pasted on his face. Colin was not the sort to smile. The man possessed an unnatural amount of self-control. He could emotionally wall himself off, which made him a superb strategist, but it seemed that after nearly a decade of being married to Makenna and becoming a father to three children, with a fourth on the way, had changed him. And not for the better, in Conan's mind.

It also did not help that Colin was right.

Now that he knew the feel of Mhàiri's skin, her scent, her passionate response, her greedy need for him, and his insatiable need for her, the idea of not being with her at night was akin to torture. Sneaking to her room might have been possible the first week, but had become very difficult the second week. After that, guests had started to arrive in staggering numbers. The castle had never been so full. Even when Conor had married Laurel, it had not touched this constant influx of people. As a result, Mhàiri and Maegan had given up their rooms and were now sleeping with Bonny and Brenna, and visiting maids now lined the halls in temporary beds. So sneaking into Mhàiri's chambers was not an option.

The torture was not only the loss of having her in his bed; it was far more than that.

He had not seen Mhàiri practically at all these past few weeks. Dinner did not count, as there were too many people present to make conversation, much less keep one. People kept asking for her attention, and the numbers of those inquisitive people kept growing every day. Conan had assumed this would alarm Mhàiri as much as it did him, but he had been wrong.

At dinner, he had groused about how few times he had had a chance to spend time with her, and Mhàiri's response had been to *laugh*. She had laughed, infecting all those around her, and then had reminded him about the two months he had pushed her away, ignoring her. That if she could wait, then so could he.

When he had returned from an impromptu trip and Mhàiri had still been as inaccessible as before, he had begun to worry. What would she be like when it was only the two of them? There would be no crowds to entertain her. It would be just her and him, sometimes for weeks at a time.

He had been so desperate, he had gone to Brenna and Bonny for help. Both girls normally loved all the activity, but even for them, it had been too much. Luckily, Brenna had known Mhàiri's schedule and when to intercept her so they could have a few minutes. The only place had been the bottom floor of the Star Tower, which also served as a storage room.

It was the smartest thing he had done in the past six weeks, for Mhàiri's actions and first words had put his mind at ease.

Mhàiri had gripped his head between her hands and kissed him with a surge of exasperation and enthusiasm. "Can you *believe* this lunacy?" she had asked. "The only one who isn't here is the King of Scotland, and I'm not sure why, for all his people seem to be camped outside your brother's castle!"

"Someone had to be responsible enough to stay home."

Mhàiri had wrapped her arms around his neck and urged his mouth down to hers once more for claiming. When he released her lips, she said, "Can you imagine if our wedding was the reason behind a string of English raids on castles left vulnerable because all the lairds are here?"

Conan had not thought about it, but she was right. If news did get down to certain leaders in England, they might realize the powerful draw of their wedding. While the clan leaders had journeyed north without the majority of their security, those who came had almost assuredly taken their best.

"All for the wedding of a woman they don't know to a man they respect but don't like," she said. Conan had arched a brow, but said nothing. Mhàiri had shrugged. "It's true, love. But admit it, you feel the same way about them."

"Aye," he had replied as he had nuzzled her neck, not wanting to let her go.

"I love you."

"I'm surprised, with all the things being said tonight."

She had pulled his head back and cupped his face in her hands so that he would look at her. "I do not care what they say or think. I only care about you and am so lucky you trust that."

Conan had swallowed at the enormity of her words and their impact. It had been damn near impossible not pummeling those who'd wanted to tell Mhàiri about women from his past, but he had remained seated. He had seen the plea in her green eyes and he had complied. For her. Unable to speak, he had pulled her back into his arms for another steamy embrace that lasted several minutes.

He should have asked about all the men flirting with her. When he was around, he ended it, usually with nonverbal threats of harm, but he was not with her much of the time. Almost every laird had brought several soldiers with them, usually their elite guard. The fact that no one knew who Conan was marrying meant that when those soldiers met Mhàiri, they became immediately infatuated. Conan wanted to make sure that she was sending them scurrying and not protecting their feelings as she was more likely to do if they were nice. But holding her in his arms, he had forgotten everything, everyone. And before he had known it, Brenna had been whispering that someone was coming into the storage room.

"Aye, I miss my woman," Conan grumbled, glaring at Colin. "She's the only person who can carry on a decent conversation, and the reason that I cannot do so right now, privately and within the freedom of the outdoors, is because of people like you."

"Me?" Colin yelped in surprise. "I've been here nearly a week! I got here even before Cole!"

Cole threw up his hands. "Blame Hamish—he only arrived yesterday."

"I was forced to bring two pregnant women!" Hamish wailed, expressing just how difficult it had been to travel with his wife and also pregnant sister-in-law in those few words. "And there were a *lot* of us."

Conan fixed a level stare on Hamish. "Why is that?" he asked earnestly. "I don't know your brother, and I don't know Laird Mackay. And neither of them know me."

Hamish's eyes flew to the end of the hall, where his brother and Laird Mackay were sitting drinking with other very powerful lairds. All three of them wished they had left a lot sooner. This gathering was unlike any before it and probably any that would come after. They had missed much by delaying their trip.

After the ice storm, the weather had been surprisingly cooperative. Scotland was not a dry land, but it had been a relatively dry spring that had come early. So the grounds had hardened, making it easier, safer, and quicker to travel. Hence, some who might have decided to stay home had changed their minds and decided to come. As the numbers of people and clans grew, more and more realized they would be the only ones not at the event and sent word that they, too, were on their way.

The training fields and those next to them had been taken over by large tents, corralled horses, and campfires. Training had been replaced with games of skill that anyone could participate in. And for those days it did rain, like this afternoon, lairds and some of their elite soldiers found their way to the crowded great hall to drink and talk. And the talk had been very interesting.

McTiernay was a large and powerful clan with several strong allies. Those allies also had strong allies, and many of them had come under the guise of seeing the most unexpected wedding ever known, but also so they would not be left out of any potential discussions. Those who were not there were noticeable. MacCoinnich, Andrias, Hamilton, and Keney were the most obvious. Hamilton and Keney were more important to Colin, as they were powerful Lowland clans. But MacCoinnich and Andrias were not. And MacCoinnich was just as powerful as the Mackays from the north. But unlike the Mackays, who had few truly trusted alliances due to their history, the MacCoinnichs had key strategic relationships in place that stretched from one side of northern Scotland through to Inverness.

Iain Mayboill strolled up to the group and wedged himself in between two McTiernays without worry that they might be offended or would not move. Conan could not think of another person in the world—including their eldest brother, Conor—whom they would have willingly shifted in their seats for. But they did it for Iain. Conan bit back a derisive comment, not to his future father-in-law, but to his brothers. He had to admit that Iain was a marvel. Mhàiri's father had sold everything of any value that he had wanted to sell weeks ago and was just as antsy to leave as Conan was.

"That was a pretty good fight you and my daughter had yesterday." Iain stared at Conan with mirth dancing in his eyes. The old man was intentionally stirring up trouble.

"Only fun if you get to make up. Which I didn't."

Iain pursed his lips together, but it did not do much to hide his smile. "That is true."

"And furthermore, I *won*. It's really not fair of Laurel not to let me spend time with my woman right after a fight."

"Worse, you probably won't win another argument for a long, long time," Cole added, speaking from experience. Another "aye" came from Colin. And the rest were bobbing their heads. "Another reason for me to hate Laurel," Conan added, directing this one to Conor.

"She loves this stuff. Not me," Conor said in his defense.

"Nor me or Mhàiri. We should have just left," Conan moaned. "Someday Scotland is going to have a place, some town, that people can rush off to in the dead of the night and wed without any fuss."

Iain took a deep breath and slowly scanned the

room. It was full and only getting more packed as the rain continued and it got closer to dinner. "I'm looking forward to tonight's meal. I'm not sure how Fiona manages with these numbers, but the quality of what comes out of her kitchen is still some of the best food I've ever had."

For the first month, hunters, falconers, and fishermen could find enough in the hills and lochs to feed everyone. Then they'd had to start butchering kyloe. Highland cattle were known for their long horns and long, wavy coats. "Thankfully, Laurel thought about food when she sent out the invitations," Cole said.

Conan snorted. "That only proves she knew *exactly* what she was doing when she sent out the invitations. The woman is a menace."

Cole's head snapped back and he put his hands in the air. "Don't look at me! I'm just glad I'm married and don't have to worry anymore about her meddling in my love life. Which is just fine by the way."

Hamish swung an arm over Cole's shoulders and gave him a squeeze. "What? Chricton is now almost two. You never know."

Cole narrowed his gaze. "I know. We agreed. Two were enough. One girl and one boy. Don't need any more."

"You need to talk to Makenna," Colin grumbled. "We have three, one on the way, and I can tell she is nowhere close to done. She loves being a mother and the chaos that comes with it."

Hamish grinned. "The McTiernay brood is growing." He then looked out the window to the steady rain. "Have you noticed that it always rains when it is our turn to use the loch?"

"Aye," Colin answered, pouring himself some more ale. He had no idea how much he had had, but no longer did it taste weak. "Looks like another cold one for us men."

With so many at the castle and staying in tents, not only were food and space an issue, but bathing had become one as well. The kitchens were always operating at a furious pace, despite tripling the help. They had no time or room to heat water, leaving all to bathe in the loch, which was also needed by servants to do the laundry. With so many needing access, and privacy and space becoming an issue, Laurel had declared the morning for the women, directly followed by the launderers, and then the men could have the rest of the day since it was impossible to predict when the weather would turn or the games would be over. It had worked, but as the rain usually came in the afternoon, every man was grumbling that it was not fair.

"I can solve that problem today," Conan muttered.

"Could you?" Hamish asked.

Conan nodded. He had been packed up and ready to go now for a month. Initially, he had actually been glad for some more time to prepare. Mhàiri's father had traveled all his life with a wagon and had many ideas to make theirs as comfortable and roomy as possible. As a result, night, storms, and cold weather would not be nearly as difficult to endure. "Since the day the cart was done and loaded, I have been ready to leave."

Cole, who had been leaning on his elbows, which were on the table, began to wag his finger as an idea occurred to him. "I'm surprised you did not leave and return in the nick of time."

"Like you?" Conan chided. "And I *did* leave. I was gone for a week and had gotten back right when you arrived. I actually thought I had arrived just in time for our wedding. I had no idea that Laurel would insist on waiting for every affirmative answer she received."

Hamish grinned. So did Colin, Conor, and Cole. Conan looked around. Everyone was smiling. "You all are loving this!" he shouted. "This is all fun for you! Keep it up and I'll make sure your trip was pointless by sneaking Mhàiri away and getting married alone."

This only brought more smiles.

Mhàiri watched the hard rain fall as she sat on one of the padded seats in Laurel's day room, which, along with Conor's day room above it and the solar on the top floor, made up the only three rooms in the castle that had not been turned over to guests or extended family.

The rain had been falling steadily now for an hour, and with all the people, the grass in the courtyard had been nearly trampled to death. Soon it would be a muddy nightmare. Before the wedding, the large bailey would have virtually emptied during such a downpour. With so many visitors and so much constantly needing to be done as a result, the commotion never ceased. Another reason the grass had no chance if the wedding was delayed much longer.

At first, Mhàiri had loved all the bustle and commotion. It reminded her of Christmastide. There were always new faces, and meal times were filled with hilarity as the group got larger. Her father was not the only one who had the gift of gab, and she found herself doubled over in stitches at least twice each meal before their plates were collected.

The additional time to make a dress had also been necessary. Laurel and Aileen had enlisted Nairne's mother, Siùsan, to help with the wedding gown. It had been beautiful, with a scooped neck, butterfly sleeves, lace, and a sweeping train. Then Ellenor and Brighid had arrived. Brighid, whose skill with a needle Mhàiri had heard of for months, took a look and insisted it needed more. And the gown had only become more beautiful.

Unfortunately, during the modifications, the five women had chatted and all concurred that the gown, while beautiful, was not the right style or color. And they had been right.

The luxurious, rich blue bliaut they had made was stunning. Brighid had created a subtle floral embroidery all over the shimmery material. The sleeves' wider openings narrowed down to the elbows, in a shape known as a bell sleeve, separated by lace. The front and back corset curved to her body, making her look even taller and slimmer. Mhàiri loved it and felt beautiful in it. All five had agreed, which was why they'd finished it, but they had also all agreed that it was still not what she should get married in.

The next ensemble had made her feel like a princess. Created out of the most beautiful material of jet black and purple crushed velvet Mhàiri's father had acquired when in Europe last fall, the five women had created something truly spectacular. The dress and outer sleeves had been made with the velvet, and the neckline had been detailed with a black braid that also adorned the arm bands. The front corset was a stunning purple shade that also lined the inner sleeves.

Mhàiri loved it, but she did not want to wear something so dark. So a final dress had been made, and even if all five had thought it, too, could be outdone, Mhàiri would have stopped them. Nothing could outshine the final lavender gown, and thankfully all agreed. Mhàiri had her wedding dress.

Mhàiri had worried about the other dresses made and that Conor wouldn't like the waste. But Laurel had assured her that Conor would have no idea, nor would he care, as long as it made all the women happy, especially his wife.

Mhàiri was very appreciative and very glad that it was over. She had helped a little, but her stitches were not as precise as Siùsan and Brighid's. And Maegan had only been able to give her reprieves periodically as she was tasked with overseeing the ever-growing brood. When Makenna had arrived with her son and two daughters—both of whom looked and acted frightening like their mother—Maegan had threatened to run away. She had not been serious, but she had told Seamus later that she did not want a large family and hoped that Clyde would be fine with that since he had six brothers. Seamus had pointed out that he had only one sibling and thought one or two children the perfect number.

Maegan had told her that the last time they had been together. It had been a week ago, and they had been out watching the Highland games. Mhàiri had been capturing on paper some of what she saw when archery had begun and she had seen Laurel take aim. The woman was massively pregnant, but that had not seemed to affect her ability to shoot, for she had soundly beat all who had gone against her. That had given Mhàiri the courage to join the competition of dagger throwing. She had been surprised when Laurel, too, had entered.

"Conor's men always go on about what I can do with a bow and arrow, but they forget what I can do with a dirk." Then she had looked at what was in Mhàiri's hand and asked, "Can you throw as well?"

The competition had soon whittled down to just a handful. That was when Mhàiri had noticed Conan was in the crowd, standing next to a scowling Conor. Neither of them had looked happy to know their loved ones were so deadly. Mhàiri had eventually won, and Laurel had said that her pregnancy was throwing her slightly off. Mhàiri had not thought so, but she would love the chance to challenge Laurel again someday and told Conan that at dinner. Unfortunately, before he could respond, she had been overheard and the topic had caused quite a stir of questions being aimed at her.

At first, all the attention had been great for her ego and self-confidence, but it had not been long before it had become old—very old. A month of answering questions about her life, her skills with a knife, her drawing, the languages she spoke, did she think she was smarter than Conan, did she really love him, how could she tolerate his company, and so many more, had made her want to sneak off, grab Conan, tell the priest their promises, leave, and break in their new cart.

She loved the new cart. It was beyond perfect, and she wished she could have joined Conan when he had taken it out for a test run. She had wanted to be there for its first use, but her man had not been happy with all the delays and she had wanted him to be. She, on the other hand, was not going to be happy until she stopped sleeping with little Bonny and started sleeping with Conan as his wife. At least she was not in bed with Brenna, who moved around in her sleep. She often woke Maegan and nearly pushed her out of the bed, despite its large size.

Maegan was one of the only reasons she had yet to tell Laurel that enough time had passed and the ceremony would be taking place immediately. Maegan and Seamus loved each other. It was etched all over their faces, but something had happened at Christmastide and they stopped talking to one another. Thankfully they were speaking again, but both were pretending that things were as they had been before. Neither wanted to lose their friendship, and neither knew how to move forward without jeopardizing it. This careful dance they were doing with each other could not be sustained forever, and Mhàiri feared that Maegan would need a friend before long if she made the wrong decision. Because soon, and Mhàiri feared that her wedding might be the catalyst, Seamus was going to give Maegan an ultimatum. One he probably did not want to give, but had to.

Giggles were coming from behind her, and Mhàiri glanced back over her shoulder. There were so many pregnant women around it was overwhelming. Laurel was due within the month, and Crevan's wife, Raelynd, who was due either in May or June also looked as if she could have a child at any moment. Not much further off was Colin's wife, Makenna, who had been born and raised in the Lowlands, but acted as if she were a Highlander through and through. Mairead, Hamish's wife, just beamed when she was not conspiring. The only wives who were not pregnant were Ellenor, Cole's wife, her best friend, Brighid, and Meriel, who was married to Craig and had had a child only a year before.

The door opened. In walked a woman whom Mhàiri immediately knew to be both kind and friendly. She had thick reddish brown hair and a smattering of freckles sprinkled over her nose and cheeks. When she smiled, her brown eyes literally twinkled.

Upon seeing who had entered, Laurel gasped. Her hand flew to her mouth just as Raelynd and Meriel squealed with delight. "*Rowena!*"

This was immediately followed by "Meriel!" and a "*Mo chairde,* Raelynd, you are huge!"

The three women hugged and laughed and danced the best they could with Raelynd being so large. It was only after several minutes of revelry and talking about how Cyric, her husband, had finally been able to break away that they remembered they were not alone and why everyone was there.

The bride. The bride whom no one knew. The bride whom everyone was here to meet. It seemed they really had little interest in Conan. They wanted to meet her. To see her and determine what kind of woman Conan was willing to marry and just could possibly be willing to marry him. Mhàiri was tired of it.

"Rowena," Meriel said, grinning and gasping for breath, "meet Mhàiri."

Like everyone, Rowena's eyes grew wide with surprise, and then what could only be labeled as a skeptical smile followed. It was as if they were surprised by her appearance and then had trouble envisioning her with Conan. "Why does everyone do that?" Mhàiri asked bluntly, pointing to Rowena's face.

"What?"

"That look of surprise. Don't deny it. You are not the only one. Practically everyone does it when they first meet me. Why?"

Rowena looked back at her friends, who seemed just as shocked by the small outburst. But her husband, Cyric, was very gifted in the ways of diplomacy, and over the years she had learned a few things. First was not to be affronted by honesty. In fact, do the opposite and embrace it. Rowena sat down beside Mhàiri. "I guess you do probably feel like a specimen being inspected, but trust me, if my expression is like everyone else's, you have not been found wanting."

Mhàiri swallowed. "Well, that is a relief. But that smile was not one of happiness. It was more amazed than genuine."

Rowena laughed. "Well, first, I was surprised at how beautiful you are. I mean, you truly are stunning. Conan may be a very good-looking man, but he is a difficult one. And since you are being blunt, I will, too. I am not a beautiful woman—"

"You are too!" came the cries from her best friends and distant cousins.

"I am far from unpleasant, but I am not a beauty and I know it. I've watched many beautiful women, though, over the past few years. My husband works directly for and with the king in diplomacy matters so I have seen too many to count around court. And beautiful women, well, usually seek someone who would fawn over them. They certainly would not be interested in a man with Conan's difficult temperament. As far as my mischievous smile, you are not just marrying a McTiernay. You are marrying Conan—*the* McTiernay everyone has heard of."

Mhàiri was not sure she could handle another story about Conan and his life before meeting her. And what she had discovered was that those who only knew Conan by reputation were spreading what they had been told, not the truth.

Mhàiri wanted to say it was physically impossible to have been with that many women, to have scorned them and left their hearts bleeding as he heartlessly walked away. She knew the truth. His eye had been caught by a pretty face numerous times, and he could count on one hand how many had turned him down for a kiss. But it had never gone beyond that because by that time he had found nothing beyond their looks of any interest. He had limited his actual sexual activities to a couple of widows. Who they were she did not know and hoped never to find out. That was his past. What was important was that Conan had not touched another woman since meeting her, including the times they had not been talking.

Despite most everyone's stories about Conan being drenched in fiction, the tales kept coming . . . usually over dinner and in the earshot of Conan himself. It had taken everything in Conan not to stand up, pummel the storytellers, and create a scene that launched a massive fight. It had happened once before, Maegan had told her, but Mhàiri knew the reason Conan did not was because of her.

What was worse were the looks from people who *did* know Conan. They just could not believe someone was willing to deal with his rude behavior. Raelynd had been the worst of them.

She and Meriel were not on bad terms with Conan,

but neither were they really on good terms with him either. They enjoyed sniping at him and pushed him to snipe back. A couple weeks ago at dinner, both women had been relentless, and when he had had something to say to Mhàiri, he had used the same tone and surliness.

"This is all your fault," he had said, the malicious tone unmistakable and aimed directly at Mhàiri. "If you had simply told Laurel no and gotten married when we first wanted to I would not have to put up with any of this, especially those two." His eyes darted to a hostile Raelynd and then Meriel, who at least looked apologetic for pushing him so far.

It was the first time that any visitor had heard Conan be rude to Mhàiri. They had all known he would eventually and stared at Mhàiri to see her response. Would she explode in anger, making him explode in kind? Would she meekly apologize?

Mhàiri had studied him for a moment and then shrugged. "What really is angering you is that I would do all of this"—she twirled her fork around in the air—"again if we had the option. I have no regrets about wanting a wedding, nor will I suddenly attain them because you, Meriel, and Raelynd cannot act like mature adults in each other's company."

Meriel's jaw had dropped, but Raelynd, who had been listening intently to see how Mhàiri would explode and rip into Conan like she would have, had sat frozen with shock. Her eyes had swiveled to her husband, Crevan, for support. He had just thrown up his hands and said, "You know it's true. You have been intentionally poking at him every night, waiting to see what will happen."

"You should have said something!" Raelynd had shouted at him. "I'm pregnant, not fragile!"

Creven had shaken his head. "Not until my babe is safely in this world." Raelynd had sat and fumed and probably would have said more if Conan had not made a threat.

"If you feel that I am so immature, maybe I should leave."

Mhàiri had bobbed her head. "That is one of the better ideas you've had in a while. Go test our cart for a week. By the time you return, everybody will have to be here and we can finally marry."

While that had been the perfect response for Conan, it had been the wrong one for everyone else. Mhàiri had been expected to get mad and yell, like all other McTiernay wives. Some had begun to wonder if her and Conan's relationship was not one of passion, but more one of convenience. The craziest rumor following that night had been that she was afraid of Conan.

Then, yesterday, all those rumors, thoughts, and concerns had been put to rest. Mhàiri had not been looking for a reason to fight with Conan, and yet that was exactly what had happened.

She had gone to her old room in the Warden's Tower to get one of her hemp books and discovered that every last book was missing. She had charged into Conan's room and found them safely among his things. Unfortunately, he had not been there to explain why he had had them moved . . . but he had been in the courtyard.

"Of course I moved the damn things!" he had yelled back. "Do you know who is sleeping in your chambers? Donald and Brighid and their *three* sons." He had waved three fingers in her face.

Mhàiri had forgotten this, but felt it did not matter if Conan had a good reason to move her things. He had done so without telling her; therefore, he should have expected she would be angry. "And what would your reaction be if you suddenly found all *your* things gone from where you knew them to be just because someone got it in their head that they weren't safe?"

"But they *weren't* safe!"

"They were mine to move!"

"Aye, and that's why I did it! But trust me, I won't make that mistake again!"

All throughout the argument, more and more people had surrounded them. Those from McTiernay Castle had stopped for a moment because it had been something new to watch Conan and Mhàiri raise their voices, but after a few minutes they'd realized it was no different from Laurel and Conor. The others, however, had been intrigued and their eyes had been completely glued on the two of them. As a result, it had been impossible to make up after their argument, which was doubly upsetting because she had won.

Rowena patted her knee with a smile, bringing Mhàiri's attention back to the women surrounding her. "Cyric told me to tell you that Laird MacInnes's group has been spotted and is less than a day away. He will be here in the morning."

Laurel clapped her hands together. "Mhàiri, he is my grandfather and Conan's godfather. Once he is here, there is no reason to wait any longer." She leveled her gaze on Mhàiri, whose heart started rapidly beating. "Tomorrow afternoon at sunset, we are going to have a wedding."

Chapter Sixteen

Mhàiri stood beside the great oak looking at Conan as they took their vows. The weather was perfect. Not a cloud was in the sky. The rain from the previous afternoon had passed on in the early hours, and since Neal's back was no longer hurting, the rain was not going to return for the rest of the day.

The massive crowd of onlookers was indescribable. Mhàiri had been told hundreds had come in, and she had seen many of them in and around the castle. The great hall had been filled with lairds and ladies from clans all over Scotland. The lower hall had been more than full with their elite guards. Tents were everywhere. When she had gone to bathe in the morning, the loch had been crowded with women. And yet she still had no idea exactly how many people had come to watch her and Conan marry until she had stood on that hill and looked out. One could not see hills or grass. Only people. It was incredible, astonishing, and almost beyond comprehension. It was also beautiful.

The only ones missing were Conan's brother Clyde and her sister, Shinae. She was too new to her vows to be free to travel, and no one knew where Clyde was. Last they had heard from him was almost three years ago. He had been among King Robert's forces who had invaded Ireland in 1315 to free the country from English rule. Both Clyde and Shinae were missed, but Conan and Mhàiri refused to let their absence rob them of any joy.

Conan had seen many beautiful women in his life. His brother Conor had married one of the most stunning females he had ever seen. Laurel with her light blond hair and blue-and-green-colored eyes could captivate a man's soul with just a look. But never had Conan seen anything or anyone who could compare with his Mhàiri.

He had seen her radiant in the past, but her beauty shined for all to see. The afternoon sun created a halo effect around her flower-bedecked figure. Mhàiri looked ethereal, almost surreal. Her dress was of the palest lavender satin, with a cream tulle overskirt— simple, elegant, and unadorned except at its hem and scooped neckline, where hundreds of seed pearls and lilac glass beads seemed to shimmer. She carried a small posy of violets and cream roses, mirroring the flowers in her hair.

Mhàiri looked at him, and Conan could feel his heart melt. Her smile could light up an area on a moonless night for miles. And today, he was the reason behind her smile. It humbled him. This beautiful, perfect creature loved him enough to be his wife. He was not worthy of her. He never would be. But then, no one ever would be.

Mhàiri's cheeks hurt. She could not stop smiling, and she did not want to. The McTiernay nobody had thought would ever marry was pledging himself to her.

She had actually found a man to love. A man who loved her fully and completely. Who knew who she was, what she needed, and how to make her truly happy.

Conan was not perfect, but he was perfect for her. They would argue and challenge each other probably daily, but they would also open each other's minds in ways no one else could. She suspected one lifetime with this man was not going to be enough.

The happy couple waved to the crowd and headed to where several large bonfires had been erected and were waiting to be lit, signifying the wedding celebration was to begin. Tonight, there would be no restrictions on the meat, the bread, or the ale. All were to feast and be merry until there was not a drop left to drink or a morsel left to eat.

Maegan had been standing near Mhàiri, along with her other closest friends up on the hill. She had been paying attention to the ceremony and the vows, but she had also been scanning the crowd as well.

A week ago, Seamus had said they were going to talk directly after the wedding ceremony, whenever it took place. The comment had left her anxious because she knew what he was going to demand. Seamus wanted a future. He wanted a wife. He wanted her to be that wife. And he wanted to know if that was a dream he needed to let go of or one she was willing to share with him.

All week, Maegan had struggled with the answer.

Her heart wanted two men. It was impossible for her to choose, but Mhàiri had pointed out an inconvenient truth. Seamus was not forcing her to choose; her heart had forced that choice upon her when it had fallen for Seamus. Because if Clyde had returned, would she not have to make a choice then? Would she give up a man she had loved for years for Seamus? Or would she choose a man she probably no longer knew over Seamus, who knew and loved her for who she was today?

Maegan was honestly not sure. She loved Clyde. She had loved him, body and soul, for so long she wondered if it was even possible to split him from her hopes, her dreams . . . her heart. She was not sure she could. And would it be fair to love Seamus, but not in the same way?

It had been a week, and all Maegan had were questions. She still lacked answers. But to Seamus, no response would be an answer.

She could not reject her love for Clyde. And yet, she could not lose Seamus. Just the thought of Seamus not being in her life made her tremble with fear and ache that physically hurt.

Maegan scanned the crowd again, looking for Seamus's tall frame and dark blond hair. Her eyes were moving from one person to the next when they landed on one face that she would always recognize she had dreamed of it so many times. It was one that, until that very moment, she had never truly believed she would see again.

Clyde.

All the McTiernay brothers had the same dark brown hair, but only two had gray eyes. The first— Conor—and the last—Clyde.

Clyde had come home.

He was here. And yet he was not, for it was clear he did not want anyone to know he was here.

He looked different. So different that people who

stood right next to him, who knew him and should have recognized him by sight, had no idea Clyde Mc-Tiernay was in their presence.

He was much larger than she remembered and he wore a full beard. His youthful lankiness had disappeared and had been replaced with a man's body. Muscles rippled underneath his leine. His arms were massive, and his hands looked calloused from hours wielding a weapon. He appeared relaxed, and yet his stance made her think he was always ready for an attack. His gaze was on the happy couple saying their vows and held a strangely detached quality that was disturbing. What had happened to him?

Then, without warning, his eyes shifted to hers. Nothing else about him moved, but in those few seconds of mutual recognition, Maegan saw it. Love. Pain. Defeat. Despair. And then it was gone. But it was too late. She had seen the truth.

In that moment, she made up her mind. She loved Seamus. She did. He was her best friend, her confidant, her support. But he was not her soul mate. Her heart was seared with anguish seeing Clyde hurting so much.

As soon as the ceremony was at a point she could move, Maegan started running. But Clyde had started moving too, and he was unnaturally adept at maneuvering through crowds. Maegan refused to give up and kept charging through, fighting a crowd that wanted to go the opposite direction she was headed in. But finally she spotted him once more and started picking up speed.

She knew that Clyde thought that he had lost her because he did not increase his gait once he was alone. She followed him as he made his way through all the tents and temporary stable setups until he reached one. He stopped, untied the reins of a horse, and was leading the animal out of the penned area when he saw Maegan.

His jaw tightened and his body froze.

Maegan, however, was not inclined to stare and launched herself at him, hugging him, tears streaming down her cheeks. "You're home. Clyde, you're home," she whispered into his chest. Nothing felt better than when his arms curved around her and held her close.

Maegan felt his mouth in her hair. She absorbed the trembles that went through his frame. She inhaled the one scent that could only be described as Clyde. He was home.

"I've waited for so long for you to come back to me." Her face was pressed into him, muffling her voice. "But I knew you would. I knew it."

And then it happened.

Clyde changed. Maegan could feel it. It was as if someone had poured ice water into his veins. He released her, gripped her shoulders, and pushed her away from him. "I did not return to you, and I am not home. I came simply to see my brother marry. Now that I have, I am leaving and I do not intend to return again."

Maegan's breath caught in her throat. "I don't believe you," she whispered. "You love me." She reached out and grabbed his forearm. She stared into mercury eyes and saw the truth. "I can see it. You can say what you want to leave, but you cannot deny that you still *love* me."

Clyde stood for what seemed like an eternity, quiet and not moving, before he spoke. "Aye. I loved you. And you loved me at one time." His eyes swept down her frame and back up. "But I am not who I was. You no longer know me. If you did, you would know that I don't have the power to love anymore. That emotion was stripped from me long ago so, if you have been waiting for my return, don't. This is no longer my home."

Maegan's hands flew to her mouth. Her eyes were wide with shock and pain. "You don't mean that."

"I do. I'm not coming back, Maegan," he said in a resolute voice. "And I am not coming back to you."

Maegan stumbled back. She had felt the impact of Clyde's words as if he had struck her physically.

She had loved him. The forever kind of love. The kind of love that could not be destroyed or killed. The kind that inspired a person to travel great distances to be reunited. The kind that one seized onto and did not let go of. She had felt that for him, and she had known Clyde had felt that way about her. She had *known* it. There had been no doubt. That was why there had never been another.

But it had all been a lie.

"You don't love me," she said.

"I don't even know you."

"You don't want me."

"I don't want anyone."

Tears brimmed in her eyes once more. She could see Clyde's pain. Hear it in every syllable. It was buried deep. So deep that it was one with him. "Are you happy, Clyde?"

Clyde's jaw twitched. "Irrelevant question, Maegan."

She closed her eyes and tilted her chin upward, hearing her name on his lips. "It isn't. I need to know that you are happy."

He looked up and refused to look her in the eye for nearly a minute. "It doesn't matter because I don't want you. Find a man who does." Using his chin, he gestured behind her.

Maegan glanced over her shoulder, knowing whom she would see. Seamus. He was standing there. Watching. Listening. Waiting. Pain was etched on his face. He knew she loved Clyde. He knew her heart was breaking. He knew that she did not love him the same way. It was killing him. And yet he remained. For her. He was there because he knew she might need him.

"Go and live your life, Maegan. You only get one. Don't waste it on me." Clyde gave a tug on the reins and led his horse to where he could jump on. Then, without another word, without looking back even once, he left.

Maegan had known Clyde almost as far back as she could remember. She knew him. She knew the truth. Clyde still loved her as much as he ever had. He was hurting. He was in pain. Something was haunting him, eating away at him, making him believe he could not make her happy. So he had set her free in the only way he knew how.

Clyde was wrong. But it did not matter.

Just as her heart had known he had loved her as much as she had loved him, her heart knew the awful truth now. Clyde was not ever coming back.

Wooden legs took her to Seamus. He said nothing. He only opened his arms and enveloped Maegan the moment her body melted into his. He had been so afraid. He had known he loved her but had not known the depth of his feelings until he had seen her running through the crowd. He had chased her to see whom she was after and had been shocked to see that it had been Clyde.

He had been hugging Maegan in a way that left no

doubt to anyone who saw them about his feelings. Clyde's love was just as deep, just as sure, as Maegan's. But when Clyde had let go, Seamus had seen something else in the man's eyes. He had seen it before, though not in one as young as Clyde, but Seamus knew that look.

War ate at a man. It hollowed him in ways that someone who had never taken a life, had never stood in the middle of a bloody field after fighting to the death, at first for a cause and then just survival, would understand. It did something. It changed a person. Doing it for years either hardened hearts or turned men into shells. Clyde was a bit of both. He had been right to push Maegan away. He loved her, but he could not love her in the way she needed or deserved.

So when Clyde looked up and stared him in the eye, making Seamus promise to love her enough for the both of them, Seamus had nodded and prayed that Maegan would let him.

And then a miracle had happened. She had run into his arms. She had sought him out and clung to him, sobbing her pain and grief for another man. But she had come to him.

He had been so afraid that she wouldn't. That she would run away and curl into herself, blocking out anything and everyone in an effort to get away from the pain. That she wouldn't let him help her.

But Maegan had come to him.

She loved him.

Maybe not the same way she had loved Clyde, but maybe that was a good thing. It had not let her see the truth. That she had lost Clyde a long time ago when he had failed to return, opting to fight, rather than seeking happiness and the love of a good woman. Seamus had almost made that same mistake. But then he had met Maegan.

She did not know it, but she had saved him. And now it was his turn to save her.

Conan carried Mhàiri up three flights of stairs before he let her down. He wanted to carry her all seven flights to the solar, and he had intended to, but that had been a foolish ambition. Especially if he wanted to do anything tonight other than recover and pass out.

Mhàiri smiled up at him and then laughed. "I guess Hagatha won." She giggled.

He frowned. "Won what?"

She reached up on her tippy-toes and gave him a light kiss. "You didn't think men were the only ones who gambled on ridiculous things? When you announced that you were carrying me up to the solar, we all knew that was never going to happen. We all picked a level that you would stop at. Hagatha had three."

Conan pursed his lips together, and he contemplated picking Mhàiri back up and carrying her the rest of the way. Three seemed like a very embarrassing number. "What number did you have? And you better not say one."

Mhàiri grinned. "Seven." When he reached down to pick her up, she scooted back. "While I have no doubt that you *could* carry me all seven flights, I have other plans for our last night in a real bed."

Conan had nearly toppled over in shock when Laurel had said that she and Conor wanted them to have the solar for their wedding night, especially as it would be some time before the couple slept in comfort again. Then Conan had seen Conor's face and realized his brother had not been so generous and was not happy that his wife had given away their bedchambers, even if it was for only one night. But Conan was not interested in making Conor happy. He only cared about Mhàiri's happiness and there was no doubt she would love sleeping in the solar. And after he got to explore every inch of her body a few times, they would take a break, go to the top of the tower, and enjoy the view. Just thinking about it made Conan salivate.

He tapped Mhàiri's bottom. "Hurry up, woman. For weeks, my body has been racked with pain without its only cure—you."

Mhàiri had started her ascent but stopped and turned around. She was on a higher step and it almost brought them face to face. She curled her arms around his neck and said in a husky voice, "I ache for you too."

"*Murt!*" he muttered. His hands were on her hips and then her bottom, squeezing her tightly against him so she could feel the evidence of his desire.

Mhàiri's eyes grew large with excitement. She gave him a quick peck, turned around, and dashed up the remaining four stories to the solar. The room was massive and very masculine, and in the middle was an enormous bed. "How did they ever get that up here?"

Conan came behind her and pulled her back to his chest. He nuzzled her neck and murmured, "They didn't. My father had it built in this room."

Mhàiri pulled free and went to look out the window. She had had no idea she would be able to see so far from this high up. She could see the tents and the campfires lit in the distance. The bonfires were mostly obstructed by the curtain wall, but she could see that the crowds had not begun to die down. The party would last for several more hours. Mhàiri was glad she did not have to wait until everyone else was ready to sleep for her and Conan to finally be together. Then, as the world decided to at last sleep, she and Conan would awake and leave. They wanted to be gone by sunrise, embarking on their life and future at last.

Conan took off his shoes, belt, and tartan and tossed them to the side. He then walked up to Mhàiri and hugged her from behind. Slowly, he began to pull pins out of her hair and then tugged free the last ties that kept the intricate weave in place. Plunging his fingers into the thick mass, he gently pulled until the dark locks hung free. Next, very lightly, he slid her gown off her shoulder, revealing skin for him to savor and kiss. "You happy?"

"I am now," she sighed, leaning back into him. "At first, planning the wedding was fun, but the last couple of weeks have been wearing." She turned around in his arms. "Pregnant women are emotional, Conan. Like *really* emotional. Probably the scariest people on earth. They are impossible to talk to or reason with. And there were so *many* of them."

Conan chuckled. It was deep in his chest, and Mhàiri could feel the slight vibration run throughout his body. "My brothers love their wives, and I suspect when you are large with our child, I will love you as well."

Mhàiri wrinkled her nose at the idea. "Let's wait. Like a long time. And if we ever decide to have a child, let's visit someone who has lots of them *and* is pregnant. I'm sure that will change our minds quite quickly."

Conan did laugh then. It was deep, warm, rich, and catching. Mhàiri could not help but join him. He held her close. Other men only thought they understood why he had broken down and asked her to marry him for Mhàiri was indeed beautiful and smart. But she was so much more—a great lover, a beautiful person, and gifted artist who possessed a razor-sharp intelligent wit. Even more importantly, Mhàiri was his best friend. Life was so much more than the shallow things of beauty and sex—though making love to Mhàiri was one of the best things he had ever experienced. But what he could not live without was her. Her friendship. Her ability to make him laugh.

He finally understood his brothers.

He finally understood what it was to have a *sonuachar*. A soul mate.

Mhàiri closed her eyes as she felt his lips brush her ear, then slide to her neck. She could feel Conan's body and how it was strung tight. He wanted to go slow for her. It had been weeks, and he wanted to make things perfect. But in her mind, perfect did not involve slow. Maybe later, but right now, slow and gentle was not what she had in mind. "Conan. I need you. Now."

Her body arched toward him as his mouth slid down her neck again. His hand was on her breast, teasing her nipple through the material. She writhed and mewled as his fingers teased, pinched, massaged, and stroked her. "What do you need, *a ruin*? Tell me your fantasies, and I'll make them come true."

"You," she whispered. "You are my fantasy. My complete fantasy. I just need you."

Conan's control snapped. His lower body hardened to the point of pain. He needed to touch her, all of her, to join with her and feel her all around him.

He stepped back and stripped off his leine. Then

she was back in his arms. His mouth descended as he went to work, undoing the laces of her dress. He pushed the garment off her shoulders so that it fell to her waist and then pulled her close. With a groan, he claimed her mouth and then traced the contours of her lips with his own. Immediately, her lips softened and then opened for him.

The feel of skin against skin caused Mhàiri's thighs to tighten, trying to bring him even closer. Her hands came up to rest on his shoulders and the tender kiss became demanding. She quivered, and Conan pulled her up into his arms and carried her directly to the bed.

Slowly, Conan lowered her onto the blanket and worked the rest of her clothes off. She was beautiful and strong, yet still fragile against his strength. After seven weeks, his need for her was almost all consuming. He needed to regain control, prepare her, or risk hurting her with his lust.

Breaking off the kiss, he eased back, looking at her lying naked in a bed. This would be the last night for a while either of them delighted in such comfort, and he intended for them both to enjoy it. Running large, rough hands up Mhàiri's quivering body, Conan shifted his gaze to her eyes. They were locked with his, and he could read the passion and arousal in those green depths.

Mhàiri was on fire. Conan was gently stroking her skin, and she needed to touch him in return. She ran her hand down his chest, tracing old scars made from mishaps in training and near misses in battle. "You're so beautiful," she whispered in awe as she followed the silky trail of hair from his navel downward.

"Men are not beautiful," he rumbled, his voice gravelly, but adoring.

"My eyesight is perfect and so is my perception. You are perfect, which makes you beautiful."

Kneeling on the bed, Conan braced a massive arm on either side of her head, sinking down for another passionate kiss. "Mhàiri," he groaned as he rolled, pulling her up and over him.

She moved to straddle him, pulling away from his kiss. Conan looked up at her with blue eyes as she knelt across his body. His gaze said that he wanted her now. His hands curled around her waist and then moved slowly down, kneading her thighs, spreading them wide so she straddled him.

Gripping her hips, he lifted her and then watched her green eyes grow hazy as he slowly lowered her, pressing against her entrance, demanding entry. She was so hot, so wet, his massive arms started to quiver. He didn't want to hurt her.

Mhàiri groaned. Conan was heat sheathed in velvet. Her glazed eyes bore into his. Her hips circled, wanting more.

"Easy," he groaned, sweat beginning to slick his chest from the strain of holding back. "It's been a while. We need to go slow. I don't want to hurt you."

Mhàiri was past all thought; only need ruled. "Conan," she whispered and pulled him up into a wild kiss that had her wrapping her tongue around his. Then she impaled herself on him. He filled her.

His hips thrusted deep. He closed his eyes as her tightness surrounded his thick shaft.

Mhàiri rocked against him, pulling him deeper into her. Conan sat up, pressing his face between her breasts.

He moaned. The sound vibrated through her chest. Mhàiri let her head loll back. She could feel her hair hanging down her back and across her buttocks. Conan took one of her nipples in his mouth again and brought the pink tip to its crested peak.

He matched her rhythm with gentle tugs of his mouth. The sensation seemed to spiral away from her, pulling her down and lifting her up at the same time. Mhàiri shuddered, rocking against him harder. Then she drew his face up to meet hers and kissed him aggressively. Her tongue explored every hot secret place in his mouth, pulling his ecstatic moans into herself.

Mhàiri dug her fingers into his hair, holding him close to her. Conan's hands curved around her buttocks, dragging her tighter, faster, and harder. Mhàiri threw her head back with a stunned cry. Freezing, Conan held her still, fearing he had hurt her.

Bringing her head forward, Mhàiri locked passion-filled eyes to his and demanded more while trying to grind her hips into his. "Oh, God, please more!"

Easing his grip, Conan allowed Mhàiri to set the rhythm. Holding on to his shoulders, she circled her hips, building the tension to an unbearable level. Pulling her to his chest, he scraped his teeth along her lower jaw as he made his way to her swollen mouth. Once there, his kiss imitated their bodies.

Mhàiri dug her nails into his shoulders and screamed at the feelings sweeping through her—tumultuous, turbulent, wild, and untamed. She was no longer with Conan in the solar, but soaring, spiraling, and spinning out of control as waves of pleasure coursed through her body.

Mhàiri fell limp in Conan's arms. Her head dropped onto his shoulder. Conan held her, running a soothing hand up and down her spine. When her breathing settled, she lifted her head and looked at him with dazed eyes. Moving to kiss his lips, she realized he had yet to find his own release.

"Conan," she whispered, moving her hips slightly. She ran her hands up his sweat-drenched chest and eased herself back. The small movement had him groaning.

Putting her hands on either side of his face, she looked deep into his wild eyes, "Take me, Conan, I'm yours." She kissed him again and his last bit of control finally broke.

Twisting her under him, he then held himself above her, bracing himself on his knees, pushing her legs further apart. He wanted to watch her face, watch himself as he slid into her, to see how much pleasure he could give her, how much love he could show her. "*A ruin*, I cannot get my fill of you," he whispered hoarsely. His hand alighted on her breast, stroking her nipple between his fingers while his tongue feasted on her mouth.

Before long, he was driving into her, encouraged by her eager cries of pleasure. Her legs widened for him. Her back arched, causing her breasts to press against him. Her appetite for pleasure matched his own. Their hips were undulating in unison, their breaths mingling.

Mhàiri could feel it again, the hot pressure, molten lava building and building until her entire body was in danger of imploding. He thrust it deep into her and suckled her at the same time. She froze, her mouth open on a silent scream as she shattered once more. Her body pulsed, hot, around him. At the same time, Conan's body shook with a fierce tension until, finally, his relief came in abundance, pulsating through him like a hellish heartbeat.

He rested his forehead on hers as he tried to regain his breath. He had never experienced a release like that. Each time got better and better.

Finally, his body slumped beside her though he did not let her go. He pulled her against him, laying kisses on the top of her head and streaking his hand down her spine. She sighed with satisfaction, burrowing deeper into his chest.

"I have a confession," he murmured into her hair. "I did not change my mind about marrying because you proved you could be happy with the life we are going to live."

Mhàiri tried to pull back, but his gentle grip was uncompromising so she sank back into his chest. "Why then did you agree?"

"Because of that first night with you. It just took me a while to remember. When I held you in my arms and we made love, it was the first time in my life my mind had ever been calm. With you, like this, is the only way I have ever known true peace and happiness. I need you, Mhàiri." He eased his grip then to look down into her loving gaze. "I truly cannot live without you. If you were ever to learn how to draw a person's soul, Mhàiri, and drew mine, you would discover that you were drawing yourself."

Mhàiri reached up and stroked his cheek. "You are mine, Conan McTiernay. All mine. Forever mine."

Conan bent down and captured her lips in a soul-searing kiss. Both decided that sleep could wait a little bit longer.

* * *

"Would you stop moving?" Laurel hissed.

Conor squirmed and put his other arm behind his head. "I wouldn't be moving if we were in our own bed," he groused.

Laurel poked him in the side. "Do not talk to me about discomfort. You have never carried a McTiernay bairn inside you for nine months."

Conor huffed. "Women always like to use that excuse. *You've never been pregnant. You don't know real pain until you deliver a baby.* Back hurts, having to go all the time . . . we husbands are very aware that the end is no fun, but you've never run into battle with a blade either."

"You and I both know that you find the administrative duties of leading a large clan much more tedious than battle."

"I just hope Conan is appreciating this little present you gave him. I'm not happy that you are out here in a tent that was supposed to be for him. You and my child need to be in a bed. Warm. Protected."

Laurel snuggled closer. "I am warm next to you. And I am protected when next to you."

Conor shifted again, and Laurel fought the urge to slap him like she would a puppy and say "*Settle!*"

"How long do you think it will be before people will start to leave?"

Laurel sighed. Her husband longed for peace and quiet. He wanted his life back. "Fortunately for you, I think it will be rather soon. Your brothers want to get their wives home as quickly as possible. They will not want to risk having a babe during the journey."

"That wouldn't happen. None of them are far enough along."

Laurel smiled and placed a light kiss on Conor's

chest. "Not if they take their time and keep the ride smooth. But all of them insisted on coming. Their wives know what they are and are not capable of. Not a single one would risk their child. I am not worried."

Conor closed his eyes. "You can keep doing that," he moaned as she swiped her tongue across his nipple. "And you better be right about everyone leaving. I miss you."

Laurel suckled and then let her hand drift downward. "Once they leave, others who might have stayed will follow their lead. Especially now that we've run out of ale."

"We didn't," he groaned as her fingers lightly caressed his shaft. "I saved some for us."

Laurel smiled. "Then you deserve a reward."

Her hand curled around him, and Conor was once again amazed at how much love he felt for his wife. And as soon as she was done with him, he would show her. "If Conan and Mhàiri find even the slightest sliver of the happiness I have found with you, they are destined for a long and wonderful life."

Laurel could not have agreed more.

Epilogue

Dugan shot straight up. His body locked and his jaw froze. He had been sleeping, deeply, physically worn out from all the ad hoc tournaments over the past few weeks. But he had been determined to mark Cole and their faction of the McTiernay clan as the best.

Then he heard what had woken him.

Screams.

Not just screams of terror. He *felt* these. These were filled with agony. Anguish of the most intense kind. Etched in every note.

Without thought, he grabbed his sword and started running. Rocks and thorns cut at his bare feet, but he barely noticed. The grief was tearing at him.

When sleeping outdoors, he did not sleep nude as was his preference when a bed was available. Tonight he had collapsed fully dressed, tartan and all. It would not have mattered, however, not with those screams, and they were getting louder with each step. Pain like that did not care about your state of dress. It just needed to end.

Heads were starting to emerge from the tents, their

sleep-filled expressions starting to be replaced with concern and then alarm. Some were starting to follow. Many of the soldiers were dressed like him, ready for battle, some were only in a leine, but more were preparing for battle.

All except one man.

He was running in the opposite direction of the screams.

Dugan hesitated. There was something about him that he recognized, and yet that was impossible. It was night and he was so far away he had not been able to discern his face before he was gone. And yet, Dugan's instinct was to follow him. Then the intensity of the cries became worse. And they were coming from nearby.

Dugan's head darted around as he saw another man dash by him. He was an old man for being so spry and agile, and Dugan recognized him as Laird MacInnes. Laurel's grandfather and the McTiernay brothers' godfather.

He turned to follow, catching up to the older man. "Do you know who? Where?"

MacInnes pointed to a tent that was set apart. "I know that scream. It's Laurel."

Dugan's eyes widened and he sprinted ahead, arriving at the same time a couple of other soldiers did. One of them was Loman, who, along with Seamus and several other of the elite guard kicked out of the castle, had been sleeping outside with the soldiers.

Loman did not even ask. He yanked up the flap and entered, followed by Dugan, MacInnes, and a growing number of men.

Dugan had fought bloody fights. He had been in battles. He had killed men multiple times and seen men killed. He hated it. Loathed it. Knew sometimes it was a necessary evil, but not once had he almost physically become ill at the sight.

But what he saw had him green and shaking.

Conor, chief of the McTiernay clan, was lying lifeless in a pool of his own blood, which was draining from a dagger that was still protruding from his chest. His head was in Laurel's lap, her hands clutching him, screaming, begging him to stay with her.

Realizing she was no longer alone, Laurel looked up, her face one of absolute terror that she was about to lose the man who was her very heart and soul. "He . . . he . . . came in. Said that Conan McTiernay could not be allowed to live. Adanel was pledged to another. And then, then he plunged the . . . the . . ." Then she looked down and started yelling at Conor. *"Don't you dare die on me! Don't you dare! Don't you leave me!"* Then, with a sob and a wail, she began to beg. "Please. *Please.* Please, Conor. Don't leave me. I need you. I need you. Please. Please. Oh, God. Please. Please don't take him. He's *mine.*"

People began to move all around Dugan. With so many pregnancies, midwives had been around, and some were well versed in medicines. He stepped back out of the tent and looked in the direction the disappearing figure had gone.

People were shouting, but Dugan blocked out all the sounds. He started to move in the direction where he had seen the figure running. Why was that man familiar? Dugan stopped. The man was not familiar. He had never seen him before . . . it was the hair he recognized. It was flame red, the same color that Conan described last fall after his attack, the same color as *hers*.

Dugan closed his eyes and gripped his sword, disbelieving his conclusions but knowing they were right. "*Adanel*," Laurel had said. "*Adanel was pledged to another.*" Until now, he had not known her name. Soon she would know his. For after tonight, there was no place she, her brother, or her father could escape.

He was coming for them. And when he arrived, he was going to be lethal.

The Mackbaythes would pay for what they did to Conor with their lives. And that included Adanel, Laird Mackbaythe's daughter and the only woman Dugan had ever loved.